W9-CMB-803

A Certain Magic

A Certain Magic

Kathleen Morgan

Five Star
Unity, Maine

Five Star Romance
Published in conjunction with
Natasha Kern Literary Agency, Inc.

Cover photograph © Alan J. La Vallee

August 1999
Standard Print Hardcover Edition.

Five Star Standard Print Romance Series.

The text of this edition is unabridged.

Set in 11 pt. Plantin by Al Chase.

Printed in the United States on permanent paper.

Library of Congress Cataloging-in-Publication Data

Morgan, Kathleen, 1950–
    A certain magic / Kathleen Morgan.
      p.   cm.
    ISBN 0-7862-2088-0 (hc : alk. paper)
    I. Title.
PS3563.O8647C47 1999
  813´.54—dc21   99-28407

To Sean, my creative, book-loving son, who was instrumental in advising me on the care and feeding of dragons. Even now, he just can't understand why I didn't take more of his advice. But, Sean, you know how mothers are.

And to his English cocker spaniel, Franklin, who provided the inspiration for Paddy. A smaller and definitely different kind of "dragon," to be sure, but just as endearing, devoted, and constantly underfoot. Even now, he's lying beneath my computer desk and I dare not move for fear of disturbing him. But then, Franklin, what are devoted dragons for?

Magic hath its own language,
Its own realities, its own laws,
And a wide realm of possibilities
For light, and darkness, and a misty "between"
Spanning a netherland of uncertain choices.

Yet though the choices bewilder
And promise naught, be it good or bad,
The wielder of magic must choose.
'Tis the price of the calling,
'Tis the price of a certain magic.

A magic that springs from the heart,
From love,
Or from the depths of a soul-deep perdition.

—from the *Grimoire of Brengwain the Wise*

PROLOGUE

Something tickled the back of Galen Radbourne's neck. He scratched the irritated spot distractedly, then resumed his intent scrutiny of the ancient grimoire lying before him on the scarred and pitted oak wood desk. *To strengthen the crystal's powers of divination,* he read, *first rub it with fresh mugwort leaves. Then, while scrying, burn an incense of equal parts mugwort and—*

A flutter of silky fibers, as light as a feather, brushed the side of his face. Galen grimaced, scrubbed at his cheek, and carefully turned the page of yellowed parchment he was reading. *Place the crystal on an altar between two white candles—*

"Ah, Galen," a sweet voice plaintively intruded. "Never have I met a more serious or obsessed sorcerer-in-training. Have you already lost interest in me, then?"

At the sound of his beloved's voice, Galen's heart gave a great, joyous leap. He glanced up from the tome of magic, turned, and smiled. "Nay, never that, sweet lass. You are everything I could wish for!"

Lydia giggled shyly, then skipped into view from behind the frayed and faded tapestry covered screen where she'd been hiding, a long peacock feather in her hand. Gazing up at her, it seemed to Galen as if the sun had suddenly pierced the gloom of the dusty, musty chamber filled with books, beakers, jars of various and sundry herbs, and guttered candles.

Flame-dark hair swirling, green eyes dancing, Lydia walked over to stand beside him. A sense of proud possession swelled within Galen. Innocent seductress that she was, she

7

had lured him not only with her softly rounded woman's body, but with her infectious laughter, playful ways, and radiant, joyous spirit.

Lured him, seduced him . . . until now he was in love—with life, with living, and with Lydia.

A charming dimple appeared in each of her rose- and cream-tinted cheeks. "Everything you could wish for, hmmm?" She took his hand, tugging on it impatiently. "Then come away from this dreary place. 'Tis spring, Galen, and the day is fresh and new. Come away with me."

Her dark auburn lashes dropped, fluttering down to fan her cheeks like some silky bird's wings. A most becoming flush stained her neck and face. "Come away," Lydia softly said. "I've a hunger for you."

The tempo of Galen's heart suddenly accelerated, sending the muscular organ pounding against his ribs. His loins tightened. His long, strong fingers closed about hers. "Aye, lass," he said huskily, "but no fierce, I'd wager, than the hunger that gnaws at me."

She tugged at him more urgently. "Then come away. Now."

He was sorely tempted. No one who met Lydia could remain cold to her for long, not even a sorcerer whose sensuality had lain all but dormant until now, buried beneath the weight of a heretofore all-consuming love for his magic. Lydia was ripe with her flowering womanhood, a lush, fragrant bloom to be plucked, a sweet, succulent fruit to be savored. And she'd chosen Galen above all the young men at Castle Radbourne. Chosen him to be the first man she'd ever lie with or love.

The swirl of Lydia's gown sent a whiff of fragrance rippling through the air. Galen inhaled deeply, savoring the tantalizing scent of her. She smelled of budding blossoms, of sweet grass, and fresh air. A longing to stand and take Lydia into his arms, to bury his face in her fragrant hair, to meld his body with hers, flooded him. With a soul-deep sigh, he firmly thrust the impulse aside.

Regretfully, Galen shook his head. "Nay, not now, sweet lass. I've another hour or two of study left me." He glanced out the deep, stone-cut window. "Mayhap, though, at two past midday. I could meet you then."

She made a wry face, her soft, full lips forming a most delightful pout. Galen tried, but couldn't drag his hungry gaze from her mouth. As if noting his avid reaction, Lydia relented with a sigh. "Two past midday then, at our secret cave. And not a moment longer, mind you. Give me your vow on that."

Galen chuckled, gave her tiny hand one final squeeze, then released it. Though he tried harder now, he still frequently forgot himself in some spell or incantation. For some unknown reason, his magical abilities had taken a great leap forward in the past weeks, almost as if, in the loving of Lydia, his powers had grown as well. But he'd not be distracted by his magic this day. Not when such a delectable prize as Lydia awaited him.

"Not a moment longer. I swear it," he solemnly assured her. He gave her a playful shove forward. "Now, begone with you. I've much to finish here if I'm to be at the cave in but another hour."

She whirled about in a flounce of silken gown and tumult of deep red curls. "Just see that you do, Galen Radbourne. See that you do." With a gay little laugh Lydia skipped from the room, her lingering scent the only evidence she'd ever been there.

For a long moment Galen stared after her. Then, with a sigh, he turned back to the grimoire. Time soon passed as it had before, as it always did, on the fleet wings of a deep, abiding fascination with the lessons he loved.

Only the resonant tones of the tower clock striking three were enough to finally penetrate his intense concentration. With a frustrated groan Galen leaped to his feet, smoothed his long, black woolen robes, and ran a hurried hand through his wavy, black shoulder-length hair.

An hour past their agreed upon meeting time. Curse it all. Once again he'd overstayed his lessons and would be late to their tryst.

He ran for the door, down the corridor that led to the Great Hall, and out into the inner bailey. Fleet limbs soon carried him from the stern, stone confines of Castle Radbourne and into yet another world and life he'd hardly noticed before.

Spring had truly burst upon the land, showering it with an abundance of fresh, green grass, achingly blue skies, and soft, warm breezes. Birds flew overhead. A bold rabbit, pink ears flopping, bounded along at the edge of the forest. A doe and her spotted fawn grazed in the meadow.

Scents of rich, damp earth and budding blossoms on the nearby fruit trees tantalized the nose, filling Galen with a re-awakened awareness of the vibrant life around him. The memory of his fascination with his magic faded, replaced by a heady, sense-stirring realization of what lay ahead. 'Twas a beautiful, perfect day—and he was in love.

As he hurried through the orchard and past the small pond, a mother duck alternately scolded, then encouraged her young ducklings into the water for their first swim. Galen smiled. Though the scenario of seasonal rebirth had played out many times in his eighteen years, never had he noted it with such perception or pleasure.

He halted at the crest of the hillock separating him from first view of the secret cave where he and Lydia always met.

Memories of the past months flooded him—sweet and poignant. They'd shared so much together, he and Lydia. Laughter, discovery, crazed escapades that had threatened the sanity of Lydia's old nursemaid and raised the brows of Galen's stolid if paternally tolerant father—and only recently come to discover the fullest aspects of the love between a man and a woman.

The warm sun beat down on Galen's face. A breeze, playful as a kitten, stroked his cheek and ruffled his darkly curling hair before scampering off to tease the budding trees and stir the grass. Galen lifted his hands to cup about his mouth and called. "Lydia? Lydia?"

She didn't reply. His brow crinkled in puzzlement. Lydia was always first to arrive at their rendezvous.

He glanced up at the sun. Already it had passed its zenith and was gliding toward the distant hills. Was he too late, then, for their appointed tryst? Had she already given up and returned home? She'd threatened it time and again.

He must check the cave, wait a short while, nonetheless. Mayhap, this time, she was the one who was late. 'Twould be amusing indeed, Galen thought, if just this once he beat Lydia to their trysting place.

"Lydia?" he called once more. "Where are you, you little temptress?"

The sound of his voice echoed weakly, swallowed in a sudden gust of wind. A dark cloud scudded before the sun, casting an unexpected pall on the formerly bright and joyous day. Galen shivered. Something, a premonition or a simple swell of nameless apprehension, filled him. With an unsteady laugh, he shook it off.

Galen scanned the meadow for one last sign of the red-haired girl, then strode down the hill to the cave. If he were indeed here before Lydia, he fully intended to make the most of his earlier arrival. Lydia, the eternal prankster, would, for once, have the prank played on her.

As he stepped inside, the cooler air of the little cave wafted over him. Save for a long, narrow slit in its rocky ceiling that permitted a ray of sunlight to illuminate its center, the chamber was dark. The light was enough, however, to ease the blackness and throw the sides of the cave into soft shadow.

Something in those shadows caught Galen's eye. He wheeled about. Sprawled in an awkward tangle of arms, legs, and loose, unbound hair, Lydia lay there, her mouth half-opened, her eyes staring blankly into oblivion. With a hoarse cry Galen ran to her, knelt, and gathered her into his arms.

"Lydia! By the Mother, Lydia!"

He ran his hands over her, searching for wound or sign of injury. There was none—no bruises, no blood. His heart racing, he lowered his face to her mouth to discern even the faintest of breaths. There was none. Frantically, he probed for a pulse. She was dead.

The shock and confusion of that terrible revelation held him in its icy throes for a long, anguished moment. He couldn't breathe, his chest so constricted no amount of effort could force the air into his lungs. Then, with a ragged sob, the breath came.

"Lydia. Ah, Lydia. Not you. Not you . . ."

He rocked her to and fro, clutching her soft, sweet body to his. Even now, the warmth of life barely clung to her. The tears welled, but the surge of anger and seething loss burned them away before they could fall.

How could this have happened? Galen raged in impotent frustration. If he hadn't been so late . . .

Had someone come before him and killed her? He glanced about the cave, searching for signs of struggle. Lydia's cloak lay spread on the floor just outside the circle of light across the cave. Aside from that, there was naught amiss. Yet somehow, someway, someone had gotten here before him and murdered her.

A brutal curse rose to Galen's lips. He'd kill the man who had done this to her! Ah, 'twas too much . . . too much. Lydia . . . Lydia, his love.

Footsteps crunched on the gravel floor. A body momentarily blocked the ray of sunlight streaming into the cave. Galen looked up. Though the face and form were shadowed, he instantly recognized him. 'Twas Dorian, his twin brother.

"She's dead, isn't she?" came Dorian's strangely flat query. "I feared this might happen."

Galen froze. Reflexively, his arms tightened about Lydia. "What do you mean? If you knew someone meant Lydia harm, why didn't you tell me, warn me so I could be here to protect her?"

"And could you have protected her against yourself?"

Fury exploded in Galen. "Against me? Are you daft? I'd never—ever—have harmed Lydia!"

"But you did, nonetheless, Brother dear," Dorian softly said. " 'Tis our special curse, the price of our powers."

"Our powers?" Ever so gently, Galen laid Lydia down and rose to confront his brother. "Play no games with me, Dorian," he snarled. "I tired of them long ago and this time . . . this time, I'm at the limits of my control."

"I play no games, Brother." A small, pitying smile quivered at the edges of Dorian's mouth. "Ah, I see now that Father hasn't told you. Mayhap if he had . . ." He gestured toward Lydia.

Galen grabbed him by the front of his long, black robe and jerked Dorian to him. "Then *you* tell me, Brother," he demanded, his voice gone low, dangerous. "Now, before I go mad with the pain and uncertainty."

Dorian eyed the big hand clenched, knuckle-white, in his robe. His own long fingers covered it, began to pry the tight fist away. "Pray, release me. The task is difficult and distasteful enough without your holding me in this stranglehold."

With a jerk, Galen freed him. "Tell me, then," he rasped, his chest heaving. "Now!"

"Our line has the potential for greater powers than most sorcerers," Dorian said, stepping back and frowningly smoothing the fresh wrinkles from his robe. "Those greater powers, however, are derived from the life essence of others. To sustain our powers, 'tis necessary to drain away that essence until it eventually kills the giver."

"What has this to do with Lydia?"

Dorian rolled his eyes. "Ah, Brother, Brother, haven't you figured it out yet? Women are the givers of that life essence we seem to need, and we gain it only through the act of mating." He cast a cool look at Lydia's lifeless body. "You've mated with her, haven't you? You killed her to augment your powers."

"Nay." Galen stepped back, shaking his head. Horror filled him. His gut roiled. "I didn't know. I never would have—"

"It matters not what you would or wouldn't have done. The woman is dead." Dorian cocked his head. "Didn't you wonder at the surge of your powers in the past weeks? Even *I* noticed your sudden growth in proficiency."

"I noticed . . . but thought . . ." Galen paused as a sudden thought assailed him. "If she died because of mating with me, why didn't she die that first time? Why now, after so many—" He bit off the bitter query, loathe to share even that special secret. "She seemed perfectly healthy when last I saw her."

Dorian gave a harsh laugh. "Did I say the dire effects were instantaneous? 'Tis unpredictable, the draining of the life essence. Sometimes 'tis quick, and occurs soon after the first mating. Other times, 'tis slower, more gradual." He shrugged. "Ask me not for details. I only relate what Father told me."

Just like that, Galen thought, freshened despair winding its cold, clammy tendrils about his heart. One moment she was alive and the next, dead. And he hadn't known, much less had a chance to prevent it. Raggedly, Galen shoved a hand through his hair. "Ah, Lydia. Lydia . . ."

"You cannot call back what was done, Brother." Dorian laid a hand on Galen's arm. "But murder is murder. The people will be up in arms when they hear." He released Galen to stroke his chin, a calculating light in his eyes. "We may have to send you away for a time. You know what store Father puts in the people's regard and—"

"I don't care!"

Galen groaned, suddenly overwhelmed with the terrible magnitude of what he'd done. He wheeled about. Walking back to where Lydia lay, he knelt and gathered her to him.

A few pebbles had ground themselves into the smooth curve of her cheek. With the most tender of touches, Galen brushed them away. Then, cupping the back of her head in his palm, he bent to capture her mouth for one final, bittersweet kiss.

"Galen," Dorian began, "you discount the mood of the—"

"I don't care, I told you!" his brother savagely cut him off. He looked up, his eyes blazing. " 'Tis over . . . my life with Lydia, my magic. There is naught left me."

"Galen, she is but a woman." Impatience tinged Dorian's voice. "A most comely one, to be sure, but still a woman. Our magic calls us to a greater destiny than any other of our kind.

Even Father doesn't possess the powers to the degree or fatal potential that we do. If a few women must be sacrificed—"

"Nay!" Galen's dark, tormented gaze riveted on his brother. " 'Tis over, I tell you. How can you expect me to accept my magic ever again, if to continue to foster and develop it I must kill others? How can *you* accept it?"

With a careless motion of his shoulders, his twin brother shrugged off the question. "I've never given it much thought, ever since Father revealed the secret to me. But then, he knew *I* would choose our heritage above all else, no matter the cost. And must have guessed, as well, that you would fall apart with the first sacrifice demanded."

He shook his head, a pitying look in his eyes. "I always knew you were lacking, that you didn't have what it took to see it through. And now Father and the rest will soon discover it as well. You won't be the favored son then, will you, Galen?"

"F-favored son?" Galen's voice wobbled in his disbelief. "Is this what it has always been? Who is more favored than the other? By the Mother, Dorian! 'Tis Lydia you speak so lightly of. 'Tis Lydia who lies here dead because of what I did to her! L-Lydia . . . ," his voice broke, "the w-woman I loved."

'Twas too much to bear, too much to fathom at a time like this. All Galen knew was his magic—his beloved magic—had betrayed him most foully. All he knew was now, instead of a life that could have been full of laughter and love, he had naught.

The floodgates of his emotions burst at last. Galen bowed his head and wept, long and hard and deep. Wept . . . until there was naught left in him but a huge, gaping hole where once had beat his heart. Wept . . . the limp form of the only woman he would ever let himself love lying cold and lifeless in his arms.

And, as he wept, he felt his magic drain away. Bit by agonizing bit it faded until, in so very many ways, he was no longer the man he'd been but a short springtide and love-laden time before.

CHAPTER ONE
FIFTEEN YEARS LATER

A frigid wind blew down from the mountains, gusting over the winter-browned, ice-encrusted grass before lifting to encompass the land in a bitter tumult of cold. High above, storm clouds, darkly bloated with moisture, obliterated the late afternoon sun. In the distance, an ominous harbinger of things to come, thunder boomed.

Yet the dark castle perched on a high, rocky outcropping far out in a bleak moor stood calmly through it all, looming over the terrain like some huge bird of prey. Foreboding it was . . . an ominous sentinel . . . ready, waiting, rife with danger.

"Well, I hope this will soon be the end of it, then," the warrior Renard said, glumly taking in the grim landscape that lay before them.

Alena pulled her heavy woolen cloak more snugly about her, tugged the hood up to cover her head, and glanced wryly over at the big man riding beside her. "Having second thoughts, are you, as to the worth of such a mission in the worst weather of the winter?" She sighed and shook her head, no more thrilled than her compatriot was at the upcoming confrontation. "Funny, but I recall mentioning something to that effect not too long ago."

Renard shot her an irritated look. "No need to harp so about it. If *I* recall correctly, winter quarters were beginning to wear thin on you as well. There's naught more nerve-wracking than a mercenary army cooped up with little to do. Besides, 'tis nearly spring. April will be here in another few weeks."

"Mayhap," she grudgingly agreed, "but, in the meanwhile, we're out in the cold, approaching a heavily guarded fortress, and soon to face a sorcerer with the most unsavory of reputations."

"Aye." Renard's frown deepened as their gazes turned, once more, to the scene of barren moor and dark castle. "But even sorcerers like money, and a ransom was the terms this Dorian of Radbourne set for the return of the Lord Hargreaves's daughter. So, a few leagues more, a brief sojourn with this Radbourne mage, and we'll soon be heading back with the young Lady Hargreaves to that snug little inn for the night."

He grinned suddenly. "I think the innkeeper's pretty daughter took a particular liking to me the last time I passed this way. Mayhap a more ardent courtship for her favors is in order."

Heartened by the anticipation of making quick work of the increasingly odious mission, Alena laughed. "An ardent courtship, eh? Well, then let's be off. I've a need for a bracing gallop and the day draws on even as we speak. 'Tis a good hour's ride back to the Boar's Tusk Inn. I'd prefer if we made it there before that storm breaks."

Renard glanced up. The clouds churned ominously, darkening even as they watched from deep gray to black. The big warrior's mouth quirked, then he urged his war-horse onward. With a wild whoop, Alena nudged her horse after him.

Down the frozen hill and across the treeless plains they rode, urging their mounts up the ice-slick rocks, pounding over the drawbridge that spanned a murky, frost-covered moat, to pull up only when they reached the castle's imposing gatehouse. A grim-faced soldier stood guard. Alena eyed his long, lethally tipped pike and wary stance. Her hand moved stealthily to free the hilt guard from her sword.

"Who do ye seek and what be yer mission?" the man croaked through cold-stiffened lips.

Alena and Renard exchanged an amused look.

"We're expected by your master, Dorian Radbourne. We bear a packet from the Lord Hargreaves," the blond warrior woman replied, turning back to the shivering man. "And we demand an immediate audience."

The guard's scrawny, beard-stubbled face twisted in a parody of a smile. "Do ye now? Well then, enter if ye dare. My master does indeed expect ye."

Once more, Alena glanced at Renard, then urged her mount on. Across a large, ill-kempt outer bailey she rode, her war-horse's iron-shod hooves echoing hollowly on the cobblestoned pavement. The area was deserted; not a sign of life stirred in the grim, brooding interior.

The fine hairs rose on the back of Alena's neck. She'd seen her share of eerie places in her years as a mercenary soldier, but this castle surpassed them all. No good would come of this, she feared, whether they succeeded in ransoming the Lord Hargreaves's daughter or not. No good at all . . .

As the wind whipped about and howled mournfully, she led the way through yet another walled enclosure into the inner bailey, before halting at the base of a broad expanse of steps leading up to an imposing keep of mottled gray stone. Black slits of windows pierced the lower levels, peering out at them like so many watchful, unfriendly eyes. There, in the cloud muted glow of sunset that washed the walls and doorway of the keep, waited another guard. The man strode down to meet them.

"Have ye the ransom?" the soldier demanded imperiously. He extended a hand as if expecting them to deliver it to him.

"Aye," Renard muttered, irritation beginning to thread his voice. "And where is your master? The money remains in our possession until I have the Lord Hargreaves's daughter."

The man gave a hollow, humorless laugh. "Then come. Radbourne waits inside." He turned on his heel and marched back up the stairs.

"A most warm and gracious welcome," Alena observed dryly. She swung down from her mount, glanced about for a stable boy to hold her horse and, when none appeared, tossed the reins down to ground tie the animal.

Renard did the same, then retrieved the two large, coin-laden sacks from his saddle and flung them over his shoulder. He joined Alena. "Best you be prepared for the worst. I don't like the feel of things here."

Alena's mouth tightened. "Indeed?" She bent to check the placement of the dagger she wore in the side of her right boot, then straightened. With a wave of her hand, she motioned Renard forward. "After you. Since you're somewhat encumbered, I'll cover your back."

The big warrior nodded curtly and strode up the steps, his free hand slipping to his own sword hilt. Into a darkly shadowed, cavernous hall they walked, the thunk of their booted feet resounding loudly off the smooth stone walls and dark, rafter-lined ceiling. The interior was barren of furniture or decoration save for the huge coat of arms hanging on the wall over the blazing hearth.

Alena took one look at it and glanced away. A silver dragon, its body pierced by a bolt of lightning, lay dying on a shield of hammered gold.

Revulsion—and something akin to a sense of utter, soul-wrenching horror—shuddered through her. Alena shook off the disturbing emotions and directed her gaze to the guard awaiting them at the set of thick, oaken doors standing to the right of the fireplace.

As Alena passed the hearth, a surge of warmth wafted over

her. She turned her face, savoring the fire's caress, the comforting crackle of the flames, the sense-stirring tang of woodsmoke. Momentarily, a fervent wish to be somewhere—anywhere—else engulfed her. There was just something . . . something very *wrong* here. Something she'd never felt before. A premonition of terrible danger prickled down her spine.

Then the doors opened. Across yet another large room, Alena caught the first glimpse of a man who could be none other than the master of the castle. She followed Leonard into the room, surreptitiously scanning the interior for any armed men or hidden traps, and found none. The doors swung closed behind them, the thick wood slamming shut reverberating throughout the chamber with a solid, mournful sound. A sound pervaded with finality.

Alena's mouth went dry. *Into the belly of the beast . . .*

He was quite a handsome man, this Dorian of Radbourne. He sat on a raised dais, his powerful, slightly fleshy, broad-shouldered frame dwarfing the carved wooden chair he indolently lounged back in. His hair was black and slightly shot with gray, thick and curling to his shoulders, his features ruggedly carved but appealingly masculine. His eyes, rich brown in color, gazed down at them with a sharp, almost predatory intelligence.

Over a long, belted undergown of shimmering amber-colored silk, Radbourne wore an intricately woven, hooded robe of bronze-hued brocade. Moonstones gleamed with a milky luster on his hands and from the large, gold-worked pendant about his neck. His was an impressive presence, stunningly attired as befitted a man of great wealth and power.

"So, Hargreaves did indeed have the money," he said when Alena and Renard halted before him. "After all that whining and crying, I was beginning to wonder how deep his affection for his daughter ran." Radbourne held out his hand. "Give me the ransom."

Out of the corner of her eye, Alena saw Renard tense, his grip about the money bags tighten. "And I say, first show me Lord Hargreaves's daughter," he tautly replied. "Those *were* the terms of the agreement, were they not?"

Something flickered in Radbourne's eyes. Something ugly and hard. Alena's weight shifted subtly to the balls of her booted feet. *Here it comes* . . .

"Ah, but that won't be possible." The sorcerer smiled sadly and shook his head. "The young lady in question took ill and died two days ago."

His mouth pulled into a wolfish grin. "Seems she wasn't woman enough to bear my vigorous lovemaking." He sighed, pausing to finger one carved end of his chair arm before once more looking up. "But then, in the end, none of them are. Yet I remain hopeful that some day I'll find a mate worthy of me . . ."

Radbourne's voice faded as he took in Alena more closely. "You look to be a strong woman, and quite attractive in the bargain. Mayhap I could impose on you to visit with me for a time?"

A spirit-numbing wave of malevolence swept over Alena. She wanted to turn and run and repressed that instinctive impulse with only the greatest of difficulty. Lifting her chin and squaring her shoulders instead, she opened her mouth to reply when Renard moved closer.

From across the room, the last rays of sunlight wavered briefly, then faded, swallowed at last by the dark force of the winter storm. "My partner isn't part of the ransom," the big warrior growled, "though it now seems the delivery of that, too, is a dead issue. We'd like some proof, however, to take back to Lord Hargreaves. His daughter's remains, mayhap, to be buried in the family cemetery?"

"That won't be possible," the sorcerer snarled before catching himself and modulating his tone. "She was cremated."

"Then some of her personal effects, mayhap?"

"They were burned with her." Dorian Radbourne rose. "Do you doubt my word on the girl's death, warrior?"

Beside Alena, Renard cursed softly. "I doubt naught, my lord. But we came for our employer's daughter and must either return with her or her body."

The sorcerer smiled thinly and nodded. "I can well understand your dilemma. Mayhap we can still sort through all of this to your satisfaction. 'Twill take time, though. Will you not accept the hospitality of my castle for the night?" Radbourne's soft, mellifluous voice was all but swallowed by the rising wail of the wind. "There's no need to venture out into the storm. The morrow's soon enough to depart."

"I think not, m'lord," Alena made haste to reply, loathe to linger even a moment more in the man's unsettling presence. "We've a long journey back and not much time to spare."

"But I *insist.*" Dorian Radbourne's gaze riveted on Alena, sharpening with sudden interest. "And you, fair lady, will be my most honored guest. On closer inspection, I find there's something about you, something I feel compelled to examine more closely. Aye," he said, his voice gone hard and flat, "*you'll* stay if no one else."

A flash of red light—of mage fire—sprang from his fingers. With a shout of warning, Renard flung the two bags of coins in the air and into the path of the oncoming beam. With a loud, crackling sound the bags exploded. Coins flew everywhere.

"Run, Alena!" Renard shoved her ahead of him in the direction of the doors. " 'Tis magic. We can't fight him!"

She shot a look over her shoulder. Radbourne stood there, motionless, but the look on his face—a look of venomous rage—now contorted his once handsome features into a mask of indescribable evil. Once again, he lifted his hand, directing it at Renard.

Alena grasped Renard's cloak and jerked him out of the way. The blast of mage fire struck him a glancing blow to the shoulder. He gasped, shuddered, and stumbled. Alena grabbed him under the arms and wrenched him to his feet. "Get up, you old goat!" she cried. "Run. Now!"

The big warrior swayed for an instant, then shoved her ahead of him once more. "The windows," he roared as a troop of guards rushed in from the now open doors. " 'Tis our only chance!"

Wheeling about, Alena raced across the room. The windows were closed and locked. She unsheathed her sword as she ran. Grasping the blade in her gloved hands, Alena swung its hilt at the glass panes. The windows shattered in a spray of glass.

She clambered up on the broad sill and glanced down through the broken window. The back of the building abutted the castle's parapet walk. They could jump to that wall, but 'twould be a long one. Beyond that lay the moat.

The wind howled and blew, its sudden, unexpected force nearly slamming her back into the room. The waning day darkened to night in the roiling turbulence of the storm. Sleet pelted the earth and castle walls. Yet the horror that lay behind Alena was far worse than anything nature could ever hope to muster.

"Renard, come. We must jump for it!" Alena turned. Renard was there, reaching up to the window. She leaned down, extended her hand.

With a howl as horrid as a demon of hell, Radbourne sent forth yet one more blast of mage fire. It arced across the room, striking Renard squarely in the back.

The big warrior's features twisted in excruciating pain. His body jerked in grotesque spasms. Yet, with one last, superhuman effort, Renard managed to lurch forward and shove at Alena.

"G-go!" he choked out the word. "S-save yourself!"

Caught off balance, it was all Alena could do to grasp her sword, whirl around, and leap for the parapet wall. She struck the stone walkway hard. For an instant Alena lay there, fighting for breath. Then she shoved to her feet and looked back to the window high above.

Dorian Radbourne stood over Renard's motionless form. As he pointed his hand at her, Alena's heart sank. There was no way to evade him this time, no place to hide on the windswept parapet. 'Twas over.

Yet, this time, no mage fire came. Radbourne shrieked; he pounded in impotent frustration on Renard's limp body; he screamed vile imprecations down at her that were all but drowned in the wind and sleet. "Come back . . . if . . . you dare. He'll . . . be waiting . . ."

Alena stared up at him for a long moment more, the scene of Radbourne stepping back from the window and his guards moving forward to drag Renard away burning hard and hot into her memory. "I'll be back, you dog of hell," she whispered hoarsely, the anguish at having to leave Renard behind almost more than she could bear. "I *swear* it."

Then, swinging about, Alena resheathed her sword, squared her shoulders, and leaped down into the murky, malodorous moat far below.

The angry sea battered the little skiff, tossing Alena to and fro. Cadvallan Isle loomed from the mists, its peaks shrouded in gray-black clouds, its rock-pillared, inhospitable shores pounded relentlessly by foaming waves. 'Twas indeed a thoroughly miserable, unhappy place, she thought as she fought the ocean that threatened, at any moment, to capsize her small boat. A miserable, unhappy place that, any other time, she'd no desire to visit. Not now—or ever.

'Twas a crazed, desperate quest, Alena well knew, her gaze fixed upon the rapidly nearing isle. Mayhap another mage of equal or greater powers lived elsewhere in the realm, but the grim fact remained that she'd no time to spare in seeking him out. Far too much time already had been lost in avoiding the search parties Dorian Radbourne had sent out after her escape from his castle, she, on foot and without gear or dry clothes in this most unfriendly and winter-barren of lands. If it hadn't been for the old witch woman, Idara, who had found her huddled, sick and shivering, in the forest beneath a makeshift shelter of pine boughs early one morn, Alena doubted she'd have survived another night.

Idara had taken her to her tiny hut a few leagues away, stripped off her filthy, frozen clothes and bundled Alena in a bear pelt before her blazing hearth fire. After filling Alena full of a rich, nourishing soup and assuring her that she was safe, secure from Dorian's pervue within a sacred circle of protection, the witch woman had woven a spell of sleep about her.

Caught up in a crazed swirl of strange and disturbing dreams, Alena had slept for a day and a half, rising finally to face the gentle questions of Idara. 'Twas then she'd learned of Dorian's twin, and his potential to defeat his evil brother. 'Twas then, at long last, the first ray of hope to rescue Renard had pierced her fever-heavy despair.

The stone sentinels of Cadvallan Isle loomed closer now, strangely misshapen and undulating through her bleary gaze.

Alena blinked fiercely, shoving the hazy remnants of her ague-battered exhaustion aside. She couldn't go on much longer, that she well knew. But, once she'd learned of Galen Radbourne, she hadn't dared spare another day in Idara's care. Every moment wasted was a day Renard came closer to death.

There was no help for it. The man, this mysterious Galen Radbourne, was said to live on Cadvallan Isle—*if* he still lived at all. Fifteen years past now, the twin brother of the foul sorcerer of Radbourne Castle had been banished to Cadvallan for some cruel and heinous crime. No one had seen or heard from him since. Yet *if* he still lived, he was her only hope to save Renard. 'Twas said this Galen was twin to his brother not only in body, but in magical powers as well.

But what if Galen Radbourne were as evil as his brother? Alena wondered fleetingly, before the sudden lift of the boat by yet another huge wave called her harshly back to the present. She fought to steady the skiff by throwing the full weight of her body against the tiller. The boat rode up and down the giant swells of several waves before finally righting. Alena expelled a sigh of relief.

'Twas *more* than likely the man she sought on Cadvallan Isle was evil, she told herself, grimly recapturing the tail end of her former thoughts. He was cut of the same cloth, born of the same flesh, reared by the same parents. But it didn't matter. She didn't dare let it matter.

Renard had been held in Castle Radbourne for over a week now, *if* he still lived. One way or another, she meant to rescue him if there was aught left of him to rescue. Partners didn't let one another down.

The waves crashed along the rocky shore, echoing ominously in the silent sunset. Alena scanned the rising darkness and curtain of sea spray and water for a place to come ashore. There seemed none.

She muttered a foul curse. She'd no other choice but to bring the skiff as close to the rocks as possible, then, make a jump for it. The small boat might or might not eventually wash ashore. 'Twas a chance she must take.

'Twas a chance, just like the chance she took seeking out some unknown sorcerer on an island in a realm rife with superstitious rumors about the male sorcerers who had dwelt there for centuries. There were no female sorcerers anymore. The males had destroyed them all, if the tales whispered over campfires and in the smoke-filled taverns were true. Tales of females who had once gained their own special powers through their unique bonding with dragons . . .

A sudden gust whipped the sail about. The boom line tied to the wind battered sail slid through Alena's hand, leaving a searing trail of abraded flesh in its wake. The boat leaned precariously to one side, threatening to capsize at any moment. In a chilling torrent, the ocean surged into the skiff. Water swirled wildly about Alena's ankles.

With a shout as much of anger as of pain, the warrior woman tightened her grip about the coarse, sea-slick cord. She jerked back hard to bring the sail to, her fever-sapped muscles straining with all their might. The skiff heaved into the air, righted, then sailed on, back on tack toward the isle once more. Her limbs quivering in relief, Alena leaned against the tiller for a brief moment of support.

The sharp, black volcanic rocks once more thrust into focus, jutting boldly from the sea, inhospitable guardians of a land long said to offer the realm's only sanctuary from the forces of magic. 'Twas also said that was why the last few dragons—if any had ever truly existed—had fled here. Here, they were safe from the sorcerers' relentless and destructive persecution. Here, this Galen Radbourne was safe as well.

Dragons and sorcerers living in peace on Cadvallan Isle. Alena grimaced wryly. She'd believe that when she saw it. *If* she lived to see it, she thought, eyeing the huge waves slamming against the rocks now towering over her. She fought to keep her balance on the boat's narrow deck, gauging the right moment to jump.

In one last, instinctive move, she momentarily released the tiller and checked her sword, assuring herself its hilt was secured to the sheath. Her dagger still nestled reassuringly within the leather boot of her right leg. Alena lifted her gaze and dragged in a resolute breath. 'Twas time. The chance might never come again.

Yet another wave slammed into the skiff, lifting it high, toying mercilessly with the boat within the clasp of its foamy swell, then pulled away. The little craft fell, striking the water with a bone-jarring crash. The sail once more spun around.

Alena grabbed for the tiller and jerked back on the boom line. Yet, even then, it was too late. The boom struck her squarely in the gut, slamming her backward. With a small cry, she flew over the stern, tumbling into the violently churning sea.

The ocean sucked her down with malevolent force. Saltwater rushed into Alena's mouth, down her throat, filling her lungs. A mindless panic engulfed her. She fought back with all her strength—against the fear, against the ocean—battling her way to the surface.

Something loomed out of that eerie silence that was the dark depths of the sea. Something big and white and heavy. It slammed into her, striking Alena a glancing blow to the head.

The skiff, she thought in that last instant of consciousness. Curse it all. The skiff . . .

The dreams came once again, more powerful, more poignant, more disturbing than ever before. Dreams of a strange magic, imbued with a shimmering, misty kaleidoscope of colors. Of powers—slipping strange about the heart and mind, yet, at the same time, oh, so hauntingly familiar, so much an inherent part of one's nature, one's soul.

Alena moaned softly, then twitched spasmodically as yet another storm tossed wave broke over her. She stirred, grinding her cheek into the gritty sand of the shore, and grimaced. The foaming waters churned wildly about her, then receded as the undertow once more pulled them back to the sea. Yet still the dream held her in its clasp.

The colors swirled crazily, coalescing at last into a pair of bejeweled eyes that were, all at the same time, the combined and separate hues of emerald, ruby, amethyst, and sapphire. Mesmerizing, iridescent eyes that bound her, yet beckoned her all the same. A sweet ache rose in Alena's chest. An ache for things long buried, for a love that transcended time and place . . . and, even, species.

She whimpered softly, struggling against the strange swell of emotions. She didn't want, didn't need, them. They would only weaken her, divert her from her true course and the only life she'd ever known.

Then the eyes closed. "Don't," Alena whispered in her dream. "Don't leave."

As if in reply, pain shot through her, sharp, splintering, agonizing. She stiffened, arching back unconsciously. By the Holy Ones, she'd never felt such pain! Yet, curiously, even as she suffered, she knew the pain wasn't her own. 'Twas the being's of the beautiful eyes.

A cry formed in her mind—desperate, pleading for her help. She twisted on the sandy beach. Her hands clenched into fists. Her face contorted in agony. *How?* she silently cried, heedless of the fear, the hesitation, the caution that warned of some ancient danger. *How can I help?*

Once more, the beautiful eyes opened, locked with hers. Once more, Alena felt the sweet, wondrous ache. *Join with me,* a voice quavered. *Give me my name.*

Alena groaned, thrashed wildly. She didn't understand. What did a name have to do with—

My name! the voice repeated, more insistent now. *I cannot find life unless you name me.* The voice dropped to a soft, plaintive whisper. *You, the heart of my hearts, the friend beloved. Neither of us can be whole until we are joined. 'Tis our destiny; 'tis how 'twas always meant to be.*

The pain came now in short, stabbing bursts, as if someone or something fought against some powerful barrier. Anger, frustration, and a rising terror filled Alena but, once again, she knew it was not her own. 'Twas the creature's of the beautiful eyes. The creature who was, even as she fought through her confusion, weakening, dying.

My name, it pleaded. *'Tisn't so hard, sweet lady, if you but take the first step. The first step that will grant me life.*

What was so wrong, Alena thought, where was the cost in giving the being what it seemed so desperately to need? She inhaled a shuddering breath, searching her memory for a name. The image of a gentle, loving old man filled her mind. *Padborn,* she sighed, somehow knowing the being for the male it was, the word rising from her lips in a wondrous rush of sound. *Your name is Padborn . . . for my father, the man who gave me life and made me what I am.*

Joy, relief, washed over her in a tide so strong as to take her breath away. *My thanks, heart of hearts, sweet friend,* the voice cried, then, in a fierce, explosive exultation, was gone. The earth trembled; rocks tumbled down the steep cliffs. A deafening roar filled the air.

Alena awoke with a start. Her eyes snapped open. There,

looming over her, was a huge, black dragon, scales glinting, eyes glowing. With battle honed senses immediately at the ready, Alena jerked to her elbows. Her hand glanced off a large stone. She grabbed it and, without hesitation or consideration, flung it into the dragon's face.

The sharp, volcanic rock glanced off the creature's nose. With a plaintive cry, the dragon reared back then scooted away. Alena lost not a moment climbing to her feet and unsheathing her sword. The dragon was certain to attack just as soon as it—

Her gaze narrowed. The dragon was but a babe, she realized, taking in its smaller size when viewed from her now upright and more clearheaded position. Newborn, as well, Alena also sheepishly noted, seeing, for the first time, the jagged remnants of a dragon-size shell lying nearby on the beach. A babe that now cowered in a mass of shiny scales and long tail curled about its haunches.

His head was long and slender, reptilian in appearance, with the buds of a pair of horns and a jagged crest of skin framing his face. But it was the eyes that recalled Alena's attention time and again to the young creature. The eyes . . . bejeweled and strangely familiar . . . like the eyes of the dragon in her dream.

She resheathed her sword and took a hesitant step forward. "Padborn?" The dragon jerked around, its brilliant eyes gone huge. Then, he threw back his head and let forth the most deafening wail.

Alena leaped back, covered her ears with her hands, and scowled fiercely. The irritated look she sent the baby dragon only served to make it wail all the louder. "By the Holy Ones!" Alena cursed. "Stop that now, I say! You'll bring down the whole mountain if you keep up that racket!"

As if in answer to her threat, a rhythmic pounding filled

the air. Her heart in her throat and hand on her sword once more, Alena glanced upward, fully expecting to see the first of the huge volcanic boulders come sliding down the mountain toward them. There was naught to be done but make a run for the sea, but how to get the baby dragon to—

Her breath solidified in her throat. There, overhead, the morning sky suddenly gone dark from their huge forms, was a flight of dragons. They floated on the gentle breeze for a moment or two, then dove straight for the beach—and Alena. With a startled yelp, she lunged out of their way. Scrambling across the sand, she headed for the shelter of the nearest big rock and rolled behind it.

When she dared peek out over the boulder, eight adult dragons had landed on the beach. All but two were males, and all were white with a curious iridescent rainbow-colored hue to their heavily scaled bodies and soft underbellies. For an instant, Alena knelt there, frozen in admiration. She'd never seen dragons before, never believed they existed, and certainly never realized how magnificent, how primally beautiful the creatures were. Then they turned their heads to gaze at her.

Once more, she was caught up in that strange fascination as she stared into their ever-changing, bejeweled eyes. There was just something about—

The largest dragon snarled and took a menacing step toward her. Alena's grip tightened about her sword hilt and she stood, withdrawing her weapon. She didn't know much about dragons or how to fight them, but she'd never backed down from a conflict before and had no intent to begin today. If 'twas a fight these dragons were spoiling for, she'd be happy to oblige. She meant to find Galen Radbourne and naught—even a mess of irate dragons—was going to stand in her way!

"If you understand me," Alena cried, stepping from behind the boulder and waving her sword in what she hoped the dragons would interpret as both a threatening and intimidating gesture, "let me pass. I don't wish any of you harm."

The big dragon eyed her with a baleful glare, then snarled again, exposing some of the sharpest and most vicious looking teeth Alena had ever seen. She widened her stance for battle and gripped her sword with both hands. Behind her the sea roared and crashed onto the shore. Before her and to both sides stood the dragons. There was no way to get past them save by going through them.

"Then come on," she said through clenched teeth, "if you've a mind for a fight. I told you I meant no harm but, if you're bound and determined, make your move."

With a sudden, sharp cry, the baby dragon hurled himself between Alena and the belligerent adult dragon. It shoved its baby fat girth as close to Alena as it could, so close its long, thick tail swung about and knocked Alena off her feet. With a surprised grunt, she tumbled backward and struck the soft sand. As her hand slammed down, her sword went sailing through the air.

"Curse it!" she muttered beneath her breath. Before the baby dragon's still erratically swaying tail could knock her over again, she scooted on hands and knees after her sword. Then, seemingly out of nowhere, a pair of black-booted feet barred her way.

Alena froze and, ever so slowly, lifted her gaze. The boots merged into snug-fitting black breeches, then a belted, dark blue tunic that fell to midthigh. Covering it all was a black, hooded robe hanging open nearly to the ground. The body beneath the clothes appeared moderately tall and impressively muscled. Alena's heart commenced a rapid beat. Was this, mayhap, Galen Radbourne, the man she'd come to Cadvallan for?

She shoved to her knees and glanced all the way up, squinting in the glare of the morning sun gleaming just behind his head to make out the man's features. His hair was dark, black most likely, brushed back carelessly from his face before flowing wavy and long to a pair of broad, straight shoulders. His eyes, as well as the rest of his features, remained shadowed from the backlit sun.

"What are you doing here and, even more importantly, how did you get here?"

The deep, rich timbre of his voice startled her. It was quiet, almost soothing, but authoritative nonetheless. A little *too* authoritative for Alena's tastes. Her gaze narrowed and she briefly considered the dagger shoved into the side of her boot before discarding that move as far too aggressive until she knew more of this man. Besides, with the dragons still at her back, her chances seemed a lot better with him.

"I'm looking for—" She stopped and tilted her head up at the man. "If 'tis no inconvenience to you, I'd like to stand. This kneeling at someone's feet isn't to my liking."

"Indeed?" A large hand with surprisingly long, tapered fingers filled Alena's vision. "Then, pray, fair lady, stand."

She ignored his outstretched hand and climbed to her feet. At this angle, her perspective of him altered somewhat. Though still imposing in build and presence, the man wasn't quite as tall as she'd originally imagined.

His eyes, rich brown and framed by surprisingly thick, black lashes, were poised now about three to four inches above hers. Not overly tall, certainly not near Renard's or Hawkwind, her former commander's, impressive height, Alena mused, but still big enough to be intimidating. And if his sun silhouetted frame was any indication of the body that lay beneath the clothing—

With a horrified gasp, Alena drew her wandering thoughts up short. By the Mother, what *ever* was she thinking? Here she was, a stranger on an unfriendly isle, surrounded by dragons and this man, and all she could think of was what his body looked like! The fever still hovering at the edges of her consciousness must have fried more than just her body.

He stared down at her, a faintly quizzical smile on his lips, and cocked his head. In that instant, Alena saw his face clearly. 'Twas Galen Radbourne to be sure. He was his brother's identical twin, from his strong blade of a nose and thick, dark brows, to his square jaw and full, sensual lips. Though leaner and without the sagging flesh about his eyelids, cheeks, and jawline of the obviously debauched Dorian Radbourne, the resemblance was still that of the man who held Renard prisoner.

"If you're quite finished with my inspection," Galen Radbourne said, "I'd still like an answer to my questions. What are you doing here? And how did you get through the spell that keeps me on the isle and everyone else from it?"

She didn't like the tolerant amusement that tinged his voice. Her fists clenched at her sides and her lips tightened. "I don't know how I got through the 'spell,' if there truly even was one. I just came across the sea in a skiff. And as to why I'm here, I came to find you, of course," she snapped. "Who else would I come for? Certainly not the dragons!"

He smiled, apparently not at all disturbed by her flare of anger. "Indeed? And how was I to know that? Some might find a visit with the dragons a far more worthwhile endeavor. Most, for that matter," he added dryly as an afterthought. "I'd wager few know I still even live—or care, for that matter."

"Well, *I* most certainly care." Alena decided a change of

approach as well as position was advisable. Though she hated to admit it, he was just too close, too overwhelming. She took a step back. "I need your help in the rescue of my friend. He's been taken prisoner by your brother, Dorian Radbourne."

"And what is that to me?" His smile never wavered.

She tamped down a surge of exasperation. Was this man truly as slow-witted as he appeared? "Isn't that obvious? He's your brother and only you have the powers to best him. Powers I need if I'm to save my friend."

"I have no powers." His smile faded. "You were misled if you were told that."

Alena couldn't believe her ears. Idara had assured her that Galen Radbourne's powers were equal to his brother's. And Idara would have no reason to lie, would she? Suddenly, Alena didn't know anything, couldn't even think straight. She felt hot, then cold, then hot again. The fever, curse it all. She should have known she couldn't hold it at bay for long.

"I don't believe you," she said, clenching her hands so tightly in an effort to keep her head clear and her body from swaying that her nails scored her palms. "Your brother is a sorcerer. All the males in your family have been sorcerers. You *must* have the power."

Radbourne shrugged. "It doesn't really matter one way or another, does it, if I refuse to go with you? Which I do." He took her by the arm and turned her around. "Now, since the reason for your visit to Cadvallan is at an end, I suggest you get back into your boat—wherever it washed up—and depart. The dragons and I cherish our privacy. We're not overly partial to—"

"Nay, curse you!" Alena wrenched her arm from his grasp and wheeled about to confront him. With a swift motion toward her boot, she retrieved her dagger. In the next instant, its razor sharp tip settled at the base of his throat.

"I don't care what you or your dragons like," she said, fighting to maintain her wavering consciousness. "My best friend, my *partner,* is being held by that vile man you call a brother. I *will* bring you back and you *will* use your magic to force him to release my friend." Alena's heart pounded in her chest and her head began to swim. "Do you hear me, Radbourne?"

"Aye, I hear you." He stood there calmly, not at all perturbed by the dagger pricking his throat. "But I say again; I have no powers. I renounced them even before I was exiled to Cadvallan Isle. I cannot assist you, even if I wished to. And killing me won't help either of us."

His face blurred; the day went dim. The ground threatened to drop out from under her. Nausea welled in Alena's gut. She flushed fire hot. "Nay, 't-twon't, I suppose," she mumbled through lips gone thick and heavy. "But then, what have I to lose, one way or another?"

"Naught it seems," came the calm reply, suddenly sounding so distant, so unclear. Then, everything went dark. Alena's knees buckled. She felt herself falling and could do naught to stop it.

"Ah, curse it all . . . ." she muttered in disgust, just before she fainted.

CHAPTER TWO

A woman . . . here on Cadvallan . . . after all these years. Even now, looking down at her sprawled in the sand, wet and bedraggled as she was, a fierce desire thrummed through Galen. Did she truly realize the danger she was in, even more so from him than the dragons? Most likely not. If she had, she'd surely hie herself off the isle, partner or no, as fast as she could.

He eyed her in languid appreciation. She was one of the most lovely women he'd ever seen, even more lovely than Lydia. But then, fifteen years, Galen belatedly admitted with a sharp twinge of guilt, could dim even the most cherished of memories.

She lay there on the beach, one arm flung out above her head, one booted leg tucked beneath the other, her long blond hair more loose from her braid than in it, and he couldn't tear his eyes from her. She was slender, with small, firm breasts and graceful curves, but still there was a promise of hidden power in the taut swell of muscle in her arms and legs.

He smiled grimly. A warrior woman, Galen thought, taking in her beige tunic, dark green breeches, long, brown-black leather jerkin laced in front, and her tall, dark brown boots. He recalled the dagger that had been pressed to his throat but a few moments ago, and the long sword with the ornate hilt he'd seen flying through the air as he'd approached her in her standoff with the dragons.

A warrior woman, to be sure. Definitely not the sort to seek out a former sorcerer, or a few sickly, powerless dragons.

Yet she was here, and the greatest mystery was how she'd pierced the spell that had kept both him and the dragons on Cadvallan Isle for all these years.

The consideration of her true motives—and the secret powers she must possess even to get this far—filled Galen with unease. He glanced up as the big white dragon lumbered over.

"Do you know who she is, or why she's here, Dragon Father?"

The dragon's long, slender head dipped and a pair of bejeweled eyes leisurely examined the unconscious woman. Then, with a sigh, the creature looked back up at Galen. "I know naught of her," he replied, his voice soft and mellifluous. "Naught save she washed up on this beach and was present for the young one's birth. She has named him and commenced an initial bonding." His glance moved to where the baby dragon stood protectively nearby, his anxious gaze never wavering from the woman. " 'Tis a most surprising set of circumstances."

"What does it mean?" Galen frowned in puzzlement. "She's a warrior, from all outward appearances. She says she came for me, to enlist my aid in rescuing her friend from my brother."

The Dragon Father's eyelids slid half-shut, as if he were pondering Galen's question. "What does it mean, indeed? Mayhap 'twouldn't be wise to send her away too quickly. Mayhap 'tis a trick of some sort, to lure you off Cadvallan. Mayhap someone suddenly has use of you."

"After fifteen years of exile?" Galen gave a self-disparaging laugh. "And what possible use could I be? My powers are all but dead. I made peace with that long ago. I'm no danger or value to anyone."

"Aye, so 'twould seem." The dragon smiled softly. "But

then again . . ." He turned back to the woman, eyed her closely. "She appears ill. You must take her to your dwelling and care for her. She cannot be allowed to die."

"Nay, she cannot be allowed to die," Galen muttered, not at all happy with the prospect of having any woman, much less one so sexually appealing, in his house after fifteen celibate years. It disturbed him greatly that the sight of a female could still stir him so easily. He'd thought he'd laid that to rest years ago, along with all the other unrequited needs and feelings . . . with all his magic.

The dragons, he was certain, imagined the renunciation of his powers originated solely from his aversion to evil and strife. He'd labored long and hard to convince them of that until, now, he almost believed it himself. But this . . . this *woman*, in but the span of a few short minutes, had again ripped aside the comforting facade of rationalizations and misty memories that had blurred, with time, the true horror of his powers.

Mayhap that was what disturbed him most about this woman's arrival. Her presence threatened to disrupt his well-ordered existence and relationship with the dragons. Though he'd made peace of a sorts with the big creatures, Galen knew how tenuous the friendship was. The dragons had been hurt enough by sorcerers. They didn't need additional issues to cloud their trust of him. *Especially* not some belated revelation of his monstrous abilities.

There was no reason for any, save his brother, ever to know the other, even more horrible basis for his voluntary exile to Cadvallan Isle. 'Twas his and Dorian's secret—the secret of their magical powers. Powers that had long ago become far too costly for Galen to bear.

For an anguished, fleeting moment, long-buried memories seared through him once more. *Lydia . . . ah, Lydia. Sorry*

. . . so very, very sorry . . .

With a savage effort, Galen wrenched his thoughts back to the woman lying before him on the beach. He knelt beside her and gathered her gently into his arms. In some instinctive move, she turned to him, her head falling naturally onto his shoulder, her body nestling against his for protection. The feel of her, her scent of ocean spray and fresh air, sent yet another shock of primal recognition—and response—shooting through Galen. He gritted his teeth, clasped her tightly to him, and rose.

There was naught he could do, however, to hide the flush warming his face. The Dragon Father cocked his long, scale-sleek head. "She disturbs you, does she not?"

Galen made a show of hefting the woman more securely to him and fiercely shook his head. " 'Tis naught. I-I'm just not accustomed to visitors, nor want them, anymore. I'll manage, though."

The dragon's lips pulled back to reveal his teeth in what could only be construed as a dragon's version of a smile. "As must we all, Radbourne. As must we all."

Turning on his heel, Galen set out down the beach with his human burden. He'd hardly taken five steps, however, before the baby dragon was bounding after him, whimpering in a low, plaintive voice. Galen stopped and glanced over his shoulder. In a spray of sand, the plump black creature slid to a halt just inches behind him. Galen shot him an exasperated look, then lifted his gaze to the Dragon Father.

The older dragon chuckled, the sound softly melodious. "She is his now. He must go wherever she goes."

Galen eyed the considerable bulk of the baby dragon. This particular species of earth dragon was quite large—even by the usual dragon standards. Newly born, the young beast easily stood as tall as he. And, to complicate an already difficult situation, if the dragon ever tried to sit back on his haunches, he'd slam his head through the roof of Galen's house.

"He can come along, but under no circumstances will he be allowed within my dwelling." Galen riveted the sternest gaze he could muster on the baby dragon. "Is that understood?"

The youngster's colorful eyes widened. He flicked his tail and bobbed his head in an awkward imitation of agreement. Though dragons eventually became fluent in whatever the local human dialect was, the skill evolved slowly at first. He'd wager his finest handmade cane chair, though, Galen thought wryly, that the words would never stop flowing once this particular dragon acquired the gift of speech. Already, there was just something . . . different . . . about this youngster.

He shot the Dragon Father a jaundiced look, then turned and strode off down the beach. Behind him, the soft galumph-galumph of the baby dragon moving across the sand filled the air.

Galen sighed. How, by the Holy Ones, could his fortunes change so rapidly? One minute he was a man without a care in the world, content and secure as he headed back from the mud pit with fresh clay for his makeshift pottery wheel, and the next, he was the reluctant keeper of an alluring if mysterious woman and her strangely possessive baby dragon.

He slowed his pace as he approached the path leading from the beach up to his secluded little house. As he did, the baby dragon, still unfamiliar with the maneuverings of his awkward young body, slammed into him. Galen staggered forward and sank to his knees, frantically clasping the woman to him. With an apologetic grunt, the dragon hurriedly backed away.

Galen struggled to stand, then glared over his shoulder at

the youthful miscreant. The young creature's eyes rolled in fright and his lower lip began a most undragonlike wobble. " 'Twas an accident," the sorcerer made haste to say before the dragon broke into yet another series of earsplitting wails. "There was no harm done. Just be more careful in the future."

The baby bobbed his head in eager assent. Galen eyed him a moment longer, then heaved a deep sigh, and set out once more. There was no fortune or misfortune to it, he thought in weary resignation. He just should've never gotten out of bed this morn.

Alena tossed and turned on the bed, vaguely aware of a soft mattress beneath her body, a blanket covering her. Hot . . . 'twas so hot. She licked her dry, cracked lips. "W-water," she heard a voice say, a voice low and rusty with disuse.

Through the dim, fire-lit haze, something moved across the room. Something cool and wet slid across her brow. Cold . . . Ah, how good, how soothing it felt! A hand touched the back of her neck. Her head was lifted and a cup pressed to her lips.

"Drink," a deep, rich voice said. " 'Tis freshly drawn from the well and icy cold. 'Twill ease your thirst."

Alena drank greedily until, accompanied by a low chuckle, the cup was pulled away. "Enough," the voice said. "You'll make yourself sick if you take too much too quickly. I'll give you more later."

She shifted onto her side to face the owner of the voice. Something stirred on her tongue. Something sharp, bitter. She licked her lips. "Bad . . . tastes bad . . ."

" 'Tis only a few herbs I added to the water to ease your fever. 'Twon't hurt you."

"I-I know," Alena mumbled and, somehow, realized that

she *did* know that about the voice's owner. He was good, kind, and gentle . . . almost . . . almost as if he cared about her. Cared . . . like Renard. Renard, her partner and dearest friend. A friend who had sacrificed himself so she might escape the evil sorcerer's castle.

A sob rose, unbidden, to Alena's lips. "Renard," she whispered softly before drifting back off to sleep. "Ah, Renard . . ."

At the sound of another man's name, Galen went still. Renard. Who was this person? The friend the woman had spoken of rescuing? Her voice had been filled with regret, anguish, even love, when she'd said his name. Was he, mayhap, more than just her friend? Mayhap even her lover?

Galen set down the cup with more force than he'd intended. What was it to him, one way or another? He wanted naught to do with this woman, save return her to health and send her on her way.

He shoved a hand through his hair. By the Mother, why did she have to come to Cadvallan? If only there were someone else here to care for her.

Briefly, he'd entertained the hope that somehow she'd managed to eliminate the spell enshrouding the isle. After he'd settled her safely into bed, he'd run down to the tiny cove where he'd secured the boat he'd built those many years ago. Unfurling the sail in the gentle breezes, Galen had attempted to set out across the sea to the mainland.

As always, a powerful wind had come up and blown him repeatedly back to shore. Just like all those hundreds of thousands of times he'd tried in the first few years after he'd tired of his exile, before he'd finally come to an acceptance that Cadvallan was where he was truly meant to live out his days.

Nay, the woman hadn't counteracted the spell, Galen thought glumly, at least not where he was concerned. Unfortunately, that also eliminated any hope he had of taking her back to the mainland and depositing her and her problems on some unsuspecting peasant. Whether he liked it or not, he was now the woman's only chance for care in her illness.

She tossed and turned on the bed, moaning softly. He eyed her with concern. She was burning with fever, a fever not even liberal draughts of his willow bark tea seemed able to control. Yet she desperately needed her body cooled.

The woman moaned again, the sound tortured, piteous. Galen flinched, her torment touching some place he'd thought long ago hardened against compassion for those of his kind. He leaned down and brushed a sweat-damp lock of hair from her face. She reacted to his touch, turning toward him.

"R-Renard . . ." she whimpered. "I'm coming, Renard. Don't despair. I'm coming."

As if burned, Galen jerked back his hand. He, too, had once known a love such as this woman had for her partner. He, too, would have sacrificed anything to be with her, save her. But instead . . . instead . . .

He stood, strode across the room, and grabbed up the bucket. Tossing the remainder of its contents into the kettle of water and aromatic herbs he kept steaming on the hearth, Galen crossed the generous expanse of the one-room, stone-and log-built house. He wrenched open the door—and nearly toppled over the baby dragon sleeping across the doorway. Biting back a scalding curse and an impulse to climb right over him, Galen forced himself instead to gently nudge the young creature awake.

"Get up," he growled. "Your 'mistress' is burning with fever and I must draw fresh water from the well to cool her."

With a startled grunt the dragon scrabbled aside, then, as Galen moved past, again took up his place of guard back at

47

the door. He'd never seen a dragon so attentive or loyal, Galen thought. Such devotion was, if the tales were true, usually reserved for a dragon and his *galiene*—that special race of human females capable of forming life bonds with dragons. But the *galienes* were gone, all of them now, systematically hunted down and killed by the sorcerers. All gone . . . which made this dragon's behavior all the more surprising.

He followed the path to the well, then lowered the bucket and drew up the fresh, cold water. If all went as he hoped, the sponging bath would help to lower the woman's body temperature until the willow bark tea could take effect. Galen heaved the bucket from the well and reluctantly made his way back to his house, so preoccupied with the consideration of bathing the woman that he narrowly avoided a collision with the baby dragon who reared up at the last minute and nearly managed, in the process, to slam his head into the water bucket.

Galen eyed the startled creature for a long moment, then sighed, shook his head, and reentered his house. As he crossed the room back to where the woman slept, an uneasy anticipation filled him. He'd never bathed a woman before, even if for purely medicinal reasons, and wasn't totally certain how to go about it. Cool cloths laid on her body, especially her face, trunk, and arms and legs, seemed the most logical way to chill her quickly.

She already lay naked beneath the light coverlet. Galen had discarded her wet clothes hours ago. That disrobement, however, had been quick, impersonal, and carried out more by feel than sight. He wasn't so certain he could handle touching her undraped flesh, even if just to lay wet cloths, quite as unemotionally.

He set down the bucket beside the bed and went to gather up some clean cloths to bathe her with. As he passed back by the window, Galen paused there to throw open the shutters and look out. The cold spring air rushed in, setting his face to tingling and his skin to tightening.

It did naught, however, to dispel his heavy, tormented confusion. Lifting his gaze to the heavens, Galen groaned aloud. The dark, star-studded night winked back at him, serene, unchanging, and heedless of his plight.

She was a human being, he fiercely told himself, clasping the windowsill. She was helpless and totally dependent on him. 'Twould be dishonorable to take advantage of anyone, much less a woman, in such a state. Despicable to find pleasure in her naked helplessness . . .

Yet even the consideration of touching her, looking at her, sent the blood to pounding through Galen's body and pooling in his groin. He had all but forgotten he was a man, a man with physical needs and desires. He'd *had* to make himself forget. To allow himself to yearn for what he dared not take again only stirred anew the embers of his long dormant powers. Powers that now sickened him.

Most of the time, Galen had managed to put aside those sweet, insistent clamorings of his body, even when, as a hot-blooded, passionate youth, he'd turned forever from the fulfillment that was so natural, so accepted for any other man of his age. No matter how brief it had been, he only wished he'd never had a taste of the pleasure of loving a woman. 'Twould have made his terrible sacrifice easier to bear.

But there was no help for it, not then or now. With a soul-deep sigh Galen shoved back from the window, pulled the shutters to, and, like a man going to his doom, headed across the room to where the woman awaited him. Pulling up a stool whose well-formed legs were carved in the tenuous swirls of some heavy-leafed vine that grew rampant on the Isle, Galen lowered himself to sit beside her.

She tossed restlessly on the bed, her cheeks flushed with the fever that consumed her. In her movements she'd inadvertently flung back the light coverlet, exposing a small, plump, pink-rippled breast. A single scar wound from her shoulder to somewhere near her breastbone before disappearing beneath the coverlet. The sight of it momentarily shocked Galen, before he recalled his earlier supposition that she was most likely a warrior.

In a reflexive motion, he leaned down to cover the woman, then realized the pointlessness of such an act. In a few moments more, he must uncover most of her as 'twas.

Forcing his gaze from the delectable sight of the woman's lovely body, Galen busied himself plunging the cloths into the water, wringing them lightly, then spreading them, one by one, across her arms and upper torso. Loathe to strip her of all modesty, he next pulled up the blanket to expose the woman's legs yet maintain a decent modicum of cover for her lower abdomen, groin, and upper thighs.

Her legs were as slender and shapely as her arms, and equally toned with a hint of well-formed muscle beneath them. Several jagged scars of various lengths transected their otherwise flawless perfection. Her skin was pale, almost the color of the moonstone he wore in the pendant about his neck, milky white and alluringly soft. Gritting his teeth against a nearly uncontrollable impulse to run his fingers down the silky length of her inner thighs, Galen concentrated on laying wet cloths over them instead.

Next, he dragged the stool closer to the woman's head and riveted his attention on her face. Her lips were slightly parted in her erratic breathing, soft and full and rosy. Galen licked his own lips, then caught himself in the act and swallowed hard. Sweat beaded his brow, his body tightened like a bow being strung.

With a savage curse, Galen turned to the water bucket and fished out the last cloth. Winding it viciously in his hands, he wrung it nearly dry before realizing what he was doing. Expelling a shuddering breath, he forced himself to fold it before plunging the cloth back into the water, this time squeezing it out more gently. Then, divesting himself of all emotion, Galen wiped the woman's face and neck with the cloth.

From time to time in her delirium, the woman murmured the man's name. "Renard. Ah, Renard . . ." Her voice seemed to soften, go deep with emotion when she said it. And, each time, Galen's heart twisted within his breast.

Memories, long and deeply buried, broke free of the tight bonds he'd woven about them, rising to encompass him in a bittersweet swell of emotion. Once, now so very long ago, he, too, had heard his name on a woman's lips, his name whispered in loving passion. By the Holy Ones, how he wished to experience that joy, that fierce sense of worth and possession just one time more!

One time more . . . before he drew his last breath, before he rotted away on this windswept isle of forgotten, rejected creatures, of lonely exiles.

She stirred, mumbled vaguely. For a brief instant her eyes fluttered open, then closed. Galen leaned down and touched the back of his hand to her forehead. It had cooled noticeably. Satisfaction filled him. The wet cloths and willow bark tea were taking effect.

As the night passed, the woman's restless movements stilled. The hectic flush receded from her cheeks. She began to mutter soft, disjointed words and phrases. Galen paid little attention, concentrating instead on the far less disconcerting task of rewetting then replacing the cooling cloths on her body.

51

"What are you doing?"

He jerked his gaze from the bucket where he was lightly wringing out another cloth. In the faint glow of dawn, turquoise blue eyes, bleary but lucid, stared up at him. He gave an unsteady laugh. "Naught more than trying to get that fever of yours to break."

She lifted her head briefly and glanced down at her body. Her lips tightened in anger. "And was it necessary to expose me so fully to do so? You have me all but naked!"

Galen released the breath he hadn't realized he'd been holding. "Aye, 'twas *more* than necessary. 'Twas vital. Your modesty was hardly the issue at the time."

"And now?"

Rather than risk a reply through a throat gone suddenly dry, Galen answered instead by removing the cloths from her legs and flipping down the coverlet. Next, he did the same for her upper torso, then poured out a fresh cup of willow bark-laced water. Lifting her head, Galen silently offered the woman a drink.

She accepted it greedily and without further discussion. "That was wonderful," she sighed when he finally laid her back on the bed. The anger seemed to ebb from her in her renewed exhaustion. Her lids lowered.

As Galen watched, she drifted back to sleep. He bent, tucked the coverlet more snugly about her, then rose and walked outside. He hadn't realized how tightly strung he was until the woman had woken and lashed out at him. He needed a breath of fresh air and a few minutes away from her, before he returned to his house. Galen's brief sojourn outside ended up lasting several hours.

Alena woke about midafternoon. She yawned, stretched, feeling quite refreshed. Her movements caught the sorcerer's attention. He was at her side in a few quick strides.

"How do you feel?" His dark eyes scanned her. "Would you like some broth? I've had it simmering over the fire for hours now, awaiting your earliest convenience."

"My earliest convenience, eh?" She eyed him consideringly. "Mayhap a bit later. First, though, I must thank you for your kindness in caring for me. After our less than cordial meeting on the beach, you could've left me lying there."

"And let that baby dragon stumble all over you in his efforts to protect you?" Galen pulled up the stool and sat beside her. She didn't seem all that angry at him anymore. "I might as well have just finished you off," he continued, a slight smile lifting his mouth. " 'Twould have been a quicker and far more merciful death."

The woman's brow furrowed. "That dragon. I dreamed of him being born . . . and then . . . then he was." She lifted one hand and massaged her forehead, a pained, puzzled expression on her face. " 'Twas so strange, so mysterious."

"Everything about you is strange and mysterious." Galen leaned forward, his forearms falling to rest upon his thighs. He fixed her with a steady stare. "To begin with, though, 'twould make things a bit easier if I knew your name. It seems you well know mine."

She lowered her hand and locked gazes with him. "A fair trade, to be sure. My name is Alena."

He arched a dark brow. "Just Alena?"

"I've been with a mercenary army since I was a child, and the warriors there only went by their first names." She managed a weak smile. "It has been so long since I used my family name, I cannot say I recall it now."

"Well, Alena will do nicely."

He said no more, only continued to grace her with an enigmatic stare. Finally, unable to bear his unsettling scrutiny,

Alena broke the silence. "Why *did* you take care of me? I didn't exactly make the best first impression, shoving a dagger to your throat and demanding you come with me."

He shrugged. "Who knows? Mayhap there's still some shred of human decency left in me?" The big sorcerer cocked his head. "Mayhap the same decency that kept you from slitting my throat when I refused to help you?"

"Mayhap," Alena admitted dryly. "Not that my plans for you have changed, no matter how kindly you've treated me. I still need you to help me rescue my partner from your brother. I owe you that much of the truth, at any rate."

"You wasted a lot of valuable time and energy coming this far. My brother may be selfish and self-serving, but I hardly think he's the monster you make him out to be."

"You haven't seen him in fifteen years. What makes you think he's the same man?"

Taken aback by her blunt demand, Galen paused. "I suppose I don't know what kind of man he's become. I just can't believe . . ." His voice faded. "Well, it matters not. You made it to Cadvallan through a powerful spell. Your own magic is sufficient to take on my brother."

She frowned in puzzlement, tried to lever herself to one elbow, and sank back in exhaustion. "I don't know what you mean. I told you before. I have no magic."

A fine sweat sheened her brow. Rather than answering Alena immediately, Galen leaned forward and raised her head for a drink from the cup he lifted to her lips. Only when he was satisfied she'd taken a sufficient draught of the willow bark-laced water did he lower her back to the bed.

" 'Tis all quite simple, really," Galen then continued. "The spell over Cadvallan still holds. I took great pains trying to leave the isle while you slept. I couldn't. You, on the other hand, seem impervious to the spell." His dark gaze narrowed. "How else is that possible, save through magical powers?"

Alena squelched the surge of exasperation his question stimulated. She'd better things to do than repeat what she'd already told him on the beach. Yet, though patience and diplomacy had never been her strong suit, she sensed this man would never be swayed by threats or physical force. "I don't know," she forced herself to reply. "I swear it. I have no powers, not for magic, at any rate. I just sailed here and landed. That's all."

"And I don't believe you." Galen set down the cup and stood. "I may be an exiled sorcerer, cut off from the rest of humanity for the past fifteen years, but I'm not stupid. You're the first human being I've seen in all this time. And no sooner do you arrive, you bond with one of the isle's dragons. *No one* does that anymore. And yet you persist in claiming you've no magical powers?"

He gave a bitter laugh. "Well, as I said before, it doesn't matter. I won't be manipulated, either with truth *or* lies. My life is best lived here now, spell or no spell, not back in a world rife with cruelty and pain. I accepted that reality long ago. Leave me in peace, I say. 'Tis all I have left."

Alena gripped the coverlet in both hands, struggling to keep the anger and frustration from her voice. "And why should you have any more peace than the rest of us? *Your* brother terrorizes the land. He takes whatever he wants, whether it be the possessions of others or even some lord's daughter. And there is naught—*naught*—anyone can do because he is a sorcerer. Yet you have the power to stop him, if not with your own magic, than mayhap because you are born of the same parents, share the same flesh and blood."

She dragged in a tremulous breath. "Ah, Holy Mother, I'm not suited for this role of diplomat! I'm a warrior, not some eloquent courtier with a mouthful of honeyed words. My sword or dagger has always spoken best when words fail me."

"You're doing better than you may imagine."

Her head jerked up. "Then . . . then you'll help me?"

He shook his head. "Nay. My mind was made long ago. Not for you nor anyone will I change it."

"Every man has his price," Alena bitterly replied. "I have only to discern what yours is." She paused to eye him closely. "You said you tried to leave the isle. What if I can find some way to get you off it?"

"Nay." Galen shook his head. "I only wished to take *you* from it. There's naught for me back in the world anymore."

"But what if I could get you money?" she persisted. "More money than you'd ever imagined? I fight for pay—lots of it— and would give it all to you. With it, you could make a fresh start. Money can always pave the way back into the hearts of others, no matter what has come before."

At her cynical offer, something in Galen hardened. Curse it all, he wasn't like the rest of them and the sooner she realized that, the better off she'd be! A thin smile twisted his lips. "So, you'd do anything, give anything, to save this friend of yours, would you?"

"Aye, *anything*."

He eyed her for a long moment more. "Well, save your breath. I need naught from you, Alena. Naught."

The challenge in his words was unmistakable, but Alena was never one to back down from a challenge. So, he didn't want to leave the isle, and he didn't want to take money? Her mind raced. She'd grown up surrounded by men. She knew them inside and out. Surely even this sorcerer had his manly weaknesses, desires of the flesh if not cravings for wealth or power. Desires he'd had no way of fulfilling for the past fifteen years. Yet to offer herself to him . . .

Renard was her friend. She couldn't let him down, no matter the personal cost. But would the sorcerer find the offer of her body payment enough? She wasn't overly generous with her favors, but she *had* lain with a few especially virile and physically attractive warriors in the past years. And many had been the others who'd offered to bed her.

"You haven't had a woman in a very long while, have you?" Alena carefully began.

His gaze swept down her body, hesitating only briefly as it passed the swell of her breasts. "And are you offering yourself to me?"

"Aye." She swallowed hard and forged on. "I'll do anything for Renard."

"Indeed?" A muscle jumped in the broad expanse of his jaw. "And after fifteen years without a woman," he silkily drawled, "I can't afford to be too choosy, can I?"

She flushed. Anger flared in her eyes. "I didn't mean it that way."

"Aye, you did, and you know it. You'd search out and seize any advantage you could find." Galen studied her in thoughtful silence, then sighed. "But it changes naught. As attractive as you are, my life and personal integrity are all the more attractive. Regretfully, I must decline your most tantalizing offer."

"Then what?" Despair filled her. Alena shoved awkwardly to her elbows, panting with the effort. "What *will* it take? I'll give you anything. Do you hear me? *Anything!*"

"Don't." Galen stepped back. "Give it up. I won't change my mind, no matter what you say or do. Let it be."

"Do you want me to beg? Is that it?" In an effort to hold back the tears, Alena's fists clenched at her sides. Tears . . . Holy Mother, she *never* cried. Yet this . . . this man had already driven her to the very edge of her control.

Why wouldn't he understand how desperate she was? She knew 'twas hopeless to pit her meager human powers against Dorian Radbourne. She hadn't a chance without Galen, and she never went to battle without first assuring the odds were in her favor.

"Well, I'll do even that, curse you!" Alena raged, feeling more weak, and helpless, and foolish than she'd ever felt in her life. " 'Tis Renard's life at stake here! Please help him. Please! There's no hope for him if you don't." She fell back on the bed, drenched with sweat, exhausted. A single, traitorous tear rolled down her cheek. "No hope . . . for him . . . or for any of us."

At her last, whispered, pitiful words, a block of ice settled about Galen's heart. He would *not* let himself be swayed, no matter what she said or did. He wouldn't let himself care. 'Twas too frightening, too dangerous, after all these years . . . for him *and* for her.

And for what? For some foolhardy warrior who'd managed to anger his brother? Did she truly expect him to go against his own brother for some stranger?

"You're singularly stubborn when it comes to accepting someone's answer," he muttered, his voice as hard as his resolve. "But 'twill remain the same, nonetheless, until the day I can send you sailing back from whence you came. The sooner you accept that, the better."

He turned on his heel and strode from the house once again, into the warm spring sun. Just a few more days, Galen told himself, and, hopefully, she'd be well enough to leave Cadvallan Isle. Just a few more days . . .

By the Holy Ones, he inwardly groaned as a fleeting memory of naked breasts and long, white legs slipped into his mind. A few more days and he might well be mad. The only blessing in all of this was his iron-clad self-discipline, a self-discipline that had served him well in all the years of his exile.

A very small blessing, to be sure, but all he had left to cling to.

CHAPTER THREE

Late the next morn, the scent of porridge cooking woke Alena. She sniffed appreciatively, snuggled deeper into her covers, and turned over onto her side. Soon, she drowsily told herself. Soon, she'd rise and have her breakfast before riding out with Renard . . .

Footsteps across a wooden floor intruded on her dreamy plans. She pulled the pillow up to cover her ears. Too early . . . too tired . . . not just yet, Renard . . .

A strong grip on her shoulder, a gentle shake, roused her. "Wake up," a male voice—most definitely not Renard's—commanded. "The day draws on and I've work to do. If you want something to eat before I leave, wake up now or go hungry until midday when I return."

Ever so slowly, Alena pulled down her pillow and turned toward the voice, her pleasant if momentary disorientation gone. She wasn't with Renard. Renard was the prisoner of Dorian Radbourne. And she was here on Cadvallan Isle to convince his twin brother to help her rescue him . . . if only she could.

He stood there, towering above her, holding a thick pottery bowl. When she did naught more than glare up at him, he set the bowl beside the steaming mug on the small table next to the bed. Pulling up a carved wooden stool, he lowered himself upon it.

"Well, what's it to be?" Galen asked, gazing over at her. "I haven't time to nursemaid you all day. Are you hungry or not?"

If the truth be known, she wanted to pick up the bowl and heave its contents into his face. Childish as 'twas, there was just something about Galen Radbourne that roused an irrational anger in Alena. Mayhap 'twas his close resemblance to his brother. Mayhap 'twas his refusal to help her, or his total control over her in that refusal. Just once in her life, she ardently wished for the cold-blooded killer instinct necessary to punish him, to take him down where he sat for his stubborn, selfish, self-centered—

" 'Twill do no good shooting daggers at me with those beautiful eyes of yours," Galen quietly interrupted Alena's violent train of thought. "The broth yestereve was a fine start, but you need something more substantial like this porridge if you ever wish to recover." He gestured to the bowl. "I haven't all day. What will it be?"

"I'm not some helpless child that I need you to feed me!" she snapped. "Begone to what must be some vitally important labor, alone as you are on this isle."

He leaned back, picked up the bowl, and shoved it in her face. "Go on then. Show me first how well you can feed yourself." He smiled. "And show yourself, as well."

Alena graced him with a look of withering scorn, then shoved awkwardly to her elbows. When further efforts to prop herself up in bed failed, thanks to a nauseating surge of weakness, she scowled up at him. "If you'd deign to help me sit, I think I can manage the rest."

"Do you now? Well, we'll see about that."

Galen set the bowl back on the table and stood. Leaning down, he grasped her beneath the arms and tugged her up. As he did, Alena was encompassed by a huge body and the scent of woodsmoke and sandalwood, by rich brown eyes and an imposing, though gentle, presence. His hands felt strangely stimulating yet soothing, his long, tapering fingers strong and sure. Confused by her response, Alena resorted to the only defense left her.

"Why must you always be so smug about everything?" she flung out the words through gritted teeth. "Isn't it enough you have me at your mercy, as weak as I am? Must you also taunt me with it?"

He released her and reared back, startled. For a long moment Galen stared down at her as a myriad of emotions flared and died in his eyes. "Each of us," he finally said, "has our vulnerabilities, vulnerabilities we defend in the best way we know how. And yours, it seems, is your abhorrence of being dependent on another, of letting yourself need someone." The sorcerer turned, took up the pottery bowl and placed it in Alena's hands. "So, prove you don't need my help. But if you can't, have the good grace to admit defeat and let me help you."

Alena's grip tightened about the bowl and she grabbed the smoothly carved wooden spoon sitting in the porridge. Grasping it, she scooped up a generous serving and lifted it to her mouth. The porridge tasted good, with a nutty, slightly grainy consistency, flavored with just the right amount of honey and goat's milk. She swallowed it, suddenly ravenous after almost two days without any food but a few bowls of broth, and shot Galen a triumphant look.

"Go on," he urged softly. "Eat it all."

She dug back into the bowl, finishing off three more mouthfuls before the spoon suddenly became too heavy. A spoonful more, and Alena fell back in exhaustion.

"Finished already?"

She riveted her gaze on him. "Not at all. I just had enough for the moment. Can't a person be allowed to savor her meal?"

He chuckled and took the bowl from her. "Here, open

up," Galen said, directing another generous spoonful of porridge toward her lips. "You can savor this just as easily if I feed you as not, and conserve what little strength you've left in the bargain."

"I'm not—" Alena let the protest die. 'Twas pointless to argue with him, when they both knew she was once more on the verge of exhaustion. She sighed and opened her mouth, accepting the porridge. Regaining her strength as fast as possible was of the utmost importance, not a petty battle of wills with a pigheaded sorcerer. And if, in the end, she found some way to convince him to go with her, despite his initial protests, the ultimate victory was still hers.

Ten minutes later, the bowl of porridge was empty and Alena was once more snuggling back into her pillow. Her lids heavy with a rapidly encroaching drowsiness, she watched Galen don his heavy black wool hooded robe, pick up what looked like a huge fishing net and head toward the door.

"A moment," she called out to him.

He paused, then turned. "Aye?"

"My clothes. Could I mayhap have them back?"

"And what for?"

Alena choked back an exasperated reply. "I may feel like getting up later."

"You'd do better to stay in bed today." He hefted the net over his shoulder and turned back toward the door.

"Wait." Alena levered to one elbow and smiled her most politic smile. "Could you at least tell me what you did with my clothes?"

"I washed them this morn before breakfast and hung them out to dry. I'll bring them back in when I return for the midday meal."

"My thanks . . . for your consideration, I mean."

He didn't reply, just continued to stare at her. After a time he cocked his dark head, his long, wavy locks brushing his broad shoulders. "Is there aught more, or may I now depart?"

She lowered herself back to the bed. "Nay, I haven't further questions . . . for now."

Galen grinned. "Aye, for now." He turned on his heel and, opening the door, strode through it, closing it firmly behind him.

In the sorcerer's wake, a flurry of cold air swirled into the room. The hearth fire flared to life in a tumult of snaps and pops. A log crashed, sparks scattered, and a surge of heat filled the room.

With a weary sigh, Alena pulled up the coverlet and extra quilt Galen had added to her bed in the night, turned on her side, and proceeded to lie there for a long while, pondering the man who, at one turn could be so kind and gentle and, the next, so stubborn and selfish. One way or another, there had to be some way of winning him to her cause. She just hadn't figured out quite how to do it.

It was past midday when Alena next awoke. She lay there for a time, savoring the feeling of refreshment, the renewed sense of energy pumping through her veins. She also recognized a familiar pang of hunger. The porridge had been good, but breakfast had been several hours ago and her body cried out, once more, for food.

She considered awaiting Galen's return, but decided that might take longer than she cared to wait. Besides, she was quite capable of fending for herself. Despite the big sorcerer's comments to the contrary, she felt strong enough for the minimal walking required to dress herself and prepare a simple meal. He didn't realize what a warrior's life was like, nor the past hardships she'd endured, sufferings that would make this brief bout with a fever appear little more than a jaunt through a flower garden.

Alena shoved to a sitting position, swung her legs over the edge of the bed, and paused as a wave of dizziness engulfed her. Once that passed, she glanced about the one-room house, seeing it in perspective and detail for the first time. It was tidy and well-furnished with a fine, hand-rubbed table and four painstakingly fashioned cane chairs, a tall, open cabinet wherein were displayed a collection of hand-painted pottery dishes, bowls, and mugs, and two intricately carved chests that sat on either side of the cabinet. The beginnings of yet another cane chair stood in one corner, alongside a potter's wheel and several greenware jugs.

This Galen Radbourne was a man of many talents, Alena mused. But then, he'd have to be to have survived so long on Cadvallan without benefit of other human assistance—assistance that, if Idara's tales were true, had lasted just long enough to deposit the sorcerer and some food and supplies on Cadvallan's shores and sail away.

Compassion flickered in her breast. He'd survived the best way he knew how, and now she came seeking him and demanding that he cast even this life aside and follow where she bid.

Yet there was no help for it. Renard's welfare, aye, his very life, hung in the balance. She couldn't spare time nor pity on Galen Radbourne's personal desires to the contrary.

Alena wrapped the quilt about her, grasped its ends in one fisted hand, and rose. A quick grab for the nearby table was the only thing that kept her from falling.

After a few moments, she felt steady enough to walk to the door and open it. There, a gust of wind nearly toppled her over. Frantically, Alena grasped the door frame, righted herself, and glanced out.

Galen Radbourne's hut was perched on a brow of volcanic

rock that thrust out over the sea. In the hazy distance, a faint outline of land could be seen, the land of Wyndymyll. Far below, the waves crashed on an unforgivingly rock-strewn shore, their dark, churning waters both foreboding and hypnotically beckoning.

Fleetingly, Alena wondered at the emotions a daily view of his former homeland stirred in the exiled sorcerer—and why he'd chosen to build in such a windswept, isolated spot. She quickly shook such considerations aside. For all practical purposes he was the enemy, and too close a knowledge and concern for an enemy always proved to be dangerous.

She'd learned that the hard way early on as a mercenary warrior, when she'd discovered that to know your enemy was to find it too hard to kill him. A quick, emotionless deathblow was far easier to deliver before one looked into an opponent's eyes or heard him beg for his life. And if one had had the misfortune to ride or fight beside a man before fate turned one against the other . . .

Alena shivered, clutched the quilt more tightly to her, and banished thoughts of her past mistakes from her mind. She scanned the area about the house, searching for where Galen had hung her clothes to dry. They flapped in the stiff breeze from a tree on a nearby hillock. Eyeing the distance, Alena decided she could make it there and back.

The actual attempt, however, thanks to the fierce winds, sapped more of her strength than she'd anticipated. By the time Alena made it to the tree, it was all she could do to hold onto the trunk with one hand and her quilt about her with the other. And, despite her repeated attempts to tug her clothes free, the tunic and breeches remained firmly fixed to the branch.

"Curse it all," Alena muttered. "Why must everything about this quest be so damned hard?"

Her patience at an end, she made a wild grab for her tunic, missed, lost her balance, and toppled over. Her hand struck a sharp outcropping of glittering black stone, slicing open her palm. Alena bit back a cry of pain, grabbed the injured hand with the other, and pressed the torn flesh together. As soon as the bleeding slowed, she used the sharp rock to hack off a piece of the bottom of the quilt and wrapped it tightly about her wounded hand.

As she sat back on her haunches, the quilt bunched and tangled around her, a faint wail reached her ears. She frowned. Where had she heard that sound before?

Scrabbling noises grew louder with each passing moment. The wail became a terrified bawl. Then, a black dragon appeared over the crest of the nearest hill leading down to the sea. Alena's heart caught in her throat.

Its beautiful, bejeweled eyes wide, the baby dragon bounded over the ground, headed straight for her at a pell-mell pace. Behind the creature, Galen Radbourne appeared, a net full of fish slung over his shoulder. One look at where the dragon was headed and he blanched, tossed the net to the ground, and, with a roar, set off at a run to cut off the dragon before it collided with Alena.

For an instant frozen in time, she watched the mesmerizing sight of a huge dragon bearing down on her. At the last minute, as the baby dragon, belatedly realizing its mistake, attempted to slide to a halt, she dove aside and rolled down the hillock in a tangle of quilt and flailing limbs. Before Alena could cover herself, Galen was upon her.

"Curse it all, woman!" he rasped between ragged breaths. "Are you bound and determined to get yourself killed? Why didn't you stay abed like I told you?"

Alena flipped the end of the quilt up to hide her nakedness, then glared up at him. "Mayhap just *because* you told me. I don't take orders well from smug, arrogant men. *Especially* ones I've no reason to obey or respect."

He squatted to meet her eye to eye. "You're on my island, staying in my house," he growled, his voice gone low and hard. "Whether you respect me or not, you should obey me, or hie yourself off Cadvallan posthaste."

Her lips tightened and her chin lifted a defiant notch. "Fine, I'll do just that." Alena paused, as the absurdity of her situation struck her at last. "But you and I both know I'm not up to any extended travel just yet, nor will I leave without you."

At her sudden change in tack, he visibly relaxed. His mouth quirked. "Then you're prepared for a very long stay, I take it?"

"Nay, as a matter of fact, I'm not." She jerked more of the quilt about her, then glanced back up at him. "Now, if you'd be so kind as to get out of my way, I'd like to retrieve my clothes and go back to the house and dress."

Galen's gaze took in her tousled mane of blond hair, the soiled and torn quilt that barely covered her breasts, and the bloodied rag bound around her right hand. "Aye, your plan is sound." He leaned down and slid one hand beneath her legs; the other moved to grasp her behind her back.

"What are you doing?"

Alena tried to scoot away, but it was already too late. In a fluid, effortless motion, Galen stood, clasping her to him in his arms. She gasped, then swiftly grabbed him behind the neck for support.

Galen shot her a quick look. "You and I both know you can't make it back to the house under your own power." He hefted her more closely to him, then instantly regretted the action. Alena's soft body pressed against his.

His flesh responded instantly, swelling, going rock hard.

Galen bit back an anguished groan, clasped her tightly to him, and strode out without further discussion. As they passed the tree where Alena's clothes still hung, flapping wildly in the breeze, he paused just long enough to allow her to pull them down, then proceeded on his way. He carried her to the house none too quickly for him. As soon as Galen reached the bed, he unceremoniously dumped her onto it.

She bounced hard, caught her balance, then scowled up at him through her tangled hair. "That wasn't necessary, you know."

"Oh, aye, 'twas." Galen stood over her, his hands on his hips. "You're impertinent and ungrateful. You've disturbed my peace from the first moment you arrived here, and I'm tired of it. Do you hear me? Tired of it!"

At the barely leashed anger emanating from him, Alena reared back. Holy Mother, he was still a sorcerer, no matter his claims to the contrary. If he should lose his temper . . .

"Fine," she muttered grudgingly. "I'm sorry. I *have* been a rather ungrateful guest. I'm just not accustomed to inactivity, nor to being ordered around."

"You must have been a trial to any leader, then." Galen's hands fell to his sides. "I find it difficult to believe you made a very good soldier with that belligerent attitude of yours."

"I'm an *excellent* warrior." Alena tossed her hair out of her eyes and raked her hand through her windblown locks. She shoved to a kneeling position on the bed and glared up at him. "Until a few months ago, I was a war captain for the finest mercenary leader in the land. But *he* knew how to motivate and lead people. *You,* on the other hand . . ." At the renewed spark of anger that flared in the big sorcerer's eyes, Alena let the rest of the sentence drop. "Well, never mind. 'Tisn't of import at any rate. I said I was sorry."

"Aye, so you did." He paused to eye her intently. "You

look a mess and you need that hand of yours cleaned and bandaged properly." He shrugged out of his heavy robe, laid it aside and gestured to her crudely wrapped hand. "Remove the bandage while I get the medical supplies."

She shook a fist at him when he turned his back and strode across the room to retrieve a bowl of water, clean cloths, and a jar of ointment. By the time Galen returned, however, Alena had done as he'd requested. Her sliced hand, palm up, lay on her lap atop the strips of torn quilt she'd used to bind it. The wound was deep and gaping. Though not overly squeamish after years of battle, Alena found she couldn't look long at it.

"Aye, 'tis bad," Galen agreed, noting her sudden pallor. "The volcanic rock up here is sharp as a blade." He took her hand gently and cradled it in his. "If your palm wasn't so callused from work, I fear the stone would've sliced clear through to the bone."

"How comforting," Alena muttered and swallowed hard. "Will I be able to use it again?"

He studied her hand for a long moment. "Possibly. But I'll have to sew it closed and you'll have to avoid using it in any way until it heals. Any movement in that area will rip open the stitches."

"I'll do whatever you ask. 'Tis my sword hand, you know."

"Aye, I know." Galen's eyes met hers. "I'll do what I can."

She couldn't tear her gaze from his. She'd never noticed before that his eyes were the shade of deep amber and flecked with bits of darker brown. She'd never noticed before how thick and long his lashes were, nor the slight beard shadow that perpetually shaded his mouth and jaw. And she'd most definitely never noticed how full and soft and sensual his lips were. Lips meant for a woman to kiss, to nibble, to suckle and run her tongue over . . .

With a start, Alena leaned back, flushing furiously. "My thanks." Nervously, she glanced away, pretending sudden interest in tucking her quilt more securely in the cleft between her breasts.

The action did little to ease the heat that seared through Galen's veins. It had been difficult enough to maintain his control over his rampaging emotions since that first instant of body contact when he'd lifted Alena into his arms. Then the sight of her, looking gloriously tousled and wanton in the tangle of her quilt when he'd tossed her onto the bed, had only stoked the smoldering fires. And just now, when she'd looked at him with those sea green eyes of hers and her gaze had dipped to his mouth . . .

He inhaled a ragged breath, forced himself to turn to his box of supplies, and opened it. Extracting a small pottery jar, Galen laid it beside the bowl of water. He quickly soaped a cloth and, concentrating on the task before him, began to gently cleanse Alena's hand.

She gave a low hiss of pain as he washed her, but neither moved nor protested. Galen avoided looking at Alena, as much from the sense-stirring sight of her as from the viewing of her pain. When all the dirt and old blood was washed away, he next flushed the wound with copious amounts of water to remove any embedded bits of rock and gravel. After patting the wound dry, Galen took up needle and thread. Only then did he finally meet her gaze.

"This will hurt."

"Get it over with," Alena said through gritted teeth. "I've been sewn up before. And I'm no puling noblewoman who faints at the first twinge of pain or drop of blood."

He clamped down on the glimmer of a smile. She was a proud one and brave as they came, but many a far stronger and bigger man had fainted from having a fresh wound sewn.

He had learned that much as a lad, helping his mother when she nursed the soldiers who had guarded their fortress home.

For a fleeting instant, Galen's thoughts flitted back to the memory of a chestnut-haired woman with soft brown eyes. His good, gentle, loving mother . . . He thanked the Holy Ones she hadn't lived to witness his crime and subsequent exile. 'Twould have broken her heart.

"Get on with it, will you?" Alena's tension fraught voice intruded into Galen's bittersweet musings. " 'Tisn't kind to keep one suffering in anticipation. 'Tis always far worse than the actuality."

"Aye, that 'tis." Taking her hand, he cupped it into its normal position of rest, then picked up the needle and thread. "Hold still now." With exquisite care, Galen swiftly shoved the needle through the flesh of one side of Alena's wound and across and through the other. Her body jerked but all the while she kept her hand steady.

Galen shot her a quick look. She was pale and a fine sheen of sweat bathed her brow. "Are you all right?"

"F-fine," she gasped. "Get on with it, I say."

He nodded and proceeded to do just that. And, amazingly, Alena didn't faint though the shudders wracked her and her breathing became harsh and erratic. By the time the last stitch was tied off, Galen was as taut and sweat-soaked as she. He hurriedly applied a generous slathering of marigold ointment over the wound and bandaged it.

She looked on the edge of passing out. Galen grasped Alena beneath her legs and slid a hand behind her shoulders. "Lie down," he commanded, swinging her over and down onto the bed. "Now, before you faint."

"I never faint." Her protest, however, was halfhearted and she didn't resist when Galen lowered her to the bed.

"So I noticed." He stood. "Rest here a while. When you're

feeling stronger, I'll bring you fresh water and cloths for cleaning up. Then, if you wish, I'll help you put on your tunic and breeches."

"I'll manage that myself, thank you," she whispered. Then, without further ado, Alena closed her eyes and promptly drifted off to sleep.

The big sorcerer watched her until a movement just outside the open door caught his eye, diverting his attention from the sleeping woman. 'Twas the baby dragon, peering in as best as his bulky young body would allow. His bejeweled eyes were wide with concern. His soft mewling filled the room.

Galen's mouth twisted ruefully. He paused for an instant more to pull a light quilt over Alena, then turned and strode across the room to the door. "She'll be all right," he informed the dragon. "She just needs to rest."

The dragon eyed him closely, then sighed and backed away. His departure only took him a few feet from the front door, however, before he dropped his considerable mass with a loud thud, laid his head on his front legs, curled his tail about his haunches, and promptly went to sleep.

"Would you like some soap and water to clean up with, while I prepare the supper meal?" Galen asked Alena four hours later when she finally awoke.

She glanced down at herself. Though the bandage on her right hand was clean, the rest of her was either dirt-smudged or covered with the tattered, bloodstained quilt. Alena's lips quirked. "I suppose I *could* do with some cleaning up." She looked back up at him. "Aye, some soap and water would be appreciated."

Wordlessly, Galen turned, fetched her a bowl of water, some cloths, and a small pottery container of soft soap. Then, his back to her to render her a semblance of privacy, he proceeded to prepare their meal. By the time Alena was washed and in her clean clothes, she found her energy sapped once more. As if equally aware of her debilitated state, Galen set their meal on the small, bedside table, then helped her scoot up in bed.

It was simple fare, two baked fishes, a loaf of crusty brown bread, a small round of goat's milk cheese, and apples. Alena surveyed the food, then took a swallow of the tangy goat's milk he'd poured in her mug. "Some ale or even wine would go down a lot better," she observed as she set her mug back on the table.

Galen placed a slice of cheese on his bread and shrugged. "Sorry. What grain I'm able to grow must go for flour for my bread. And I have as yet to master wine making, though there are a few wild grapevines growing on the other side of the isle. There's fresh water, though, if the milk's not to your liking."

"Nay, 'tis fine." Alena smiled. "I'm being the ungrateful guest again, aren't I?"

He eyed her cautiously. "It doesn't matter. I, too, frequently long for a cool swallow of ale or a goblet of a fine wine."

"There's wine and ale aplenty in Wyndymyll." She took a bite of her fish before surreptitiously glancing up at him.

His mouth twitched. "You won't give up, will you?"

"I can't, Galen." Alena laid down her fork. "If I don't help Renard, he has no one. Could you live with yourself if you left your dearest friend to rot in some dungeon or worse, let him die?"

He studied her in thoughtful silence. "Nay, I suppose not. But it has been a long time since I've known human friendship, or had to face such issues." He took a bite of his bread and cheese, not continuing until he'd chewed and swallowed it. "I admire you for your devotion. I encourage you to do what you feel you must to rescue your friend. I just don't want to be involved in your life or problems."

"But what chance do I have against—"

Galen lifted a silencing hand. "I'm not the man you need, Alena. You must believe me when I tell you that I'd be of no use to you, even if I were able and so inclined to follow you off Cadvallan. And, just as I respect your commitment, you should also respect my desire not to involve myself with the world. And respect, as well, my wish not to discuss this subject again."

She opened her mouth to dispute his words, then clamped it shut. 'Twould do no good endlessly to debate this issue with him. She needed time to regain her strength, to reassess the situation and search out the chinks in the armor of his resolve.

In the end, his continuing kindness to her notwithstanding, if all else failed she'd just force him to leave Cadvallan whether he wished to or not. He was a big man, but even a big man could be felled—if not by overt means, then by something more covert like an herbal sleeping potion. She hadn't spent time with Maud, their army's healer, without having learned a few tricks along that vein.

Alena finished off her last bite of the deliciously seasoned, perfectly cooked fish and nodded. "Fine. I'll say no more for the time being. I owe you that much for what you've done for me in my illness and recent injury." She picked up her mug of milk and emptied it, wiping her mouth clean with the back of her hand. "This meal was wonderful but I feel the need, once more, for a short rest."

The sorcerer rose and gathered up the dishes and mugs. " 'Twould mayhap be the wisest course."

"What will you do this evening?"

Galen's mouth quirked. "Naught of much import, save the cleaning and drying of the rest of the fish I caught. The wind has died while we've been supping and today's sun has warmed the flat rocks on the protected side of the house where I dry my fish and fruits and vegetables."

"I could help."

He cocked a quizzical brow. "I thought you wanted to rest."

Alena shrugged. "I can rest sitting propped against the house as easily as I can in bed. Besides, I've a wish to repay some of your hospitality."

"And what does a warrior woman know of preparing food?"

"As much as a sorcerer knew when he first began, I'd wager, but I can easily learn." She grinned. "Afraid I'll do better than you, mayhap?"

"Hardly." Galen hesitated, torn between the urge to accept her most appealing offer and the realization that her presence would only serve to rekindle his barely banked desire for her. Logic finally won out. The woman needed no additional advantage over him and, though she'd agreed to a truce on the issue of Renard, Galen well knew 'twould only be temporary. "Your generous offer notwithstanding, I think you'll do better resting a bit more. On the morrow, if you're up to it, you can accompany me on my next fishing expedition."

"You fish every day?"

Galen smiled ruefully. "Not every day, nor solely for myself, you can be sure. If I didn't supplement my fish diet from time to time with some of the isle's wild fowl, I'd have long ago given up fish altogether. But the dragons need meat and there's little else on the isle to feed them, save my goats, which I'm loathe to part with."

"The cheese was quite tasty," Alena admitted. "I just didn't realize how deeply involved you were with the dragons."

"We help each other. If 'twasn't for them, I'd have lost my sanity years ago." He inhaled a deep breath. "Now, enough of the talk. Rest. You need it more than you realize."

Alena started to dispute his assessment, then thought better of it. 'Twouldn't hurt to take his advice just this once, she thought, settling back against her pillow. After all, the sooner she regained her strength, the better. Even now, precious time was being wasted while Renard languished in Dorian Radbourne's vile prison. Quashing a sudden surge of anguish that memory stirred, Alena turned to face the wall and closed her eyes.

Galen fought his own tormented battle as he strode back outside. The sun was beginning to set over the sea in a brilliant explosion of crimson and gold. For a long moment he stood there, his mind in a turmoil. What was he to do about Alena? Try as he might to distance himself from her, emotionally if not physically, some event always seemed to arise to force them together again.

Just when he'd thought he'd finally regained control of his wayward desires after nursing her through her fever, she injured herself and he was forced to care for her again. And the intimacy of the act, the emotional toll it had taken on him in having to cause her pain, had bound him to her once more. He was beginning to wonder if he'd ever totally be free of Alena again.

"She disturbs you, does she not?"

Galen wheeled around. There, in the light of the dying sun, was the Dragon Father. The sorcerer ran a hand through his hair, his exasperation all but palpable. "Didn't we have this same conversation yesterday?"

The big dragon lowered his long, slender head until he was eye-to-eye with Galen. "Aye, that we did. But you've been with the woman over a day now and still I sense great agitation in you."

"And what do you want me to say?" Galen growled. "That she's a beautiful woman and I find my passions stirred? That I want her and would almost sell my soul to have her?"

"If that is what you truly feel, then why are you fighting it so? She wants your help. She'll give her body to you for it."

Galen's gaze narrowed. "And how do you know that? Have you been spying on us?"

The Dragon Father's lips curled back in a fearsome smile. "There is naught that goes on on Cadvallan Isle that I am not aware of. You know that, Radbourne. And this woman's mysterious arrival is most interesting, most entertaining."

"Then take her back to your cave and see to her yourself," Galen snapped irritably. "I don't find her presence interesting *or* entertaining!"

"Yet she is here and must be dealt with." The dragon stretched his huge wings, then settled them once more against his iridescent scaled body. "And I think, in the end, 'twill change naught no matter how you rail or fight against it. You must go with her, do as she bids."

"Must I now?" In spite of himself, Galen felt his anger rise. 'Twas too much, first Alena and now the Dragon Father, pushing and prodding at him to leave Cadvallan. "And am I to have any choice in this matter, do you think?"

His huge companion sighed and slowly shook his head. "Nay. Though you have been an invaluable aid to us and our survival all these years, I now see your destiny calling you elsewhere. You must follow it, Radbourne, wherever it beckons."

Galen stared up at the dragon in disbelief. "And toss aside

my life here? I think not. No one, neither some half-crazed warrior woman nor a dragon, no matter how powerful, is going to make me leave Cadvallan. This is *my* home—though not originally of my choosing—and where I wish to live out my days. And that's all I care to say on the subject!"

The Dragon Father watched Galen stride off toward his house. Then the creature slowly turned to gaze back out over the sea. In the distance, the sun sank into the ocean in a blaze of fire and light, washing the isle in soft, shimmering colors. The dragon stood there for a long while, considering the events of the past two days.

"A pity, Radbourne, that you must leave Cadvallan," he finally said, his voice low and melodious. "Sorcerer and blood enemy that you be, you indeed were an invaluable ally all these years. But the woman is even more special to us, and her needs cannot be denied."

At the anticipation of the woman coming into her powers, a fierce hope swelled in his dragon breast. "Nay, you'll soon have no choice in the matter, Radbourne," he whispered softly. "No choice at all . . ."

CHAPTER FOUR

The late morning sun felt good on Alena's face. Though the day was cool, only a slight breeze ruffled the tall grass growing in the cracks and crevices between the black volcanic rocks. As she made her careful way along the steep trail leading down to the narrow strip of shore below Galen's house, Alena inhaled deeply of the rich, salty air. 'Twas a beautiful day, a glorious day, and she was happy to be alive.

Close at her side, Galen kept a firm hand on one elbow, seemingly determined she not suffer any more accidents, while, with the other, he grasped a basket filled with their midday meal. Behind them, at a considerable distance back to preclude causing any unexpected mishaps of his own, followed Padborn—whom Alena had decided to more appropriately nickname Paddy. Though under normal circumstances Alena would have been insulted, if not angered to be treated like some delicate, helpless woman, this time her pride wasn't the issue. Her full recovery and use of her hand was.

It throbbed and ached fiercely each time she forgot and moved it in some way, but seemed to be free of infection and beginning to heal. Galen had insisted on tending to it earlier that morn, bathing the hand in warm, salted water then gently patting it dry and applying more of his marigold ointment before rebandaging it. She only hoped she'd regain full use of it when 'twas healed. If she didn't, she didn't know what she would do.

For the moment there was naught more to be done save allow Galen to care for her hand and take all precautions not to reinjure it. In the meanwhile, Alena meant to enjoy the day—and use every opportunity to get to know the big sorcerer better. 'Twas the only hope she had of divining his weaknesses and finding some way to use them to her advantage.

Once on the sandy strip of beach, Galen released Alena. "Sit over there by those rocks. You'll be out of the wind and water and still get a full view of everything."

Alena glanced to where some moss-covered rocks rose from the sand. Far enough from the waves breaking on the shore, it indeed seemed a comfortable spot to watch Galen from. She ambled over and sat down.

The rocks, though hard, were adequately cushioned by the thick growth of the rich green moss. A faint scent wafted to her nose, of fresh earth and a tangy, grasslike essence. Alena smiled and settled back, strangely content.

Galen threw off his woolen robe and, lowering himself to the beach, pulled off his boots. Next, he rolled up the sleeves of his dark blue tunic to above his elbows and his pant legs to just below his knees, then proceeded to gather up the big fishing net and stride out onto a narrow promontory that jutted far into the water. With a surge of powerful muscles, Galen flung the heavy net up and out over the water.

The net fell, settling gently, almost caressingly, over the rocking waters, then sank into the sea. When the catchline had stretched to its fullest, Galen heaved back on it. The broad, flat muscles of his back straining, he slowly pulled in the net.

Fish of all sorts and sizes wriggled within the prison of woven rope, their moisture-slick scales glinting silver in the bright sunlight. Once Galen had the fish-laden net on the promontory, he squatted, hoisted the squirming burden over his shoulder and headed back to shore.

Before he even had the fish dumped on the beach, Paddy

was there. Greedily wolfing down the wildly flapping creatures, he consumed over half the net's contents before pausing to emit a loud belch and swallow a few more. Galen eyed him wryly, then glanced over at an awestruck Alena. "And that's only one dragon, albeit a very hungry and growing baby dragon. Generally, this 'vitally important labor' of mine takes a full three to four days out of every week. Fifty dragons of various sizes and ages eat a lot of fish."

At the reminder of her irritable jibe at him yesterday when he'd offered to feed her, Alena flushed. "So I now see. And why can't the dragons fish for themselves?"

"They aren't in the best of health." Galen flung the net over his shoulder. The wet ropes quickly seeped water onto his shirt, staining it a crisscrossed pattern of dark blue. "As you've probably noticed, this particular form of earth dragon's adult scales are usually white overlaid with a rich, shimmering iridescence. Yet the scales of most of the adult dragons on Cadvallan are pale and opaque, a sure sign of ill health. And, though they were formerly capable of flying great distances, their strength has long ago waned until 'tis insufficient for most tasks. More than likely many would've drowned by now trying to catch fish."

"Then they have you to thank for their current existence. Is that what you're saying?"

Galen glanced away, suddenly unable to meet her gaze. "As I said before, we help each other."

"Mayhap," Alena agreed. "But what will happen to them in the end? Sorcerer though you be, even you can't lengthen your lifespan indefinitely, and dragons are said to live five hundred years or more."

He lifted his gaze to hers. A soul-deep sadness burned in his eyes. "I don't know, Alena. But until I do die, the dragons need me. They're too weak to leave this isle and most can no longer even perform the traditional mating flight." He smiled sadly. " 'Tis one of the most glorious of sights—a female dragon, beautiful and full of the wisdom of the ancients, pursued by hundreds of adult male dragons."

"Then you've seen the dragons mate?"

Alena couldn't quite hide the twinge of envy that crept into her voice. She, too, had heard tales of the magnificent creatures' mating flights, of the heart-stirring scene of a flight of dragons high overhead, but, like everyone else, thought the tales were just that—tales. One way or another, it hardly mattered anymore. The dragons were all but extinct, an obsolete part of a mystical, magical, wondrous time.

"I've seen them mate only about four or five times in the past fifteen years," Galen said. "And that's not often enough to replenish their species."

Alena frowned. "What happened to them? To cause the dragons to weaken and die?"

Galen shrugged. "What else? The same things that eventually corrupt all peoples and set all societies on the road to destruction. A growing mistrust that feeds on one's insecurities, a self-centered and obsessive hunger for power, a loss of moral responsibility and sense of self-sacrifice."

"And I thought the all-wise dragons and sorcerers were above such common weaknesses." Alena's lips twitched. "Obviously not."

"Obviously. Even those called to a higher standard cannot always reach such lofty heights. And magic, for all its potential for good, also has a darker side. 'Twas the morally weak and misguided among the dragons and sorcerers who fell prey to that dark side." Galen's gaze swung out to sea. "The balance of magic shifted ever so subtly at first with small disputes, then outright battles, until the dragons and sorcerers found themselves at war. And with their destruction, so went the land."

"But what of the fabled *galienes?* Why didn't they attempt to use their influence at least to restrain the dragons?"

A pair of dark eyes locked with hers. "They tried but failed," Galen replied softly. "The dragons had become as enmeshed in the battle for power as had the sorcerers. Finally, sickened by the growing rancor and evil and hoping to at least force their beloved dragons to reconsider the terrible course on which they'd set themselves and the land, the *galienes* turned from their ancient role and disappeared. Unfortunately, without the dragons' protection, the brave women fell easy prey to the sorcerers. Because of the *galienes'* influence over the dragons, and their potential power over them, the sorcerers set out systematically to destroy the *galienes.*"

"And with their deaths," Alena finished for him, "the dragons began to weaken until, finally, the remaining ones were forced to flee to the holy sanctuary of Cadvallan Isle. Only there could they finally be at peace."

"For what that peace was worth," Galen muttered. "Without the life-sustaining force of their *galienes,* most became too weak and sickly to mate and repropagate their species. The dragons, it seemed, needed their *galienes* as much as the *galienes* needed them. And now, as the few remaining female dragons age, hope for the creatures' survival grows less and less." A look of deep sadness darkened Galen's eyes. "Yet to watch even once that mating flight . . ."

He smiled softly. "It fills one with hope they might yet overcome the terrible fate of extinction."

"What is it like, the mating flight, I mean?"

He cocked a dark brow. "How explicit do you wish me to be?"

Alena scowled. "I'm not some sheltered maiden, Radbourne. I've grown up surrounded by the crudities of coarse warriors. I asked but a simple question and require but a simple, straightforward answer."

"I beg pardon for my oversight." He paused, gave a low chuckle, then continued. "Only the most powerful of the males can keep up with the female on her nuptial flight. Finally, the most agile male dragon claims her. The female extends her wings to their maximum span, the male slides beneath her belly, and enfolds her in an embrace of wings and talons. Thus entwined, the lovers reach their climax while plunging straight down to earth. Only when they're but a few yards from the ground do they part and spread their wings to land."

Listening to Galen's mesmerizing tale, Alena couldn't help but be drawn once more into the wonder that was the dragons'. He spoke so impassionedly about them that she knew at last the depth of his devotion to the massive creatures. 'Twas more than just his own selfish concerns and personal fears that kept him on Cadvallan. And that realization made her decision to force him to leave all the harder.

Knowing now the depths of his devotion to the dragons, Alena briefly considered using the dragons in some way to coerce Galen into leaving Cadvallan. But that plan seemed an impossibility. Even if she could get Paddy to go with her in the hopes the big sorcerer would follow to bring him back, Alena knew the baby dragon was far too heavy for her skiff—*if* she ever found it and 'twas still intact—and he was quite evidently still too young to fly. And she hadn't the time to spare for him to grow up, as if she even knew how long *that* would take.

"It seems risky, the way they mate, I mean," Alena said, casting aside a flare of frustration as yet another plan died an ignominious death.

"But well worth it. Even dragons feel affection for their

mates, all issues of procreative imperatives aside." Galen ran his hand up and down the catchline in a thoughtful, considering manner. "This particular species is also unique in that they mate for life. There is but one female for a male, and one male for a female. The first mating determines their lifelong love."

Alena gave an unsteady laugh. "Thank the Holy Ones such a rule doesn't hold for humans. Frequently one's first lover is hardly the stuff of an enduring relationship."

A shadow crossed Galen's face, then was gone. "Aye, and sometimes one's first love is the stuff of dreams, dreams of such grandeur and magic that 'tis impossible for any other lover ever to hope to fulfill."

At his words, uttered in a soft and wondering voice, jealousy stabbed through Alena. He spoke of a woman he'd once known, a woman with whom he'd experienced the heights of pleasure. A woman he'd loved and had been loved by.

She knew she shouldn't care, shouldn't feel such envy for the unknown woman who'd possessed Galen's love. 'Twas irrational. She had chosen the men she had for lovers exactly *because* they neither expected nor desired commitment.

'Twas how she'd wanted it, too. Wanted it that way to avoid any ties, any man ever having a hold on her heart. They all became too demanding in time, expecting a woman to sacrifice everything for them.

Nay, there'd been no man—save one—who could have asked for and received such devotion. Thankfully, she supposed, he'd never considered her as aught more than a little sister. After she'd gotten over him and seen to what lengths her overwrought feelings would have led her, Alena had been grateful that things had turned out the way they had. Nay, she told herself, let Galen Radbourne mourn what might have been, dream his futile dreams of a woman to mate with for life. She cherished her independence far too dearly ever to let another person dictate the terms of her existence.

Almost as if sensing the change in Alena's mood, Galen grinned sheepishly. "I wax a bit too eloquent at times. Fortunately, it has mostly gone unheard." Without another word, he turned and strode off back toward the promontory.

The rest of the morn passed quickly. Galen caught and hauled in six more loads of fish to dump onto the beach. With each load, three or four dragons would swoop down from their perches on the cliffs above, devour the fish, then fly back to their rocky aeries. At midday, Alena called a halt for lunch.

As she set out the repast of cheese, bread, apple tarts, and a jug of goat's milk on the quilt, Galen ambled over, threw himself down, and rolled onto his back. Pillowing his head beneath his hands, he stared up at the cloud-strewn blue sky. The last of the dragons finished their own meal. In a mighty surge of powerful wings, they flew away.

It was silent save for the roar of the waves slamming onto the beach and the faint cries of the gulls flying far out over the ultramarine water. A cool breeze caressed Alena's cheek. The sun beat down, warming the sheltered little cove enclosed by the rock walls.

'Twas peaceful, soul-soothing, sitting here by the sea, she thought, and mayhap the most relaxing and inactive time she'd ever known in her life. She should feel guilty that she wasn't busy training a young soldier in the proper battle techniques, or riding out on a mission, or exercising at her own warrior skills. But the only guilt that could be fanned into any semblance of life was that of the disparity of her current situation compared to Renard's.

She glanced at Galen. Stretched out on his back with his eyes closed and his rugged features tranquil, his big body looked loose and languid in repose. His blue tunic, soaked with a combination of sea spray and sweat from his recent exertions, clung damply to the broad planes of his chest and his hard, flat belly.

Alena's gaze slid lower, past his belted waist to take in the equally damp length of Galen's groin crowned with the prominent bulge of his manhood, before moving down his tautly muscled thighs and well-shaped calves and feet. He was surprisingly fit for a man who reputedly lived by his mind and magic rather than by the sword, but the frequent all-day fishing expeditions, plus what must be nearly nonstop work just to survive, had admirably maintained the magnificent physique nature had granted him.

There appeared to be a lot of things different about the two brothers, Alena realized when she paused to consider it, from their level of physical fitness, to the difference in their aging—Galen easily looked a good five or six years younger than his twin—to the dissimilarities in their personal outlook and relationships with others. Indeed, Galen Radbourne seemed nothing like his brother, save for outward appearances and the common heritage they shared.

He stirred, exhaled a deep breath, then turned his head to look at her. His teeth flashed white in a lazy smile. "The day sits well with you, doesn't it?"

Alena eyed him—suddenly wary—then slowly nodded. "Aye. I rarely have the opportunity to loll around on some beach. 'Tis quite pleasant, if pointless."

"Pointless?" Galen shoved to a sitting position. "Life isn't meant just to be one endless whirlwind of activity, Alena. Life is to be indulged in, to be seduced, then captured, to be gloated over, and savored." He gestured to the sky. "Have you ever seen such a brilliant, heart-stopping shade of blue? Or noticed how achingly pristine the white clouds can sometimes be? Or watched the waves pound the shore and wondered at the power and majesty of the sea?"

"They are there," Alena muttered, growing uncomfortable with Galen's sudden, poetic turn of the conversation. "One cannot help but see them."

"But have you *felt* them? Allowed yourself to join, to blend your spirit with them? Experienced that part of you that is equally a part of them, as well?"

He smiled at her with a gentle understanding. Alena didn't like it. Didn't like it at all. Somehow, someway, he edged too close to her greatest fears and deepest secrets. Didn't he realize that to care too much left you needing, open . . . vulnerable?

"It lessens that eternal sense of loneliness and restlessness," Galen continued, forging on despite the warning glower Alena sent him, "that haunting conviction there should be more in life than mere existence."

"I'm a warrior. I've no time for philosophizing. Fighting for survival permits little leisure for cloud gazing and the like."

"Then you aren't truly living," Galen softly said. "And I feel sorry for you."

At his words, something in Alena snapped. Why, the arrogance of the man to think, just because he had all the time in the world to contemplate the mysteries of life, that he was better off than she! "Save your pity, Radbourne! 'Tis an easy thing to judge from your insular little world where no cares or conflicts assail you. But where is there any courage or honor in that? Nay," she went on, vehemently shaking her head, "I say, instead, that you've chosen the coward's way and aren't worthy to claim any kinship, whatever there may be, with life or nature!"

For a long moment, Galen studied Alena in thoughtful silence. Then, he gestured toward the food. "Shall we eat? I've only fed half the dragons and the time is fast drawing on. They'll be in a sorry mood if some go hungry this day."

She bit back a scathing remark regarding his refusal to defend himself, suddenly spoiling for a fight. "Aye, of course," Alena muttered instead, and hurried to uncover the cheese and tarts.

By the Mother, she wondered, what was wrong with her? She'd never reacted so boorishly or labored so hard to antagonize someone in her entire life. And 'twasn't an approach, at any rate, sure to win over a man like Galen Radbourne. But she also wearied of tiptoeing about him, too.

Galen busied himself pouring out two mugs of foaming goat's milk, then handed one to Alena. She accepted it, drank deeply of the pottery chilled milk, then turned to the rest of the food. The meal was finished in a tense if polite silence before Galen exhaled a deep breath, then rose.

"If you'll take no offense in the request, would you clean up here while I return to the fishing?"

Alena glanced up at him, her earlier rancor gone. "And why would I take offense? We do what we're capable of and, at the moment, that is all my strength will permit."

His mouth twisted wryly. "Why, indeed?" He turned to leave.

"Galen. Wait."

He looked back. "Aye?"

"My words . . . earlier." Alena hesitated, loathe to apologize but knowing she must. She'd never win him over at the rate she was going. "I was . . . tactless and unkind . . . when I called you a coward. I'm sorry."

"You spoke what was in your heart." Galen shifted uncomfortably and a slight flush crept up his neck and face. "And mayhap, just mayhap, though I'm loathe to admit it, there's some kernel of truth in what you said."

Without further ado, he turned on his heel and strode back out to the promontory. Alena watched as he tossed out the fishing net once more, unaccountably shaken by his admission. Shaken, and hopeful, for the first time in the past three days. With a puzzled frown, she turned her attention back to cleaning up the remnants of the midday meal.

The afternoon wore on as the big sorcerer caught and deposited load after load of fish on the shore. And, in groups of three or four, the dragons swooped down to feed.

'Twas her first time to view all the dragons on Cadvallan, and Alena marveled at their variety and number. 'Twas also true what Galen had said about their overall poor health. Though in hue they ranged from pure white to a soft cream, with an overlying metallic luster, their scales had a flat, almost colorless appearance. Only the shimmering white Dragon Father, black baby Paddy, and the few adolescent dragons who varied from a deep gunmetal gray to a silvery white, showed signs of the true vigor of a healthy dragon.

A deep sadness filled Alena. 'Twasn't fair the dragons should come to such a fate. They were gentle, happy creatures, she thought as she watched Paddy cavort in the surf, leaping in the air, trying his wings which were far too small and weak as yet to support the bulk of his young body, then crashing into the water with a great surge of spray and sand.

He was such an awkward, if well-intentioned creature. His constant shadowing of her, however, was already bordering on the irritating. One would think she was Paddy's mother, for as close a proximity as he always kept near her.

Down the shore on the jutting of volcanic rock, Galen tossed the net out yet another time. Alena marveled at his tireless strength. Some time ago, he'd shed his tunic and now labored in only his rolled up black breeches. Though the breeze blowing off the ocean was cool, sweat glistened on the muscled planes of his back and arms.

Alena was glad he kept his distance, save for the necessary trips back to the beach to deposit his latest catch. All day as she'd watched him work, his physical appeal had grown.

Her fingers ached to thread through the dense tangle of his dark chest hair, to lightly stroke the satiny bronzed skin that lay beneath the wiry crispness. Her gaze roved over his rippling, hair-whorled abdomen, hungrily eyeing his taut buttocks, smooth flanks and steel-tempered thighs. And, as she watched, the hot sun beating down on her, the wind stroking her own flesh with sensuous, seductive fingers, desire swept through Alena like flames through dry tinder.

She wasn't a stranger to the pleasures of the flesh. She well knew the hot, agonizing hunger of passion and the sharp ecstasy of physical fulfillment. But Alena was also a disciplined warrior and, in the past, had always carefully chosen her men and the optimum occasions for coupling. Yet for all his physical perfection, Galen Radbourne wasn't the man for her, nor was this the time to indulge in some mindless rutting.

Offering her body in a cold-blooded business deal to save Renard was one thing. Allowing oneself to become enamored, nay, *obsessed,* with the need to mate with some mysterious sorcerer was another. Yet the heat, the need, the hunger grew until Alena thought she'd go mad, sitting there on the beach, watching Galen and his beautiful, magnificently masculine body.

As the sun made its descent a storm formed on the horizon, swallowing the fading orb in its blustering maw before next turning toward Cadvallan. Galen tossed out the net one last time, pulled in a sizable catch, then grabbed up his shirt, flung the net of fish over his back, and headed for shore. As the Dragon Father flew down from the cliffs, he deposited the fish on the beach and stepped back.

The big creature had perched overhead all day, watching as his subjects fed, allowing each and every one to take their fill before he ate. Now, at last, 'twas his turn.

Galen stood there, but several yards away. A tiny tremor coursed through Alena. He was dwarfed many times over by the huge white dragon, both in size and physical attributes. If the dragon should ever decide to turn on him . . .

But Galen was their friend, sorcerer that he was, she reassured herself. He was in no danger from the gentle dragons. Yet why, time and again as she watched the Dragon Father feed, was she overwhelmed with the strangest sense of the dragon's long and carefully hidden animosity toward the dark-haired man standing nearby?

She shook the unpleasant feelings aside. She was but tired and confused after her first full day out of bed—and her even stranger and still worsening desire for the big sorcerer.

Deciding action was just the thing to drive away the increasingly irrational emotions, Alena gathered up the food and dishes and replaced them in the basket. She climbed to her feet, folded the quilt, and put that in the basket as well. Then, after inhaling a fortifying breath, she took up Galen's robe and ambled over to him.

He turned at her approach. His long, dark hair was damply matted to his face and neck. His torso and arms glistened with moisture. His breeches were soaked, molding most tantalizingly to his—

She firmly quashed her fresh surge of arousal. "Why don't you wash off a bit in the water, then dry yourself and put on your robe? Your shirt is wet and of no use, and you'll soon be chilled with the sun setting and the storm on its way."

Galen stared at her for a long moment, then wordlessly turned and headed toward the surf. He walked out in the foaming waters until he was knee deep, then bent and laved himself clean. Returning, Galen took the cloth she offered and quickly dried off before accepting his robe.

"My thanks," he finally said. Something dark, smoldering, flared in his eyes. He averted his gaze to the storm churning overhead. "We'd better head back to the house. Those clouds bode a downpour if naught else."

"A-aye." Alena forced the word past a throat gone suddenly dry. Holy Mother, she thought with a wild elation, knowing the look Galen had sent her and its meaning. He desired her as fiercely as she did him! The realization both excited and terrified her. And fear was one thing that angered Alena more than anything else.

"Let's be gone then," she snapped. Without awaiting his reply, she turned and strode toward the trail leading back to the house. At that moment, Paddy, with a squeak of dismay that Alena was leaving without him, bounded into her path. If not for Galen's quick response in pulling her back, she'd have tripped over the baby dragon and fallen into a small tide pool on the side of the trail.

She clamped down on a string of curses and, instead, shot Paddy an irritated glance. His colorful eyes widened; his tail flicked, and he hastily backed away. Shrugging off Galen's steadying hand, Alena stomped up the trail.

High overhead, the storm clouds gathering above him, the Dragon Father sat, watching it all in silent, brooding anticipation.

The tension grew as the night burned on. It simmered over the supper meal, taking on an almost palpable aura before arcing across the table between Galen and Alena. The air grew still, heavy, as the storm halted directly over the isle and hung there, laden with moisture, inexorably pressing down on every living thing. Thunder rumbled in the distance.

Lightning slashed from sky to sea in silver bolts of fiery discharge that died far out on the roiling water.

Neither of them said much throughout the meal. Finally, Galen rose and began gathering up the dishes. Alena jumped to her feet, upsetting her chair. Her face burning, she bent to right it, then turned to face Galen.

"Let me help." She quickly picked up the wooden spoons and knives.

"Nay." Galen halted her with his free hand. She jerked back, his touch too stimulating to bear. His jaw went taut, save for a muscle twitching furiously in the broad, shaven expanse of his cheek. "Go to bed," he said, reaching across the table once more to take the spoons and knives from her hand. "It has been a long day for you and you're overtired. I'll clean up."

Alena considered a protest, then thought better of it. 'Twas wiser to place as much distance as she could between them right now. Though she desired him ardently, more than she'd ever desired any man before, Alena also sensed, with a certainty so strong it took her breath away, that 'twould be her downfall to mate with Galen this night.

Such soul-searing passion was far too dangerous, too fraught with commitment and emotion for one such as she. Too much stood to be lost—one's freedom, one's integrity, aye, even one's sanity.

"Aye," she mumbled, not daring to look at Galen a moment longer. "Your words have merit. I bid you good night." Gathering up the clean tunic he had offered her earlier as a bed shirt, Alena quickly disrobed while Galen busied himself, back turned, with washing the dishes. Surprisingly, she felt herself drifting off to sleep almost as soon as her head hit the pillow.

Thank the Mother, Alena offered up a silent prayer of

gratitude just before slumber claimed her. On the morrow all would be well. On the morrow, these strange, unnatural passions would be gone. All she needed was . . . just a little . . . sleep. . . .

Galen finished washing the dishes, dried them, and replaced them in the cupboard. Then, without looking Alena's way, he wiped the table, straightened the chairs around it and proceeded to sweep the floor. Naught, however, helped soothe his rising tide of tension.

'Twas but the storm hovering overhead, the storm that had been building since late afternoon, he told himself. 'Twas the storm that made his skin tingle and go damp and clammy. 'Twas the storm that made him feel so restless, so out of sorts, so . . . so hot and cold, so alternately angry and yearning. 'Twas the storm that had caused it all.

He paced the room for a time, then banked the hearth fire in the hopes of cooling the room a bit. He settled down to work on the pot he'd been planning to throw all week on his potter's wheel. The clay felt cool, soothing, running through his fingers.

For a time, Galen thought he'd vanquished the restless, indefinable feelings. Then the bursts of fire exploded once more beneath his skin. His muscles twitched with strange spasms. His groin filled with blood and his sex thickened.

With a savage curse, Galen smashed his newly thrown pot on the wheel and rose. 'Twas too hot in the house, that was all there was to it. He needed a bath. Some cold water from the well would more thoroughly cleanse him from today's labors as well as cool him.

He shot Alena a swift glance. She was sound asleep. 'Twas too cold to bathe outside and no harm would be done if he took a quick bath by the light of the smoldering coals of the fire. She'd never know.

The wind gusted into the room when Galen opened the door. Good, he thought, the storm was nearly ready to break. He grabbed up the bucket sitting beside the door and strode out. The wind whipped at his clothes, tore at his hair, but Galen welcomed the distraction. Let it blow, let the storm rage, let rain pelt the earth and lightning strike. Anything, if only this pressure, this bowstrung tautness within him would ease.

Paddy lay nearby, keeping devoted guard as always. The young dragon lifted his head as Galen passed, murmured something dragonlike and unintelligible, then went back to sleep. Galen sent the bucket plummeting into the well, then pulled it back up. At that moment, the moon broke through its cover of roiling clouds. Light bathed the rugged, rocky terrain—highlighting the form of a huge dragon unexpectedly perched on a nearby volcanic outcropping.

Galen froze. After fifteen years, the silhouette was familiar. 'Twas the Dragon Father. Galen stood there for a long moment, torn between the urge to go to him and ask why the dragon was so far from his cave on a night like this and a loathing to do so, fearing the answer to his questions. He didn't know why he felt that way; he just did.

Finally, Galen decided against it. He was too tired, too overwrought right now to make civil conversation at any rate. He headed back to his house, nodding briefly to the Dragon Father as he passed, then went inside.

Alena slept on. Galen deposited the bucket beside the fire, then retrieved a big pottery bowl which he placed on a chair he dragged over to stand by the bucket. Next, he gathered up a washcloth, a jar of soft soap, several drying cloths, and a clean tunic and breeches.

Quickly stripping out of his clothes, Galen poured some of the well water into the pottery bowl then wet a washcloth and soaped it. He lathered his arms, then his chest, scrubbing fiercely to rid himself of the heated sensations prickling once more beneath his skin.

Rinsing the soap away, Galen decided not to dry himself, hoping the moisture on his skin would help cool him. Next, he turned to his legs, propping first one foot, then the other on the edge of the chair to wash himself. The sense of heaviness, of oppression returned, all but smothering him. He fought past it, trying mightily to ignore the turgid flow of blood throbbing in his sex, the tightness building in his groin.

'Twas the storm, Galen told himself for the hundredth time, even as the red-hot mists of his passion swelled and grew. 'Twas the storm or he was slowly going mad. He rinsed himself, his actions jerky and quick now, then soaped the cloth one more time and reached out to cleanse his stiffly jutting organ.

The feel of the wet cloth on his shaft and hair roughened sac filled him with a wild rush of pleasure. He soaped himself quickly, afraid to prolong the stimulating friction on his passion heated sex. He shoved the cloth back in the water, wrung it out, and wiped himself clean.

As he did, the image of Alena flashed across his mind, of her naked breasts and long, white legs. Of her wild tangle of blond hair. Of the silky flesh of her inner thighs, and the tantalizingly damp curls of her woman's mound.

With a low groan, Galen threw back his head. His eyes slid shut. He grasped himself, hard.

By the Holy Ones, but he was so engorged it hurt . . . hurt, and there was naught he could do about it. Just this once, in all these years, a woman lay sleeping but a few yards away, and naught would satisfy him but the tight, sweet pleasure of her body.

Naught . . . and he didn't dare have her. 'Twould surely

end like the last time he'd laid with a woman. 'Twould surely *be* the end of the both of them. . . .

A low, anguished sound woke Alena. She lay there in the dimly lit room, all her warrior senses alert. Someone was near and in pain. Had it been but a dream? Had she imagined she'd seen Renard suffering in his prison cell?

Then, a movement caught the corner of her vision. She turned her head and nearly gasped aloud. Galen stood across the room, stark naked save for the pendant he wore about his neck, his big, hard-muscled body wet and glistening in the firelight. His head was thrown back in what looked to be agony and his hand—she noted as her glance slid down his body—clasped his manhood. A manhood stiff and swollen with arousal.

An impulse to close her eyes and turn away filled her, to permit him his privacy in his self-pleasure. Alena had seen warriors find their release in such a way many times when no willing woman was about. 'Twas naught to be ashamed of or disparage in another. Still, there was something about Galen's face and the rigid stance of his body that gave her pause.

He fought the pleasure, rejected it, she realized with a flash of insight. 'Twasn't *what* he wanted or *how* he wanted it. And, watching him, Alena felt her own tension—the tension she'd fought all day—explode into an intensely uncontrollable desire. A desire that only Galen could ever hope to fill.

Suddenly, all caution, all fears of the consequences, fled. All Alena knew was that she wanted Galen and must have him or die. The fire within her grew, consuming her until all she saw was a magnificently, exquisitely desirable naked man gleaming in the firelight. A man who was as needing as she.

She threw back the coverlet and climbed out of bed. "Galen," she said, her voice as deep and dark as the mysterious spell that had enveloped her. "Come. Come to me; love me."

CHAPTER FIVE

Galen jerked around, his whole body rigid in his surprise. His hand fell from his hardened shaft. The bathing cloth dropped, unnoticed, to the floor. But he made no other move, neither to cover himself nor to walk toward Alena. 'Twas as if something held him there, frozen to the spot.

As she rose from the bed and moved across the room, Alena's overlarge tunic sagged open, revealing an enticing glimpse of the curve of her breasts. The shirt's hem lifted in soft waves to expose the gentle, silky swell of her inner thighs.

She didn't appear to notice, but Galen did. He choked back a tormented groan that was all but swallowed in the roar of the wind rising outside the house. What was she about, to so blatantly, so wantonly tempt him? he wondered, awash in a wild riot of sensations and fevered impressions. Didn't she realize . . . ? But she couldn't. No one but Dorian and he knew what mating with them would risk.

He lifted a hand to keep her from him. "Nay, Alena," Galen rasped in a passion thickened voice he hardly recognized as his own. "It cannot be. I cannot do this."

She halted before him, her hair tumbling long and wild about her shoulders and down her back, her fair skin flushed, her woman's scent, musky with her desire, hovering like some heavy, heady cloud around her. "Cannot?" She smiled, her eyes deep and dark—and full of a woman's understanding. "Are you a virgin, then, Galen?"

"Nay." He shook his head fiercely, in as much to deny her supposition as to ward off the encroaching mists of his bur-

101

geoning need. " 'Tisn't that. I just . . . cannot . . . mate with you."

In a quick move, Alena dodged his outstretched hand. Before Galen could react, her arms slipped behind his neck and her fingers entwined, capturing him. "Yet you want me all the same," she breathed, pressing close to his passion heated body. At the touch of his distended sex against her, Alena shuddered in delight. "And never have I known a man as big, and thick, and powerful."

Galen grasped her wrists and tried to pull her away, but Alena's hold was suddenly fierce, forceful. He knew he'd hurt her if he exerted the strength necessary to free himself. With a ragged breath, Galen released his grip. His hands fell to his sides.

"Let me go, Alena. Now."

She glanced down at him, saw the straining arousal that gave lie to the true meaning behind his words, and met his gaze once more. "Nay, Galen. Though your mouth may say one thing, your body says another. You want me. Admit it." Alena pressed close once more, rubbing her breasts and woman's mound against him. "Admit it, Galen."

The wind was like some unleashed beast now, beating against the thatched roof, rattling the windows. Thunder exploded overhead. The air fairly crackled with static, setting Galen's skin to tingling. Or was it but the delicious feel of Alena's flesh so close, so ardently pressed to his?

A shudder racked his body. His eyes clenched shut. "Aye, I want you," he whispered, the admission torn from him against his will. He felt his resistance shred, splinter, scattering in a wild tumult of broken resolutions and mangled self-discipline. 'Twas too many years without a woman, and Alena knew it. And knew, as well, that she was exquisitely alluring, and he wasn't strong enough to resist her.

Yet he *must,* an agonized voice cried out. Must, or 'twould be the death of her. And he'd vowed never to kill again.

With an enraged cry, Galen wrenched her arms away and turned. Alena's warrior training, however, had prepared her too well. She flung her arms about his waist, then slid around to kneel at his feet, clasping him about his hips.

"Nay, Galen," she cried, her face but a hair's-breadth from his thrusting sex. "I'll die if you turn from me. I cannot help how I feel, nor do I know how to contain it, but I need you." She turned her face to nuzzle him, her lips soft and knowing. "I need you . . . no matter the cost."

Galen groaned softly. He couldn't help himself—or deny the temptations her nearness offered. He clasped her head, guiding her yet closer to the heated core of his desire. Just for a moment, he thought. Just for a moment . . .

"Alena," he said on a ravaged whisper.

Her mouth closed about him, sliding up, then down in a languid, sensuous motion. Galen shook violently. His head fell back and his face contorted in ecstasy. His fingers clenched in her hair.

Never had he known such glorious, such exquisite sensations. They wrapped around him, lifting him to a place of rarefied experiences, of sheer, ardent pleasure. He felt his control slip away, to be replaced, bit by bit, by a savage intent. And he found what had satisfied him but a few moments ago wasn't enough anymore.

With a primal growl, Galen pulled Alena from him and, grasping her hands, lifted her to her feet. Before she could respond or offer protest, he swung her up into his arms and carried her over to the table. Placing her on its edge, he tore aside her tunic and shoved between her legs. His shaft, so hot and hard and swollen, pressed against her now exposed groin and flat belly.

Galen slammed his mouth down on hers. As he plundered her lips until she opened to him in an equally frenzied response, one hand slid around Alena's hips to anchor her while the other closed over a lush white breast and squeezed. She moaned against his mouth, pumping her hips wildly, frantically.

"Galen!" she gasped when he pulled back for a brief instant. "Ah, Galen!"

He'd never thought to hear another woman cry out his name in her passion and need. Never thought to taste the honeyed ambrosia of a woman's mouth nor feel again the yielding softness of a tender breast. A fierce, sweet anguish rose within him. Ah, for just once more, for one last time, he wanted to be a man and love a woman!

Gone were all constraints, all admonishings of a conscience honed to a white-hot integrity by years of regret and loneliness and deprivation. The fire within him, the hunger for Alena, would not be denied.

In all truth, Galen couldn't have stopped himself if he'd tried. A force outside him seemed to control him now, pressing down with insistent power, power both alluring and mystical. The recognition plucked at the edges of his memory. 'Twas familiar, this power. It spoke of fire and ice, of starlit splendor and a soul-deep satisfaction, of light and darkness, good and evil.

It spoke of . . . *magic.*

Directly overhead, thunder cracked, shaking the house, setting the wooden floor atremble. The scent of sulfur, then burning wood filled the air. Yet Galen didn't care, *couldn't* care.

Horror roiled within him, building in force and intensity as the seconds passed. Galen's mouth opened, moved soundlessly, but no words would come. His muscles clenched, jerked with fine tremors, refusing to respond. Yet he could no more push Alena from him, no more prevent his mouth from lowering to suckle a pouting pink nipple, than he could stop his heart from beating or the blood from surging hotly through his veins.

A spell. The truth could no longer be disguised, no longer be attributed to the mounting storm or the years of self-denial. A spell encompassed both him and Alena, and there was naught, for all the potency of his former powers, that he could do to halt it. But who? Who on Cadvallan was capable of such ability? There was only him and Alena . . . and the dragons.

Desperately, Galen searched for the caster of the spell, scanning the rippling layers of dragon magic that had always surrounded the isle—and slammed into a wall of such strength it took his breath away. He felt the magic grow, felt its insidious tendrils entwine about him, beguiling him, dragging him deeper and deeper into the mind- and body-drugging allure that was Alena.

Alena. Her eyes locked with his and there, in their blue-green depths, Galen saw her own yielding, her powerlessness to recognize, much less overcome, the magic that encompassed them. He fought mightily against the enchantment, summoning up powers he'd thought long dead, powers weak from disuse, but still there.

He fought to protect Alena if naught else. Fought to protect her from himself

Fought—and failed.

She gazed back at him with such openness, such trust, that Galen knew he was lost. Her beautiful eyes ensnared him in a prison of wonderment. Within their mesmerizing, ever-changing depths, he caught a glimpse of her soul.

A soul that was brave, good, loyal to a fault, and profoundly passionate. The soul of a woman a man could bury himself in and take comfort from when life was unkind. A woman with the courage to fight at his side, a woman capable of great joy and generosity.

Galen's heart swelled with the knowledge, with the bonding he felt drawing him to her. He knew, no matter what came of this night, that he'd never want or need another woman like he wanted and needed Alena.

She whimpered beneath him, lifting her hips with frantic little thrusts, rubbing herself against his throbbing shaft. She needed him, *wanted* him. And, as the spell tightened around them, Galen saw the last of his control shred, then disintegrate.

With a low, guttural sound, he grasped her hips and pulled her to the very edge of the table. She flung her arms about his shoulders. Her fair skin glistened with sweat; her breath came in sharp little pants. "Now," she cried, glancing down to where his big glans flared at the soft, damp curls of her womanhood. "Now, Galen. I beg you!"

She opened wide to him then, heedless of her total nakedness and vulnerability. He caught a glimpse of her slick, pink flesh, moist with desire. "Aye, now," he growled, his passion totally consuming him. Grasping himself, he thrust into her.

Over and around them the storm broke at last. Rain pounded down, clattering against the door and walls and windows. The wind whistled and howled, twisting and turning, hammering at the house and land. It plucked at the windows, shaking and rattling them until it found a weakness in one window latch. Tearing it apart, the storm flung open the shutters and roared into the room.

Water poured in. The wind surged past and filled the chamber with deafening sound and a soul-numbing cold. The coals in the hearth flared to life, scattering fire-red motes into the air. Yet the two lovers, joined as they were in passionate union, were oblivious to anything but each other.

Alena arched back, her mouth opening in soundless ecstasy. Galen slammed into her in a crazed rhythm. It only seemed to excite her the more, for she thrust back at him in a wild, ardent abandon.

She trembled; she jutted her breasts forward to rub against his coarse chest hair. Her nails dug into the thick muscles of his shoulders and upper arms, clenching deeply to score his flesh. She leaned back, suspended only by the strength of his hands, seeking the maximum depth and penetration.

Watching her uninhibited response, it was all Galen could do to hold back his climax. His own fingers gouged into her flaring hips as he fought to stay the force, the sensations building within him. The sensations—her sheath, tight and hot, clenching around him, pulling him ever deeper. Her wetness, slathering over his throbbing sex, intensifying the exquisite sensitivity, the ever burgeoning pleasure. Never, *never* had it been like this!

Then Alena arched up. An expression that was both agonized and ecstatic tautened her face. She screamed out her climax, jerking wildly, her release total, her legs wide, her body yielding, her breasts thrust high, peaking with pleasure.

Galen thought he'd go mad. He bucked against her. He writhed and plunged, his body drenched with sweat. He panted, gasped, moaned. And all the while he watched her, relishing his power and potency, his reawakened manhood. Thrusting into her, again and again and again.

He worked Alena with intense concentration, loathe to surrender to his release, savoring the moment and the anticipation of the explosion to come. "Sweet . . . ," he groaned. "So very, very sweet . . ."

She came to him then, her own climax spent at last, pressing to his sweat-slick body, cradling his head to her breast. Still, Galen thrust on, until he thought his heart would burst. Alena crooned to him, stroked his dark, damp head, whispering fevered words and erotic promises.

And, at last, Galen felt his seed spew forth, flowing through him and into Alena in sharp, rhythmic bursts. He cried out, went rigid, and shook with the intensity of his release. A release that went on and on and on, flooding him with the fiercest joy and satisfaction he'd ever known.

Galen rode the tide of ecstasy until, with a choking sob, he fell against the woman who held him in such tender, loving possession. Fell against her . . . spent, satiated, and astounded. There was naught more to be imagined or asked for, he thought in a sleepy, contented haze.

Naught this night, or any night ever to come.

The storm faded, withdrawing to slink away like some shamefaced miscreant. Through the open window, something moved. Something large yet agile.

Outlined once more by the moon breaking through the tattered remnants of the clouds, the creature lifted its wings and shook off the rain. Its bejeweled eyes gleamed with triumph as it scanned the scene within the house, of naked, sweat-sheened bodies locked in an ardent embrace, savoring the aftermath of their lovemaking.

A fierce joy swelled within the creature's breast. " 'Tis done, then," the Dragon Father whispered. "The life mating sealed, the woman's powers set into motion. 'Tis done, and destiny will now take us all where it may."

The early morn breeze was cool and damp, laden with the remnants of last night's storm. It swept across Alena's naked breasts, tautening the nipples and sending a skin-tightening chill coursing through her. She stirred restlessly on the bed and, eyes closed, grasped at the quilt to cover herself.

Instead of the quilt, however, her fingers glanced off something hairy and warm. The alien sensation sent a warning prickle through her. She froze. Her eyes opened.

There, lying beside her and equally naked, slept Galen Radbourne. As her glance skimmed his broad, hair-roughened torso, shock, then a growing horror filled Alena. What, by the Mother, was he doing lying next to her in bed?

Full awareness rushed back—and with that the memory of heated, writhing bodies joined in passionate lovemaking. Last night . . . the storm . . . she'd mated with Galen. Stifling a moan of distress, Alena carefully sat up and scooted to the edge of the bed, taking the greatest care not to disturb her sleeping companion.

Last night . . . By the Holy Ones, had it, could it truly have been as wildly pleasurable, as emotionally stirring as she re-membered? Their first joining, overlaid as 'twas by the growing pressure and intensity of the storm, had been a crazed, agonizingly rapturous, lust-driven union.

Yet, as intensely satisfying as it had been, the rest of the night until the waning hours before dawn, had been just as sweet, just as fulfilling, if less frenzied. She had never known a man like Galen Radbourne. Never known that lovemaking could be so intimate, so warm, so giving, so . . . so bonding.

With a soft, wondering sigh, Alena glanced down at Galen. He slept on, relaxed, at peace, a small smile quirking one corner of his sensuous mouth. She smiled in response, thinking he should always look so happy. So much had been revealed last night, the most surprising of which was an in-sight into Galen's true character.

He was a man beset with questions and self-doubts, hesi-tant and unwilling to venture back into a world fraught with cruelty and selfishness, tormented by secrets he kept tightly guarded. But he was also a good man, a kind and gentle man who was capable of the most surprising generosity. Time and again as they'd made love last night, he'd sacrificed his own pleasure, prolonged his own release, until she'd plumbed the depths of hers. Even now, remembering how it had been between them, Alena felt yet again the stirrings of desire.

She didn't know if she could ever tire of a man like Galen . . . nor ever again desire one as much as she desired him.

Yet, what, in the end, had it gained her? a more practical voice demanded, intruding on her misty reverie. She had come to Cadvallan Isle not to find the perfect lover, but to secure help in rescuing Renard. Not to experience the heights of sensual delights, but to enlist a sorcerer's aid. And could she honestly say she was any closer to her goal, despite what she and Galen had shared last night?

He had promised naught, offered no assurances that the taking of her body sealed their bargain. Mayhap he had never intended to, sensing quite accurately that she was so smitten with him, so governed by her lust, that only the simplest of acts like having her waken to find him standing there, naked and aroused in the firelight, would be enough to shred the last of her control.

But, on the other hand, what of her insights into his true character last night? Was he truly that manipulative to know she'd rush to mate with him if she found him standing naked before the hearth? How could she balance that new knowledge of Galen gained last night with her doubts about his true motivations? By the Holy Ones, she didn't know *what* to think anymore! It had been so much easier when she'd viewed him as an enemy, an opponent to be bested.

Alena climbed off the bed and stalked over to the chair where she'd laid her clothes. How indeed could she sort through it all, after last night? she asked herself, her emotions and mind in a muddle as she quickly dressed. What did it matter, one way or another, what Galen Radbourne *or* his motivations were? Renard was what counted. She had known him, fought and suffered alongside him, for nearly ten years. And she had spent but three days with Galen.

Nay, one night of lovemaking, however body- and heart-stirring, didn't mean more than what she and Renard had shared. 'Twas exactly why she had shied from emotional attachments with any of the warriors she'd taken as lovers in the past. Why she had never jeopardized her partnership with Renard, as good and attractive a man as he was. And why she must quickly and forcefully forget what had transpired last night. It meant naught in the total scheme of this quest—and her life.

Yet 'twas hard, so hard, to close her heart to him, Alena thought tenderly, gazing down at Galen once more. He had been such an exquisitely satisfying lover, both in his moments of tender passion and in his savage lust. He'd stirred emotions she'd never known she possessed.

A movement outside the open window snagged her attention. Alena turned, frowned briefly at the puddle of water standing beneath the window, then lifted her gaze. There stood Paddy, his bejeweled eyes bright with concern.

Are you all right? he mentally asked. *After last night, I mean? He seemed quite . . . rough.*

She gave a start at hearing, for the first time since her dream, the dragon's voice in her head. Then she sighed. *Aye, I'm no maiden unused to a man's passion. He didn't hurt me.*

Good. He has been kind to us. I would not have wished to punish him for harming you.

"Why would you wish to harm him?" Alena asked aloud, forgetting herself in her surprise. "I can well take care of myself."

He is a sorcerer. And you are mine, as I am yours. We are vowed to protect each other.

"Nay." She walked over to the window. "You are mistaken. I am naught to you. I'll soon leave this isle and you, as well. There is *naught* between us."

The young dragon's eyes darkened in pain. *Naught? But don't you know after last night? Don't you understand how it truly is between us?*

There was the softest whisper of cloth across the wooden floor, then Galen stood behind her. "Nay, she doesn't understand," he said, his voice still rough with sleep. "And neither did I until last night. 'Twas your magic joined with the Dragon Father's that cast the spell, wasn't it? He hadn't the power without you."

Alena wheeled around, glancing from Galen to Paddy. "What are you two talking about?"

The big sorcerer stood there, clutching the quilt about his waist, his upper torso bare. With his black hair tousled and the shadow of a beard darkening his jaw, he looked both boyish and delectably masculine all at the same time. Alena's heart gave a small leap of delight before she firmly quashed her response. Curse him for looking as good as he did, for last night!

"I ask again, Galen Radbourne," she said, irritation beginning to thread her voice. "What are you two talking about?"

Galen's glance met Paddy's. "I think 'twould be best if the explanation came from me. She has a tendency not to think too highly of magic, however much she now needs its assistance."

Paddy eyed him warily, then slowly nodded. Turning, the baby dragon ambled over to a nearby, sun-warmed rock. Climbing atop its massive expanse, he lay down and closed his eyes.

"Well, I'm still waiting," Alena prodded when the sorcerer riveted his attention back on her. "And you're right. I don't think highly of magic. I've rarely seen it used for much of anything good."

He reached out to take her by the arm. Alena jerked back. "Don't. I don't want you touching me."

A dark brow quirked and a smile twitched about his mouth. "Indeed? That hardly seemed a problem last night."

Alena's gaze narrowed. "After listening to you and that dragon, I begin to wonder how much of what I did last night was actually of my own free will."

"We were both ensorceled last night. And most of what we did was the result of magic."

"Most?"

"I may be presumptuous in speaking for you, but I wanted you and enjoyed what we did very much. I just never would have mated with you if it hadn't been for the spell."

"Spell?" Once again, confusion assailed Alena. Though she deeply regretted her unthinking abandon in coupling with him last night, until now, she'd thought it the result of two passionate people's attraction for each other. But was it possible? Had her surprisingly intense response to Galen been a result of magic, rather than a momentary loss of control? If 'twere, then she'd been manipulated, used. And there was naught Alena hated more than being used.

She gave an unsteady laugh, still loathe to lay the entire fault at his feet. "If your words are true, who but you was capable of casting that spell? Do you claim you used your magic to take advantage of me? A magic you say you no longer possess?"

His mouth went grim. His eyes flashed in anger. "I thought my powers were gone. I wanted them to be until last night, at any rate, but I was wrong. Not that it did much good. They were too weak to best the enchantment cast about us.

"But, be that as it may, I've never used my magic purposely to take advantage of another. And, in answer to your question as to did I cast the spell, the answer is nay. Have you mayhap forgotten the dragons are capable of magic, as well as yourself?"

"I cannot use magic, curse you!" Alena took a threatening step forward then caught herself. 'Twouldn't be wise to get too close to him. Possible spell or no, last night still lay too fresh, too potently, between them. "When will you get that through that thick skull of yours?"

Galen shrugged. "Mayhap when you begin to believe me, too. And when you give me a truly plausible explanation not only as to how you came through the spell enshrouding this isle, but how you came to bond with that young dragon. That is what you did, whether you realize it or not."

"By the Mother, not that about the spell surrounding this island again!" Alena rolled her eyes and heaved a deep sigh of exasperation. "Why do I even try to convince you I've no magical powers? All you do is lay more and more at my feet." Her lips curled in derision. "And now, on top of it all, I'm bonded to a dragon."

She made a move to walk past him when he grabbed her arm. Alena went rigid and looked down at his hand. "Let me go, I say. Now."

"And I say, nay." Galen met her stormy gaze with an equally stormy one of his own. His fingers clenched in the flesh of her upper arm until his hold was fierce, controlling. "You claim I took advantage of you, that I used magic to lie with you. But you don't know how far from the truth that is. I would have never—do you hear me?—*never* taken you to my bed if it had been within my power! Though I know not how it happened that you survived, I thank all that is holy that you did."

She relaxed in his grip. Confusion clouded her eyes. "I don't understand. Why wouldn't I have survived mating with you?"

Galen stared at her for a long moment, a myriad of emotions flaring, then dying in the dark depths of his eyes. Then he sighed, the sound wrenched from some secret place, some rarely examined part of his soul.

"Come, let us talk about this in more decency"—he glanced down wryly at the quilt-covered lower half of his body—"and more comfort. 'Tis a long and difficult tale but, after last night, I think you've the right—and need—to know."

"Fine," Alena muttered, unaccountably unsettled by the sudden change in Galen's mood. "I'll prepare us a breakfast while you dress."

He nodded and released her. Turning, he strode back across the room to where he'd left his clean clothes by the hearth last night. Before he could drop the quilt, Alena wheeled about and walked over to the cupboard to fetch two plates and mugs. By the time she had a simple meal of brown bread, butter, and cheese laid out and two mugs filled with cool goat's milk from the covered jug stored in the spring cooled compartment beneath the floor, Galen was dressed, his hair combed and face and hands washed.

She sat warily on the other side of the table from him. When he proceeded to slather butter on a piece of bread and slap on a slice of cheese, Alena quickly busied herself doing the same. Finally, though, when Galen finished with his first piece of bread and cheese and made a move to prepare himself another, Alena had had enough.

"Are you going to eat everything in sight before you tell me what happened last night?"

He glanced up, bemused, to find an irate woman glaring at him from across the table. "What? Oh, nay, I suppose not. I just didn't realize how ravenous I was until I took my first bite of food." His mouth quirked. "I'd forgotten how hungry I get after a passionate interlude."

"There are things of more import here, I'd wager, Galen Radbourne, than your appetite!" Alena grabbed the plates of bread and cheese and pulled them out of his reach. "Now, will you talk to me or not?"

Galen shot the food one last, longing look, then exhaled a resigned breath. "Aye, I'll tell you. I must warn you beforehand, however, that everything I say is the truth—at least as I see it—and I expect you to treat it as such. I'm in no mood for any more of your sarcastic snipes."

"Sarcastic snipes?" Alena half-rose from the table, furious all over again. Only the tightest self-discipline pulled her back into her chair. She needed to know what secrets he held so securely clasped to him, if she were ever to pierce the armor of his resolve.

"Fine. Fine." She waved his insulting warning aside with an impatient movement of her hand. "Just get on with it, will you?"

He arched a dark brow, his gaze narrowing. "Alena . . ."

She sighed. "Please, Galen. I'll listen. I swear it."

"A most heartwarming consideration, you listening for a change." He took up his mug and emptied it, then wiped his mouth with the back of his hand. "As I said before," he finally began, "we were both bespelled last night to mate with each other. For reasons I'm not entirely certain of, the Dragon Father joined his powers with those of your Paddy's to fashion a magical spell strong enough to compel us to mate."

"Indeed?" Alena's lips twisted mockingly. "Too powerful

for you, were they? These dragons you claim are fain to dying and without any magical powers left?"

Galen graced her with a withering look. "I didn't say they were entirely without magical powers. But, until now, none of them had sufficient strength to accomplish what was accomplished last night. Somehow, someway, though, your Paddy isn't like the rest. He's completely healthy and, if I'm not mistaken, possesses full dragon powers. He must still come into more maturity to fully utilize them himself, but 'tis possible the Dragon Father was able to draw on them nonetheless."

She gave a disbelieving laugh. "Do you know you have a most annoying tendency to contradict yourself?"

"Contradict myself?" Galen stared at her, momentarily dumbfounded. Then, recognition flared. "Ah, you mean about what I first told you of the dragons?" He shook his head. "I only shared what had been fact—or at least until you arrived. So much, in such a very short time, has changed regarding my perceptions of the dragons. And you wonder why I suspect you of magical powers, of motives deeper than what you care to share?"

"I can understand it from your viewpoint. But if it isn't me causing all these changes in the dragons, who is?"

Galen frowned. "I'm not sure." He shook his head. "And that makes you and me pawns."

"Nobody uses me!"

He smiled at the savage vehemence in her voice. "I don't know too many people who enjoy being used. And when they go so far as to risk your life . . ."

Her head snapped up. "Aye, you said something about our mating endangering me. How is that possible? Though I made no mention of my prior experience with men, surely you grasped that quite early in our lovemaking."

At the memory of her mouth settling around his hardened shaft, Galen's lips twitched. "Aye, that I did. And 'twas most pleasurable—your experience, I mean."

"Well, be that as it may," Alena muttered, flushing in spite of herself, "it doesn't explain what you meant."

"Nay, it doesn't," Galen admitted. He hesitated, finding sudden fascination in the raised leaves and vines he'd painstakingly carved around the edge of his plate.

Finally, he lifted his gaze to Alena's. " 'Tis a hard tale to tell and mayhap doesn't matter at any rate. Suffice it to say, there were other motives, aside from my bitterness against my people, for why I chose to turn forever from the way of magic and live out my life on Cadvallan Isle. Despite your earlier remarks regarding my courage and manhood, these are the real reasons why I refused to accept the most tantalizing offer of your body and go with you to rescue your friend."

When he didn't immediately continue, Alena shifted restlessly and leaned forward on the table. "Aye, and those reasons were?"

"Both my powers and those of my brother's," Galen hoarsely forged on, "are nourished and intensified by the life essence of others. Eventually, though, we take so much from them that they die."

Puzzlement furrowed her brow. "And what does that have to do with me, or with our having lain together last night?"

He sighed and shook his head. "Don't you see, Alena? Dorian and I gain our powers through women in the act of lovemaking."

She paled and leaned back. "Like last night?"

"Aye," Galen said, his mouth going flat, his eyes bleak. "Like last night."

CHAPTER SIX

Alena laughed unsteadily. "Well, I feel no worse for the wear. Is it possible you may be mistaken in this?"

"Nay." Galen's eyes held hers in a prison of fierce anguish. "I'm not mistaken. I killed the only woman I ever loved."

His admission took her by surprise. Galen had killed the woman he loved? 'Twasn't possible. Though she'd only known him a few days, she'd always prided herself on being a good judge of character. Naught about Galen gave her any suspicion that he wasn't exactly the man he appeared to be. And after last night . . .

Once more, Alena leaned forward. "Tell me how it happened," she urged. "I must know it all, must understand if I'm to help get us off this isle."

"Is that all you care about? Getting us off the isle?" His voice was harsh and rasped thickly in the suddenly heavy tension. "Better still, count yourself fortunate that I've given you fair warning. Count yourself fortunate that you survived. The drain on another is unpredictable and there's no way to know when the fatal experience will occur. But if you mate even one time more with me, Alena, I can't promise you 'twon't be your last."

"There's no need for us ever to mate again."

Galen stared at her in disbelief, then laughed bitterly. "In that case, I suggest you hie yourself off this isle as fast as you can. The Dragon Father, for whatever his reasons, could well ensorcel us again. Are you willing to risk that?"

"I've said it before and I'll say it again," Alena stated

firmly. "I'm not leaving here without you."

"Little fool!" He stood, shoved back his chair and strode across the room to stare out the window.

Alena watched Galen for several minutes, then rose and walked over to him. His shoulders were hunched, his arms rigid, his hands clenched into fists at his sides. "Galen, there has got to be a way to work this out." Hesitantly, she placed her hand on his arm. "We can—"

At her touch, he wheeled around. Agony tautened his features and burned in his eyes. Startled, Alena lurched back. "Galen? What's wrong? What did I—"

"You still don't understand, do you?" he cried. "If what you say about my brother is true, he may be using women to feed his magic. And that makes him far more powerful than I. Even if I wanted to, I can't go against Dorian without those same enhanced powers, and the only way I can replenish those powers—powers that fade very, very fast—is to mate frequently. How deep does your loyalty, your love for your friend go, Alena? Deep enough to sacrifice your life in feeding my magic?"

She stared up at him, her face gone white, speechless.

"Do you see what you risk in asking for my help?" he ground out hoarsely. "Do you finally understand why I repeatedly refused you?"

"Aye," she whispered, and turned away, suddenly too full of confusion and a bittersweet, if irrational sorrow, that she couldn't think straight.

Galen watched her walk toward the door, open it, and stride through it, his heart twisting within his chest. *At last,* he told himself, hurting so badly he thought he'd die from the pain. At last she knows and sees me for the monster I truly am. And, at long last, she will finally leave me.

The realization brought him little comfort, though Galen

knew 'twas for the best. Mayhap 'twas his lonely, longing exile, but Alena had managed, in but the course of a few days and one, exquisitely passionate night, to capture his heart. A heart that, for her continued safety, must shun the newly awakened emotions now coursing through it.

His hands clenched at his sides, grinding his nails into the callused flesh of his palms. His chest heaved with pent up pain and frustration. Ah, curse the unkind fate that had ever brought her to him! Curse his foolish, fatal vulnerability!

Whether Alena left or stayed, he would never, ever, regain the peace he'd had before.

After several hours and no sign of Alena, Galen went out to find the Dragon Father. He found the big dragon perched on a smooth tumble of boulders down where the underground spring finally broke the surface to form a small pond. The warm liquid bubbled and churned, the morning sun glinting off the agitated waters in scattered bits of light. 'Twas a peaceful, soothing place, the tall willows drooping low to dip their early budding arms, birdsong filling the air.

But today Galen found it a place of seething questions and barely leashed emotions. A place where he'd have his answers at last—and plumb the heart of a creature he'd thought he'd always known.

He strode over to stand before the big white dragon, and lifted his gaze to meet that of the mesmerizingly iridescent one of the Dragon Father. "Why did you ensorcel us?" Galen demanded, eschewing, in his anger and frustration over Alena, a more tactful approach. "What did you hope to gain?"

The Dragon Father shrugged, arched his huge wings briefly in a flare of tautly stretched white skin and sinew, then settled them snugly against his scale-slick body. "What else?

To bring you and the woman together. I said before that your destiny now lay with her. It seemed a most expedient way to bind you to her so you would follow on her quest."

"You called her through the spell surrounding Cadvallan, didn't you?"

"Aye, that I did. I sensed there was something about the woman from the beginning."

"What exactly *is* so special about Alena, that she is now of more import to you than I?" Galen's jaw clenched. His stance altered, widening imperceptibly, as if steadying himself for the blow to come. "What has become of all the years we labored together to help your kind, of the trust and friendship we shared? Is it now of naught, when some woman suddenly appears on Cadvallan?"

"Trust? Friendship?" The Dragon Father gave a bitter laugh. "You, too, have kept secrets from me, Radbourne. Secrets that precluded any hope of truly trusting each other."

"Secrets?"

"Aye, of why you turned from your powers, sorcerer that you be." The big creature lowered his head until his long, slender face was a warm breath away. "I listened this morn when you told her of the vile consequences of your powers. Do you think I'd have risked the woman bonding with you, expedient mate though you were, if I'd known you nourish your evil kind of magic with the life essence of women?"

He jerked back his head in a motion of anguish, his eyes clenched shut. "But now 'tis too late. She is yours as much as you are hers. There is naught left me but to trust whatever is good in you will prevail. That, and send the young one with you to protect her."

"Don't trouble yourself. I'm not leaving Cadvallan!" Galen snarled, furious that the dragon had once again eavesdropped.

He was glad now that he'd never shared his secret with the big dragon. After this revelation of the Dragon Father's true feelings for him, there was no telling what he would have done. "But, even if I *were* to go with her, Alena needs no protection from me," Galen said. "I'd sooner cut out my heart than harm her."

The Dragon Father's eyes opened and he cocked his head. "So, you *do* care for the woman. 'Tis good, but you must not mate with her again. It could be her death."

Galen laughed harshly. "You should have thought of that before you bespelled us. What you set into motion will now be doubly hard to control."

"She needed to mate, to form a life bond with one of her kind, for her powers to blossom and mature. And without those powers . . ."

"Aye?" Galen prodded when the dragon paused. "What *are* Alena's powers and why are they so important?"

The Dragon Father eyed Galen. "Haven't you discerned the truth yet? Haven't you felt even the faintest stirrings of antipathy toward a woman destiny has made your mortal enemy?"

"Nay. Alena is aggravating, headstrong, and stubborn, but I bear no hostility toward her."

"Good. Good." The dragon nodded in satisfaction. "Though I had no choice, I feared bonding a sorcerer and a *galiene*. But mayhap you—"

"Alena?" Galen cut off the big creature before he could go on. "A *galiene*?" He shook his head in disbelief. " 'Tisn't possible. You dream too much in your waning years, hope for the return of times long dead."

The Dragon Father arched a brow. "Do I, Radbourne? Mayhap, but think a moment before relegating me to the dragon's graveyard. The woman arrived here, breaking through a spell that neither you nor I could breach. She bonded with the young one even before his birth, and gave him his name. And the young one flourishes, grows larger and stronger with each passing day, rather than weakening and turning puny like all the rest."

His wide mouth quirked. "You've seen our young ones and how quickly they turn sickly and their growth becomes stunted. Haven't you noticed this one's exceptional progress?"

There were many strange occurrences since Alena's arrival, only one of which, Galen realized now that he paused to consider it, was Paddy's amazing health. He felt a fool not having seen it sooner, but he'd been so preoccupied with Alena, the baby dragon had been but an irritation and nuisance.

He sighed. Shoulders slumping, Galen turned and ambled over to a rock to sit. Alena . . . a *galiene*. The thought was mind-boggling. Mind-boggling and disturbing.

For hundreds of years now, the *galienes* had been the sorcerers' fiercest enemies—even more so than the dragons—for only through the *galienes* could the dragons' powers be intensified into the significant threat that had once made the dragons the sorcerers' equal in magic. The women had other powers as well, abilities but whispered about among sorcerers, but ones Galen knew were equally feared.

There was so much to be considered and sorted through. How would Alena's powers affect the dragons on Cadvallan? What would the sorcerers do, once they discovered who Alena really was? And was she about to embark on a quest that suddenly seemed more than a simple rescue? Galen was beginning to wonder.

He shoved a hand raggedly through his hair and met the Dragon Father's gaze. "I'd thought all your dragon ladies were gone. Thought those of my kind had killed them all."

"A few escaped and went into hiding. Obviously the woman's mother was one of them." The Dragon Father shuffled to the edge of his rock and leaned down toward Galen. "What will become of the woman, once she reaches your home? Your brother will surely kill her if he learns of her powers."

"Dorian isn't the monster you and Alena make him out to be!"

"And I say you have been away too long, and mayhap never knew the man your brother was destined to become. He hates the dragons. He uses others to feed his magic, if what the woman says is true. And *he* is the one who kept the spell about Cadvallan all these years."

"You lie!"

The Dragon Father gave a snort. "Do I? And have you never wondered, in all this time, who cast the spell?"

"Aye, I've wondered, but finally accepted that it mattered little if I couldn't break through it."

"Well, now you can, Radbourne."

"Can I?"

A huge, leathery wing lifted and pointed toward the sea. "Why not try it and see. Just remember to return for the young one and the woman."

Galen rose, hesitated, then squared his shoulders. He turned and strode off, back up to the hilly knoll above the spring, then down the trail that led to the beach and the spot where he'd secured his little boat.

As he walked along, doubts and questions roiled in his mind. Was today the day he'd finally sail from Cadvallan and reach the distant shores of Wyndymyll? Was today the day he'd at last set foot on the land of his birth, see the quaint little villages once more, smell the rich, earthy scents of a town crowded with inhabitants, hear the harsh shouts of the farmers and happy cries of the children?

Galen's steps slowed, the old, painful memories flooding him once more. How would the people accept him if he returned from Cadvallan after all these years? What would he say to Dorian when they next met? If Alena's and the Dragon Father's words were true, how would he convince his brother to release Renard and mend his evil ways?

The world in the past fifteen years had changed, gone on, and Galen feared he'd not know it—or like what he saw. He could well be a misfit, as isolated in the midst of his people as he'd been alone on Cadvallan. And he could fail—miserably, shamefully so—in the process.

Yet what other choice was left him, now that he knew the truth about Alena and her link with the dragons? What other choice had he, if he truly meant all his fine words and aspirations for the dragons? He wouldn't live forever. The dragons' best hope for the future now seemed to lie in Wyndymyll, not on Cadvallan Isle.

In the end, there were too many unanswered questions out there, questions about his brother and his part in the continuing destruction of the *galienes* and dragons, in his potential misuse of his magic. Questions about good and evil, right and wrong. Questions even he could no longer ignore.

No man of honor could ignore them, or turn his back if he had any power to change what was awry in the world. Though he wouldn't willingly use his magic, after what he'd just learned from the Dragon Father, Galen knew he couldn't hide away any longer in his safe, secure little life here on Cadvallan. Nay, not anymore and, most likely, never again, no matter what happened.

But to turn again to his magic, to go against the brother, their long-standing rivalry notwithstanding, who had helped him with such compassion and consideration through the most difficult, heart-wrenching time in his life . . . Ah, neither Alena nor the Dragon Father knew what they asked of him. He could barely face it himself.

Galen reached the spot where the boat was stored, dragged it out, and pulled the vessel across the beach and into the water. Climbing in, he raised the sail, grasped the tiller, and guided it out to sea. A breeze blew, strong and stiff this morn but, this time, 'twas a breeze that blew *away* from Cadvallan Isle. As Galen neared the point where the spell always forced him back, he tensed, awaiting the inevitable, disheartening change in the wind's direction. He dared not allow his hopes to rise, knowing how unpredictable the winds were this time of year.

Yet the wind never lessened or varied. A wild exultation filled Galen. Whether his unwavering course toward Wyndymyll was a result of his newly enhanced powers or Alena's influence, he didn't know. It mattered not. The spell was broken at last.

The tall, towering oaks overlooking the sandy shore of the land of Wyndymyll grew close, until Galen could make out the faint buds of green that heralded spring and the stiff, proud little shoots of the daffodils and hyacinths that grew wild in the forests. Patches of snow dotted the land, but the warmth of the late morning sun was already melting them away. The scent of rich, damp earth and growing things wafted to Galen on an errant breeze. His pulse quickened; his throat went dry.

Home. He was almost home.

Then, with a surge of powerful muscles, he turned his boat about and headed it back across the sea to Cadvallan. Soon, he silently vowed, he'd return, but there were still a few issues left unresolved back on Cadvallan. A few issues yet to be settled with a beautiful, alluring woman named Alena.

A woman who had never been what she'd seemed.

Alena still wasn't back when Galen returned to his house. After a thorough search, he found her down on the beach, sitting in the secluded, moss-covered rocks. Her chin resting on her drawn up knees, she gazed out to sea.

Galen made no sound or gave notice that he was nearby, just turned and silently climbed back up the trail to his house. Though he knew now he must leave Cadvallan and journey with her, there was naught he could say or do to ease her concerns about him. As difficult as it had been for even him to accept, he was what he was.

For a time after he'd learned what he'd done to Lydia, he'd been suicidal. To protect Galen from himself, Dorian and their father had had him locked high in a tower room without access to anything he might have used to harm himself.

Even now he remembered the long days and endless nights of horror. How he'd screamed out his anguish until his throat was raw, how he'd pounded his frustration against the unrelenting stone walls and thick wooden door until his hands were bleeding and mangled. How he'd refused both food and water until he was so weak he could barely crawl, and then they'd come and forced it down him anyway.

Finally, Dorian, in a desperate attempt to save his brother, had cast a spell of repose about him. Galen had slept for weeks while time, the ultimate healer, had mended his shattered mind and heart. When he'd eventually awakened, Galen had still remembered what he had done, but the pain was far more distant, even bearable—and he had known he would go on living.

There was no hope, however, of salvaging his promising

talents as a sorcerer-in-training. Though the proud tradition of magic had been passed down from father to son through many generations of Radbournes, Galen had refused to work his spells ever again. The intensive intermingling of blood-lines had reached its pinnacle of magical abilities in the birth of him and his twin, but the cost had been too great. To be the most powerful sorcerers of all required the eventual deaths of any women brave—or foolish—enough to mate with them.

Galen had even refused to settle for a position of minor sorcerer with the skills he'd acquired through training and intensive practice. To tread even lightly again in his magic would only drag him down, bit by bit, into that darker, seductive side. Even then, Galen had known he was a man driven to perfection, and his exacting nature eventually would lure him to try again what he feared most. Even then, Galen had known his ambition—and had known he'd sacrifice almost anything for it. That much about him hadn't changed over the years.

His humanity, however, was more than even he cared—or dared—to risk. 'Twas why he'd finally chosen to accept his life on Cadvallan and turn his energies to other things, denying his magic and driving all thought of it from his mind.

Until Alena, Galen had thought he'd come to terms with his self-imposed fate and the potential horror that would always be a part of him. But hardly had he met her than he knew the fallacy of that imagining. Had she stirred him so quickly, so easily just because she was a comely woman? Or, though it sickened him even to contemplate it, because her life essence stirred anew his magic?

Shutting out further consideration of the reasons for his attraction to Alena, Galen turned his bittersweet musings, instead, back to last night. Could any coupling between a man and a woman be as wondrous, as intensely pleasurable, as heartbreakingly intimate, as had the couplings they'd shared? Mayhap 'twas just his inexperience with women. He'd been but eighteen when he'd first laid with Lydia. And before Lydia, all there had been was his magic.

His magic. Ah, how he still loved his magic! Even now, stoked by last night's mating, Galen felt it stir, coil within him with the insidious power of some imprisoned serpent. Growing, rising, demanding release.

But he didn't dare give it its freedom. It had killed Lydia and 'twould surely kill Alena sooner or later. Nay, no matter what the upcoming quest held for them, he dared not accept either—neither his magic *nor* Alena.

She didn't return until sunset. He'd started a fire in the hearth to ward off the evening chill and put a pot of soup on to cook just as she'd returned. Galen shot a quick look over his shoulder, saw she was calm and composed, and turned back to the slicing of a few more wild onions into the soup. He listened, nonetheless, as the sound of her footsteps moved across the room and over to the table. A chair scraped along the floor, her clothing rustled, and she sat.

Silence settled over the house, save for the crackling of the fire and the occasional thunk of Galen's spoon against the sides of the pot as he stirred the soup. The broth began to simmer, the vegetables and chunks of wild fowl to cook, and a fragrant aroma wafted to his nostrils. Another fifteen or twenty minutes, he thought, and 'twould be ready.

With a resolute straightening of his shoulders, Galen shoved to his feet and turned. His glance settled on Alena's, sitting there, fingers knotted before her. "Supper will be ready shortly."

She looked away. "I'm not hungry."

"Yet you should eat," he persisted. "You aren't so long from your sickbed and need to rebuild your strength." He gestured toward her bandaged hand. "And I haven't re-dressed that, either, since yesterday."

Alena's head jerked around and Galen was momentarily taken aback by the angry, anguished look she sent him. "How can you be so . . . so good, and still be capable of killing? Possess evil powers that are such an inherent part of your nature, and yet be so tender . . . so loving?"

He stood there before the fire, half of him hot, the other half ice-cold, and found he wished, with all his heart, for the courage to go to Alena and take her into his arms. But after what he'd told her this morn, she couldn't possibly trust him anymore—if indeed she ever had—and, more importantly, he didn't dare trust himself. If he touched her now, as hurting, as needful as he was, he feared he might lose control again. And, this time, have no spell to blame it on.

So, instead, Galen shrugged and forced a halfhearted little smile. "We all make choices, Alena. I chose not to be the man my destiny called me to, no matter how much I loved my magic. The price 'twas higher than I cared to pay."

" 'Twasn't too high for your brother, though, was it?" she muttered bitterly. She cocked her head and studied him. "Did you know that, Galen? That your brother's magic grows with each passing day? After what you told me this morn, 'tis now evident how he feeds that magic."

She averted her glance. " 'Tis more than likely what happened to the Lord Hargreaves's daughter, the one Renard and I were sent to ransom from your brother. It all falls into place now, his words, his actions." Alena shuddered. "He wanted me, as well. Had attacked us with the intent of killing Renard and taking me prisoner."

Alena laughed, the sound hollow, humorless. "And now I know why, and know my eventual fate if I dare go back to rescue Renard alone. But I won't go back alone, Galen," she continued, her voice taking on a hard, determined edge. "Have your powers returned after last night?"

He didn't answer immediately. "I'll tell you true, Alena. I was never without some powers. I just chose not to use them ever again. But," Galen sighed, "thanks to last night, they've indeed become greatly enhanced."

"Good. If I must be the source of a sorcerer's powers, I choose to be yours, not your brother's. And, I say again, though I may well risk my life in the act, I'll do anything to save Renard—and that includes mating with you if need be."

She paused, then forced herself to go on. "I am strong. You won't drain me as quickly as you might other women. I feel certain 'twill be enough to get you to Castle Radbourne and assure the defeat of your brother. Will you help me, Galen?"

Help her? By the Holy Ones, he wanted to take her into his arms, into his heart and life, and never let her go! "Aye," Galen said instead, "I'll help you."

At the sudden, wild look of joy that flared in her eyes, he raised a silencing hand. "I said I'd help you, but consider carefully what I next tell you. How can you be certain that the same magic that has corrupted my brother won't eventually corrupt me as well?" he asked, forcing words to what had been just a shameful fear lurking in the darkest corners of his mind. "I was obsessed with my magic before, would have sacrificed almost anything for it. If it hadn't been for my sweet, beautiful Lydia . . ."

He dragged in a shuddering breath. "She called me from my magic and, for a time, I learned of other things—of flowers and birds, of the beauty of the heavens, and how wonderful and fulfilling the love of a woman was. I also began to realize just how dangerous and seductive an obsession could be. It frightened me, Alena, how close I'd come to shutting out everything but my magic."

And how tempted I was, even after what I did to Lydia, he silently added, *to taste again of that heady surge of power.* But *that* admission was too deep, too dark, too shameful ever to share with anyone. Nay, Alena knew enough, had been forewarned. He'd not bare it all to her.

"And now I ask you to face your magic, to test the limits of your courage and wield that which nearly corrupted you before," Alena softly finished for him. "Ah, Galen, I find no pleasure in asking this of you. I realize now that, in taking you with me to rescue Renard, I risk destroying you as well as losing him."

She pounded her fist on the table in frustration, the old, hard resolve filling her anew. "But what choice have I? I cannot turn from my obligations, no matter how difficult, how painful, they may be."

"And neither can I, it seems."

Galen walked over to stand across the table from Alena. What choice, indeed, was there for any of them anymore? he thought. He could never have Alena—that he well knew—but he couldn't turn from her or deny that somehow, someway the plight of the dragons and their continued survival might well lie in her hands. Nay, 'twasn't a simple rescue anymore, no matter how simply it might have all begun. 'Twasn't simple at all.

"I see now I cannot hide away or avoid the world," he continued, his determination growing with each word he spoke. "My destiny, whether I wish it or not, now calls me out of exile, if only temporarily. But I cannot promise you how 'twill go, either, be it good or bad. You must also know that, Alena."

"You can only do the best you can, Galen. 'Tis all any of us can do."

He smiled. "Aye, I suppose you're right." Silence descended upon them again and, within that silence, the burbling of the soup plucked at their consciousness. Galen gave a start, then turned and hurried over to the hearth. Taking up a thick cloth, he grabbed the pot and lifted it off the fire.

"Is the soup scalded?" Alena asked from close behind him.

He wheeled about, unnerved by her unexpected closeness. "Nay. There's still hope for it, but 'twill require a bit of cooling before 'tis safe to eat."

Alena grinned. "Well, the eve's still young. Come, put the soup aside and we'll talk. We've plans to make and time is short."

"Aye, I suppose so," Galen agreed. "But first, let me tend to your hand."

As if remembering it at long last, she lifted her bandaged hand and stared at it. " 'Twould be wise, I'd imagine. I may well need my sword hand sooner than I'd expected."

CHAPTER SEVEN

"Nay, Paddy is *not* going with us!" Anger threaded Alena's voice and spilled over into her rigid, fists-on-hips stance the next morning as they worked together on the beach. "This quest is danger-fraught and difficult enough without lugging a big, awkward, baby dragon along. And how do you imagine we'll avoid undue notice or talk if we're accompanied by a creature most have never seen before save in their worst nightmares?

"Nay," she firmly shook her head, "no dragon."

Galen glanced up from the hollow-log raft he was lashing together. "If I make careful use of my powers, both my former ones as well as my now more enhanced ones, I can cast a spell of invisibility over Paddy so that no one but I see him. My skills are rusty and I can't promise how long I can maintain the spell, but it should help us when we pass through more populated areas. Besides, how do you think you'll keep him from following?" He motioned toward Paddy, frolicking nearby in the surf.

With a sigh of exasperation, Alena looked over at the young dragon. Round of belly and strong of body, he bounded about in the foaming waves that crashed onto the shore, the sunlight glinting off a scale-sleek body, blue-black with health. Paddy lifted his meager, immature wings, flapped them fiercely in an attempt to chase after a gull who'd foolishly cut too low after a fish. His inexperienced efforts in attempting to fly, however, were enough to cause him to lose his balance and topple over, headfirst, into the sand.

"Do you see, as well," Galen continued, "what would

happen if we refused to take him and he tried to follow us? Paddy would drown in the sea attempting to fly to Wyndymyll."

Alena scowled. "Don't they know how to swim?"

Galen chuckled. "You're thinking of water dragons. These earth dragons aren't known for their swimming abilities."

"Well, I don't care!" Alena rose to her feet. "I'm not Paddy's mother nor his nursemaid. I'm a warrior, curse it all, and that's all I'll ever be!"

"Nonetheless, I'm taking Paddy along. If he doesn't go, neither do I."

"Galen, don't threaten me."

He ignored the veiled warning in her words. "Fine, I won't threaten you." Without another word, he went back to lashing the logs together.

Alena stood there for a long moment seething, Galen well knew, then whirled about and, in a spurt of sand and indignation, stomped off down the beach and back up the trail to the house. He shot Paddy, who had halted his play when he'd heard the anger begin to tauten Alena's voice, a commiserating look, then went back to his work.

She doesn't want me, does she? Paddy's plaintive voice echoed in Galen's head.

Galen looked up. "She doesn't know of her special powers or the significance of her relationship with you yet."

But she needs me!

"She doesn't know that yet, either."

Dragon Father said not to tell her. Why is that?

"The time isn't right, Paddy." The big sorcerer finished lashing one end of the raft and knotted the rope off. "Alena must come to a gradual realization and acceptance of her powers on her own. I'm not sure she's the kind of person to welcome such a startling revelation from us. She might view it as us trying to tell her what to do. In this, at least, I agree with the Dragon Father."

Will she want me then? When she accepts her true destiny?

"I hope so, Paddy. She's one of the very last of her kind." Galen glanced up and smiled sadly. "I truly hope so. The survival of the dragons may well rest with her." He scooted down to the other end of the raft.

You will help me with her, won't you? You are her mate now. She will listen to you.

Galen paused in the act of beginning to weave the stout hemp cord around the logs at the other end. *You are her mate . . .*

The words struck a curious chord. Her mate . . . By the Holy Ones, as strange, as foreign as the concept was, the more he considered it, the more he turned it over and over in his mind like some precious jewel, examining all its sparkling, surprisingly startling facets, the more the idea gained a certain allure.

What would it be like to be the mate of a woman like Alena? She was a warrior, brave, forthright and assertive. She had survived countless battles, fought men twice her size and strength, seen death and destruction and horrors he couldn't even begin to imagine. And, beautiful as she was, she could have any man she wanted.

Any man . . . like Renard.

The realization stabbed through Galen, leaving a gaping hole where his heart should have been. Renard was a warrior, most likely big and brave and strong. Hadn't Alena said they'd been together for years? More than just a partnership most likely bound them. Most likely they were lovers.

The truth, as hard as 'twas to face, was that Alena hadn't willingly chosen to bed him. Her initial offer was based on enlisting his aid in rescuing Renard. Her eager response the other night was the result of a spell. And if 'twas necessary to couple with him again, 'twould only be to sustain his powers.

. . . I'll do anything to save Renard—and that includes mating with you . . .

Though he'd chosen to hear only her plea for help at the time, and gone on to explain how it had been between him and Lydia and his magic, he'd rolled Alena's words around in his mind ever since. Though she'd seemed more kind and concerned toward him since their mating, he knew she'd not dare couple with him again unless 'twas to save the man she truly loved—Renard. She was a warrior. She did what was expedient and no more.

Nay, Galen forced himself to face the truth, however painful 'twas. He was her mate only to advance the Dragon Father's plans and serve as a catalyst in the maturation of Alena's own unique powers. Above all, the fact still remained that he wasn't the man for her. A normal life with a woman could never be his, no matter how he yearned for it.

Galen jerked the hemp cord tight and glanced up at Paddy. The dragon stared back, his expression expectant, guileless. Paddy would never understand the complexities of the situation, nor was it necessary that he did. Some problems were best kept to oneself.

"Aye," Galen sighed, " 'tis true. I am her mate. But I don't own her, nor can I force her to do what she doesn't wish to do."

But you will help me, won't you, in winning her heart?

Galen smiled grimly. One of them, at least, should experience Alena's love. 'Twas fitting it be a *galiene* for her dragon. "Aye, I'll help you. But only because it seems her destiny. She'll choose, in the end, though, the course her life must take. Destiny or no, 'tis her right."

My thanks, Galen Radbourne. With you at my side, I am cer-

tain to prevail. My lady has a special affection for you and will listen as you direct.

"Like she just did when I told her she must take you along?" The big sorcerer's mouth quirked. "You're young yet, Paddy. You've a lot to learn about females."

The baby dragon flapped his wings, managing to lift himself a few inches off the ground in his excitement. *Your words are true, Galen Radbourne. Time is short. Pray, teach me what I need to know.*

Galen shot Paddy a disbelieving look. " 'Twill take more than a few days to teach you about women. 'Tis a lifelong endeavor, to be sure, and I'm hardly more than a novice myself."

At the crestfallen look on the dragon's face, Galen sighed. "Come close while I finish this raft, and we'll begin the lessons. Though I'll warn you now that even I haven't all the secrets when it comes to a woman—and especially not one as complex as Alena."

They set out the next morning at low tide, Galen sailing his boat, Alena towed behind on the raft to soothe the terrified Paddy. The journey began well; the seas were a bit choppy, but manageable. Paddy, however, couldn't seem to sit still. He constantly moved from side to side on the raft, tipping it precariously until Alena, in an attempt to quiet the anxious creature, stood and walked over to him.

At that moment, a large wave crashed into the raft, dousing both Alena and Paddy with frigid water. Paddy squawked in distress and swung about. His long tail slammed into the warrior woman's legs and knocked her over.

With an outraged squawk of her own, Alena tumbled into the ocean. Paddy, quickly realizing what he'd done, wheeled around and nearly fell himself when he raced to the edge of the raft and tilted it precariously once again.

"Paddy! Halt!" Galen shouted from the boat. "Don't make it any worse!"

The baby dragon skidded to a stop, then backed away into the middle of the raft. His fearful gaze, however, never left the spot where Alena had fallen in.

With a sputter, she surfaced. Alena flung her sodden hair from her face and swung about, looking for Paddy. He sat there forlornly on the raft, gazing back at her. Furiously treading water, Alena graced him with a baleful glare.

Galen threw back his head and laughed.

Alena paddled around until she faced him. "What's so funny, Radbourne?" she cried peevishly. " 'Twas your idea to take this . . . this troublesome dragon along, and yet I'm the one who must repeatedly suffer for it!"

The big sorcerer shrugged. " 'Tis but one of the joys of parenthood. And he bonded with you, fair lady, not me."

She swam over to the raft and grabbed hold of the nearest log. "Do you know how sick I already am of being reminded of that? You're the dragon-lover, not I!"

"Well," he called back to her, not at all chastened by her snarling words and foul looks, "sometimes our destinies call us where we've no wish to go."

Alena climbed up onto the raft, shot Paddy a warning look when he made a move to hurry over to her, and shoved to her feet. Seawater dripped from her hair and clothes, puddling at her feet. A small fish flopped frantically from the top of her right boot. Alena bent, pulled it loose, and tossed it back into the sea.

"A novel way of catching fish," Galen shouted from the safe, dry confines of his boat. "I should have thought of that sooner. Then we wouldn't have had to spend the past week fishing to build a stockpile of dried fish for the dragons to eat while we were gone. I could have just dunked you into the ocean and pulled you back up, laden with fish."

"Enough, Radbourne!" Alena stomped over to take her place back in the middle of the raft. "No more of your jibes, I say. Just direct your efforts to getting us to shore as quickly as possible."

And Galen, noting the rising anger clouding her face, decided to do just that.

Aided by a stiff breeze at their back, they made landfall two hours later. Galen beached his boat, then hurried back to the edge of the water to pull the raft into shore. A still damp Alena wordlessly climbed down when the raft hit the shallows, followed almost instantly by Paddy. Unfortunately, the young dragon's eagerness resulted in his missing the beach.

Paddy landed in three feet of water just behind Alena and Galen. The ensuing wave created by a five-hundred-pound baby dragon knocked them off their feet. Both rose to the surface, sputtering and soaking wet.

Galen shoved his long, dark hair from his face and glared over at Paddy. "Next time, will you wait until I tell you what to do and when to do it?"

"Don't like it so well, do you, Radbourne, when the boot is on the other foot?"

He wheeled about to confront a smirking Alena. "Most definitely not at this time of year!" He took her by the arm. "Come on. Let's get out of these wet clothes."

She jerked her arm from his grip. "You forget yourself, Radbourne. I'm quite capable of taking care of myself."

"Fine," Galen gritted. "Then you won't mind if I don't linger here with you?" With that, he turned on his heel and strode toward the shore.

Alena quickly followed, then helped him pull the raft onto the beach. They unloaded the packs of clothes and food, then hid both the boat and raft in a dense thicket of bushes growing in a nearby stand of trees. Returning to the packs, Alena pulled out dry clothes for Galen and herself.

"Here," she said, shoving his apparel into his hands when he strode back up to her. "You take the trees over there," she indicated the forest to her right, "and I'll dress behind the bushes."

His lips lifted in a wolfish smile. "There are no other people about, fair lady. And our bodies are well known to each other. What's the harm in changing right here?"

"Don't even ask," Alena muttered. "Don't even start with me, Radbourne." She stalked off toward the bushes.

A short while later and dressed again in dry clothes, Alena and Galen met back on the beach. As she settled her belt more snugly about her trim waist and fastened the cuffs of her long-sleeved, burgundy tunic, Alena surveyed the leather packs that lay at their feet.

" 'Tis an hour's walk to the village of Elmsdale." She bent and picked up two of the four packs, slinging one over each shoulder. "I hope to buy two horses there so the rest of our journey won't be on foot." Her glance skittered off their scaly compatriot who had shuffled up to stand behind Galen. "What do you propose we do with Paddy in the meanwhile?"

Galen considered that for a moment. "Can we take a path through the forest and off the main road?"

Alena scowled. "Aye, if you've a wish to increase the journey an extra hour. I thought you said you could make him invisible."

"I can, but I'd prefer to conserve my powers for as long as possible."

Her gaze narrowed. A small, niggling doubt flared within her. "Indeed? And you haven't been, er," she struggled for a tactful way to phrase it, "misleading me as to the true extent of your abilities, have you? Though I know you've powers, I've yet to see any magic from you."

He looked definitely irked. "Alena, first you force your way into my life and demand I use my magical powers to aid you, and now you act as if I've been some charlatan all along. Make up your mind before I drag out my boat and sail back to Cadvallan."

"Well, I wouldn't mind a small display of your powers," she muttered, not quite able to meet his gaze.

Galen studied her for a long, exasperated moment. "Fine. Just remember, I haven't used my magic for fifteen years. 'Tis bound to be a bit rusty."

"Have no fear. I'm easily impressed." She set the packs at her feet and looked up expectantly.

He glanced around, his gaze settling on Paddy. Why not try his spell of invisibility? He'd learned the rudiments after several years of minor spell casting and had managed to master that particular talent with small objects just before he gave up his magic altogether. But with a large, living creature?

Well, he'd told Alena he could do it and his enhanced powers should provide the extra ability he needed. Mayhap 'twas best to try it out now and work through all the problems before 'twas really needed.

"I'm going to cast a spell over you," he said, turning to Paddy. "You should feel no different, nor even realize you're invisible when the spell is complete. But if, for some untoward reason, you feel strange or experience pain, let me know."

The young dragon glanced to Alena, his eyes wide and anxious. His big tail swept the beach, dragging the sand back and forth.

" 'Twill be all right, Paddy." Her voice dropped to a low, soothing tone. "Galen won't harm you and 'tis important that he be able to cast his spell to make you invisible quickly and accurately." She paused, her mouth twisting in a wry smile. "People hereabouts aren't used to seeing dragons anymore."

I trust you, my lady. And your mate.

As the words echoed in Alena's head, she had to bite back a sharp retort that Galen Radbourne wasn't her mate. Wherever did Paddy get the idea that one night of coupling made for a lifelong commitment?

She looked at Galen to see if he, too, had heard Paddy's comment. He stared hard at the young dragon, his hand clasped around the strange pendant he always wore about his neck, apparently already in the first stages of spell conjuring.

Relief filled her. She didn't need Galen, on top of everything else, getting the idea he was her lord and master.

Galen's mumblings of some archaic words jerked Alena from her unsettling thoughts. As he spoke, he reached out and touched Paddy on the chest. The young dragon rolled his colorful eyes and shuddered. Then, the lower half of his body began to disappear.

From his clawed feet and long tail, Paddy faded from view. Up his body the spell went, erasing his chubby belly and the beginning of his wings until it halted at midchest. Paddy looked down. He squealed.

Alena's gaze met Galen's. "What happened? Only half of him is invisible."

Galen arched a brow and eyed the dragon in puzzlement. "I don't know. I guess my skills have degenerated more than I realized." He stroked his chin and frowned in thought, never taking his eyes off Paddy. "Mayhap the key is to concentrate on making him disappear from the head down, rather than the other way around. I could have been mistaken in my recollection . . ."

"So, not only are your skills rusty, but you aren't even certain if you remember your spells accurately." Alena sighed and shook her head. "Well, can you at least get all of him back?"

"What?" He shot her a quick glance. "Oh, aye, that part is easy. I just have to stop concentrating and . . ."

As the sorcerer's voice faded, the lower half of Paddy's body came into view. The young dragon rolled his eyes, then shuffled over to stand behind Alena. He peered at Galen over the top of her head.

"I told you no harm would come to you, Paddy," Galen tried to reassure him. He waved him back over. "Come on. I'll get it right this next time."

Alena twisted around to look up at the anxious, tail-swishing dragon. "Go to him, Paddy. We can't set out on the quest until he gets this invisibility thing right."

That's easy for you to say, my lady. You're not the one who just had half his body cut off.

She smiled. "Nay, I wasn't and I find it quite brave of you to let Galen try out his skills on you. Would you prefer he practice on me for a while?"

As if considering that for a moment, Paddy paused, then shook his head. *Nay. My fate is to protect you from all harm. And 'tis me he needs to make invisible, not you.*

Unaccountably touched that Paddy thought he needed to protect her from anything, Alena hid her laugh behind her hand with a cough. Her glance met Galen's and he smiled. 'Twas a small smile, but it made his brown eyes dance and his already quite handsome face seem almost beautiful.

She jerked her gaze away. 'Twas business and naught more, Alena told herself for the tenth time today. She'd worked with attractive men before without letting that attraction distract her. She could well do it again.

"Then get on with you," she ordered the dragon, her exasperation with her unruly feelings for Galen sending an edge of annoyance into her voice. "We haven't all day while you cower behind me."

At the look of hurt in Paddy's eyes, Alena bit back a curse. The dragon imagined 'twas him she was angry with, when 'twas really with herself. She turned back to confront the true source of her frustration—Galen. "Could you possibly hurry this along a bit? 'Tis already midday. The journey to Castle Radbourne is long enough without whiling away another hour or two here on the beach."

Unperturbed by her outburst, Galen shrugged. "As you wish." He turned to face Paddy who now reluctantly stood before him. He grinned up at the baby dragon. "Shall we try the top half this time?"

Paddy rolled his eyes and nodded, but his most undragonlike expression of dread belied his acquiescence. Galen closed his eyes, clutched his pendant, and began muttering the strange words. His brow furrowed in intense concentration. As Alena watched, Paddy disappeared from the head down—all of him.

Excitement filled her. Galen had spoken true when he'd said his skills were awkward with disuse. Yet though she'd accepted Idara's assurances of Galen's powers on faith alone, 'twas still good to have some tangible proof that Galen was indeed a sorcerer.

"Can you bring him back now?" she asked in a breathless voice that surprised even her.

"Aye . . ." Galen opened his eyes and turned toward her. "But first let us gather up our packs and ready ourselves for the journey."

"But Paddy . . ."

He held up a hand to silence her. "I need to test my powers of concentration while I move about and work and converse with you. 'Tis the only thing that maintains the spell."

Alena frowned. "What? Moving around and talking with me?"

"Nay. Concentrating while I do other things." Galen strode over, picked up the other two packs, and flung them over his shoulder. "I must accustom myself to doing simple things while I work to maintain the spell. I can't have myself getting distracted and let Paddy reappear in the middle of some town square sometime, can I?"

Alena laughed. "I suppose not, but 'twould make for some interesting sights—what with the people's reaction and the resulting bedlam."

"Aye," Galen solemnly agreed, setting his two packs more comfortably on his shoulder, "but think of what 'twould do to poor Paddy."

That consideration was too much for Alena. She threw back her head and gave a shout of laughter.

Galen grinned. A deep chuckle rumbled in his chest. He gestured toward a dirt path leading up the beach and into the forest. "Shall we be on our way, then?"

"Aye." Alena squelched her merriment with a final chortle. "Just as soon as you bring Paddy back."

Galen nodded. As suddenly as he'd disappeared, the young dragon flashed once more into view. With a look of great relief, Paddy bounded over to them.

"Satisfied that my magic is functioning well?" Galen asked Alena, looking, at that moment, every bit the proud and resplendent sorcerer.

"Aye." She scrutinized him closely, her mind racing. "Mayhap 'twould be wise to disguise yourself a bit. Any who know your brother will quickly recognize your relationship to him. And I don't think it wise to advertise our progress and purpose in journeying to visit him."

"What do you propose? A warted nose and eye patch? Changing my hair color to bright red?"

Alena scowled. "Nay. A full beard should suffice. The rest of your clothing is unremarkable and shouldn't draw attention." She cocked her head, eyeing his beard-shadowed jaw. "Can you use some of your magic to hasten the growth of your beard?"

Galen sighed and nodded. "Aye, but have a care how often and much you demand I draw on my magic. I'd like to sustain this power you gave me until we reach Castle Radbourne. 'Tis only a week's journey and my powers, if used judiciously, should last."

"Aye, 'tis a week's journey, but 'twill be a lot longer if you're recognized and your brother sends out his minions to stop us."

"You worry overmuch, Alena. Dorian won't try to stop me from reaching him. After all these years, I'd wager he'll be happy to see me."

She gave a snort of disbelief. "Don't bet on that. But that's another subject altogether. Could you grow that beard so we can be on our way?"

He smiled. "No sooner asked then done." Galen grasped his pendant and closed his eyes. As he did, the black stubble on his face began to lengthen and grow. In the space of five minutes, Galen's lips, chin, and jaws were covered by a lush, dense growth of short black hair.

Releasing his pendant, Galen opened his eyes. Noting Alena's intent focus on his face, he chuckled. "Does everything meet with your approval?"

"What?" Alena jerked from her scrutiny of Galen's beard. "Oh, aye. 'Tis quite satisfactory."

"Then let us be on our way." He turned to Paddy. "Come along, young one. We've a journey to Elmsdale before us."

Paddy glanced around, plainly relieved that he'd survived the magical spell, then bounded up the beach after Alena and Galen. *The things a brave and loyal dragon did for his lady,* he thought with no small amount of bluster and self-congratulation. Then he promptly stumbled over a half-buried rock and fell flat on his face.

A league outside Elmsdale, they left Paddy hidden in the forest. The young dragon wasn't at all pleased to be forced to stay behind without Alena, demanding to be made invisible so he could accompany them into the town. Galen, however, was firm. The spell of invisibility required too sustained a drain on his powers, and would only be used when absolutely necessary.

Yet only after Alena assured the dragon they'd return with food for him before nightfall did Paddy finally acquiesce. The thought of three or four fresh chickens seemed to be just the thing to soothe his fragile feelings. He watched them leave, sending warnings to have a care and call for him if ever they were in danger echoing in both Alena and Galen's minds, then made himself a nest in a pile of leaves and settled down to a long wait.

The town of Elmsdale was a bustling, crowded, and quite aromatic place. Galen's nose, long stranger to all the pungent scents of civilization—rotting garbage, human waste, and close-packed and frequently unwashed bodies—revolted long before they drew close to the center of town. He fought back his swell of nausea several times, barely controlling an urge to retch, before finally deciding it the better part of valor to stop breathing through his nose.

Alena, for her part, offered little sympathy, even when she finally noted the slight tinge of green that colored his skin. "Welcome back to the world, Galen Radbourne. 'Twill be an adjustment, will it not?"

He managed a wan smile. "Aye. That 'twill. I'd forgotten some of the more unsavory aspects of living in such close contact with others."

She smiled as they navigated the narrow streets with their half-timbered houses pressed so close they actually loomed over the byways. "Before your exile, you lived in a castle, didn't you? Your life was one of luxury. Even then, I'd wager you'd little occasion to experience life on so 'basic' a level."

"And I thank you for providing me with the opportunity to do so," he muttered dryly. "Somehow, though, I think I could've lived a long and happy life without experiencing a lot of this."

Alena shrugged, then agilely dodged a torrent of wash water cascading just then from an overhead window. She shot the inconsiderate housewife who'd dumped the dirty water an irate glance, then turned back to Galen. " 'Tis any world, even if 'tisn't yours. And, since 'twouldn't do to attract unnecessary attention to ourselves traveling together in dangerous lands, 'tis wiser to maintain the facade of two simple warriors."

"Warriors?" Galen gave a wry laugh. "Mayhap that'll be an easy task for you to pull off, but I'm not and never have been of the soldierly inclination."

"Ah, but you will be of a more soldierly inclination when I'm done with you," Alena assured him, drawing up at last before a well-kept stable on the other side of town. "Just as soon as I procure some horses, get the blacksmith to fashion you a sword, and give you a few lessons. This particular smith is quite talented in weaponry, so we're in luck."

She sent him an admiring glance. "You're big and strong enough to handle a sword well, and I'm an excellent teacher."

"But you don't understand," Galen began, before Alena

cut him off by turning and striding into the stables. He had no choice but to follow her.

The air inside the stable was warm and smelled of horse and manure. Galen's nostrils twitched but, surprisingly, he found the scents here not half as repulsive as back in the midst of town. Mayhap, he mused, it had something to do with his long acquaintance with the dragons. Honest animal smells were honest animal smells.

In one corner at the back of the barn the sound of clanging metal upon metal could be heard. As Galen caught up with Alena, a blast of superheated air engulfed him.

A short, squat, but very brawny smith, bare-cheated save for the leather apron covering his torso and legs, worked over a forge. He pumped a set of leather bellows and the air-fed fire leaped once more to a small, intense blaze. Alena stood nearby, waiting patiently for a break in his activity.

The smith was repairing broken links in a set of chains. He heated an iron rod by shoving it into the fire-hot forge, withdrawing it only when the rod glowed cherry red. Then, placing the rod on the anvil, the smith used his hammer to beat out a narrow bevel on one side of the rod. After cutting the rod slightly longer than the length of the other chain links, he reheated the iron, then beveled the other end.

Finally, the smith looked up. "Well, what can I do fer ye?" His lank brown hair clung damply to a sweat-sheened and grimy face. "I'm a busy man and haven't time to lollygag all the day."

"We need two strong, sound horses," Alena hastened to say. "Have you any available for sale?"

"Aye, that I do." The smith gestured to two stalls in the far corner of the barn. "I've a fleet gray mare and a big bay gelding. The gelding can be a bit stubborn at times and puts up a fuss for the first mounting o' the morn, but once he settles down, he can go for days without stopping."

"They sound like they might be adequate for our needs. Do you mind if I take a few minutes to look them over?"

"Nay, take yer time." The smithy went back to his work, reheating his beveled rod in the forge, then fashioning it into a curved link.

Alena turned to Galen. "Do you want to look over the horses with me?"

He grinned. " 'Twouldn't matter if I did. I know naught of horseflesh."

She eyed him closely. "Do you at least know how to ride?"

"Does a fat pony who could barely extend past a fast walk as a young lad count? After some harrowing falls from its broad back, I gave up hope of ever learning to ride and took to, er, other less usual means of transporting myself from place to place."

Alena sighed. "I see I must teach you everything."

"Nay, Alena." He laid a hand on her arm, his voice gone deep and laden with meaning. "Not everything."

She flushed crimson. "Well, I didn't mean . . ." Reminded yet again of their night of passion by the heated look in his eyes, frustration, quickly followed by anger, flooded her. She jerked away. "Just stay here, will you? I'll be back in a few minutes." She quickly stomped off toward the stalls.

The two horses were sound and strong. By the time Alena returned to Galen's side, she was once more in command of herself. She gave the big sorcerer a brief, neutral smile, then turned to the blacksmith. "How much for the two of them, plus saddles and bridles?"

The smith paused to plunge his curved chain link in a bucket of water. The hot iron striking cold water sent a hiss of steam and cloud of mist into the air. "How much?" he repeated. "They be fine animals. I'm thinking mayhap five gold crowns for the two o' them."

"Three," Alena countered.

The smith laughed. "And where would ye be finding other mounts, if not here? I'm the only stable in town. But, being the fair man I am, I'll go down to four crowns and three shillings."

"I'll give you four crowns and that's my best offer. I'd also like to buy a sword," Alena added. She motioned to Galen. "One that would suit a man of his size and stature."

The smith eyed Galen up and down. "Well, I haven't any o' his size waiting for yer perusal. I'll have to fashion ye one."

"How long will that take?"

"I'm backlogged, I tell ye. 'Twill have to wait two or three days."

"I need it on the morrow." She held up a pouch of coins and shook it. The gold pieces clanked suggestively. The blacksmith's eyes widened. "I'll pay extra if I can have it then."

"And extra 'twill certainly cost ye. I make some o' the finest weaponry in these parts." He thought a moment. "Another four crowns, I'm thinking, but ye'll have it by midday."

"Midday will be too late. Make it dawn and the four crowns are yours."

Once more, the smith eyed the bag of coins. Alena tossed it lightly in her hand.

He finally nodded. "Dawn 'tis then. And I'll be having two crowns payment in advance."

Alena exhaled an irritated breath, then dug in her coin pouch and tossed him the money.

"Er, if I may be so bold as to interject here," Galen said, "none of this discussion nor the payment for the sword is necessary."

"Indeed?" Alena asked coolly, irritated at his interference

after a deal had just been made. "And why not?"

"Because I don't need or want a sword, whether you teach me how to use it or not."

" 'Tis just your hesitation at learning a new skill, Galen." Alena laughed, relaxing. "As I told you before, I'm an excellent—"

"Nay, Alena. You didn't hear what I said." The big sorcerer cut her off, his mouth tightening. "I *will not* use a sword or any other weapon. Though I agreed to come with you on this quest, I'll never do harm or kill again. Not for you or anyone."

He fixed her with a resolute stare. "And that's my last word on the matter."

CHAPTER EIGHT

Alena stared at him for a long moment, not certain she'd truly understood what Galen had just said. Then, as realization flooded her, a flush crept up her neck and face. Beside them, the blacksmith gawked.

"What do you mean," she slowly enunciated the words, " 'you'll never do harm or kill again'? Do you mayhap think we embark on some frivolous excursion to see the countryside and pay your brother a social visit?"

Galen stood his ground. "Nay, I think no such thing. But I'll not take up arms to harm another."

A rough clearing of a throat jerked Galen and Alena's attention back to the smith. "Begging pardon, but I've a farmer who needs the chain on his ox yoke repaired so he can plow his fields for the spring planting. If ye could kindly make up yer mind one way or another . . ."

Alena tossed Galen a fierce look, then glanced back at the smith. "Make the sword. I'll be back at dawn to pick it and the horses up."

At Galen's narrowed gaze, the man laughed and ambled back to his forge. "As ye wish. Just make certain ye're here first thing on the morrow with the rest o' the money."

"I'll be here," Alena muttered. She motioned ahead of her. "Shall we be on our way?" She shot Galen a cool glance.

He answered with a curt nod of his head. "Aye." Wheeling around, Galen strode out of the stable, his long strides never slowing even after they were headed back down the narrow streets.

Alena finally had to run to catch up with him, her hand clasped firmly on her sword hilt to prevent its wild banging against her leg. "Galen, curse you!" she cried. "Wait up, I say."

At her harsh plea, he stopped and turned. Alena slid to a halt to avoid slamming into him.

"What did you mean back there," he growled, "ignoring my request not to buy me that sword? We'd better get one thing clear right now, Alena. *No one* forces or intimidates me into doing what I don't wish to do. Not even you."

"I've never wished to force or intimidate you, you big, thick-skulled son of a sorcerer," she raged back at him. "But you said you wished to conserve your magic as much as possible, and I only thought to provide you with a more conventional form of protection to supplement your powers. A good warrior tries to anticipate all contingencies and provide a backup plan, if at all possible."

His rigid stance relaxed a bit. "I appreciate your greater expertise in matters such as these. But there are some principles I will not betray. If that doesn't suit you, I'm sorry, Alena."

Her jaw clenched and, for a long moment, Alena's battle to control her temper teetered on the brink of defeat. Curse the man, she thought. At every turn he revealed yet another aspect of his personality—and each revelation seemed to throw another obstacle in the path of her determination to see Renard free.

"What will you do then," she finally asked in a tautly modulated voice, "if you're set upon by enemies and your magic has drained? Will you let yourself be killed rather than defend yourself?"

"I've never faced such an eventuality and hope never to do so."

"But what if you do?" Her voice was little more than a furious, disbelieving whisper. "You can't wait until it happens and then wish you'd had a sword at your side and knew how to use it. Let me teach you, Galen. If the occasion never arises, so be it. But if it does . . ."

"Nay, Alena. A sword is too easy an answer. A man does best if he's forced to search for a better solution, rather than grasp at the easier if more violent one too quickly. Pride can lead to tragic consequences if not firmly restrained. I'd rather walk away and sacrifice a bit of that pride, than take another's life."

"Fine words, Galen Radbourne," Alena cried, so angry and frustrated with what she saw as his smug, stubborn, superior outlook that she wanted to punch him in the face. *Never* had a man enraged her like this one did! "But *your* way can also be construed by many as cowardice, and set the heartless jackals on you with even greater fervor. A strong, fearless front is the best approach."

"And are you now saying I'm a coward because I choose not to fight?" he asked, his voice gone soft and dangerous. "That I'm incapable of supporting you on this quest?"

"It doesn't matter what I think. But 'twill be what others, our potential enemies, will believe."

"Nay, I think not." Galen stepped close, taking her by the arm. "It *does* matter what your thoughts are on this. I ask again. Do you think I'm a coward?"

" 'Tis hard to think anything else, if you refuse to defend yourself." She wrenched her arm free and returned his piercing stare, her hands fisting on her hips. "I'm a warrior. Fighting is all I know. How else *could* I see it?"

"How else, indeed?" Something fleeting and anguished flashed through Galen's eyes. "And mayhap I am. I was content to distance myself from the world all these years. But only time will tell if your fears are well-founded."

His gaze caught on a vendor's stall where several butchered chickens hung. "In the meanwhile, we promised Paddy a meal and the day draws on. If you've naught further to say . . . ?"

"Oh, I've plenty to say, but know, as well, how intractable you are when your mind is made." Alena motioned impatiently toward the chicken vendor. "Come, let us be on our way to yon butcher's stand, then return to Paddy and make certain he's safely sheltered for the night. 'Twill soon be dusk and we've still a room to hire and a meal of our own to eat."

"Aye," Galen muttered under his breath as he strode out once more, "and here's to a night spent in relative peace between us. If that will ever again be possible."

The Hogshead Inn, with its attached tavern, was hot, noisy, and overcrowded. But the ale was renowned and the food passably good. It was also the only inn left in town with a vacant room, thanks to the annual Spring Fair that had just arrived in Elmsdale. Before returning to the tavern for their evening meal, Alena and Galen fed Paddy, concealed him in a nearby cave just outside Elmsdale, then made a brief detour to their room in the inn to wash up.

The room was small, with a window so tiny it would have been difficult for a man of Galen's size to squeeze through. The window was covered by a stringy piece of lacework that supposedly served as a curtain. The bed was narrow, its sorry mattress sitting on an even sorrier wooden frame covered by a well-worn but surprisingly clean blanket and lumpy pillow. It was also only large enough for one person.

Alena eyed the bed with a jaundiced look, then tossed the packs onto the floor beside it. "Well, I guess 'twill be the floor for me tonight."

"You can have the bed," Galen said stiffly, not yet over his anger at her high-handed maneuverings at the blacksmith's. "I'm not without some honor when it comes to women."

She wheeled around. "And I'm not some pampered little lady, either," she growled, "who needs you to look out for her. You can have the bed."

Galen glared back at her. "Well, I don't want the bed!"

At the look on Alena's face, he thought she might physically attack him. Strangely, Galen found the idea a most pleasant consideration. After the tension building within him in the past days since the night of the storm, the thought of finally finding relief for that tension, however hostilely, actually seemed appealing. She would strike him, mayhap even claw his face, but 'twould be well worth it if only he could hold her tightly to him, feel her body squirm, her soft curves press into him. Aye, 'twas worth even the consequences of her anger.

Yet Alena didn't move, didn't even speak for the longest time. Her face flushed; her body went rigid. Her hands fisted at her sides. Then, at long last, she exhaled a shuddering breath and gestured to the door.

"Shall we be going? Naught is served standing here arguing about the sleeping arrangements. Mayhap after a meal we'll be in a better frame of mind to discuss this."

Though he didn't want to, Galen accepted her unspoken offer of truce. "Aye," he muttered. "A meal would be best."

He followed her out of the room and down the stairs. The Hogshead Tavern was dark, dingy, and odiferous, reeking of rancid ale, sweat-laden bodies, and the cooking smells of the evening's meal. The ancient hearth, a huge mass of poorly laid stone with a chimney that seemed to blow more smoke into the room than it drew, took up half of one of the walls. Another wall fronted the street, its grimy, smoke-scummed windows emitting little light. The other two walls were adorned with various stuffed hogs' heads and rusted weaponry, as well as one door that opened into the kitchen and another into the inn's entry area where stairs led up to the sleeping chambers.

Rough-hewn wooden planks set upon trestles, along with their accompanying benches, jammed the tavern in semiorderly rows. Patrons packed the benches and those without a place to sit stumbled up and down the narrow aisles, sloshing ale on any not vigilant enough to watch his back. Galen stood, taking in the noise and surging mass of people until Alena tugged on his arm.

"Come on," she yelled over the din. "I see a table along the back wall with room for us."

He followed without protest, quite willing to let her take command in such a foreign environment. Weaving through the throngs of close-packed, coarsely clothed bodies, once more Galen had to fight down a surge of nausea. Alena glanced back at him just then and, by the sardonic smile that twisted her lips, he knew she'd noted his distress. With a scowl, Galen shoved through the narrow aisles, pushing aside the men who lurched back in his way, and forged resolutely onward.

The table Alena had chosen stood along the far wall opposite the front door. She gestured to a spot on the bench that backed the wall, a spot that looked barely adequate for one person.

"Climb in," she said. "I'll sit on the end."

He eyed it with misgiving. To be crowded in between some stranger and against Alena . . . Galen shook his head. "I'd prefer to sit on the end."

"Have it your way." She sat on the bench and slid over. Patting the spot remaining—about six inches if that much—

Alena smiled up at him. "Have a seat."

Gingerly, Galen lowered himself onto the bench, half on, half off. That uncomfortable perch lasted only long enough to cause a muscle spasm in his right thigh. With a sigh, he shifted until his back was toward Alena and his legs were planted firmly on the floor.

"Here," he heard Alena say over his shoulder. "I'll scoot over and make a bit more room."

For her efforts, he was able to pivot around and face the table at an angle. "My thanks," Galen muttered.

At that moment a buxom serving maid waltzed over. She was dark of hair and eyes, ripely rounded, and provocatively dressed with her low-cut, dingy white chemise worn well off her shoulders to reveal the ample swell of her full breasts and her leather bodice laced tightly to accentuate her tiny waist and the womanly curve of her hips. As she approached, she swayed sensuously, swirling her red skirt about her ankles.

"Well, what will it be?" she asked, gracing Alena with a cursory glance before directing the full force of her sparkling brown eyes onto Galen. "We've a fine mutton stew or a pigeon pie. There's also brown bread and sweet butter and our special dark ale." She paused to look expectantly down at her chest, then back up at Galen. "Does aught mayhap catch yer fancy, my handsome lad?"

Galen smiled, well aware of the serving maid's double meaning. "Aye, a lot catches my fancy," he replied, laughing, "but 'tis best if I restrict myself to the food. I'll have the pigeon pie and a tankard of your ale. The lady"—he glanced at Alena—"will have . . . ?"

"The mutton stew and bread, plus a tankard of your ale," she ground out the words, then looked away.

"As she says," Galen finished, puzzled by Alena's response.

The serving maid smiled. "I'll be back with yer meals post-haste. Ye can be certain o' that." She paused. "My name's Emma. What's yers, handsome?"

"Emma, is it?" He grinned. "My name's Galen."

"Galen." As if savoring it, Emma rolled the name about on her tongue. "A noble name for a noble man." With a saucy laugh, she wheeled about and walked away.

Briefly, Galen watched her sensuously swaying hips, then turned back to Alena. "A pretty lass, is she not?"

"I wouldn't know or care," the warrior woman snarled. "She's trouble, though, mark my words. A woman like her lives for the thrill of provoking men to fight over her. And I'd wager at least one or two of the regulars here already fancy her theirs. Leave her be, Galen, if you've a shred of sense about you."

Her words, and the scathing sarcasm she uttered them in, struck a chord of anger in Galen. First, Alena came to Cadvallan Isle and demanded he accompany her on a quest to rescue her friend. Then, she ordered him a sword he would never use. Finally, she tried to lecture him on who he could and could not talk with. Did the woman think to control his life?

He opened his mouth, then clamped it shut. Dragging in a ragged breath, Galen said, "I'm capable of deciding which woman I care to make the acquaintance of, and which to not. I'll thank you to stay out of this, Alena."

"Fine," she muttered. "Suit yourself. And suffer the consequences of your foolish actions as well."

"I usually do," Galen retorted. "Or at least until I met you."

They sat there in silence, the raucous shouts and singing of a group of farmers over in the corner drowning out further opportunity for conversation. The seductive serving maid finally returned, two tankards of foaming ale in her hands.

"I brought yer ale. The food will be out shortly." She placed Galen's mug before him with a pretty flounce that provided him a full view of her breasts and cleavage before thunking Alena's mug down and shoving it over to her. The ale sloshed over the sides of the pewter cup.

Alena scowled, started to tell the careless woman what she thought of her service, then thought better of it. The woman deserved what she got—which was naught more than the frustration of wanting a man she couldn't have. Though Galen might savor her freely displayed favors, he would go no further. He didn't dare, if he truly meant what he'd said about his magic killing any woman he dared mate with. And somehow, though 'twas difficult to fully fathom why, Alena believed his tale and the sincerity of his intent to avoid further involvement with women.

Apparently satisfied her initial foray into seduction had worked, Emma leaned back, shot Galen one more smile, then turned and walked away. The big sorcerer chuckled and picked up his tankard of ale. As he did, his glance snared on a pair of pale blue eyes staring at him from across the room.

Galen paused, his mug halfway to his lips. Whatever was the matter with the man? He knew no one in Elmsdale but Alena and the blacksmith, yet the man's gaze was bright with interest—and a fierce calculation. But interest in and calculation of what? With his full beard, no one should recognize him as Dorian's twin—unless that person was in his brother's employ.

"Here's yer food," Emma said, arriving suddenly to stand beside him. " 'Tis best ye eat it while 'tis hot." She leaned over once more to place Galen's plate in front of him, smiling sweetly. "Would ye like me to cut yer pigeon pie to cool it a bit?"

"Nay. But my thanks for your prompt and most generous service." He smiled up at her. "Would you like payment now for the food and drink?"

Her heavy-lashed lids lowered in a sultry look. "Nay, I can wait. And mayhap we can talk a different kind o' payment later."

Alena slammed a gold crown on the table beside Galen's plate. "We'll pay now. My friend and I might well be finished and gone up to bed before you next return."

The serving maid arched a slender brow. "Indeed? And how sad for him if he does." She smiled sweetly. "Leave and go up to bed with ye before I return, I mean."

"Imagine what you wish." Alena's teeth clenched. "But the fact remains I'll be the one with him this night, not you!"

"Er, if you two ladies wouldn't mind," Galen carefully intruded, "I'd like very much to eat my meal."

"And well ye should, my handsome lad." Emma lightly, sensuously, ran her fingers through Galen's hair. "I made certain cook gave ye the best pigeon pie left in the kitchen." She twisted a wavy lock around her finger, tugging on it playfully. "Mayhap I'll return in a while and see if there's aught else I can do for ye?"

Galen, already cutting into the flaky crust to spear a thick chunk of pigeon, glanced up. "Oh, aye. That would be nice."

The serving maid graced Alena with a triumphant look, then flounced away. Alena sat there, itching to leap up and go after the arrogant woman and throttle her. Instead, she watched Galen eat his meal. He finally looked up after yet another swallow of ale and noted her stew was still untouched.

"Why don't you eat? The food is quite tasty, if this pie is any indication."

"I'll eat soon enough." Alena's attention, however, was

riveted on the seductive serving maid as she worked her way around the tavern.

Several patrons made grabs for her which she nimbly eluded with a teasing little laugh and toss of her wantonly tousled hair. A big, blue-eyed man sitting almost directly across from them on the other side of the room, however, staked his claim to her most forcefully when she swept by. An arm bulging with muscle shot out and jerked her to him. Emma made a short show of struggle, then settled down onto his lap and gave him a long and deep kiss.

Alena's mouth twisted in disgust. She turned back to her own meal. The goings-on across the room, however, soon drew her attention once more. The couple's amatory pursuits had quickly degenerated into an argument. The big, blue-eyed man made a great show of gesturing toward Galen, then grabbed the serving maid by the arm and gave her a shake. She pulled back, jerking her arm free, and stood. Though Alena could hear little of the conversation, 'twas evident she was setting the big man straight on his attempts to order her around.

The warrior woman smirked, shot a quick look at Galen, who was occupied in devouring his pigeon pie, then turned to her own meal. 'Twas a savory concoction of tender chunks of mutton, root vegetables, and an herb-seasoned gravy. The bread was hot and fragrant, fresh from the oven, and the sweet butter she slathered over each slice melted instantly.

As she ate, a warm sense of lassitude encompassed Alena. 'Twas partly, she realized, the work of the good food and partly her first real opportunity to relax, back in her own world, the first part of her mission—to procure Galen Radbourne's assistance—at last complete.

She cleaned her bowl with the last slice of bread, emptied her tankard, and leaned back against the wall. At that moment, the man sitting beside her turned and glanced her way. He was old, his scraggly hair streaked with gray, and several sockets gaped black where some of his yellowed teeth should have been. He hefted his mug of ale to his lips, swilled a big mouthful, then grinned drunkenly over at her.

"Ye're a fair lass to be traveling through these parts," the old man said, slurring his words. "Have a care. Our lord has a penchant for a comely wench, and those he takes to his evil castle are never seen again."

Alena's interest rose. She leaned forward. 'Twas likely the man spoke of Dorian Radbourne. She noted that Galen had stopped eating and was listening surreptitiously. "Indeed?" She turned the full force of her smile on the old man. "And which lord might we be talking about?"

"Why, the Lord Dorian Radbourne, and who else?" her table companion said. He finished off the contents of his mug and refilled it from the pitcher on the table, emptying that as well. The foam rose with the liquor, swelling up and over the sides of the tankard.

"He's a bad one, and no mistake," the old man continued, oblivious to the mess he was making as he gulped down several more swallows. " 'Tis said he takes the young lasses and drains the life from them, jest like his twin brother did many years ago. They're a sorry lot, the Radbournes are. If only the Lord Dorian had died off in exile on Cadvallan Isle like his evil brother had.

"Nay," he muttered forlornly into his mug, "Wyndymyll can't bear much more o' their ilk. And neither can we."

"Is there naught anyone can do?" Alena asked carefully, noting the sudden pallor to Galen's features. It must hurt him to be spoken of so disparagingly, but she must be certain he understood the truth about his brother. "To rid the land of such a malevolent presence, I mean?"

The man lifted his mug of ale and once more drained its contents before continuing. "Nay, naught that any o' us o' the more mortal persuasion can do. He's a sorcerer, one o' the most powerful there is, and only those o' great magic could hope to have a chance against him."

He frowned blearily. " 'Tis said, though, that an old book, a grimoire written by the *galiene* Brengwain the Wise, holds answers to the tragedy that twines tighter and tighter about us each day. But the grimoire has disappeared, never to be seen again. Some say Brengwain took it with her when she disappeared, over a hundred-odd years ago. Most say it doesn't matter one way or another." He shrugged. "Without the *galienes,* or the dragons that feed off their powers, to help us . . ."

"Then mayhap the sorcerers must settle the problems amongst themselves," Alena offered, shooting Galen a sideways glance. "Mayhap they must at last claim responsibility for what they have wrought—and put an end to the evil once and for all."

At the old man's besotted if disparaging laugh, Galen went rigid, but never looked his way. "And the mythical dragons o' Cadvallan Isle will fly again before that day dawns," the old man said. He sighed and shook his head, then took up his empty tankard and rose. "Ye're an innocent to think such things, lass. Just remember my words and beware. And stay far afield from the Lord Dorian Radbourne."

He climbed over the bench and staggered away then, disappearing into the crowd of laughing, raucous revelers and hazy, smoke-filled room. Alena shot Galen a pointed glance and, noting his tight-lipped, narrow-eyed expression, decided further attempts at pushing her point about his brother were unwise. She leaned back against the wall, suddenly overcome with a heavy sense of weariness.

The small bed, though she'd been bound and determined to give it over to Galen, suddenly assumed an enormous appeal. I wonder, Alena thought drowsily, her lids slowly sliding shut, how I can gracefully back out of—

"Finished with yer meal, are ye?" came the husky voice of the serving maid.

Alena's eyes snapped open. The dark-haired woman bent down, shoved Galen's plate and tankard aside, and lowered herself onto his lap. Her slender arms encircled his neck. She scooted closer until her breasts pressed against Galen's chest.

"Now, isn't that much more comfy?" Emma purred. "Ye're such a big, strong man. Ye make me feel all warm and trembly and weak inside, ye do."

"Do I now?" Smiling, Galen reached up to disengage her hands and bring them down to hold them in her lap.

She glanced down at where his own hands lay, and giggled. "Aye. And ye rouse me greatly, too." Lifting her dark and dancing gaze, she squirmed restlessly. "Do I, mayhap, rouse ye a bit, my handsome lad?"

Galen lifted his eyes and, over the woman's shoulder, met Alena's. She watched him with an intent, almost predatory light, as if . . . as if she were a she-lioness about to strike. But was it against him, or the serving maid? Galen wondered. Suddenly, though he knew 'twas foolhardy to goad Alena, he wanted to know.

"You're a fine woman, and no mistake," Galen replied, turning back to Emma. "I'd wager any man would find you desirable."

"Aye, that they would." The buxom maid bent and delicately stroked the curve of Galen's lips with her tongue. "And I never fail to please, either."

In spite of himself, Galen felt his sex harden. Though the woman was far less appealing than Alena, there was still something earthy and elemental in her ripe, wanton sensuality. Something a man would be tempted to taste without thought or reason, and wonder the next morn why he'd done it. Yet, though her favors were freely and eagerly offered, Galen knew he dared not—for her sake at least—accept them.

With a sigh, he grasped Emma by the arms. "Most regretfully, though, I—"

"Get yer filthy, pawing hands off my woman!"

Alena went rigid. She glanced up. Instinctively, her hand went to her sword. Towering over Galen was the big, blue-eyed man. Behind him, glowering fiercely, were two of his equally big compatriots. An impulse to rise and stand by Galen filled her. With only the strongest of efforts, she tamped that down.

He'd said he wouldn't take up arms to harm another, that he'd rather walk away and sacrifice his pride. He'd said those words, she well knew, in the throes of an idealism fostered by fifteen protected years of exile. Yet 'twas past time he had a taste of reality. This tavern, with its rough and feisty men, was a prime opportunity to teach Galen the error of his ways. Let him stand up for himself, or, if worse came to worse, use one of his magical spells to extricate himself.

With a small sigh, Alena forced herself to relax. Galen might suffer a few bumps and bruises for his ideals, but 'twas better now than later, out on the road.

The big sorcerer stared up at the man looming over him. Then he chuckled and glanced down at the serving maid. "It seems your companion has need of you, sweet lass."

She flounced about on his lap. "Well, I've no need o' the likes o' him!"

The blue-eyed man snarled a savage curse. Grabbing her arm, he jerked Emma up and away from Galen. "Ye don't know what ye need, save to stir men to a jealous frenzy!"

"Do I now?" The woman smiled up at him. "But that's yer problem, not mine. I prefer this fine gentleman to ye and yer pawing ways."

"Mayhap ye do." His grip tightened and he flung her back to his friends. "But we'll jest see how well ye like him once I've smashed up his face a bit."

The big man turned back to Galen, who still sat at the table, calmly staring up at him. "Well, will ye stand and fight, or not?"

"Nay," Galen replied. "I see no sense in it. You've got your woman back."

The man's mouth widened into a wolfish grin. "Aye, that I do. 'Twasn't hard, either. But I've still a mind to thrash ye for yer arrogance." He leaned over the table and grasped Galen by the front of his tunic. "What say ye? Do ye want to fight man-to-man, or shall I whip ye 'afore the others like some sniveling coward deserves?"

Galen clamped down on the other man's wrist. "I'm not fighting. Unhand me now."

"Or ye'll what? Slap my face and start bawlin'?" He jerked Galen to his feet and dragged him halfway across the table. "Come on, my handsome lad," the big man taunted. "Show my sweet Emma what ye're really made of."

Alena gritted her teeth and kept her hands clenched beneath the table as Galen was pulled down onto the floor. He struggled to his feet, only to receive a quick uppercut to the jaw, followed by a vicious blow to his abdomen. Gasping for air, he immediately sank back to his knees.

"Well, will ye fight me now or not?" Galen's assailant shook him roughly. "My Emma likes her men to be brave and strong. Ye wouldn't want her to be going and getting the wrong idea about ye, would ye?"

Galen's grip tightened around the man's wrist and he tried

to stand but couldn't. "I-I don't want to fight you o-over this," he said, still struggling for breath. "I already s-said the woman is y-yours. I never wanted—"

With a foul curse, the man slammed his fist into Galen's mouth. The sorcerer's lip split. Blood welled, dripping down his chin.

"Insult my lady, will ye?" The blue-eyed man glanced over his shoulder. "Come, help me, lads. Hold him while I teach him what it means to shame one o' our women."

The man's two friends hurried up and, grasping Galen under each arm, wrenched him to his feet and twisted an arm behind him. Once he was standing, the blue-eyed man plowed into Galen with all his might, raining blow after blow into his abdomen.

Galen grunted in pain but, aside from twisting in the other two men's grips in an attempt to protect himself, did naught to fight back. A vicious cuff to his face broke his nose. Blood spewed forth once more to mingle with that of his cut lip. A side blow to his jaw snapped his head back. Yet another fisted thrust into his abdomen doubled him over.

The crowd of men around them edged closer, stirred by the scent of blood and battle. "Teach the dirty coward a lesson, Jarvis," one onlooker yelled.

"Make 'im beg ye to quit," cried another.

"Take 'im apart!"

"He deserves it—and more!"

The voices rose, swelled around Alena, rising to crude shouts and laughing jibes. The spiraling tension, the mounting hunger to view and savor another's pain and suffering, encompassed her, imprisoning Alena in a suffocating cacophony of noise and crazed sounds. 'Twould only grow and worsen the longer it went on, she well knew, drawing all into a frenzy of unthinking blood lust and brutality. And still the man called Jarvis battered Galen, mercilessly, savagely.

He wouldn't give in, Alena realized. Galen, for reason of either principle or cowardice, refused to fight back—*just like he'd said he would*—and wouldn't use his magic, either. Though she dearly wished he'd act otherwise, she knew now that Galen would allow himself to be beaten to a bloody pulp rather than defend himself. 'Twas up to her to do what he'd no stomach for.

Alena rose in one fluid motion. She unsheathed her sword, the harsh, metallic sound slicing through the din of rough voices and coarse laughter. A sharp pain shot through her right hand as her grip tightened about her sword hilt, and she cursed softly. Her hand. She'd most likely broken open the wound.

Forcing herself to ignore the pain, Alena carefully laid the razor sharp tip against the back of the big man's neck. "Unhand him now, Jarvis," she growled, her legs widening in a warrior's stance, both of her hands now gripping her sword. "Unhand him—or see that brutish head of yours severed from your body."

CHAPTER NINE

Jarvis froze. The room fell silent. Then, ever so slowly, the big man glanced over his shoulder. Ice blue eyes locked with Alena's.

"Have a care, wench, who ye threaten with that sword," he said softly. "I may be a simple traveling wheelwright, but I've taken on better men than ye."

Meeting his gaze, Alena was struck with the sudden, if inexplicable certainty that this Jarvis was far more than he made himself out to be. A ripple of heightened awareness set the hairs on the back of her neck to rise.

Galen's rescue might be more difficult than she'd first anticipated. Three unarmed men she could take on. But if the whole room, at Jarvis's urging, turned on her . . .

"He's not worth your time," Alena said lightly, deciding to defuse the potentially explosive situation by belittling the concept of two men fighting over a woman that only one of them wanted. "You already have the serving woman. She but meant to use my friend to make you jealous." She smiled. "Emma must love you very much to attempt such a transparent feminine ploy. I'm surprised you didn't see through it immediately."

As if realizing the inanity of their earlier aggressiveness, the men in the tavern began to shuffle restlessly. "Aye, Jarvis," an elderly man cried out. "Ye've only been in Elmsdale a week. Ye wouldn't know o' Emma's tricks."

"Aye," shouted another. "She's a tease, and no mistake."

"Let it be. The poor sot has had enough."

173

One by one, the voices that not long ago had been raised to call for Galen's blood now cried for an end to the bloodshed. 'Twas the way of men, Alena thought grimly, taking in the sudden swell of support. They blew as wild and unpredictable as the wind.

Jarvis's mouth tightened. "And ye think that was what 'twas, do ye?" he demanded of Alena.

Almost imperceptibly, his body relaxed. He knew as well as Alena that his scheme, whatever 'twas, was over.

"Aye." She nodded slowly. "I'm a woman. I fathomed her game long ago."

He studied her for a long moment, then glanced down at the sword. "Ye've won this one, wench," he breathed so softly only Alena heard him. "Ye won't be so lucky next time."

With that, Jarvis turned back to the men who held Galen. "Release him. From the looks of him, I'd wager we've taught him not to fall for Emma's games again."

Galen was immediately—and unceremoniously—dumped onto the floor. Alena waited until Jarvis and his two compatriots headed back to their table before resheathing her sword and walking over to Galen. He'd managed to shove to his knees, where he swayed awkwardly.

Alena squatted before him. "Galen, can you stand? We need to get you up to the room."

He groaned and lifted his gaze to hers. His face was bloody and bruised, his nose off-center, one of his eyes beginning to blacken and swell shut, his upper lip, where it had been slammed against his teeth, swollen and oozing blood. "Aye," he rasped. "If you can help me."

An anguished guilt lanced through Alena. She'd let Galen be beaten just to teach him a lesson and assuage some of her own frustration at what she'd imagined to be his stubborn and shortsighted refusal to see things her way. Vainly, she tried to justify her actions that 'twas better for him to suffer a beating now rather than refuse to fight later when the stakes might well be higher. But, this time, even that rationalization failed.

She leaned down and took him by one arm. "Come, once you're standing, I can support you better." She tugged him up and, with an unsteady shove, Galen stood. Alena swiftly moved to his side, grasping his arm with one hand to lift it to rest over her shoulder and slipping her other arm about his waist. Her right hand began to throb fiercely and she saw fresh blood stain the bandage.

She swallowed a frustrated curse. Though she deserved the pain, after allowing Galen to be beaten so badly, at this rate her hand would never heal. But that was but another problem, and she'd more pressing things to consider just now. Problems like getting Galen up to their room.

Together, they made their halting way across the tavern and out the door leading to the inn. Climbing the stairs was a painfully slow process but, at last, they stood outside their room. Alena unlocked the door and kicked it open, then helped Galen over to the bed.

He took one look at it, then shook his head. "I told you the bed was yours tonight."

Exasperation filled her. "Don't argue, Radbourne. The bed is yours. I've no taste for nursing you, bent over on the floor."

His swollen lips twitched. He turned to stare at her out of his one good eye. "Well, when you put it so nicely . . ."

Something exploded in Alena. "And what good would it do to be nice to the likes of you? You had your magic. You could've at least cast a spell of some sort over those men to halt their attack. But, nay, you . . . you chose rather to *let* yourself be beaten!"

He took a step forward to balance himself, then drew in an unsteady breath. "Nay, Alena, you are wrong in this. I didn't have my magic. 'Tis yet another secret Dorian and I shared, a secret that affects all male sorcerers. Our powers fade to naught when the sun goes down."

She stared at him, struck speechless for a long moment. "You are magically powerless at night?"

"Aye."

" 'Tis a terrible flaw. A potentially *fatal* flaw in your powers."

"Aye." Galen's calm brown gaze locked with hers. "But I trust you never to use it against me. I also felt, for the sake of our quest, that you should know."

Clamping down on a savage curse, Alena lowered Galen to the mattress. Silent and seething, she divested him of his hooded robe and tunic, then assisted him to lie down. After quickly pulling off his boots, Alena stepped back and surveyed the condition of his torso.

Curse his magic-crippled hide, he was badly bruised over his ribs and abdominal muscles. He'd move awkwardly and with great pain for several days to come. And be a poor traveling companion, she belatedly realized, in the bargain.

She should've thought of that before she allowed him to be beaten so badly. Where, oh where, Alena raged, lifting her eyes to the ceiling, had been her common sense? She was beginning to think like some unseasoned girl, rather than the experienced warrior she was.

Her glance riveted back on Galen. 'Twas his fault. He drove her to the brink of madness with his stubborn, illogical acts.

But that was no excuse, a more levelheaded side of her protested. No excuse . . . no matter what the man meant to her. She certainly hadn't let her feelings for Renard interfere with her plans to rescue him. But then, Alena admitted with a small ripple of unease, she'd never reacted to any man like she did to Galen Radbourne.

That revelation frightened her. Ever so quickly, before the sudden insight could sink its claws into the unprotected belly of her conscious perception, Alena slapped it away. 'Twasn't of any import at any rate. Galen's injuries needed nursing. If at all possible, he must be ready to set out on the journey on the morrow.

She strode over to the small table that held the water pitcher and washbasin. The pitcher was chipped, the handle cracked, but the water within looked clean. Alena placed the basin and pitcher on the floor, then dragged the table over beside the bed. Retrieving the pitcher and washbasin, she placed it back on the table.

The packs lay where she'd left them by the bed. She rifled through them, pulling out several clean cloths she could use to cleanse Galen's wounds and tear into strips to bind his bruised ribs. There was also a jar of marigold salve and another of soft soap. Alena set all the equipment on the table, then dragged over the room's single chair. After quickly wrapping her own hand with a few of the cloth strips she'd torn to reinforce the blood-soaked bandage, she filled the basin with water, sat and dipped a cloth into it.

"I'm going to wash your face now, Galen." She leaned down toward him with the damp cloth. He grabbed her wrist before she could touch him.

Puzzlement darkened her eyes. "Aye, Galen?"

He fixed her with a piercing stare. "You made a grave error in judgment this eve, didn't you?"

Alena went still. "I don't understand."

"Don't you?" He made an attempt at a smile, then gave it up when his battered lip pained him. "Well, though it makes little sense, I suppose it really doesn't matter why you did what you did. You must live with the consequences of your decisions as must I." He shrugged and released her. "Your outlook on most things has always been different than my own."

Her hand, still hovering in the air where Galen had left it, clenched. "My outlook makes more sense than yours in refusing to defend yourself."

"Nay." He shook his head. "Yours, I'd be willing to wager, was one of simple vindictiveness."

" 'Twas no such—"

"Don't lie to me, Alena. Don't *ever* lie." With a grimace, Galen levered himself to one elbow. "You were angry and frustrated with me, with what you saw as my foolhardy determination not to raise my hand in battle. You thought to teach me a lesson."

Alena made yet another move to protest, then sighed and leaned back in her chair. All the fight, all the simmering frustration, drained from her. "Aye. I thought to teach you a lesson. But 'twas only for your own good."

She slumped forward and cradled her head in her hands. "By the Mother, Galen! I only want us to survive this quest."

"I still have my magic," he softly said. "I may not choose to use it in every situation you deem appropriate—and never to harm another—but there are still ways . . ."

Alena looked up. "You should've told me before that your magic is useless after dark. If I hadn't stopped that Jarvis and his friends, they could've killed you. And they weren't even using magic. What will you do when you go up against your brother?"

"I truly don't know what I'll do when Dorian and I next meet. I still hope . . ." His mouth twitched. "Well, I'll deal with that issue when the time comes. In the meanwhile, my actions with Emma were unwise and I paid the price, as any man might. That is all that needs to be faced this night."

Alena gave a snort of exasperation. "Aye, you were a fool, and no mistake."

A thoughtful look clouded Galen's brow. "All jesting aside, there was something about those men—and Jarvis in particular—that would've made me hesitate to use my magic even if I'd been able." He shook his head. "I'm not certain what 'twas, but he disturbed me greatly. He looked at me the first time across the room as if he were trying to recall something. I fear he's not all . . . what he seems."

"I felt the same." Alena couldn't calm the sudden acceleration of her pulse. "We must beware, Galen. Someone—either Dorian or some other—may not wish us to reach Castle Radbourne."

"Or it may be something altogether different, like the dragons . . ."

Alena frowned. "What are you talking about?"

"Strange things have been set into motion since your arrival on Cadvallan, things not set awry for over fifteen years." He sighed and lay back on the bed with a wince. "You'll have to face the truth sooner or later."

"And what truth is that, Galen Radbourne? What you'd like me to believe?"

"Aye, what *I* believe and *you* should believe, too. You have powers, Alena. You have a special bond with a dragon. You can communicate with him." His mouth went grim. "Only those of magic, be they male *or* female, can do that."

Unconsciously, Alena twisted the cloth in her hands. "Aye, magic. And how am I truly to know if that magic arises in me, or is yours? You could bespell me to think I hear Paddy speak in my mind, when it really came from you."

"And when you finally hear him speak aloud, will that, too, be a spell? And is his unswerving devotion to you also the result of a spell?" Suddenly too weary to argue further, Galen closed his eyes. "I haven't the strength to discuss this further, Alena. But we must consider all possibilities, anticipate all contingencies." His lids lifted, and a tiny smile hovered on his lips. "That *is* what a good warrior does, is it not?"

"You come to that particular lesson a bit tardily." Alena turned and dipped the cloth back in the basin of water. "But 'tis better than never at all. Mayhap there's hope for you yet."

"And for you, as well, sweet lady."

She paused, a look of uncertainty flaring in her eyes. Then, Alena shook her head, firmly and with finality. "I am all that I ever want to be. Let that be sufficient, Galen. Don't try to change me."

"Nay, Alena. I'd never try to do that. But you must be willing to make your own changes if destiny calls you down a different path than where you once traveled."

She began dabbing gently at the cut over his left cheekbone. "I've always made my own destiny."

"Isn't the creation of one's destiny but a series of choices? And aren't the consequences but the fruit of those choices, be they wise or foolish, good or bad?"

"Aye," she prodded impatiently. "What is your point?"

"Make the wise choice, the good choice, Alena." Galen gazed up at her, knowing, even as he spoke, she was yet unready for the full disclosure of her wondrous powers and heritage. Soon, though, she must be told. Soon, there'd be no more time to shield her, to ease her into it. "No matter if you fear the changes," he continued softly, "no matter if 'tisn't the path you originally envisioned your life as taking."

"And what of you?" she demanded, consumed with terror that he once more sought to encompass her within his spell and force her to believe what she'd no wish to believe. "What of your destiny, Galen Radbourne? What if this quest sets you on a path that will take you from everything you used to hold dear?"

A haunted, anguished look flashed across his face. "Aye, what then?" he softly murmured. "What then, indeed?"

The early morning sun peeked through the open bed chamber window, piercing the gently flapping, threadbare lace curtain to dance on the floor in shimmering puddles of light. A tender breeze, kissed by the chill of the waning night, swirled around and around, stirring up dust motes and bits of feathers that had long ago escaped the lumpy little pillow. Birds chirped in the tree outside, bright, cheery heralds of the new day.

Alena stood in the room's open doorway a moment longer, wondering at the simple beauty of the sun drenched morn. Then, with a soft sigh, she slipped back in, pulled the door closed, and quietly walked over and placed the cloth wrapped hunk of brown bread and tankard of ale on the table beside the bed.

Her glance shifted slightly. Galen slept on, free, at least for a time longer, of the torment of a painfully battered body. If she hadn't known from experience how much worse a man could look the morning after a severe beating, she wouldn't have believed what she saw.

Galen's left eye was swollen shut and blue-black. His upper lip, beneath his thick black mustache, was bloated, the cut crusted and red. His cheek was purpled, his nose, where she'd set it, puffy and distorted. He looked a mess—and in no shape to ride anywhere today.

Yet they must, if 'twas at all possible. Idara's hut was but two days' journey and, given the possibility that Jarvis and his men might yet attempt other foul and underhanded tricks against them, lingering here was dangerous. Out on the road, 'twould be easier to outdistance or outmaneuver them. Out on the road, Alena would once again be in her element.

Reluctantly, she squatted beside Galen and shook him awake. He stirred, groaned, then slowly opened his good eye.

"A-aye?" he croaked.

" 'Tis morn, Galen. 'Tis time to depart."

He shoved to one elbow. The effort it cost him wasn't lost on Alena. His chest heaved. He coughed carefully. "Give me a moment to wash and dress, and I'll be ready."

Standing, she slid her arm beneath his and helped Galen sit. Pouring out a cup of water, Alena offered it to him. The big sorcerer drank greedily, then gingerly wiped his mouth with the back of his hand. He attempted a smile. Thanks to his swollen upper lip, it turned into a lopsided snarl.

"Here, let me help you wash and dress," Alena said, unaccountably moved by his brave efforts. "Then, while I visit the smithy and retrieve my, er, purchases, you can break your fast on the bread and ale I brought up from the tavern."

He glanced at the cloth wrapped parcel. "I'm not hungry."

"Yet you must eat something to maintain your strength."

Galen shook his head. "I don't think I could chew it."

Alena took up the parcel of bread, laid it in his lap and unwrapped it. Swiftly and efficiently, she tore the chunk into small, bite-size pieces. Next, she slid the tankard of ale close. "Here," she said, demonstrating. "Dip a piece of bread in the ale to soften it, then swallow it. That way you won't have to chew and you'll gain the added advantage of whatever ease the ale provides your aches and pains."

He cocked his head. "Have a care. You don't want me too drunk to ride a horse, do you?"

She smiled. "Hopefully not. Just pleasantly relaxed." A sudden thought struck her. "The night is gone and your magic returned. Is it possible for you to mayhap heal yourself?"

Galen couldn't seem to meet her gaze, finding sudden fascination with the bits of bread in his lap. " 'Tis possible, but not this time."

There was something about his tone and evasive actions that snagged Alena's attention. "And why *not* this time, Galen? What's so special about this time?"

He didn't answer until he'd dipped a piece of bread in the ale and carefully shoved it between his sore lips. "Because"—he paused to swallow—"I must conserve my magic."

Her gaze narrowed and her hands fisted on her hips. "Galen, I tire of hearing how you must constantly conserve your magic. There are few things more important than your physical well-being, yet you refuse to heal yourself. There's more to this than some miserly wish to preserve your magical abilities, isn't there?"

He didn't answer.

Alena's suspicions grew. What could Galen fear that would keep him from using his magic? Surely, there was no danger to him, so what—

" 'Tis me, isn't it?" she cried. "You fear losing your powers too soon, before we reach your brother, and having to mate with me again. That's why you risk so much to conserve your magic!"

"And what if 'tis?" He jerked his gaze up to meet hers. "You survived our mating once, Alena. There's no guarantee you'll survive again."

"But you're hurt, can barely move, and we've a long ride ahead this day!"

"My body will heal and, in the meanwhile, I'm alive," he rasped in a voice gone harsh with pain. "I can bear the discomfort of a bruised body. What I can't bear is harming you—in any way!"

The mounting tension of the past days shattered. Once more, Alena knelt before him. "Ah, Galen," she whispered, stroking his bearded, bruised face with infinite tenderness. "I don't want you to suffer or be harmed, either. Yet we seem to be constantly at odds with each other, battling instead of working together."

"Aye, 'tis true enough." He turned his face to fleetingly kiss her palm. "Yet 'tis also safer than . . ."

Galen's voice faded. Loathe to say more and reveal feelings he knew he dared not share, he instead let the admission die. She was Renard's, Galen fiercely reminded himself. He *must* believe that. He was sorcerer, she, *galiene*. There had never been any chance for them.

In her heart, Alena must know that. And he must accept it as well. 'Twas better than fostering hopes that would eventually be dashed against the jagged rocks of a cruel reality. Call him a coward in this if in naught else but, fact that 'twould eventually become, Galen didn't think he could bear her outright rejection.

"What?" Alena prodded, lowering her hand. "What is safer?"

"Naught," he growled. "Naught." He leaned back from her. "Haven't you errands to run while I finish my breakfast? Unless you wish to while away half the day here in this room?"

She stood, rebuffed, yet strangely relieved that their conversation—and the emotions it had stirred—had taken an abrupt and different tack. "Aye. The blacksmith awaits." Alena glanced down at the packs. "Can you be dressed, with all our gear stowed in the packs, by the time I return? I can help you down the stairs to the horses then."

"I can make it down the stairs under my own power," he growled, his expression clouding. "I'm not a child."

As if wishing to say more, Alena stood there a moment longer, then turned and left the room. Methodically, Galen forced himself to finish his bread and ale, feeling a bit better as the effects of the heady brew gradually insinuated itself into his system. Finally, he stood, washed himself as best he could, and dressed. By the time Alena returned, the bags were packed and he was teetering on the verge of mild inebriation.

She took one look at him and shook her head. "I should have realized that a man without ale or wine for fifteen years would have little tolerance for even a tankard of the brew." She bent and retrieved the packs, then strode over to Galen's side. "Come," Alena said, slipping an arm about his trim waist. "You may well need some assistance navigating the stairs after all."

He graced her with his asymmetric smile. "Do you think so, sweet lady?"

"Aye, I definitely think so." Alena sighed and rolled her eyes. Then, directing him toward the door, she followed him from the room.

They rode out of Elmsdale without problem or interference, a half hour later than planned. True to the blacksmith's predictions, Galen's horse, the big bay gelding, put up quite a fuss when Galen attempted to mount him. It didn't help that Galen couldn't seem to find the stirrup or commandeer sufficient strength—thanks to the effects of the ale—to make the saddle. But with the horse shying and sidestepping, and Galen toppling over every time he made an attempt to reach the saddle, they soon drew a crowd of townspeople.

Finally, in exasperation, Alena gave him her mare and swung up on the gelding. Once he felt her weight on his back, the horse immediately settled down. With a wry glance back at Galen, she headed the gelding out of town.

Paddy was anxiously awaiting them when they reached his hiding place in the forest. He bounded out of a thicket right in front of the horses, startling himself *and* the horses. Alena maintained her seat. Galen didn't.

He slid back and off the mare's rump, landing in a heap on the ground. If not for Alena's quick reaction in grabbing for the gray's reins, the horse would have galloped off down the road. Once she had both horses calmed, if still wild-eyed and nervously watching a chastised Paddy, Alena glanced down at Galen.

"Are you all right?"

He shoved painfully to his knees. "No bones are broken, but I think I may have added a few fresh bruises to the old ones."

"Are you capable of mounting your horse by yourself this time, or must I dismount and give you a leg up?"

A decidedly offended expression spread across Galen's face. He climbed to his feet and stomped over to retrieve his horse from Alena. "I'm not helpless, you know."

"Mayhap not," Alena muttered under her breath, "but you're definitely one of the most unskilled horsemen I've ever met."

He must have heard her. Galen wheeled about from his attempt to lift his foot into the stirrup. "What was that?"

"Naught," Alena hastened to reply. "Naught at all."

Surprisingly, Galen managed to mount his horse on his own after only the third try. With Paddy following behind, once more a safe and hidden distance back in the trees, they set out down the road.

From a spot high in an ancient oak, a pair of pale blue eyes watched it all. "A woman, a dragon, and the sorcerer's twin brother," Jarvis muttered. His lips lifted in a feral, calculating smile. "I wonder what my lord Dorian will say, once he hears who is now abroad in his lands? I wonder what he will do with a brother he thought safely—and permanently—disposed of?"

CHAPTER TEN

Jarvis reached the appointed spot at the ancient scrying pool just as the sun swung to its zenith. He left his two compatriots to await him back on the road and out of sight. Heading to the pool, the big man knelt beside the gently rocking waters and muttered the strange, if detestable words his master had instructed he use to summon him.

For a long moment the water remained as it was, a shimmering reflection of Jarvis and the sky and the budding trees overhead. Then, almost imperceptibly at first, the pool changed. It smoothed to the consistency of glass, blackening to a flat, opaque surface like some dark mirror without light to reflect an image. A mist rose in the midst of the magical mirror. From the center of that mist, a face appeared.

'Twas Dorian Radbourne, the most feared and powerful sorcerer in the land. Dorian Radbourne, his master. Jarvis cast off the superstitious shiver of horror he always experienced whenever he came face-to-face with the indisputable evidence of his master's powers. His innate response would serve little purpose. There was no escape from Dorian's reach if any dared go against him. 'Twas better to obey—mindlessly and without conscience—and not question aught else.

"You have information?" Dorian's mellifluous voice pierced the silent woods. "You have found the woman?"

"Aye, m'lord." Jarvis shifted back to sit on his haunches. "But 'tis her traveling companions that might be of even more interest to ye."

"Go on."

"She travels with a young dragon and another sorcerer. Both of which recently disembarked from Cadvallan Isle."

The sorcerer's eyes flashed. His mouth tightened and a considering frown furrowed his brow. "Do you play games with me, Jarvis? There is but one sorcerer on Cadvallan, and he's my twin brother."

"Aye, m'lord. He is one and the same man who journeys even now with the woman."

"Galen . . . free at last of Cadvallan." Dorian stroked his chin. "And how can that be?" he asked, half to himself. "How did he escape the spell I cast over the isle? And why does he now travel with the woman?"

He paused and, like the sun dawning over a darkened land, realization gradually came. *She went for him,* he thought. *Someone told her of his potential powers, that they could be a match for mine, and she convinced him to help her rescue her friend. But who would've told her, and who would've helped them both escape my spell? Has Galen now regained his powers?*

There was only one way his brother could have done so. This Dorian well knew. He'd had to mate with a woman to feed on her life force.

At the consideration that the woman might be Alena, the woman he'd so avidly sought for the past weeks, the first ember of jealousy—long banked since his brother's exile—sparked and flared anew. Was it possible? Had Galen, so long denied the pleasures of a woman in retribution for stealing the woman Dorian had always desired, once again taken what Dorian coveted?

The sorcerer's hands clenched in the folds of his ornately brocaded black robe. If Galen had, Dorian vowed his brother would pay the price yet again for his arrogance. Pay the price—and more.

But, this time, Galen's punishment must be handled more

carefully. A dragon traveled with them. A creature who hadn't stepped foot off Cadvallan Isle for almost half a century.

What did it mean, Dorian wondered, to have one free in Wyndymyll now? Had he come in the guise of friendship for Galen, or was there some more sinister reason? Had some *galiene* somewhere called to him? Had the dragon bonded with one already?

The danger was great if the beast had. Even one *galiene* bonded to a dragon was a formidable threat, especially with the Night of the Dark Moon drawing near. The powers that could be unleashed that night . . . Powers against the sorcerers . . .

He shivered, then remembered himself. "The woman and my brother must be allowed to reach me unharmed." Dorian smiled thinly. "The dragon, on the other hand . . ."

"Aye, m'lord?" Jarvis stood, sensing the spell summoned meeting was nearing its end. "What of the dragon?"

"The dragon must be destroyed. It cannot be allowed to fulfill whatever purpose called it off Cadvallan." The sorcerer stared at his henchman, his eyes taking on a fierce, eerie light. "Kill the dragon, Jarvis. Before it reaches me. Before it ruins everything."

Though Galen tried mightily, his strength wasn't equal to a full day's journey. About midafternoon, as they skirted a small town, Alena made the decision Galen, who could barely stay astride his horse, still stubbornly refused to make. She reined in her mare, forcing Galen to do the same, and glanced over at Paddy.

The young dragon cast her an inquiring look. *Aye, lady?*

You must hide yourself and stay here for the night. Galen is too weary to travel further this day. I'll take him into town and find us a room. Then, I'll return with your supper.

Paddy's lips twitched. *You care for the sorcerer. 'Tis good.*

Alena shot him an indignant look. *Indeed, and how so? My concern is but a practical consideration. Galen will be no good to either of us if he falls ill or is too weak to use his powers.*

And be no aid in the flowering of your own powers, either. But first, your affection for him must grow.

Paddy, what, by all that is holy, are you talking about? In her exasperation, Alena's legs tightened about her mare's belly. The horse shied. With a low curse, the warrior woman quickly brought the animal back under control, then glared up at the dragon. *I tire of both you and Galen insinuating I have powers. I also tire of being made to feel I owe Galen more than I care to give. Don't speak of these things again to me. I-I don't wish to—*

Hear what, deep in your heart, you know to be truth? the dragon asked gently. *But how can we ever hope to destroy the evil Dorian and save the dragons if you don't accept your destiny? 'Tis your birthright, lady, whether you were raised to it or not.*

He moved close, excitement flaring in his colorful eyes. *Don't you even wish to know what that birthright is? I could tell you, if you but ask.*

She gazed at him in frigid silence, the awful certainty in the dragon's words sending her heart to thudding wildly beneath her breast. Her birthright? Was it indeed something far different than what she'd been raised to be?

Her father had been naught more than a simple farmer before the famine came, and he was forced to leave behind his lands. Taking her, his motherless young daughter with him, he'd set out to join a mercenary army. She knew little of her mother. Her father had been singularly closemouthed about her, sharing only the fact that he'd loved her dearly.

Was it something passed on from her mother that Paddy

so baldly hinted at, some powers that now seemed to call her to a strange and frightening future? A shiver coursed through Alena. Some realization, a wisp of a memory, plucked at her. Of women . . . dragons . . . magical powers . . .

"Nay," she fiercely muttered. " 'Tisn't possible."

At her softly spoken words, Galen, who'd been all but dozing atop his gelding, jerked awake. "Wh-what? Did you say something, Alena?"

The sight of him, swollen of face and exhausted of body, plucked, once more, at her heart. Her expression softened. "Nay, Galen. I was but talking to myself." She sent Paddy a quelling look. *Not one word of this to Galen. Do you hear me?*

He nodded. *'Tis yours to command, lady, as 'tis your choice to make. But I would be a poor companion to you, indeed, if I said naught. We are bonded till death. What choices you make affect me—and my kind—profoundly.*

Once again, the shiver rippled through her. Once again, the vision came, cloudy, muddled, but laden with a poignant, bittersweet call. By the Mother, Alena thought to herself, I'm going mad. 'Tis as simple as that.

She shook her head to clear her mind, riveting her attention back on Galen. "Come, yon town is sure to have an inn. The day draws on. 'Tis best if we take a room for the night."

The big sorcerer glanced up through the trees. " 'Tis only midafternoon. We can easily ride on another three or four hours, and make camp in the woods if we fail to find another town then."

She eyed him skeptically, then shook her head. "Nay, Galen. You're at the end of your strength, whether you're willing to admit it or not. If you don't rest soon, you'll be no good at all on the morrow. And, if we get an early start, I hope to reach Idara's hut by the next eve."

He frowned. "You've told me little of this Idara. Why is it

so important we even visit her on our journey?"

"She is the old witch woman who rescued and hid me when Dorian's men were out tracking me. I was near death when she found me. She nursed me back to health, safe from Dorian's magic. Idara was also the one," Alena added, "who told me of you, and gave me hope of at last finding a sorcerer of equal powers to fight Dorian."

As Galen listened, his instincts stirred. There was something about this Idara that intrigued him. Though Alena seemed to accept the old woman's help as one of coincidence, he wasn't so sure. Too much had been set into motion with Alena's arrival on Cadvallan.

Somehow, someway, he suspected Idara's hand in it, just as he'd belatedly come to realize back on Cadvallan that the Dragon Father had taken an active purpose in Galen's bonding with Alena. The Dragon Father's motives were clear, however. At all costs—even to the jeopardy of their friendship—he wished to save his kind. To that end, he saw Alena and Galen as the instruments for doing just that. Idara's motives, on the other hand, if she also meant to use them, were still shrouded in secret.

"This Idara may well be able to help us, 'tis true," Galen admitted, deciding it best—at least for the time being—to keep his doubts to himself. "I confess, though, to a certain curiosity about meeting her. But your observations on my physical state are true, too. I *am* weary and my body aches something fierce." He smiled wanly. "I just didn't want to let you down."

"You're not a warrior, Galen, and, though in admirable condition, I'd wager you'll discover muscles you never realized you had on the morrow." She grinned. "Riding a horse on an infrequent basis can do that to a person."

"Aye." He shoved a hand wearily through his hair. "Not to

mention all the times I've fallen off today." He glanced at Paddy. "Will you be comfortable awaiting us here? There seems adequate coverage for you to hide over there." He gestured to a distant cave, nearly hidden in the shadow of the trees and half-buried in the earth.

"He'll be fine, Galen," Alena hastened to reply before Paddy inadvertently blurted out to Galen more than he needed to know about their earlier conversation. "I already promised him I'd return later with his meal."

The sorcerer eyed the two of them, then nodded. "Good, then let us be off."

The small town, which they soon learned was called Margate, had been built on the ruins of an ancient walled city. Some of the tan-colored sandstone walls still stood and, where they offered stability, half-timbered houses were built into them. At other parts of the town, stalls displaying produce, meats, and the goods of various craftsmen were fashioned into the more crumbling parts of the outer walls. The simple addition of crude, pole-supported awnings shaded the proprietors in their open-air booths as they hawked their wares. The middle of the town sported a huge fountain built over an artesian well. From all the women gathered around it with big pottery jugs, it was evident that this was also Margate's primary water source.

As Alena and Galen pulled up before the town's only inn, all the women paused in their work. Myriad pairs of eyes watched their every move. Though Galen, in his exhaustion, seemed oblivious to it, Alena wasn't.

"We seem the brunt of today's entertainment." She chuckled. "Margate must be so far off the beaten track that they get few visitors."

Galen glanced at her. "They'll be sorely disappointed then. We can do little to enliven their existence."

"Aye," Alena agreed. " 'Tis strange, though, that I passed this way on my journey to Cadvallan and never came across this town."

"But you said 'twas off the beaten track. 'Tis likely you by-passed it without even knowing of its presence."

She dismounted and looked back up at him. " 'Tis possible, I suppose. 'Tis just such a strange little town—"

At that moment, Galen swung off his horse so awkwardly that he lost his balance when he touched ground, and stumbled. Alena hurried to support him, all thought of the town of Margate forgotten. After depositing their horses in the stable behind the inn, they entered the inn and took a room for the night.

This inn was far better kept than the Hogshead in Elmsdale had been. Their room boasted a good-size bed capable of comfortably holding two people, and covered by a fluffy down comforter and two pillows. There were also two cushioned chairs, a bedside table set with a candlestick, and a small tapestry depicting a battle of an army of knights against a dragon hanging on one wall. The single window was open and pristine white, lace curtains undulated in the late afternoon breeze.

Scanning the room, Alena was tempted to doff her boots and lie down for a short nap on the bed herself. But she squelched that impulse. Instead, she urged Galen over to the bed and, shoving him down on the edge, pulled off his boots. Next, she removed his hooded robe and belt, then helped him to lie down. Covering him with the comforter, Alena stepped away.

"I'm going to purchase a few chickens for Paddy's supper and deliver them to him, then I'll be back," she said. "I'll awaken you at sunset and we'll go down to the tavern for a meal."

He smiled up at her, already drowsy. "Paddy will appreciate the chickens. Dragons quickly weary of fish."

"Sleep well, Galen." Alena turned and strode across the room to the door. Twenty minutes later, four plump hen carcasses in a burlap bag tied to her saddle, she was riding out of town.

Paddy's hiding place lay a good fifteen minutes travel from Margate. As Alena rode along, the wind stirred, bringing with it the scent of rain. The air grew damp and cold. The clouds darkened to smoky gray, blotting out the sun. The trees swayed to and fro, their budding branches clattering and snapping together.

Alena shivered as a chill finger of air found its way down the back of her tunic, and fervently wished she'd had the foresight to bring along her warm cloak. But the past few days had been balmy and there'd been no reason to think the weather would change so swiftly. Then another chill finger stroked its frigid way down her spine.

This unpleasant sensation, however, wasn't just another harbinger of the mounting storm. It heralded, instead, she realized in a sudden swell of certitude, something dark and dank and evil. As Alena surreptitiously glanced around, her hand slipped to the hilt of her sword and she freed the thong that bound it. Yet, though her practiced gaze scanned every tree and bush along the way, she could find naught to justify her strange premonition of danger.

'Twasn't here, she realized suddenly. The danger lay elsewhere, farther in the forest . . . somewhere near . . . Paddy! With an anguished cry, Alena spurred her mare forward. She didn't know how she knew, but suddenly, with a terrifying surety, she knew Paddy was in the gravest danger. Fleetingly, she considered riding back for Galen, but just as quickly realized there wasn't enough time. If she didn't reach the young dragon soon, it might well be too late.

The mare, as fleet as the blacksmith of Elmsdale had promised, raced down the road. Gripping her sword tightly with one hand, Alena flattened low along the mare's neck urging her ever faster and faster. She couldn't have explained why her heart beat so frantically, or what had happened to her breathing, or why her throat had gone tight with terror. She just knew, with a certainty that sprang from a deep, heretofore untouched place, that naught must happen to the young dragon.

Naught . . . or she would near to die of the pain.

Sounds of struggle reached her ears. Cries of pain, of shrubbery crackling, and the shouts of hoarse male voices. As Alena turned her mare off the road and into the densest part of the forest leading to the cave where they'd left Paddy, a long, keening wail filled the air.

Pain, sharp and stabbing, lanced through Alena. For an instant, the world spun giddily around her. Only her strong legs and her grip on the reins kept her from falling. And only the strongest of mental efforts managed to contain, then control the horrible sensations pulsing through her.

'Twas as if she'd been pierced with a lance, Alena realized. Yet there was no weapon, no injury, no blood. 'Twas almost as if . . . as if 'twere a wounding of the mind, the soul, instead!

She caught a glimpse of movement through the trees. Saw three, brawny men leaping about, long, lethally tipped spears clenched in their hands. They shouted in fierce exultation, rearing back with their weapons then plunging down, over and over and over again.

Plunging their spears into a helpless, cowering, whimpering Paddy.

A blood-red mist exploded before Alena's eyes. She screamed out her rage and pain. As her horse broke through the trees into the small clearing where three men attacked a gentle baby dragon, she unsheathed her sword.

The closest man fell in a gurgling gasp of agony, his head half-severed from his body. Then Alena was between the other two men who ran forward, their bloody spears aimed straight for her. She recognized Jarvis and one of his other companions. The man she'd just killed may have well been the third, but it no longer mattered.

Jarvis's compatriot thrust at her. Only her battle honed reflexes protected Alena. She deflected the spear with a skilled blow from her sword. The spear skittered off, slicing a deep gouge in her mare's shoulder.

The horse screamed in pain and reared. Momentarily distracted, Alena fought to steady the crazed animal. Jarvis used the diversion to his advantage. He flipped his spear and used the pole end to strike Alena hard on her sword hand. The unexpected ploy sent the sword sailing into the air. It landed several yards from Paddy.

With a cry, Alena leaped off her pain-maddened horse and ran for the sword. Jarvis's compatriot suddenly stood before her, blocking her way. He grinned, a leering, gap-toothed smile, and motioned toward her with his spear.

"Ye're not getting back to yer sword, lovey. We've got other plans for ye."

"That's what you think," Alena growled and, in a blindingly swift motion, bent, withdrew her dagger from her boot, and flung it at her assailant.

The blade sank deep in the man's chest. With a strangled cry, he lurched backward, dead before he hit the ground.

"I wouldn't try that again." A low voice, ominous with warning, rose from behind her. The prick of a spear point in the middle of Alena's back added emphasis to the command.

Alena froze. *Jarvis.* "What now?"

"Kneel down—don't turn around—and ye'll live a bit longer!" came the rough demand. "If ye don't—"

"What? You'll skewer me like you did the dragon?"

Jarvis gave a harsh laugh. "A most pleasant consideration, to be sure, though I'd prefer a much blunter kind of spear. Unfortunately, though, I must save ye for another." He jabbed her a little more sharply in the back. "Now, down on yer knees. Ye're too sneaky for me to trust ye for long."

As Alena knelt on the ground, the storm broke overhead. The wind whipped through the trees. Thunder boomed. Lightning flashed. And the skies released their burden of moisture.

Yet Alena scarcely noted the frigid drops of rain falling to strike her and the earth around her. All she saw was Paddy's eyes, locking with hers. All she knew was his voice in her mind, crying out to her to help him, pleading with her to join her powers with his. Telling her, in words without sound, 'twas their only hope . . .

"Nay," she whispered, the fear of the hot, roiling *thing* that even now rose within her all but paralyzing her even as she fought against it. 'Twas hers, that she well knew, a dark and fearsome part of her that she'd known, yet never faced until now. A part of her that had been with her all her days. She didn't want to face it even now, but if 'twould save her and Paddy . . .

Survival—that, in the end, was all that mattered. Her warrior's instinct took precedent over all else. Survive the battle. Deal with the consequences later.

With a groan, Alena clenched shut her eyes and opened herself to the shadowy, awesome forces burgeoning within her. From deep in her mind she heard Paddy's dear, sweet voice, calling her, leading her on.

'T-tisn't so bad, lady, he quavered, his voice weak and

pain-laden. *'Tis but the natural way of things . . . for beings such as you and I. Feel the power . . . the magic grow. Feel it swell and join with mine until our two forces combine into an even greater force. We are one, now, in the freedom of our magic. One . . . as 'twas always meant to be.*

A fierce elation filled Alena. She did indeed feel the power grow within her. Felt it turn to a white-hot force, begging, nay, demanding, release. But how to free it, how to contain and focus such an unruly, seething thing?

Center your power, lady, Paddy once more urged. *Then feed it . . . back to me. You are the source, the inferno which needs no fuel . . . save the sustenance of a loving lifemate. I am the channel through which that power flows. Together, we are a force . . . few can ever vanquish.*

"Come, put yer hands behind yer back now," Jarvis's voice, rough with irritation, penetrated the exultant power rising in Alena. "I haven't time to waste on the likes of ye."

Now, Paddy cried, desperation edging his voice. *Give it to me now!*

With a sigh that was part panic, part elation, Alena opened her eyes and let the surging, mesmerizing, terrifying power go. It exploded from her, arcing in a blinding burst of light to where a bleeding, dying dragon lay, the whirling iridescence of his beautiful eyes the only sign of life still in him. It struck Paddy, encompassing him fleetingly in a glittering coruscation, in bright, flashing beams of light that seemed to surround and nourish and heal him. And, all the while, Jarvis stood there, mouth agape.

When the dragon shoved to his feet, opened his jaws in a toothy, intimidating grin, and extended his wings, the last of Jarvis's faltering courage fled. "By . . . by the Holy Ones!" he sputtered. Dropping his spear, he wheeled about and disappeared into the forest.

Alena shoved to her feet. For a fleeting instant she considered going after Jarvis. Then concern for Paddy superseded her need for revenge. Her glance locked with the dragon's. Though the memory of the past moments were already fading, gilded with a kind of misty unreality, she saw the truth in Paddy's eyes.

"Are you all right?" she forced out the words through a throat raw with unshed tears.

"A-aye," Paddy struggled to reply. As he heard his own voice for the first time, a childish and tentative voice, his eyes widened. He reared back in surprise. "You saved me, lady. And faced your powers at last."

The admission was too much for Alena to face. She stepped back hastily, shaking her head and rubbing the back of her hand across her eyes. "Nay. What I did, I did out of desperation. I did it only to save you."

Paddy sighed. "But don't you understand, lady?" he asked, gaining confidence and fluency with each word he spoke. "Once the power is released, it cannot be called back. And, like that power, you cannot call back the life you once had."

"I did naught but help you fight Jarvis!" Alena cried, beginning to tremble so violently her whole body shook. "I made no other choices, chose no other destiny than that which was already mine!"

Bittersweet understanding gleamed in the dragon's eyes. "Yet 'tis changed, no matter how you deny it. Naught will ever be the same, not for you, nor for me. Don't you see how it has always been for us, lady? How 'twill always be?"

"Nay, I don't," Alena whispered, suddenly, inexplicably wanting to cry. "And I won't."

The wind whirled about them. The rain fell. Then, in the midst of the storm's tumult, Galen appeared. One minute the grassy spot before them was empty, the next, the big sorcerer was there. As the force of his magic swirled about him, whipping at his hair and robe, he stood there healed and whole, fiercely beautiful, enveloped in a shimmering aura.

He glanced about him and saw the two dead men. His expression darkened, turned thunderous. Galen's gaze lifted sharply and locked with hers.

In his eyes burned a mixture of savage possession and white-hot anger. Alena's heart twisted within her breast. Ah, by the Mother, she thought, never had she wanted a man as badly as she wanted Galen Radbourne!

The truth of it filled her with the sharp exhilaration of a freshened breeze. Yet it could never be. Not only the terrible price of his magic stood between them, but the realization he was not and would never be the kind of man she needed.

The tears, long held in check, fell then as Alena wept with the storm for a man and a life she hadn't the courage to face. A man and a life she had never, in her wildest dreams, ever desired. Yet both now stood before her—and she was simply, utterly, terrified.

Galen strode over to Alena. He stared down at her for a long, heart-stopping moment, his gaze warm with affection and understanding. Then the big sorcerer gathered her unprotesting form to him.

With a soft cry, she came to him. Her arms encircled his neck; her body yielded to his. They stood there for a long while, as the rain softened to a gentle patter, then stopped.

Around them, the sounds of the forest returned. The wind clattering in the trees. A hawk crying out high in the roiling, cloud-strewn firmament. An irate squirrel chattering at his neighbor.

Finally, Galen pulled back. He took Alena's chin in one strong, long-fingered hand and wiped away the remnants of her tears with the other. He smiled.

"Come, sweet lady. 'Tis past time you knew and understood all the explanation I can give you." Galen released Alena and took her by the hand. "Come, hear of the destiny that was always your birthright. Only then can you truly choose which path to take."

CHAPTER ELEVEN

Alena pulled back, suddenly wary not only of what Galen would tell her, but what the eventual consequences of such a revelation might be. Then, reason overcame her instinctual aversion to the magic even she now knew stirred within her. No decision could be made until she heard the full truth—a truth, it seemed, both Galen and Paddy had known all along.

"Aye, I'd like to hear it all," she said, gazing up at Galen with narrowed eyes. "But this hardly seems the spot. Though the rain has stopped, 'tis damp and cold, and I'm soaked clear through to the skin."

He glanced down at her sodden clothes and smiled. "You're right. The inn would be warmer and provide us with the privacy we need. 'Tisn't an issue that's best discussed where any might overhear. However"—his gaze lifted to Paddy—"after what just happened, I'm loathe to leave him behind."

"Can't we find some spot in Margate to keep Paddy? And place some magical circle of protection around him? Idara did that to her hut and its existence was invisible to the naked eye. Even Dorian couldn't find her."

"Magic circle or no, he'd have found her if he'd known whom he was looking for," Galen muttered. "Of that you can be certain. But, in most instances, a magic circle of protection does work." He stroked his jaw, deep in thought. "There's a spot behind the stables where few go. Several broken down wagons and carts are stored there. It should be safe for Paddy, and our room overlooks the area."

"Good." Alena tugged on his hand. "Place a spell of invisibility over him and let's be off."

"Mayhap you could do it yourself, if you'd a mind to?"

Alena glared back at him. "Well, I don't—have a mind to do it, I mean. I don't even understand how I did what I did to rescue Paddy, much less how to cast a spell of invisibility. And I've wrought about all the magic I can stomach this day."

"Aye, I suppose you have. I was just curious what kind of magic . . ." Galen let it drop and followed her over to Paddy. He met the young dragon's inquiring gaze. "Can you handle another spell of invisibility?"

Paddy nodded. "Aye. The closer I am to my lady, the better I'll feel." He paused. "Er, if I may be so bold, my lady cannot cast spells herself. She feeds me the power and I create the magic."

The big sorcerer cocked a dark brow. "Ah, so you can talk now, can you?" He frowned consideringly. "So, if you're the true magic wielder in this partnership, with Alena's help, can you make yourself invisible?"

Paddy shook his head. "Not yet. I am still too young and unseasoned. But as my lady's powers grow and mature, so will mine. In time, though, 'tis possible I could cast a spell of invisibility."

Galen shot Alena an arch look. "You advanced greatly in your powers today, but it seems you've still a ways to go."

"I haven't any idea what you're talking about," Alena snapped.

"Don't you?" He shrugged. "Well, I'll soon see what I can do to rectify that." He grasped his pendant and murmured the archaic words. In the blink of an eye, Paddy disappeared from view.

Alena eyed him closely. "That was quick. Your skills improve rapidly."

"Aye. They've come back disconcertingly quickly. I can only surmise that once you've learned them, they stay with you forever." Galen smiled thinly. "Whether you care to face that fact or not."

"You arrived here quickly, too. How did you know—?"

"That you and Paddy were in danger?" he smoothly cut in. "I don't know. I just did. After that, 'twas easy enough to summon my powers and magically transport here."

Galen eyed her for a moment longer, then motioned that they should set out. "Shall we be on our way?"

"Aye." She looked around for her mare. The animal grazed in the trees but a short walk away, nibbling greedily at the first tender shoots of grass.

Alena strode over. The wound on the horse's shoulder had stopped bleeding. At closer glance, the spear cut appeared painful, but superficial. She moved slowly to take up the reins.

"Think you should ride her back?" Galen asked from behind her.

"Nay. 'Twould be best to spare her as much as possible."

"Will she be ready to ride on the morrow?"

Alena shook her head. "Nay. I'll have to trade her for another mount. Luckily, she's a fine piece of horseflesh. It shouldn't cost us too much extra in the bargain."

"I could heal her."

She glanced over her shoulder. "You'll use your powers to heal a horse, but not yourself?"

Galen's mouth quirked wryly. "We need the horse. I managed with my injuries."

Alena considered his offer. Then, she nodded. "Aye, 'twould be the best of all options. She's a good animal."

"No sooner requested than done."

Once more Galen clutched his pendant and, closing his

eyes, whispered yet another strange stream of words. The mare gave a snort of surprise and jerked up her head, her ears pricked, her body poised for flight. As Alena watched in wonderment, the long wound on the horse's shoulder slowly faded until naught remained but a thin, white scar.

She was still staring when Galen took her by the arm and began to lead her away. "Come," he said matter-of-factly, as if he hadn't just performed a miracle. "If we don't hurry, 'twill be dark before we reach Margate, and, though the spell of invisibility will remain in effect since 'twas set before dusk, the rest of my magic will be useless if we've need of it." As they strode off, he looked over to his right. "Are you coming, Paddy?"

There was naught there, save the sound of something heavy squishing across the waterlogged ground. Alena stared, trying to make out a shadow, a faint outline or form, but could see naught. 'Twas Galen's spell, she thought. 'Twas why only he could see the dragon.

Briefly, she considered the effect of Paddy's footprints, to some unsuspecting peasant they might pass on the road, appearing out of nowhere on the muddy ground. Well, there was naught that could be done about it, she finally decided. They'd just have to deal with those consequences if and when they occurred. Just like all the other consequences that seemed frequently to be rearing their unpredictable heads on this quest.

With a sigh and small shake of her head, Alena followed Galen, leading the mare behind them.

"Nay, 'tisn't possible." Alena's shake of her head was as vehement as her denial as she flung herself into the nearest chair in their room. Unmindful of her muddy boots, she stretched out and propped her feet on a little wooden stool.

"You've lived too long on Cadvallan, mired in dreams of a time that will never come again. The *galienes* are as dead as the dragons will soon be!"

" 'Tis true," Galen calmly replied. "Most of those women *are* dead. But all the evidence points to the fact that you are one of them, Alena. After all that has happened in the past weeks, surely even you can't deny that."

"I have powers. I have a dragon that has decided to bond himself to me." Alena shoved an errant lock of hair out of her eyes. "Yet, as strange as all that may be, that's no reason to think I'm part of some extinct race of witch women."

"But to whom else would those sorts of things happen?" Galen strode over and sat in the chair opposite her. At the set, stubborn look on her face, he sighed in exasperation. "Alena, think about this for a few minutes. You came to Cadvallan through a spell that neither I nor the dragons could break. Almost as soon as you landed, you were caught up in a dragon birth—through your dreams, you say—and you not only named Paddy, but freed him to be born. The Dragon Father immediately recognized there was something special about you, and conspired to force us together. Then, just as soon as we mated—"

"Enough, Galen!" Alena held up a hand in protest. "Coincidences or outright manipulations, each and every one. And I can explain away most, if not all, of them."

"And what of this Idara?" he demanded, leaning forward. "Can you explain her part in this, too?"

Puzzlement crinkled Alena's brow. She became still, wary. "What do you mean?"

"If she truly *is* the witch woman you claim she is, she knew of the spell surrounding Cadvallan. Yet she still sent you there, mere mortal that you supposedly were. Was she but playing a cruel trick on you, raising your hopes that you might reach me and enlist my aid in rescuing Renard, knowing full well you'd never break through the spell?"

His voice took on a taut, impassioned edge. "Or did she know, rather, that your own powers, combined with that of the dragons who eagerly awaited you, would be enough to pierce the spell? Mayhap, just mayhap, she never cared one way or another if I agreed to help you or not. Mayhap she just wanted you to reach the dragons."

"Oh, aye, lay all this on the back of a kind old woman." Alena gave a disparaging snort. "You pluck at answers like a starving man at an apple tree. And I still don't understand why 'tis so important to you. What have you to gain from this if I truly am a *galiene?* You're a sorcerer, whether you choose to use your magic or not. And sorcerers are supposed to hate *galienes* as much as they hate dragons."

Galen leaned back, his expression gone impassive. " 'Tis a mystery, to be sure, but do I hate you, Alena? Have I done aught to harm or obstruct you, save for my initial reluctance to join you and leave Cadvallan Isle? Indeed, what could *possibly* be my motives?"

She didn't answer immediately, and Galen could almost see the thoughts and questions churning in her mind. As he awaited her reply, he wished she *would* tell him why he was becoming so increasingly involved with her. Why he cared who or what she truly was anyway. But if *he* didn't even understand his motives, how could he expect her to?

Some primal instinct—an innate one of survival—told him he could well be playing dangerously close to the edge in pushing Alena to examine her powers, to face her true destiny. What if, in finally accepting her own magic, she turned on him for what he was, sorcerer and enemy? What would he do then?

Galienes and sorcerers had been mortal enemies for so

long 'twas difficult to imagine them any other way. Yet so were dragons and sorcerers, Galen reminded himself, and he'd never harmed a one. Nay, far from it. He'd striven for the past fifteen years instead to win their trust and friendship, to try to save them. And Alena had never once shown herself to be easily swayed by other's decisions. She was a woman of principle and courage. That much he knew.

A soft sigh escaped her, drawing him back. "Nay, Galen. You've done naught to harm me *or* the dragons. 'Tis just . . . just that everything has become so confusing . . . ever since I met you."

She rose and began to pace the room, her shoulders hunched, her head lowered. Then, as if she found little comfort in her pacing, she returned and sat in her chair. "Ah, by the Mother, I should be overjoyed that I, too, have magical powers," Alena moaned. "It only increases the odds in our favor when we go up against your brother. But all I can think of, instead, is what is happening to me, to my life."

Stirred by the tormented sound wrenched from some place deep within Alena, Galen stood, walked over, and knelt before her. Guilt swamped him. Mayhap he'd told her too much, too soon after her discovery of her powers. It must all seem so overwhelming to her.

Ever so gently, he took Alena in his arms. "Hush, lady," he soothed, stroking the wild tangle of her hair. "It has been a hard, confusing time of late for the both of us. I wish I could answer your questions. I wish I *knew* the answers, but I don't. All I know is that, up until now, fate has manipulated us both to bring us to this point in our lives. 'Tis past time—don't you agree?—for us again to take charge of our lives and destinies. And the only successful way to do that is to be even more knowledgeable, more in control, than those who seek to use us."

She lifted her eyes, some of the old anger and defiance beginning to flare anew in their luminous depths. "And who wishes to use us, Galen? Tell me so I may defend us against them."

He smiled softly. How like Alena to revert back to her warrior ways. "The Dragon Father, to be sure. 'Tis also possible that Idara, Dorian, or mayhap someone else we have yet to discover also has a stake in what we do or don't accomplish. 'Tis too soon to be certain." He stroked the side of her face, gently, tenderly. "But believe me when I swear to you that I have and will never seek to use or harm you in any way, sweet lady. Believe that, if naught else."

"I believe you, Galen." She captured his hand as it moved down her cheek. Her lips tightened. "I don't like the idea of being anyone's pawn, though. Don't like it at all."

"Neither do I, sweet lady," he murmured, his voice going deep, husky. "Neither do I."

She met his gaze, stirred by the softer tenor of his voice. The touch of his hand on her face, the look of tender yearning in his eyes, plucked at some carefully guarded needs of her own. She was angry, confused, her emotions all in a turmoil. And Galen, just now, wasn't helping to clear her mind. Nay, far from the contrary.

Throwing all caution to the winds, Alena lifted Galen's hand and brought it to her lips. For at least a few moments, she told herself, there wasn't harm in escaping all the decisions that must soon be made. For at least a few moments, she needed to drown herself in something other than logic and reality.

Turning the callused length of Galen's palm to her lips, Alena kissed him there, savoring his scent and taste, before lifting his hand to press her mouth against the pulse throbbing in his wrist. He felt so warm, so alive. She nuzzled him briefly before a stronger, more basic need drove her further.

She nipped him with her sharp, white teeth, gently at first and then more aggressively, before opening her mouth to kiss him wetly, then run the tip of her tongue over the hot, suddenly erratic beating in his wrist. And, all the while, her glance met his, saw the fire leap in his eyes, saw them burn with reawakened desire, saw the remembrance of that night of the storm explode in his dark, beautiful, mesmerizing depths.

Galen's response stirred an answering one in Alena. She pulled him to her, took his face in her hands, and, leaning down, kissed him. He stiffened in surprise, his mouth momentarily hard and unyielding against hers. Then, with a moan of sheer, unmitigated desire, he roughly pulled her down to him.

They tumbled together on the floor, a tangle of arms and legs and barely banked desire. His mouth opened over hers. His hands moved down her back, molding her tighter and tighter to the hard length of his body. Then, in a bold and demanding move, he parted her lips and thrust his tongue into her unresisting mouth for a deep, hot, languorous kiss.

Alena's response was as savage as her desire. She growled low in her throat, a husky and primally feminine sound. Her long legs twined about Galen's, capturing him in a sweet prison of slender, well-toned muscles that clenched tighter with her rising passion. The feel of her woman's mound, pressed hard and hot against his groin, threatened to drive Galen over the edge.

He wanted her, now, on the floor, without thought or care for right or reason. She wanted him. There was no mistaking her eager response, or the way her hands grasped at his buttocks, jerking him to her in the rhythmic thrust of mating. There was no way his own body could help but respond. His sex hardened to a throbbingly painful fullness, engorged with his blood, ready to explode.

Yet Galen didn't dare give in to the seductive promise of ecstasy. If the immorality of taking Alena's life for a brief if highly pleasurable mating weren't enough reason for restraint, the added responsibility of protecting her budding powers—powers that might well mean the dragons' salvation—dwarfed everything else by comparison.

And his role . . . Later, he told himself, he'd ponder his role, and seek to determine whether 'twas one of good or evil. Only that answer could determine what he must do next. But now . . . now, Galen thought in savage anguish as Alena's hands stroked his buttocks and the insides of his upper thighs, now he must end this wild, delicious joining of their bodies before 'twas too late.

He captured her hands, brought them 'round to imprison them on her chest. "Stop it, Alena." He ground out the words harshly. "Stop it now!"

She froze. Confusion darkened her eyes to the deepest ultramarine. The struggling of her hands in his stilled, and she leaned back.

"Don't tell me you don't want this as much as I," Alena said, her eyes narrowing in suspicion. "Already I know your body, can read its response as well as my own."

"You know we can't mate. 'Tisn't safe."

"I'm not so certain I believe that."

He wrenched her legs off and away from him, shoving back. "Well, it doesn't really matter what you think about it. As long as there's any doubt in my mind, that's all that matters. Unless you plan on tying me down and raping me."

She leaned up on one elbow, a wry smile quirking her lips. "A most intriguing consideration. But I'm not in the habit of forcing my men. I like them warm and willing."

The easy way she spoke of her former lovers plucked unpleasantly at Galen. "And you've had so many of them, haven't you?"

Fleetingly, surprise widened her eyes. Then, her smile widened. "More than you, to be sure. Not that that would be so difficult."

Galen shoved to his knees. "I fade appreciably in comparison to your other lovers, to be sure. It almost makes me wonder why you waste your time on me."

She saw she'd hurt him and fervently wished she could call back her earlier words. Alena sat up. "Galen, I didn't mean—"

"Don't!" He cut her off with a savage vehemence. "It doesn't matter. What matters is that we put a halt to a pointless and dangerous act. We cannot hope ever to make aught of our physical desires for each other. You know that as well as I. Let's just keep it strictly businesslike from now on."

"And what do we do, when the time comes to replenish your powers? Shall we mate then in a strictly businesslike manner?" Alena shoved aside the hair that had fallen into her face. "By the Mother, Galen, you can't turn desire on and off like that!"

I need more than desire, he wanted to shout back at her, but didn't. *I need . . .* Galen paused, alarmed, suddenly unsure exactly what he *did* need from Alena.

Surely 'twasn't love. His capacity for love had died with Lydia. He didn't dare stir that painful emotion to life again. Lust for a woman was difficult enough to deal with. What would become of him if he allowed himself to yearn for, to cherish, to heart-deep *need,* a woman again?

He didn't want to face that answer, not now or ever. And there was no reason to. His fate had been decided a long time ago. There was no turning back, no matter how dearly he wished it.

"We won't need to turn our desire off and on, Alena." Galen shoved to his feet. "I conserve my magic just so there won't be any necessity of mating ever again. We'll reach Idara's on the morrow. Castle Radbourne is but two days' journey from there. If all goes well . . ."

"Aye, if all goes well." Angrily, Alena rose and glared at him. "And if it doesn't? What then, Galen?"

He gazed down at her, hardening himself to her anger *and* her need. "Then we'll have to make a decision, won't we? Decide whether to attempt to rouse that elusive desire we feel for each . . . and take yet another chance with your life."

Alena tossed and turned on her pallet on the floor. Her fevered dreams, thanks to her wound that was open and inflamed once more, were strange, unsettling, and overlaid with a sense of danger, of impending doom. Faceless forms hovered over her, looming heavy and ominous and suffocating. She struggled harder, fighting to stir her passive, unmoving limbs. She cried out silently in her sleep, begging for help.

A voice answered, far away. A faint, sweet, childish voice. Paddy? Alena fought wildly now, her cries growing frantic, desperate. The voice moved closer, became stronger.

My lady? My lady? MY LADY!

Alena jerked awake. Blackness filled the room, save for a thin sliver of moonlight that pierced the curtained windows. She looked around. Dark, shadowy forms moved about, undulating and disembodied. Alena blinked hard, banishing the lingering cobwebs of sleep.

The forms took shape, materialized into bodies—human bodies. Bodies looming over the bed where Galen still slept. Alena jerked up, her hand snaking to the sword she always slept beside. In a swift move, she rose to her knees and unsheathed her sword.

The harsh, metallic rasp as steel escaped sheath filled the night shrouded room. The forms froze, then slowly turned. There were ten or fifteen bodies who, as one, moved toward her. Alena climbed to her feet, her stance widening, both hands gripped about her sword.

"Galen!" she cried. "Galen, wake up!"

At her words, he bolted straight up in bed and, through the blackness, she saw him glance her way. "Your sword," Alena shouted, knowing it hung from the bedpost by his head. "Arm yourself. Now!"

There wasn't time to say more. The dark bodies advancing on her leaped forward. Alena found herself cornered, her own sword the only deterrent between her and capture. "What do you want?" she tersely demanded, even as she swung her weapon back and forth before her. They were hopelessly outnumbered and Galen had no magic. 'Twas up to her to get them out of this. "If 'tis money, I'll give you what little we have."

Her attackers said naught, only moved closer. Unease prickled down Alena's spine. 'Twas obvious they were here for a more sinister purpose than theft. But was it one of abduction or of death?

There was a sudden movement, then a big body hurtled toward her. She staggered back, slamming into the wall behind her, and instinctively thrust out with her sword. Soundlessly, the man fell, sprawling at Alena's feet.

Another stepped forward, and another, to take his place. Alena slashed at one. Her sword bit into flesh, drove deep, yet not a cry or groan escaped the man's lips. As he fell, he grasped the razor sharp blade in both hands, dragging Alena off balance.

Three more men moved up to join the fourth man and, in an eerie silence, surrounded Alena. Two grabbed her arms, the other two wrenched her now immobilized sword from her grip. She struck out, kicking wildly at unprotected shins, twisting savagely. She managed to break free one arm, swing down and grab for the dagger she kept beneath her pillow. A booted foot knocked the knife away.

Her arm was recaptured and wrenched viciously behind her back. Slowly, inexorably, she was forced to her knees.

"Galen!" Alena cried. "Help me!"

At the desperation in Alena's voice, something in Galen snapped. He'd backed into the far corner of the bed, swinging at his attackers with his sheathed sword. Though he knew the act served only to keep the men at bay, 'twas all he could think of to do.

His magic was useless, and dawn was still several hours away. He couldn't use the sword blade on the men. That would most likely do harm. But now . . . now Alena needed him, was mayhap in danger of her life. She, proud warrior that she was, would never have called for help otherwise.

Yet still Galen hesitated, torn between his need to aid Alena and his soul-deep repugnance of ever again taking a life. As he wavered in his moral dilemma, the men confronting him leaped forward as one, burying him beneath an avalanche of bodies. The sword was knocked from his hand. His arms were imprisoned at his sides. And, though he fought back with all the strength he possessed, Galen was flipped over onto his belly like some sack of flour, and his hands wrenched behind him and tied.

Despair flooded him. Despair and a bitter frustration. Curse his indecision! As terrible as the choice would have been to make, he had now lost the chance to decide either way. And, because of his hesitation, Alena would suffer.

Fear for her stabbed through him. Panic swirled in to crowd out the fear. Think, he commanded himself, fighting to regain control and find some way free of the ever-worsening dilemma. Think, you fool, who once said there were better ways out of a situation than force and bloodshed. Think, before 'tis too late.

His feet were bound, then Galen was roughly turned over and dragged from the bed. He caught a glimpse of Alena still fighting on the floor. Saw a fisted hand rise and fall, striking her. Saw her go limp, then groan softly.

By the Holy Ones . . . Alena.

With all his heart, Galen wished for his magic. Wanted, needed it—not for himself—but for Alena. His magic . . . but the night had robbed him of all his powers. He was helpless, impotent when he wanted his magic more than he'd wanted anything else in his life. Impotent . . . as were all sorcerers in the dead of night . . . but not so the women, the *galienes*—and their dragons.

"Paddy!" Galen cried, the realization filling him with a fierce exultation. "Call upon Paddy, Alena! Join with him and send your power to him. 'Tis our only hope."

Through the fog that threatened to encroach on her consciousness, Alena heard Galen call. Paddy . . . She hadn't thought, hadn't considered . . . Yet the union of their powers against Jarvis had saved them once. Could it mayhap do so again?

She saw their attackers pull Galen off the bed and drag him toward the door. Knew a similar fate would soon be hers. And knew, as well, that as much as she dreaded facing the consequences of her powers, she must. Survival, winning against all odds, was what mattered. For this quest, at least, she must fight with different weapons, accept changes, compromises she might never accept again.

She couldn't let anything happen to Galen. For his sake. For Renard's sake. For *her* sake.

That knowledge flooded her, pounding through Alena with renewed power and determination. *Paddy,* she silently called. *Come to me. Help me.*

The sound of crashing timbers and scrabbling claws filled the air. *I come, my lady. I come.*

Alena was flipped onto her belly. Her hands and feet were tied, yet she was barely aware of the rough handling. Paddy came. Paddy, her brave and loyal little dragon.

Joy swelled within her, a curious aching, arcing emotion she'd never experienced before. A bonding joy . . . a fierce certainty of shared hearts and purpose . . . of a union that transcended time and place and species. 'Twas familiar and oh, so right, and yet foreign in its unique sense of belonging, of a heritage at last fulfilled, and a destiny finally accepted.

The glass panes of the window shattered. The wooden frame, snared on the body of the enraged black dragon, split and splintered. At the sight of Paddy, half-in, half-out of the room, Alena released the white-hot force building within her. In a bolt of light it arced from her to the dragon in bright, flashing beams.

Paddy took it in, gathering it within himself, feeding the power until it became a thing of greater strength and force than it had been before. Then, with a high, shrill sigh, he released it.

The magic filled the room, became a horrifying, swirling force, spilling out from the dragon in ever-widening circles. With terror-stricken screeches, the dark men clambered over each other and scrambled away. They left Galen where he fell just outside the room, leaping over his prone body in their frantic haste to escape. Alena was released with a jerk. With her hands and feet bound, she could do naught more than sink to her knees.

And still Paddy's magic drove them on, until the inn fell

silent and the terrorized cries faded into the night. "Enough, Paddy," Alena finally said. " 'Tis enough."

The black dragon wheeled about, his bejeweled eyes gleaming triumphantly in the darkened room. "We did it, my lady. We are truly one now, *galiene* and dragon."

At the term *galiene,* Alena stiffened. The unreality of it all—to awaken in the night and be set upon by attackers, then call on a dragon and join powers with him—rushed back, filling her with an unnerving sense of disbelief. It had happened, nonetheless, as had her rescue of Paddy yesterday. And both had come about through the forces of magic.

"Aye, Paddy," she grudgingly admitted, still both startled and overwhelmed with what they'd just accomplished. "We did it. Now," Alena added, suddenly aware of her bonds and the danger they still might be in, and not ready to linger overlong on the emotion-fraught topic of her powers, "can you use that magic for something a bit more simple, like freeing us from our bonds?"

The young dragon's head bobbed in eager assent. "Oh, aye, my lady. Pray, turn around."

Alena quickly complied. There was a crackling sound, her wrists felt momentarily warm, and then she was free. By the time she'd tossed aside the ropes, Galen was also struggling out of his bonds. She spared him a cursory glance, saw he was unharmed, and strode over to her pallet.

"Get dressed," she called back to him. "We need to ride out of here as soon as possible."

Alena pulled on her boots, then rose, buckled on her sword belt and resheathed her sword. Gathering up the few items they'd used last night to cleanse and rebind her hand, she shoved them into a pack.

"Ready?" she then tersely demanded, swinging two of the packs over her shoulder.

"Aye." Galen walked over and eyed her closely. "Are you all right? I saw one of them hit you. I'm afraid I wasn't much help. I—"

"I'm fine." She cut him off before he could go on. He *hadn't* been much help. If it hadn't been for her magic . . .

But she'd no time to dwell on his continued reluctance to fight, much less on what had transpired in the past day, and certainly no inclination to delve into all the ramifications. But, Alena knew, as well, the time would soon come when she must.

There was no denying the truth anymore. If she wasn't a *galiene,* she was as close to one as any living being could get today. And she was beginning to suspect—as had Galen—that old Idara might well possess some important knowledge on that subject. There were just too many coincidences surrounding the subject of her newly discovered powers. Too many unanswered questions.

They left the inn, made quick work of saddling up their horses, then rode out of the ancient, walled city of Margate. Once they'd cleared the drawbridge, Alena glanced back. The town shimmered in the faint glow of torchlit windows and moonlight, then grew dim.

Alena blinked, thinking her eyes betrayed her. They didn't. Margate disappeared into the mists, back into the thin air from whence it had first been conjured.

CHAPTER TWELVE

He watched them ride out of Margate as if the devil were pursuing them, then, with a vile string of curses, picked up the scrying crystal and threw it against the wall. The ancient stone shattered in a loud explosion sending glittering shards spraying across the room. Curse them. Curse them all! Dorian inwardly raged. The woman was a *galiene*. Not only did he have the issue of his brother to soon confront, but now, a *galiene*, as well.

A *galiene* and her dragon. And the Night of the Dark Moon was drawing near. It could well mean the end of him, if the woman discovered the ancient ceremony. It could well mean the end of all the sorcerers. And the end of Galen, too.

Dorian's mouth twisted. Did his naive, long-sheltered brother have any idea what forces he might unleash if he supported the woman? Did he even care?

'Twas possible the woman had beguiled his twin in some way. Mayhap, with the aid of her dragon, she had fashioned some spell around Galen. If he could free Galen from such a spell, their combined powers might be enough to destroy the woman and the dragon before 'twas too late.

Joining forces with Galen, needing him.

Dorian turned the idea over in his mind, marveling at it. The concept was as foreign as the ability to experience love, or compassion, or concern. Useless and draining, they were no more than trifling obstacles on the road to power and glory. Trifling obstacles . . . just like his brother was and would always be.

But Galen, like all the rest, could be used to further his

own plans. 'Twould be a simple enough task to enlist his aid. Galen had always been idealistic. Dorian would just have to decide how best to approach him.

He was older, wiser now in the way of the world and the weaknesses of people. Skilled in manipulation and intrigue. Though their youthful rivalry had been fierce at times, 'twould be a simple enough thing to convince Galen 'twas now dead. 'Twould be simple to assure him that filial loyalty now was of the utmost importance.

In the end, all that mattered was that he prevailed. 'Twould be the final victory over his brother—the brother who, solely due to the good fortune of being born a few minutes before Dorian, was the heir, the favored son, the shining paragon of virtue. Or had been until Lydia's death, he added smugly. *That* had changed everything—for the both of them.

He'd played well the solicitous brother to Galen in his time of grief. It had all been his machinations, including convincing their father of the wisdom of sending Galen away for a time, that had exiled his brother to Cadvallan Isle. His poor, sorrowing father had never been the man he was since the death of their mother. But he was gone these ten years past and no longer a problem of any kind. Now, there was only Galen left to deal with, to seal the inheritance that had always rightfully been his.

Nay, Dorian thought, 'twas an easy thing, indeed, to manipulate men governed by love. And why he'd never, ever, allowed himself *to* love. Not even the beauteous, vibrant, ill-fated Lydia.

His satisfaction lay now in deepening his magical skills, in gaining unlimited power. And power he would have, over Galen, the *galiene*, and her dragon. 'Twas all but a matter of time—and a well-honed and practiced treachery. If the woman meant something special to his brother, he would take her as well, flaunting that power as he rammed into her beautiful body, driving home to Galen and her alike who was the true master. Master of magic . . . master of Wyndymyll . . . master of all.

They rode through the night and into the day, not stopping until early afternoon. Finally, Paddy begged for a halt. Though Alena was loathe to rest until they reached the safety of Idara's house and her magic circle, she also realized the young dragon's stamina was all but gone.

A small pool a short ways off the main road offered the ideal resting place. As Alena watered the horses and Paddy plopped down on the flat sheets of sun-warmed rock encircling the pool, Galen set out a repast of their remaining food. The meager pile of dried fruit and even drier bread wasn't the most appetizing of meals, but Alena forced it down. There was no way of knowing what further dangers lay ahead, and she might need all the strength she could muster.

Galen was unusually quiet, finishing his own meal and cleaning up with only the most necessary of speech. She wondered if he was still shaken by the events of last night, or if something else bothered him. An impulse to ask him filled Alena and only the firmest of self-discipline squelched it.

'Twasn't her right to pry, nor demand he share his private thoughts with her. If the truth be known, she actually feared getting any closer to Galen than she already was. 'Twas danger enough—not only emotionally but physically—in desiring to bed him again, she thought, marveling yet again at the broad swell of his chest and powerful body, his long, strong fingers, his dark, ruggedly attractive countenance.

Unwilling sorcerer and warrior that Galen was, still he emanated a restrained power and masculine vitality she found so very appealing, so very, very seductive. But to allow herself to begin to care for Galen, to love him, was folly of the greatest kind. Yet if she spent much more time with him . . .

Alena shook off the disquieting thoughts and rose. "If you'll pack away our things, I'll water the horses one last time and we'll be on our way. Idara's hut is but another five hours' ride and I'd like to reach it before nightfall."

"Do you think Paddy is up to another five hours on the road?" His glance swung to where the dragon lay, head upon his front legs, dozing. A few inquisitive flies buzzed about him, and only an occasional tremor of his scaled hide betrayed his reflexive awareness of the insects.

"I hope so," Alena said, glancing down to brush away a scattering of bread crumbs on her breeches. "I don't want to spend the night in these woods. We'd be too vulnerable."

"And do you truly think we'd be any safer in Idara's clutches?"

Alena's gaze swung to his. "What are you talking about?"

"Don't play the fool with me, Alena," Galen growled. "You know my misgivings about her."

She glared down at him, immediately on the defense at his sudden change of mood. "I play no fool, but I doubt she'll be any danger to us. I think her intentions to direct my destiny, if that is what they be, are to my good."

"Are they?" He laughed bitterly. "Good intentions don't justify someone's deception and manipulation of another."

" 'Tis true enough. But I still prefer to hear Idara out before condemning her."

"Just have a care, Alena. I was betrayed by the Dragon Father after fifteen years of devoted service to him and his kind. In the end, I was but a pawn in a larger game. I don't want that to happen to you."

"The only game that concerns me is the one to rescue

225

Renard." She eyed him closely. "Never forget that, Galen. I haven't."

"Nor have I, Alena," he quietly replied, his mouth a tight, grim slash in the rugged expanse of his face. "Nor have I."

She hesitated a moment more, unsettled by the shuttered look he'd sent her, then turned and strode back to the horses. Paddy, awakened by the fresh flurry of activity, climbed to his feet, yawning hugely. He ambled over to Galen.

"Is it time to travel on?"

"Aye." Galen finished shoving the last of the food into the packs and rose. " 'Tis another five hours' journey to Idara's. Can you manage it?"

The dragon stretched his wings and arched his back, easing the tightness of stiff muscles. "If need be. I must go where my lady wishes."

A sudden thought struck Galen. "The dragons seem to follow their *galienes* without question or hesitation. What would happen if a *galiene* ever turned bad and demanded her dragon use his magic for evil?"

Paddy's brow furrowed in thought. "I don't know. Dragon Father never spoke of such a thing."

"Do the dragons have free will?" the big sorcerer persisted. "Can they choose to disobey an evil request? 'Tis certain the *galienes* did, when they turned their back on the dragons and their destructive war with the sorcerers."

"We have free will," Paddy carefully replied. "But to turn against our *galiene* . . ." He shuddered and shook his head. " 'Tis a terrible thought. Our bonding eventually becomes so strong, so intense that to deny our *galiene,* to leave her, would be a most painful experience. I wonder if a dragon could long survive it. Look what has happened to us since our *galienes* left us."

"And what of the Dragon Father?" Galen knew he was

treading on delicate ground now, but he had to know. Too many, it seemed, had their hand in this quest and he must discern where the loyalties of all lay. "What if he demanded something of you that you felt was wrong, even evil?"

Paddy's colorful eyes went wide and he took a step back. "What are you asking, Radbourne? Dragon Father warned me to beware of you on this quest, reminded me that, for all your kindness to us, at heart you were still a sorcerer. Do you now seek to undermine my loyalty to the dragons and my lady?"

"Nay, Paddy." Galen sighed and shook his head. "What purpose would that serve, so long as we all strive to do what is best for the land? I only wonder at the decisions that lie ahead for us, and question if any of us have the wisdom and the courage to make the right ones, however difficult they may be. Better creatures than we, be they dragons or sorcerers or *galienes,* have trod this path before and failed."

"Then we must have even greater wisdom and courage and trust in ourselves," the dragon said, thrusting his scale-slick chest out in a youthful show of bravado. "What else *can* we do?"

"Indeed," Galen muttered, slinging the other two packs over his shoulder. "But youthful idealism isn't always enough. I learned that most bitter and painful of lessons long ago. One must think not only with one's heart, but with one's head, and pray one makes the right decision. But first, one must know all the rules of the game."

Understanding flared in the young dragon's eyes. "And which rules which players play by."

Galen smiled. "Aye. You advance in wisdom, young dragon."

Paddy flapped his wings, his lips parting in a toothy grin. "Aye, that I do. Do you think my lady will notice?"

"Alena?" The sorcerer cast a glance her way. She had finished watering the horses and was leading them back toward them. The sunlight filtering through the trees caught her just then, bathing Alena in a luminous glow. Galen's throat tightened. She was so beautiful.

"I think she has much to concern her of late," he forced himself to reply, fiercely shoving aside his painful swell of emotions, "but she is ready at last to begin to consider the implications of her powers, and her relationship with you. Be patient with her, Paddy. She'll need our support and patience in the next few days."

"She is my lady. I will give her whatever she desires."

As would I, Galen thought, once again inundated with a stirring tenderness and fierce possessiveness as he watched Alena walk up and halt before them. *As would I, if only she'd let me. If only I could.*

Idara's little hut sat deep in the midst of a huge forest of towering pines. Already the setting sun had faded, giving the day over to the dark secrets of night. If not for the smoke curling from the tiny stone chimney and the light shining from the windows, Alena doubted she'd have found it at all that night.

Though her and Paddy's combined magic had managed to dispel the illusion cast by Idara's circle of protection so they could locate her hut, the journey through the forest had been difficult. All were exhausted and Alena and Galen were barely able to stay astride their horses. Paddy limped along beside them, his feet sore and tender.

As Alena halted her horse before the little house, excitement momentarily banished the mists of her weariness. Here, she might discover the truth at last. Here, she would find a kindred spirit, for if Idara wasn't a *galiene* herself, she at least

228

understood magic and could mayhap guide her in its proper use. A use, Alena hastened to reassure herself, that would extend to Renard's rescue and no further.

Dismounting, she turned to Galen. "Come along. Get down and stand at my side when I first greet Idara."

He leaned over and all but slid from his gelding. With an effort of abused muscles, Galen straightened and slowly hobbled over to Alena.

She couldn't help a tiny smile at his condition. "You rode well this day. No man could've done better, even a seasoned warrior."

His mouth quirked. "You think so, do you? Well, I only hope your Idara will permit us to rest with her for a day or two. I fear I won't be able to stand, much less walk, on the morrow."

Alena grasped his arm and gave it a reassuring squeeze. "Have no fear. Between Idara and me, we'll find some way to ease your aches and pains. But come. 'Tis past time we greeted her."

Galen obediently followed Alena up the narrow stone steps and halted at the door. A wreath of juniper, entwined with the protective plants of angelica, mistletoe, rosemary, and fennel hung there. They exchanged a glance, then Alena lifted her fist and knocked. There was a pause, then the sound of slippered feet dragging across the floor. The door opened, hearth fire and candlelight spilling onto Alena, who stood a step above Galen.

For a moment the old witch woman stared in surprise, then gave a cackle of laughter. "Welcome, child. Yer magic must be strong to have pierced my spell without my having known it." She hobbled forward and took Alena into her arms. As she did, her glance caught Galen standing there, only dimly lit by the flickering light from within the house.

It must have been enough, however, for Idara to see him for what he was—sorcerer and direst of enemies. She gave a hiss of terror and lurched back from Alena, her eyes blazing.

"Who do ye bring to my dwelling now? Have ye lost yer senses, girl? The man's a sorcerer and will be the death of us! Ah, by the Mother, have ye ruined it all, before it could yet begin?"

Alena stiffened. Her chin rose. "And did you not send me to find this very man? I wonder at your motives, Idara, now to take such offense at his presence."

The witch woman's eyes narrowed fleetingly and her mouth tightened. Then she forced a smile. "Aye, I did send ye to him, but I thought at the time 'twas a hopeless quest. I never imagined one of his ilk would help ye."

"Then you misjudged without knowing that I was and will always be," Galen said from behind Alena, "a man of honor if naught else."

Idara gave a disparaging laugh. "Fine words, coming from a sorcerer! 'Tis worth little to my kind."

"Then *I* give you my word Galen is an honorable man," Alena calmly offered. "Is that enough or must we turn now and ride away?"

Surprise flared in the old woman's eyes. "Nay, 'twill be enough, child. I meant no offense, but 'tis hard to change one's impressions, after all we've suffered at the hands of Dorian Radbourne and his kind." She stepped back, motioning them in. "Come, come. Partake of the comforts of my simple home. Ye're both welcome."

Alena made a move to enter, then hesitated. "We bring a dragon with us. Is there some place he might also take his rest? And have you a fowl or two we might butcher to feed him?"

"A dragon? Ye have a dragon with ye?" Seeking to pierce

the darkness and ascertain the truth for herself, Idara craned her neck to look around Alena. "How did ye—?" She caught herself. " 'Tis a miracle, child, but we'll talk more of that later. Yer dragon can make his bed on the backside of the house. There's a pile of hay there that I use to feed my milch cow. And I've plenty of fat hens. I'll prepare two for him after I've a chance to get the both of ye settled in."

"Three or four hens might be more to Paddy's liking," Galen drawled. "He's a growing dragon, you know."

Idara's gaze swung back to Alena. "A young one? Did ye mayhap bond with a babe then? Ah, 'tis more than I dared hope. But come," she said, grabbing Alena by the arm, "come into my house. I've a stew simmering over the fire and a fresh loaf of bread from my weekly baking. We'll have a fine meal, then talk."

Knowing Paddy had heard their conversation and could find his own way to the back of the house, Alena obediently walked past the old woman and inside. Galen followed, but not before Idara's frigid glance raked him from head to toe. It chilled him to the bone, unnerving him. Never had he experienced such open animosity, as he'd just felt from Idara.

There was a history behind such a blistering enmity. A history he must plumb sooner or later, if for no other reason than 'twould likely reveal the old woman's motives for helping Alena. Motives he must know if he was to have any hope of protecting them from further manipulation and harm.

Save for the light of the hearth fire and a thick, yellow candle stuck on an iron candlestick holder sitting on the long wooden table, the witch woman's hut was dimly lit. More by scent than sight, Galen made out bunches of drying herbs hanging from the low rafters. The familiar aromas of tarragon, basil, rosemary, vervain, and betony filled the air. Jars full of other dried herbs were stacked on shelves that lined one wall. The overflow spilled onto the floor two- or three-jars deep. Against another wall was shoved a bed topped by a plump comforter covered by a cloth in the most unlikely colors of purple, red, and yellow.

To all appearances, 'twas the house of a healer, but Galen knew differently. Though 'twas night and his powers were gone, he could still sense the aura of magic hovering about the room. But was Idara a simple witch, or something more, mayhap a *galiene* who had long ago lost her dragon?

Recalling the venomous look she'd graced him with earlier, Galen doubted she'd willingly reveal her secrets to him. Yet with the right opportunity, Idara might well share them with Alena. Share that, and more, he grimly realized, if her plan was now to nurture the powers Alena had just recently discovered.

But would the witch woman's motives be those of good or evil? One way or another, Galen was determined to find out. No one would use either him or Alena again.

"Come," Idara said, closing the door and indicating a spot beside it. "Set down yer packs and take a seat at the table. I'll brew ye a nice cup of tea to warm ye until the stew is ready."

Galen set aside his two packs, then held out his hand for Alena's. As if debating the significance of allowing him to assist her, she eyed him for a moment, then shrugged and gave Galen her packs. Though he tried hard to keep his expression inscrutable, he couldn't help a small twinge of pleasure. Alena was slowly but surely relinquishing her protective warrior's ego if she could accept his help without protest or defensiveness.

The witch woman set out three cups on an ancient sideboard that stood before the shelves of herbs, then took down two jars of dried leaves. Galen watched her dig out a handful of leaves first from one jar and add some to each cup, then do the same from the other jar. She next hobbled over to the fireplace to retrieve an iron teapot. When Galen shoved back his chair in a move to come to her assistance at the hearth, Idara quickly shooed him away.

"I've done quite nicely without ye for all these years. I think I can still make a cup of tea by myself, thank ye very much."

Galen nodded and sat back down. "As you wish, wise one," he said, rendering her the highest term of respect. "I meant no insult to your abilities."

"And best ye not underestimate them, either," Idara snapped. "Ye may be a sorcerer, but I'm not without a few tricks myself."

He smiled thinly. "I never doubted that for an instant. Your magic lays heavy on the air."

Idara grasped a thick cloth she kept hanging from the mantel and, wrapping it about the teapot's handle, lifted it from the fire. A thin jet of steam billowed from its spout. She carried it over to the sideboard and carefully poured boiling water into each cup. Then, after swirling the concoction, she turned and approached the table.

"This is a special brew, rich with rose hips and juniper berries," Idara said, placing the cup before Alena. "And to yours," she added as she set the cup before Galen, "I added a bit of willow bark to ease yer aches." The old woman arched a graying brow. "I noted yer stiffness when ye walked into my house. Ye're not much of a horseman, are ye?"

Galen exchanged an amused glance with Alena. "A shortcoming quite evident to all, it seems." He took the cup in his hands and inhaled deeply of the tea's rich aroma. "There's more in here than just rose hips, willow, and juniper berries." He frowned in thought. "Mayhap a bit of cowslip and feverfew, too?"

Idara's mouth quirked. "For a sorcerer, ye've a goodly knowledge of the herbs. Aye, 'tis a bit of cowslip and feverfew in the tea as well. Enough for a good night's sleep, but no more."

"I would hope so." He smiled grimly, determined to set Idara straight where things stood between him and Alena. "Alena still has need of my particular talents."

"Mayhap, but I'd wager only until she has time to fathom the depth of her own," the old woman muttered darkly. "Then, there'll be no sorcerer in the land who'll be able to harm her."

"I don't wish to harm her now, nor will I ever, wise one. Be assured of that, if naught else."

"Well, *I'd* be content if the two of you would stop talking about me as if I'm not here." Alena put her cup down on the table and glared from one to the other. "You both sound as if you're fighting over the remains before I'm even dead."

Galen flushed. "I beg pardon. Mayhap I'm overtired and short of patience this night." He picked up his cup, swished the liquid about for several seconds to cool it then drained the contents. "My thanks for your sleeping potion," he said, glancing up at Idara. "Mayhap we can talk further on the morrow."

"Aye, if ye wish." She glanced toward the hearth. "Ah, I think the stew is ready. Spare me but a few minutes more and I'll have yer meal steaming before ye." With that, she hobbled over to the shelves and took down some pottery bowls and eating utensils. A rich stew was soon on the table.

The next twenty minutes were spent in relative silence as Galen and Alena wolfed down two bowls of the savory stew and four slices each of the fresh brown bread. Two flaky tarts, rich with apple and a sugary, cinnamon filling, completed the meal. Finally sated, they leaned back in their chairs.

"A fine meal, wise one," Galen said, heaving a contented sigh. He glanced toward the single bed shoved against the far wall. "I must admit the combination of your food and the tea is fast beckoning me to sleep. Is there some spot you'd prefer for me to make my bed?"

"Ye can sleep before the hearth, if ye wish. The nights are still cold and since I cannot offer ye my bed, what with my old bones and rheumatism, at least a spot near the fire will be warm. Do ye have need of a few extra blankets . . . ?"

Galen shoved back his chair and rose. "Nay, I've enough in my pack. But a bit of water to wash in would be appreciated."

"The pitcher on yon table," she said, indicating the small table standing on the far side of the hearth, "is full of water and ye can wash in the basin it sits in."

He nodded and strode over to the packs. Extracting a clean tunic, rag, and jar of soft soap, Galen headed to the little table. Though he felt the two women's eyes on him, he nonetheless stripped off his robe, belt, and tunic and proceeded to lather up the cloth and wash himself.

Alena watched him avidly, drinking in the sheer masculine beauty of hard muscles rippling in the firelight, sheened with an alluring dampness as he washed, then rinsed himself. It seemed so long ago now that she'd seen Galen even partially unclothed, and the sight of him stirred memories of another time in a firelit house. Of Galen, naked, aroused, and damp from his bath, of a storm beating not only overhead, but at their hearts and minds and bodies.

It had been so beautiful that night, a time of wondrous, unforgettable passion and loving, and Alena was suddenly overcome with an intense yearning to experience that again. But they were but two days' journey to Castle Radbourne. Two more days and 'twould all be resolved—one way or another. She'd either be dead or have rescued Renard. One way or another, there would then be no further place for Galen in her life.

Once Renard was safe, she'd have no other choice but to ride away and never see Galen again. A mercenary army awaited her and Renard, an army already growing restless, eagerly anticipating the next battle as spring drove the snow and chill winds of winter away. There was no reason to linger a moment longer in Wyndymyll. 'Twasn't her land or people, after all.

A bony hand settled over hers. Alena looked up, startled. Concern gleamed in Idara's eyes.

"Ye must let him go," she softly said. "Before 'tis too late. Ye must, child. Ye've no other choice."

Anger flared in Alena. "Must I? And who are you to tell me that? I take orders from no man—or woman!"

"Hush. Enough, child," the old woman soothed, shooting Galen a worried glance. Relieved to see he'd paid them little notice, she turned back to Alena. "We'll talk more once he's asleep. I've so much to tell ye." Idara rose and cleared off the table.

Galen finished his brief bath, donned his clean tunic, then laid out his bed before the hearth. After settling in beneath the blankets, he shot Alena a quick smile. "Good night, lady."

She forced a wan little smile in return, wanting to join him so badly she thought her heart would break. "Rest well, Galen."

He stared at her for a moment more, something dark and emotion-laden flaring in the depths of his rich brown eyes. Then he turned on his side, his back to her, and lay there, staring into the fire, until he finally fell asleep.

While Alena took three butchered chickens that Idara had

hanging outside over to Paddy, the witch woman brewed them both another cup of tea. When the warrior woman returned and sat down at the table, Idara settled herself opposite her.

Her smile was bleak as she met Alena's gaze. "The sorcerer sleeps soundly at last. My herbal sleeping potion will keep him from awakening until morn. 'Tis past time we talk."

"Indeed?" Alena arched a dark blond brow. "Then pray, allow me to go first. I have one question that cries above all others, for an answer."

Idara sipped carefully from her tea. "Ask it, child. All questions tonight lead to the same destination."

Alena gripped her cup. "You sent me to Cadvallan Isle, knowing full well there was a spell around it, knowing as well that Galen was there. Yet you seemed quite distressed this eve when he showed up with me at your door. Why is that, Idara? And what was your true purpose in sending me to Cadvallan? Somehow, I now doubt 'twas ever to procure Renard's rescue."

" 'Tis true enough, child."

"Then why? Why, Idara? What was your reason?"

Calm, old eyes, laden with a lifetime of sadness and haunting memories, lifted to hers. "What else? To save the land if 'tis even possible," she whispered. "To destroy the sorcerers, once and for all. And ye, child, ye and yer dragon, are our last and only hope."

CHAPTER THIRTEEN

Alena stared at Idara for a long, stunned moment. Though she'd feared that her newly discovered powers possessed some special significance, never, in her wildest imaginings, had she envisioned this. She set aside her cup of tea. Inhaling a ragged breath, Alena locked gazes with Idara.

"You lay an impossibly heavy burden on my shoulders," she finally said. "I am only one woman."

"Aye, 'tis true," the old witch woman admitted gravely. "But ye are also the last remaining *galiene* bonded to a dragon. Only ye, in union with yer dragon, have the power to go against the sorcerers, against Dorian Radbourne in particular. And the way is simple, for one of yer ilk. 'Twill only take the ceremony on the Night of the Dark Moon to do it."

Alena cocked her head, puzzled. "What is this ceremony of the Night of the Dark Moon? How can that solve all the problems between the dragons and sorcerers?"

" 'Tis an ancient ceremony, little used and nearly forgotten, child." Idara took a sip of her tea. "Where once 'twas used by the *galienes* as a symbolic means of driving out evil in the land each year, over time it grew in power and influence until, eventually, the ceremony was capable of eradicating evil, be it in the magic, or the magic wielder. And, when that day came, the sorcerers saw the true potential of the *galienes*—and their threat. If they chose, the *galienes* could use the ceremony on that one night each year to destroy them."

" 'Twas then that the sorcerers first made their decision to kill the *galienes*, did they not?" Alena offered, beginning to

238

discern yet another facet of the centuries-old feud. "But they couldn't accomplish that without also antagonizing the dragons."

"Aye, 'tis true enough." Bitterness laced the old woman's voice. " 'Twas then that they set out to destroy the *galienes* and their dragons. 'Twas then that the destruction of the land and people began."

"But the dragons were well able to protect their *galienes,*" Alena protested. "The sorcerers could have done little damage—"

"The sorcerers didn't directly attack the *galienes,*" Idara was quick to correct her. "That would have been too overt. Instead, some of the more corrupt sorcerers set about manipulating the dragons, playing on their fierce pride and sometimes overly sensitive feelings. Only by undermining the bond between the dragons and their ladies could the sorcerers ever hope to prevail."

It all began to fall into place now, Alena thought. The doubts and fears of the powerful had eventually gnawed away at the very underpinnings of the land—the proud, ancient alliance between the sorcerers and the dragons. And, like the sappers who tunneled beneath the castle walls during a siege to weaken them, what began insidiously eventually undermined the whole foundation of a society's defenses.

"So, to save themselves from what they perceived as a potential threat from the *galienes,*" Alena finished Idara's story for her, "the sorcerers chose to send the land and the people into chaos."

"It could have happened no other way." Idara nodded her most vehement agreement. "The sorcerers are the essence of evil."

Alena stared at her for a long moment, torn by conflicting emotions. 'Twould be so easy to lay all the blame on the sorcerers, to justify their final destruction with this mysterious ceremony, but the easy answers weren't always the honest or correct ones. "Mayhap if I hadn't met Galen, I'd have arrived at the same conclusions," Alena softly said. "Mayhap if I'd been raised as a *galiene* all my days, rather than become a warrior and seen the truth of life in the world, I'd agree. But I'm not a *galiene* in outlook or upbringing. And I don't see it as you do."

"There's no other way *to* see it, child." The old woman leaned forward on the table. "What other reason is there, save the sorcerers are evil and wish our kind dead?"

"Our kind?" Alena smiled. "I thought as much. You're a *galiene*, too, aren't you, Idara?"

The witch woman flushed. "Aye. I suppose there's no sense in keeping it from ye any longer."

She shot Galen a furtive look. He slept on. "But don't, I pray ye, tell the sorcerer. For whatever reason he continues to treat ye well, he has no reason to spare me. He will see me as a threat, for I tell ye true, child, I will seek ceaselessly to turn ye from him. He is of the same flesh, the same spirit as his brother, and, in the end, a sorcerer will cleave to his kind. Survival is what matters to them above all. No matter the cost, he *will* survive."

"And isn't it that very attitude that got us all in this terrible mess to begin with?" Alena demanded. "Though the sorcerers erred in attacking the *galienes* through the dragons, the dragons' pride made them easy pawns in the sorcerers' manipulations. 'Twas only the *galienes,* from what I've been told, who had the courage to stand up to the both of them and tell them they were wrong. And, when that failed, to turn their backs and walk away from it all."

"Aye, and where did their courage get them?" Idara rasped, her face gone white, her skin stretched tautly over her cheeks and forehead. "The sorcerers still achieved their goal of separating the *galienes* from their dragons, to the destruction of all. They were fools—*I* was a fool—to have followed the women who led us in this."

She buried her face in her hands. "I lost all in my foolish, idealistic attempts to bring peace to the land. I lost my beloved dragon and my lover—he was a sorcerer, ye know, and turned against me to stand with those of his kind. Now, I have naught to live for, save the hope of revenge."

She lifted an anguish-ravaged face. "Ye are our last hope, what few of us remain, for only a *galiene* in full bonding with her dragon can perform the ceremony on the Night of the Dark Moon. And, though not raised in our ways, the blood flowing through yer veins is the same. The mother that bore ye was of our kind. Ye cannot turn yer back on us now, child. Ye cannot!"

"Can't I?" Alena leaned forward on the table, her shoulders stiff with her effort to contain her anger. By the Holy Ones, she didn't want this, had never wished for this! "You forget what brought me here to begin with. I'm determined to rescue Renard. He's my partner, my best friend. In the end, he is all that matters to me."

"And what of the sorcerer?" the old woman demanded. "What is he to ye? He's yer lover, is he not? 'Tis the only way yer powers could have so quickly come to fruition after ye bonded with yer dragon."

"Aye, and what if he was?" Alena found she couldn't quite meet Idara's gaze. "It doesn't change my determination to rescue Renard."

"And do ye think he'll so easily relinquish ye to yer Renard? Ye are his now, and sorcerers are dreadfully possessive of what is theirs. What makes ye think he even intends to free this partner of yers, once he gets ye to Castle Radbourne?

'Twas yer latent powers, in union with those of the dragons on Cadvallan, that got ye to the isle. 'Twas yer powers that ultimately got ye both off it, too. But now that he's free once more, what do ye think he wants most in the world?"

"I don't know, Idara," Alena challenged, an edge creeping into her voice. 'Twas too much. First Renard, now Galen. Would the woman never cease? "Why don't you tell me?"

Hurt flared in the witch woman's eyes. "Ah, child, don't get angry with me now. Ye must know it all, consider it all, if ye're to make the best decision."

With a supreme effort, Alena bridled her rising anger. "Fine, Idara. I'm but overtired and my patience wears thin. I meant no offense."

"I know, child." Idara reached over and patted her hand. " 'Tis hard to hear what I say this night. But though ye may have lived in the world, seen the good and bad of it, I know sorcerers far better than ye. And I tell ye true, this man ye travel with will forget everything save the lure of his magic, once he returns to Castle Radbourne and his brother. They aren't strong enough—none of them are—to separate the good and bad of it. And he won't be, either."

"Did you know he turned from his magic after it killed the woman he loved?" Alena asked, stopping short at revealing the true cause of the tragedy. There was no need to add further to Galen's pain by Idara knowing it all. "That he refused to help me for the longest time, admitting that he, too, feared his powers? 'Tisn't the way of a man who'd forget everything he believed in to return to his magic."

"Mayhap," Idara muttered doubtfully. "But have ye asked him, then, what he plans to do to help ye with Dorian Radbourne, once ye reach the castle? Surely ye can't imagine Dorian will easily give up yer friend? Or, for that matter, that he'll be willing to let ye go. He wanted ye for himself, if my memory serves me correctly. Ye did tell me that when I first found ye, didn't ye? And, for that matter, have ye asked this brother of his how he now feels about his magic? Now that he's back in the world, and mayhap has had a chance to use it again?"

"Nay, I haven't." Wearily, Alena rubbed her eyes. "There's so much to consider, to think about, after what you've told me this night. But naught more can be done until the morrow." She glanced up. "Where would you like for me to make my bed? By the fire?"

"Nay." Idara smiled. "The hearth is drafty, once the fire fades. Ye'll be more comfortable near me, I'd wager." She rose from the table. "Come. I have some old quilts that'll make yer bedding a tad softer and yer sleep sounder. The morrow is indeed time enough to ponder all this further."

Alena cast one longing glance in Galen's direction. He slept on, deep in the throes of Idara's herbal potion, one arm beneath his head, his other at his side, his expression peaceful. How she longed to slip over to him, to brush aside the dark lock dangling in his face, to kiss him gently on the cheek and wish him sweet dreams. Or, better still, crawl into bed with him, snuggle close, feel his warmth and solid male strength encompass her like some protective, comforting cloud.

But 'twas not to be. With one last, yearning look, Alena turned and followed Idara across the room.

Galen slept late into the morning. Until he rose, Alena busied herself helping Idara prepare a simple breakfast of porridge and milk, then assisted in the cleanup of the dishes. Afterward, strangely restless, Alena couldn't help but keep from pacing.

"If ye can manage it," Idara said, watching her with

knowing eyes, "I could use a few loads of wood for the cook fire."

Alena shot her a grateful glance, then headed outdoors. The morn was fresh and clear, with only a tang of the chill night still lingering. Wood violets peeped through piles of pine needles. A raucous jay shrieked overhead. Squirrels, foraging on the forest floor, chattered and scolded.

'Twas a fine morn, but Alena was too burdened with questions and difficult decisions to much care. Preoccupied, she all but ran into Paddy who just then ambled around the side of the house. Alena reared back.

"M-my pardon, my lady," the young dragon stammered, equally nonplused. "I didn't see—"

" 'Twasn't your fault, Paddy," Alena hastened to soothe his sensitive dragon feelings. "I wasn't paying attention."

The dragon lowered his long, slender head and eyed her intently. "That isn't like you, my lady. A warrior cannot afford to lower his vigilance for even an instant."

"Aye, you're right," she grudgingly admitted. "I just have . . . a lot to think about."

"The old woman is a *galiene*. I sensed that when first I saw her."

"She told me as much last night." Alena met his inquiring gaze. "And what of it? You wish to make some point, do you?"

"Though she is one of your kind and loyal to the dragons, her actions and impressions could well be tainted by her past experiences. Have a care how she may guide you."

"Your words border on the treasonous, don't they, Paddy, to speak poorly of a *galiene?*" She smiled and cocked her head. "What would the Dragon Father say?"

He looked decidedly shamefaced. "He'd be very angry, I'd wager. But my first loyalty is to you. And as you waver between the past and the future, so do I. In my short time since birth, I have watched and listened and pondered all that I have seen and heard. Things once accepted as indisputable don't seem so certain anymore, do they?"

Alena's first impulse was to deny she knew what he was talking about. But then she remembered how close their psychic link had always been. Paddy but put into words what she was feeling. "Nay." She sighed. "They certainly don't. But I must work my problems out in my own time and way."

"Some things, 'tis true, cannot be rushed. Especially the quandaries of the heart."

Leaving her to contemplate his words, Paddy turned and ambled back the way he'd come. Irritation rose in Alena. Was he, too, seeking to influence her now by playing the matchmaker? He'd liked Galen from the start, thought they were meant for each other. 'Twas but Galen's knowledge and authority over the dragons, she told herself. That was all 'twas. Paddy was still young and inexperienced in the ways of men.

'Twould never work, Alena thought. Not between her and Galen. Though she refused to accept Idara's assessment of Galen's inherent immorality solely because he was a sorcerer, she also wasn't going to be swayed by Paddy's softhearted urgings, either. She'd make up her own mind, curse them all, *and* in her own good time. She slammed her fist hard against the house.

"You seem a tad out of sorts this morn," Galen's voice intruded into her frustrated thoughts, "to treat your poor hand so badly."

She wheeled around, her face gone white.

Galen stared down at her, startled by her reaction. Finally, he reached out, took her chin in his hand, and lifted her face to his. "Alena, what's wrong? I've never seen you react to me like this before."

A sudden thought assailed him. Idara. The two women had had time to talk last night after he fell asleep. What had she said to Alena? Curse his foolishness in taking that sleeping potion!

"Naught." Alena wrenched her face away. "Naught is wrong with me. You just surprised me, that's all."

The averting of her gaze and the step she took back belied her words. A cold determination rose in Galen. He'd not lose her to the witch woman's lies. He'd force her to talk to him, to work things through between them, if 'twas the last thing he did!

"Come." Galen stepped forward and took her by the arm. She froze. Her glance narrowed. "Please, Alena," he said, softening his command to a request. "I need to speak with you. Please come away from the house so we may talk in privacy."

"You mean, away from Idara, don't you?"

He released her. "Aye. Is that so bad? After what we've been through together and may well go through in the next few days, don't I deserve an equal chance to tell my side. Before," he added grimly, "Idara turns you against me."

Alena's hands fisted at her sides. "There you go again, Galen Radbourne, treating me as if I'm some mindless child who lacks the sense to see things clearly and make her own decisions. But hear me and hear me well—neither you nor Idara will make me think or do what I don't want to. No one has ever been able to accomplish that before, and I'm certainly not ready to let anyone begin now."

"Alena, I meant no such—"

"Aye, you did, Galen," she fiercely cut him off. "From Idara, I can mayhap understand. She doesn't know me well. But from you? Do you know how much that hurts? Do you?"

"Fine," he growled, the heat rising in his face. "I'm sorry. I just don't want to lose you . . ." As the implications of what he'd just said flooded him, Galen's voice faded. He shoved a hand roughly through his hair. "By the Mother, Alena, I didn't mean it to come out quite . . . that way."

She stared up at him for a long moment, dumbfounded. Then, a slow smile spread across her face. "And if you did—mean it the way you said it—where's the harm in that? If 'tis truly what you feel?"

As if he found sudden interest in the pine trees overhead, his glance skittered away. A muscle worked furiously in his jaw.

"Galen," Alena prodded. "Will you please answer me? Truthfully, I mean?"

"And what would you have me say?" he demanded hoarsely, swinging back to her. "That I care for you, Alena? That I want to lie with you again? But, even more important, that I want you to care for me as much as I care for you? And t-that . . ."

His voice broke and he wheeled about so she wouldn't see the sudden tears that sprang to his eyes. "And that," he forced himself to continue in a more controlled tone, "that I yearn for a life together—a *normal* life—after all this is done."

"Aye," she said softly, coming up behind him to place her hand on his shoulder, "if that's what you truly feel. Do you think I'd make light of it, of your honest feelings? Do you imagine me some monster?"

"*I'm* the monster, Alena." Galen shrugged off her hand and turned. "Ah, what does it matter anyway?" He stared down at her. A soft, wondering smile trembled on her lips. He bit back a savage curse. If she dared pity him . . .

"You and I both know the truth of it," Galen forced himself to go on. "All you care about is rescuing Renard and I'm well aware I can never again have a normal relationship with a woman. So, let's just drop this subject while we both still retain some shred of our pride and dignity."

"And run away from the truth, from our feelings for each other?" Ever so gently, she reached up and stroked his bearded cheek. "Nay, I say instead, let's summon the courage to speak freely this day. Of our doubts, our fears, our deepest needs. And of plans made that now must mayhap change."

He captured her hand. Lowering it, Galen held it at her side. "But the wanting, especially in my case, doesn't justify the risk. I almost killed myself—tried to, but Dorian and my father wouldn't let me—when I realized what I'd done to Lydia. Do you think I could survive this time if I was also responsible for killing you? Let it be, Alena." He sighed. "I made a grave error in even bringing this up."

"Nay, you didn't," she whispered achingly, "but 'tis evident the time is not yet right for you to discuss this further. 'Twill be soon, though, Galen. It *has* to be."

"Mayhap." He released her hand and stepped back. A wan, sheepish little smile twisted his lips. "I have yet more to confess."

She smiled in return. "Indeed?"

His smile faded. Though the admission cost him dearly, Galen forced himself to go on. "That night in Margate . . . when we were almost taken prisoner. I almost used that sword you bought me. But, at the last moment, I hesitated, torn between the morality of taking lives and the need to protect you. I hesitated too long but, though 'twas too late and I was overrun, I made my decision."

"And that was?" she softly prodded.

"I would fight for you, no matter the cost, if ever you need me again. I would use my magic to kill, if your life was in danger." He paused, so at odds within himself even now it nearly tore his heart asunder. But 'twas right to stand up for those he loved. To honor Lydia's memory in some bold, forceful manner rather than continue passively to mourn her and turn from life and living in the process. Lydia, so vibrant, so full of life, would've wanted it that way.

"And does that willingness to protect me extend to protecting me from your brother?" Alena's gaze, wide and full of anticipation, locked with his. "Will you use your magic even against him if need be?"

"I will do what is right, what is needed, and no more. But, to the best of my ability, to the very sacrifice of my life, I won't let anything happen to you. We'll leave Castle Radbourne alive and with Renard, or not at all."

"And what will you do then?" Alena asked. "You don't wish to stay in your home? Afterward, I mean?"

Galen considered her question for a moment. "I don't know, Alena. 'Twill depend on what happens, on how I feel about things." He grinned. "Too much has happened too fast. I need time to think on it all."

A mischievous twinkle danced in her eyes. "In the meanwhile, would you now be interested in learning a bit about swordplay? You did say you would fight for me, didn't you?"

He frowned. "Well, I had my magic more in mind when I said that . . ." Galen cocked his head consideringly. "I suppose it couldn't hurt to learn a bit about the sword. In case I ever needed it again at night, if for naught else."

"Exactly." She took him by the arm and tugged. "Come along. The day is still young. We can easily get three or four good hours of lessons in."

Galen dug in his heels, suddenly apprehensive of taking sword in hand. "No promises, Alena. I make no promises I'll be adept at this."

She gave an airy wave of her hand and tugged again. "I've taught all sorts of men. Have no fear, Galen Radbourne.

You'll be thrusting and stabbing with the best of them when I'm done with you."

"I can hardly wait," he muttered under his breath, then followed where she led.

After the evening meal, Idara brewed them all a cup of herbal tea and sat down opposite Galen and Alena. When he shifted slightly in his chair, her mouth quirked wryly at Galen's pained expression. "Ye're not much of a swordsman, either, are ye?"

"Nay," he equably agreed. "Until now, I never dreamed of being challenged like Alena has challenged me in the course of a few weeks."

"Not everyone has to be a warrior," Alena said, noting the derisive twist to one corner of the witch woman's mouth. "Besides being a sorcerer, Galen's a fine craftsman, cook, and farmer. If you could only have seen the house he built on Cadvallan and the—" She stopped short, as two pairs of eyes leveled on her, Galen's mildly amused, Idara's puzzled and overlaid with a rising concern.

"I'm flattered you thought me so talented," he began carefully, "considering my decided lack of warrior's skills."

"Well, you are," Alena muttered, flushing crimson. "It just took me a while to realize that."

" 'Twill make little difference, one way or another, once ye reach Castle Radbourne," Idara said. "Yer magic must surely suffer for want of practice these past fifteen years. Ye can't possibly hope to equal yer brother in powers."

Galen shrugged. "Mayhap not. But, if things go as I hope, there won't be any need for magic."

"Indeed? And do ye intend to ride in and find a grand welcome awaiting ye?" The old woman cackled. "Ye're a dreamer if ye do—and 'twill be the death of ye in the bargain."

He smiled thinly. "One less sorcerer for you to worry over then."

Idara shot him a seething glance. "Aye, and if 'twere only yer life at stake, 'twould worry me little. But ye take Alena with ye."

"I never intended to send Galen in to rescue Renard alone." Calmly, Alena met the old woman's gaze. "I don't hide away and let others do my work."

"Then take the dragon with ye, for pity's sake!" Idara cried. "Together, yer combined magic might be strong enough to thwart Dorian Radbourne."

Alena turned to Galen. "What do you think of that idea?"

He considered it briefly, then shook his head. "Nay, Dorian would see it as a threat. 'Twould set the wrong tone. We should go in peace, and a sorcerer wouldn't view a dragon in his castle as a peaceful act."

"And how long do ye think 'twill take for him to discern that Alena is a *galiene*, if he doesn't already know it?" Idara indignantly demanded. "Ye risk her life, I tell ye, if ye take her in that den of evil without her dragon!"

"Nonetheless, that is how 'twill be." Galen looked at Alena. "If you agree, of course."

"It seems the wisest, even if not the safest, course." Alena leaned across the table and took up one of the old woman's bony, gnarled hands. "Think about it, Idara, without the veneer of emotion laid from past injustices and pains."

The certainty that, though she had entered this quest solely to save Renard, she was now inexorably being drawn into the conflict between the dragons and sorcerers filled Alena with a strange determination. " 'Tis past time this terrible feud end. So long as one side continues to feel threatened by the other, 'twill never be over. 'Tis also past time for those of courage to step forward and risk all, be it their very lives, to save Wyndymyll."

"Ye'll never convince Dorian Radbourne of that," Idara hissed. "Remember my words, just before he kills ye."

"I'm no fool. I've seen the blackness of Dorian's soul. But I also trust that Galen's soul is strong and good, and that he won't let us fail." She smiled at Galen. The look he sent her set her heart to pounding. "I tell you true, Idara. I've never been so certain of anything in my whole life."

"Then I suggest ye fortify his powers in every way ye can. And yers, as well, through the act of mating with him." Idara pulled away from Alena. " 'Twill be yer only chance in the confrontation to come." With a deep sigh, she rose from the table. " 'Tis late and teaching ye this day has wearied me. The morrow will require yet more of yer instruction if I'm to prepare ye for what's to come."

"There's no time left, Idara," Alena gently contradicted. "We leave on the morrow."

Horror filled the old woman's eyes. "Nay, 'tis too soon. And the Night of the—" She stopped short, sending Galen a nervous glance.

"I cannot wait for that. 'Twill do naught for Renard or increase the powers I need to rescue him." Alena shoved back her chair and stood. "I won't squander another day in getting to him. 'Tisn't right that I lollygag about, while he languishes in some dank, filthy dungeon."

"But 'tis only a week away," the witch woman protested. "If ye but wait a week more . . ." Her voice faded. She motioned impatiently toward Alena. "Come, we need to speak privately."

"Nay." Alena firmly shook her head. "I told you before, Renard comes first, not some dubious ceremony to drive out evil. Afterward . . . well, I'm not sure what I'll do afterward."

"Then I must journey with ye, child. I cannot stand by and

await the outcome of yer battle with Dorian Radbourne. I must be there, as well."

"And do you plan on riding into Castle Radbourne with us?" Galen challenged. "Of using your feeble magic against my brother?"

"Galen!" Alena wheeled about to stare down at him, shocked at his bluntness. "You've no cause to insult Idara like that."

He cocked his head to gaze up at her. "I meant no insult. I but spoke the truth. Idara knows her magic isn't what it used to be when she was bonded to a dragon."

The witch woman gave a low hiss of surprise. "How did ye—" She shot Alena a furious look. "Why did ye tell him? I warned ye not to!"

"She didn't tell me, Idara," Galen calmly interrupted her. " 'Twas simple to discern from all you've said. I'm no fool. I'm also not your enemy. You're in no danger from me."

"Aye, mayhap not now, but what will happen when ye return to yer home, reunite with yer beloved brother?"

Galen's mouth went tight and a bleak haunted look flared in the depths of his eyes. "I don't know, Idara. Does any of us truly know what they'll do, how they'll react, until they're tested. And, as terrifying as 'tis to consider," he said, his gaze swinging to meet Alena's, "my test may well be yet to come. I only hope that I am equal to the trust and confidence placed in me."

"And if ye're not, Galen Radbourne? What then?"

"Then we all die, I fear, and with our deaths die the last hope for the dragons—and the land."

CHAPTER FOURTEEN

"Your hand does poorly," Galen said the next morning as he cleansed her wound, applied yet another generous slathering of marigold ointment, and began to rebandage it. "You tore it open yet again yesterday during our sword practice."

"Aye," Alena muttered, her voice as tight as her body as she viewed the unhealed flesh of her right hand. "That I did. But I cannot spare further time for the cursed wound to mend. Too much is at stake here and the dangers too great constantly to consider my hand."

"Alena, you could well lose the use of it if you persist—"

"Don't you think I know that, Galen?" she cried, frustration threading her voice. She rolled her eyes to the ceiling of the little house. "All I need is just a few more days. Then I can let my hand be for a time to heal."

"It may well be too late by then, if it isn't already."

"Then heal it yourself, Galen, and be done with it!" she cried, inexplicably hurt he hadn't offered on his own to do so.

He made a great show of wrapping her hand. "I can't, Alena. My magic is rapidly waning. We'll be at Castle Radbourne in two days and I need to conserve what I have left. Afterward, though . . ."

"Aye, afterward," she whispered, eyeing him closely.

Galen glanced up. In his eyes, though he struggled to hide it, burned his true desire. More than anything, he wanted to heal her. Wanted to, but didn't dare. A sudden realization filled Alena. He'd said his magic was waning. He'd lied. His magic was gone.

"Galen, I—"

He cut her off before she could put words to the truth, "We've gone over this before, and I grow weary of discussing it," he rasped, tying off the bandage and climbing to his feet. "Risking your life in another mating isn't worth the healing of your hand right now. 'Tis hard-hearted, but I must conserve what powers I still have. And that's exactly what I intend to do."

"Then, so be it!" she snapped, at the end of her patience. Curse his stubborn hide! If he thought to shut her out, he thought wrong. She glared up at him, flinging the only barb she could think of at him. "Whatever it takes, 'tis worth the price of Renard's life!"

One corner of his mouth pulled into a slight, sad smile. "I grow more and more eager to meet your Renard. He seems to be quite a man."

"He is," she said pensively, the memories of their years together flooding her anew. "Loyal, brave, with the driest, most entertaining sense of humor. And one of the finest warriors in the realm, too. We were war chiefs together for the famed mercenary leader, Hawkwind."

"I can't recall ever hearing of him."

Alena chuckled. "That would've been difficult, I'd wager, hidden away on Cadvallan as you were."

"Aye." Galen leaned down and picked up his medicinal supplies. "I missed a lot in those fifteen years of my exile."

"Then you don't resent my efforts to call you away from Cadvallan so much now?" Though she shouldn't have asked it, Alena wanted to know that, whatever happened, she hadn't ruined Galen's life. That some good would come of it all.

He studied her in thoughtful silence. "You called me from

my safe, if insignificant life, a life I'd come to accept with all its limitations. I could've gone on to my dying day thinking I'd found a purpose there—and working with the dragons *was* worthwhile—while all along in the world our kind continued to slowly destroy each other. I was a naive fool to think I could make any real impact on Cadvallan, when the true battle lay waiting me in Wyndymyll. But do I resent you?"

Galen stroked his chin. "A small part of me still does, especially when I think of what lies ahead. I'm afraid, Alena. And I don't know if I'll be equal to the task."

She laid her bandaged hand on his. "None of us does, neither you, nor I, nor Paddy. The only ones who seem sure of themselves and what must be done are Idara and Dorian. And I don't like what either of them wants to do."

"The choices are uncertain, as are the consequences, for those like us." Galen paused, chewing his lip in consideration. "I'll tell you true, Alena. I fervently pray that Dorian can be brought to see our way of things. If I can't win over my own brother . . ."

"You lay too great a burden on yourself, and too great a confidence in Dorian that he wants to change or is even capable of it."

"Nonetheless," he firmly stated, "that is my hope—and plan. If I fail, I fail not only my brother and myself, but all of our kind. 'Twill mean there is something so innate, yet intrinsically evil in sorcerers that none of us can overcome it. If I fail, I also jeopardize any hope of ever finding some way back to a normal life."

"You place unreasonable expectations on this," Alena muttered uneasily. "You set yourself up for failure, even if, in the end, Dorian is defeated. Things are never so simple as you wish to make them. Convincing Dorian of the error of his ways isn't enough to solve this age-old problem between the sorcerers and dragons. It goes far deeper than the power-hungry machinations of just one man."

"Aye, that it does." Galen replaced his supplies in one of the leather packs. "But 'tis a start." He fastened the pack closed, slung it over his shoulder, and rose. "The morn draws on. 'Tis past time we depart."

Alena climbed to her feet. "Aye, you're right. Little more can be accomplished here. The challenges lie ahead."

She shot Galen a wry glance, then, with her left hand, picked up the other pack. Heading outside, Alena found Paddy waiting, his eyes bright with excitement.

"Ah, my lady, 'tis a fine morn for an adventure, wouldn't you say?" As he spoke, the young dragon danced around, barely avoiding tripping over his own tail and causing the horses tethered nearby great consternation. They snorted, rolled their eyes, and sidled away as he leaped and cavorted about.

Alena's mouth quirked. "Aye, I suppose so, Paddy, but the day's journey is long and, if I were you, I'd conserve some of that energy. You'll need it by nightfall."

Paddy halted, a crestfallen look stealing across his face. "My pardon, my lady. I was just so excited—"

"I know, Paddy," Alena hastened to soothe his dragon-sensitive feelings. "I understand."

The dragon looked appropriately mollified and fell quietly into place beside the bay mare and gray gelding. Galen chuckled softly, coming up beside her. Alena turned. "Pray, what's so funny, Radbourne?"

"Naught. I was but amused how swiftly your attitude toward Paddy has changed in the past weeks. I recall that 'twasn't so long ago that you saw him as naught more than an irritating nuisance. And now . . ."

"And now what?" Alena demanded, scowling slightly at

the possibility of Galen laughing at her.

"Now," he smilingly explained, "you treat his feelings with great care. You worry over his health and comfort. You love him, don't you, Alena?"

Her face flushed crimson. "He's but an animal, Galen. I but care for him like I would any . . ." Her voice faded. Before she even finished the sentence, Alena knew she was lying as much to herself as to Galen. "Aye," she softly said, watching as Paddy playfully butted heads with Galen's gelding, "I suppose I *do* love him.

" 'Tis strange," she murmured, turning back to the big sorcerer, "how much has changed in such a short time. I never thought to care so much for a dragon, or to wish for . . ."

She exhaled a deep breath and forced a bright smile. The gentle question in Galen's eyes nearly shattered her resolve not to reveal her true feelings for him, but just then Idara hobbled over, leading her mule behind her. Grateful for an excuse to break eye contact with Galen, Alena wheeled about and strode over to the old woman.

"Packed and ready to go, are you?" she asked Idara with a forced brightness.

"Aye," the witch woman grumbled. "My old friend Rawley promised to look in on my animals, and all else is prepared. But I tell ye true, 'tis a foolish, hopeless quest ye embark on. If only ye could wait until after the Night of the Dark Moon, everything would be so very simple then."

"But I cannot and won't," Alena gently countered. "Do you think Dorian Radbourne would stand by and allow us to perform the ceremony, at any rate? I suspect he knows what I am by now. He certainly knows of Paddy, if Galen's suspicions as to Paddy's assailant's true allegiance are correct. And the attack by the villagers of that magical town of

Margate . . . nay." She firmly shook her head. "The longer we linger, the more time Dorian has to fashion some plan to thwart us."

"Have it yer way then." Idara dropped her mule's reins. "Would ye give a leg up to an old woman?"

Alena grinned. "Aye, that I would." Slipping around to the animal's side, she helped Idara onto her mule, then handed up the reins.

Her own mare was swiftly mounted. Galen soon followed. Then, after a quick survey to assure herself that all was in order, Alena urged her horse forward. The last leg of the journey—wherever it might lead—had begun.

They rode hard that day and made camp in a circle of monoliths that night. Idara said the location was perfect, for within the sacred ring of standing stones no evil would befall them. Though Alena expressed her doubts by suggesting they still break up the night into three equal watches, Galen, for once, was in accord with Idara. They were safe. The magic of the ancients protected all within their circle.

The next day dawned bright and clear, if briskly windy. As they rode along, excitement vibrated through Alena. The terrain, bleak though it increasingly became, possessed a familiarity that plucked at memories of a time not long past.

'Twas here, Alena recalled as they passed a small grove of linden trees and the blackened remains of a campfire, that she and Renard had made their night camp for the last time. 'Twas here, she thought several hours later, that they halted beside an ice-cold torrent of water to eat their last meal together. 'Twas the same route she'd taken through the frigid, winter-barren land when she'd fled Dorian's pursuit. The memories then, however, hadn't been as pleasant.

Yet the further she rode and the closer they drew to

Radbourne lands, the more pensive Alena became. What had become of Renard? she endlessly fretted. Indeed, did he still even live? And what would happen to her and Galen, before all this was over?

Gingerly, she flexed her right hand. 'Twas stiff and pained her greatly. Galen had been right. She could well lose the use of it, at least as far as wielding a sword was concerned. If she survived this encounter with Dorian Radbourne and rescued Renard, her days as a mercenary warrior were still most likely numbered. What would she do with her life then?

Though Galen feared the more savage aspects of his magic and what it might do to her, Alena knew now he cared for her—mayhap even loved her. She marveled how quickly she had come to know him, respect him for the man he was, even as different as he was from all the men she'd been raised with and fought beside. There was such goodness, such kindness and patience in him, and he had been such a wonderful, yet passionate lover.

For the first time in her life since Hawkwind, Alena wanted a man for more than just his physical attributes, for more than just how well he could please her in bed, before casting him aside and moving on. She wanted to spend long winter nights in his snug little cottage with him, dozing before the fire while he whittled away at some new project. She wanted to lie in his strong arms, feel his mouth slant hard and hungry over hers, bask in the warmth of his big, powerfully built body. And, she wanted to stand on that windswept promontory that jutted out into Cadvallan's sea someday, and watch with Galen as the dragons once more flew high overhead in that awesomely magnificent mating flight.

"Ye dream too much and too hungrily, child," Idara's voice intruded suddenly on Alena's wistful reverie. " 'Tisn't wise, leastwise not about what could have been with yer sorcerer. Like all of his kind, he'll betray ye in the end."

Alena jerked around, her hands clenching, knuckle-white, about her reins. Galen rode a short distance behind but the way the wind was blowing, 'twas unlikely he could make out much of their conversation. "You interfere where you've no right, Idara," she muttered. "What is between Galen and myself is none of your concern."

"Ye stand to risk it all because of yer feelings for this man." The witch woman nudged her mule to hasten its pace and keep up with Alena's swift-moving mare. "All, child. The dragons, the few of us that remain, the land and the people."

"And what would you have me do then?" Alena demanded tautly. "Summon Paddy's power to join with mine and kill Galen? Is that what you want?"

Idara shot Galen a look over her shoulder. "Nay. He is still of use for a time more. Yer bonding with the young dragon has progressed well, but 'twill still take a time to mature to its fullest. We'll reach the Boar's Tusk Inn by sunset. I want ye to take a private room with the sorcerer and seduce him this night. Even one more night of coupling will strengthen yer powers immeasurably."

Alena couldn't quite help a small laugh. "You speak bluntly for an old woman. And if I mayhap have no further wish to lie with Galen? What then, Idara?"

"I may be an old woman, but I've yet to become blind and stupid," Idara snapped. "Ye want him and he wants ye. Why not give him what he wants and, in the giving, gain what ye so desperately need yerself?"

Why not indeed? Alena thought. 'Twould strengthen her magic but, even more importantly, 'twould replenish Galen's rapidly fading powers. Though he seemed determined she not discern it, Alena knew Galen was once more weakening magically. 'Twas surprising, this certainty, but she supposed it had something to do with their mating bond. Already, the special powers he'd gained through her that night on Cadvallan were gone. Gone, just when he needed them most, when they were to go up against Dorian on the morrow.

But Idara didn't need ever to know that. Let the old woman think, instead, that she laid with Galen this night for the benefit of her own magic. Nay, Idara would be no problem to convince. 'Twas Galen who worried her.

"Your words have merit. However, I am not so skilled at seduction as some women might be," Alena carefully continued. "Though I am loathe to ensorcel Galen this night, have you some simple spells of love magic I might use to—shall we say—set the mood? For all his desire for me, he can be a most difficult lover."

"Aye." Idara cackled gleefully. "That I do, child. But know, as well, I cannot use my magic to force even one such as he. But I hoped ye would consider my words in time, so I made ye a lover's sachet of dried rose petals, a pinch of catnip, half a handful of yarrow and a touch of mint, coltsfoot, strawberry leaves, ground orris root, tansy, and a bit of vervain. Tonight, I'll divide it into three parts. The first part ye must take with ye when ye go outside this eve—naked, mind ye—and throw it up to the moon and ask that love be sent to ye."

"Idara," Alena quickly interjected. "I've no intention of frolicking outside naked before the moon near such a public place as an inn."

"Well, then stand in the window of yer room after moon rise and toss it out yer window toward the moon. 'Tis the ceremony that counts."

"Fine," Alena muttered. "I suppose I could do that, though even that makes me feel the fool."

"Ye asked me for a love spell," the old woman hissed. "If

ye wish it to work properly, ye must follow the rituals that accompany it. If ye don't, 'tisn't magic."

"Get on with it then." Alena made an impatient movement with her hand. "What are the other two parts to this spell?"

Idara met her gaze with a jaundiced eye. "The second part of the sachet ye must scatter around the room where ye'll be coupling. And the third part, ye must wear on yer body in a pink cloth I'll sew up for ye. And, of course, ye must bathe . . ."

The next hour or so passed in a feminine sort of scheming, as Idara explained all the intricacies of love magic to Alena. And Alena, well aware of Galen's reluctance ever to mate with her again and determined to save him from his own foolish pride and overblown protectiveness, was as avid a student as there ever was.

Just outside the village of Gathersby and the Boar's Tusk Inn, Alena had called a halt to their journey. Galen had pulled up beside her, a questioning look in his eyes.

"What now, Alena? Having second thoughts about taking our rest so near Castle Radbourne, are you?"

She glanced back at where Idara had halted her mule. The old woman was well out of earshot. "Aye, I am. But since 'twill soon be night, there's no sense in traveling on to visit your brother. Your powers will be gone and, though Dorian's will, too, he has the considerable might of an armed fortress to compensate. We, on the other hand . . ." She grinned wryly. "Suffice it to say, though your swordsmanship has improved greatly, we are still too small a force to best a castle full of soldiers."

"Aye, that we are," Galen admitted. "Then why the stop, if you still wish to bed down in Gathersby?"

Once more, Alena's gaze strayed, this time to Paddy,

halted ahead in the trees to the right of the road. He snuffled and dug through the fallen leaves, rooting for delectable fungi and grubs. His huge tail swung to and fro, slapping the nearby trees with enough force to make the newly budded leaves shimmer and shake. She suppressed a chuckle. He was such a lovable young creature, for all his awkwardness and lack of awareness of the might of his big body.

"We need to do something with Paddy for the night," she said, indicating the dragon. "After Jarvis's attack, I'll not risk him staying out in the forest alone, especially so close now to your brother. You need to cast another spell of invisibility so we can take him to town with us."

"Nay." A set, implacable look stole across Galen's face. He shook his head. "I told you before. I must conserve my magic for what lies ahead. Do you think I spoke lightly when I refused to heal your hand, or that I cared so little for your healing?"

"Galen, we've gone through this before." In spite of her best efforts to contain it, an edge of irritation crept into Alena's voice. "You and I can mate and—"

"And *I* told you before," he growled, his hands clenching in his reins, "I refuse to risk your life. There's no need, at any rate, if you allow me to use my magic as I see fit."

"Your magic—at least what you gained from me—is gone, and you know it!" Though she knew this wasn't the time nor place for this accusation, Alena blurted it out, nonetheless. Thankfully, Idara was now engrossed in digging through a pack tied to the back of her saddle and appeared oblivious to their conversation. "That's the real reason you pretend to conserve your magic rather than use it."

"Are you calling me a liar?" Galen's expression darkened like some thundercloud.

"I'm calling you a man who, because of some misguided

sense of self-sacrifice, will end up killing us both in the bargain."

"Think what you want," he muttered. " 'Twon't change my mind."

She eyed Galen with narrowed gaze, so frustrated with him she wanted to knock him off his horse. "Nay, that much is certain. I've learned that about you if naught else. But what do you suggest we do with Paddy in the meanwhile?"

He considered that for a moment. "Mayhap Idara could cast another circle of protection, around him this time."

"Aye, 'tis possible," Alena admitted grudgingly. "But this issue between us isn't over, Galen Radbourne. Mark my words on that."

"I'll mark them, for what 'tis worth. And, in another day, 'twon't make much difference—one way or another." He indicated Idara with a jerk of his head. "Now, best you get on with it. If we're to leave Paddy here, he needs that spell of protection."

She shot him a seething glance, then wheeled her mare about and rode back to the old witch woman. The circle of protection was soon laid and they were once more on their way.

Galen's foul mood, however, lasted all the way into the inn. A plump, pink-checked older woman, a garish red and purple shawl wrapped about her shoulders, bustled over from behind the scarred oak counter that served as a desk. Even her brightest smile, however, couldn't seem to ease Galen's scowling demeanor.

"I'm Twyla, the innkeeper's wife. What can I do for ye?" the woman asked. "Do ye wish a room for the night?"

He glanced at Alena and Idara. "We need *two* rooms for the night. One for myself, and one for the ladies."

Alena cast Idara a startled look. The witch woman smiled and put a finger to her lips in a silencing gesture. Alena bit back her protest and nodded.

"We do have two rooms left, but at separate ends of the hall upstairs." The innkeeper's wife cocked her head. "Will that be to yer liking?"

"Fine," Galen muttered. "That'll be fine. The price?"

"A crown for each room."

He slammed down two gold crowns, then stooped and picked up his two packs. "If you could show us our rooms? I'm tired and would like to wash up before I come down to your tavern." Galen looked back at Alena and Idara. "I assume you'd like to take supper in the tavern?"

"Aye," Alena replied. "But a short time to wash up sounds good to me, too."

They followed Twyla up a steep, narrow set of rickety stairs and down an equally narrow hall. She stopped at the room nearest the stairs. "Which of ye would like it?"

"Is there aught different about them?" Galen asked.

"Nay." Twyla unlocked the door and shoved it open. "Both have ample-size beds."

"Fine." He turned to Alena. "Why don't you and Idara take this room then?"

She nodded. "When would you like to meet for supper?"

"In an hour's time, if 'tis suitable to you."

"Aye, 'tis suitable."

Galen looked to Twyla. "My room next, if you please."

Alena watched his tall, broad-shouldered form disappear down the dimly lit hall, then turned back to Idara, motioning her in. Once the door was closed and locked behind them, the warrior woman rounded on Idara. "What am I supposed to do now? He refuses to talk with me and has made it more than evident he has no wish to bed me."

"There's still the sachet. And I know a spell to unlock doors. Ye can still get into his room anytime ye wish."

"Mayhap," Alena grumbled, "but I'm not so sure 'twill do any good once I get in. At least not in the mood Galen's in."

"Have no fear, child." Idara hobbled over and took her hand. "He wants ye still, no matter how hard he tries to fight it. And, sorcerer that he is, he's still no match for two determined *galienes*." She smiled up at Alena. "Now come, let's wash the grime from our hands and faces, then prepare the sachet. The night draws on, and we've work to do."

The tavern of the Boar's Tusk Inn was a clean, if somber place. Though the room was as crowded as any other tavern, the patrons were subdued, even nervous, as they talked in low voices and drank their ale. There was something amiss here, Alena thought, as she brought up the rear behind Galen and Idara. She wondered if it might have something to do with the close proximity to Castle Radbourne.

A meal of roast pork, potatoes, and carrots was served along with a pitcher of dark ale. Galen said little as he ate, content to drink deeply from his tankard and gaze about the room. Alena watched as well, and noted the lowered heads and voices, the careful glances to see who was lingering about before they next spoke to their table companions. These people were afraid. The more she watched, the more she decided she needed to know why.

" 'Tis a quiet tavern," she ventured, directing her gaze to the man sitting across from her at their table. "Are you always such a well-mannered lot?"

The man, a farmer if his threadbare clothes, sun bronzed skin, and work roughened, dirty nailed hands were any indication, eyed her over his mug of ale. "Ye're a stranger to these parts. Where are ye headed?"

Alena nodded and smiled genially, hoping 'twould encourage him to talk. "Aye, we're strangers, and just passing through."

"Then 'tis best if ye keep on passing through and ask no questions. 'Tisn't wise to ask too many questions in these parts."

"Indeed?" She paused to take a swallow of her own ale, aware that Galen, sitting beside her, had gone tense as he eavesdropped on their conversation. "Your warning seems a bit unfriendly, when all I did was make an observation on the people of this tavern."

"Norwin meant no harm," Twyla said, entering into the conversation as she halted at their table, yet another foaming pitcher of ale in her hand. "He has just learned the hard way to avoid any semblance of disloyalty to the mage of Castle Radbourne."

"And ye haven't?" Norwin countered bitterly. "Ye've lost that pretty daughter of yers to that monster. What more will it take to teach ye to hold yer tongue?"

The innkeeper's wife went pale. As she proceeded to refill the tankards on the table, her hands trembled. "He hasn't had her too long yet," she whispered. "Mayhap there's still hope—"

"There's no hope and ye know it, woman!" Norwin stood and, in his abruptness, knocked against the pitcher in Twyla's hand. Ale sloshed over the sides and dripped onto the table in large, frothy dollops. For the longest moment, no one spoke. Then Galen broke the silence.

"You speak as if Dorian Radbourne took this girl with dishonorable intent." He fixed a dark gaze on Twyla. "Is that true?"

The woman stared back, her eyes filling with tears, and said nothing.

"Aye," Norwin snarled, finally answering for her, " 'tis true enough. And the lass wasn't the first of the maids that monster has taken. 'Tis a gross abuse of his noble prerogative as lord of these lands, yet the saddest part of all is that he never returns them."

"Then what does he do with the maids?" Unease twined about Galen's heart. "He surely doesn't keep collecting women to fill his castle."

Norwin gave a harsh laugh. " 'Tisn't obvious? He kills them when he tires of them."

Galen stiffened. "I find that difficult to believe."

"Believe what ye want, stranger." Norwin leaned forward on the table, his face reddening in anger. "Ye haven't lived here these fifteen years past, and seen the horror and destruction the man has wrought. And these ten years past, since his lord father died, have been the worst of all. But why should ye believe us, why should ye care? 'Tis naught to ye, one way or another." He stopped short, dragged in an unsteady breath and straightened. "Are ye happy now? Have ye heard enough?"

"Aye, I've heard enough." Galen watched Norwin turn and walk away, saw the strained heartsick look on Twyla's face. He'd indeed heard enough and *had* enough.

Galen stood, the dark, smoke-filled room, rife with the odors of food and unwashed bodies, suddenly too much for him. He felt sick, smothered, and strangely disoriented. He had to get away to put all he'd heard into some sort of perspective. He had to. He'd meet his brother on the morrow. And the doubts and fears Galen had harbored for the past weeks had just been slammed into a reality he wasn't so sure he knew how to handle.

"I'm weary." He glanced down at Alena. "I bid you good night."

"Galen, wait." Alena made a move to climb to her feet, when Idara clasped her arm to halt her. Galen looked from Alena to the witch woman, his mouth twisting. Then, without another word, he turned and strode across the tavern.

"Let him go, child," the old woman said. "He needs a time to mull all this over. He's not ready for ye just yet."

With a sigh, Alena sunk back onto the bench. "Aye, 'twas evident that Twyla's and Norwin's words upset him. But mayhap that is for the best. 'Tis past time he realized once and for all what manner of man we're up against."

"Aye, not that I've much hope 'twill make any difference in the end." Idara rose. "Come, child," she said, smiling down at Alena. "We've work to do to prepare for the night to come."

To fortify her for the task ahead, the warrior woman took one last swallow of her ale, then stood. Silently, she followed Idara out of the tavern and up the stairs to their room, her mind churning. Once inside, she turned to the old woman.

"Idara," Alena began, the concerns that had nibbled at her all evening since they first spoke of casting a love spell over Galen now rushing to the forefront.

The old woman glanced up from the packets of sachet she had taken and begun laying out on the bed. "Aye, child?"

"I know this will sound strange, especially since I was the one who first broached the subject, but I don't feel comfortable using magic to force Galen to mate with me."

Slowly, the witch woman straightened. She riveted a piercing gaze on Alena. "Indeed? And why not? Yer need to fortify yer powers is more important than some passing concern over the right and wrong of it. He's a sorcerer, child. He matters not to us, save to use to our best advantage."

"Nay." Alena walked over to stand before her. " 'Tis part of the problem, the problem that has dragged us all—dragons and *galienes* and sorcerers alike—down to the depths we all are now mired in. Mistrust, unprincipled manipulation, a narrow-minded selfishness, that is what has gotten us to where we now are. And it must stop, Idara. Stop now, before 'tis too late!"

"Ye choose a fine time to get so righteous on me. And for such a paltry reason as whether or not to manipulate a sorcerer." Idara picked up one of the sachets and held it out to her. " 'Twill do no harm, child, and ye want to couple as much as he does. 'Twill only help the cause along."

"Aye, *'twill* do harm. The last and only time we mated we were under a spell of the Dragon Father. I won't let that happen again. Either we lie together of our own free wills, or . . . or we won't lie together at all, no matter the ultimate consequences. I refuse to be used or use another again!"

With a strength and vehemence surprising for a woman of her age, Idara flung the sachet at Alena. "Then die, both ye and yer reluctant lover. For 'twill surely happen if ye fail to strengthen yer powers before going up against Dorian Radbourne. And, with yer death, dies the last hope for us, and for that young dragon who follows ye so devotedly. Just remember that, when ye go to him this night. Just remember that, when he turns ye away!"

CHAPTER FIFTEEN

Flickering bits of light filled the ebony canopy of the heavens, familiar denizens of the night, predictable, comforting, heart-easing. Yet, this night of all nights, the stars mocked rather than soothed, reminding Galen yet again of all he risked—and stood to lose. His hands gripped the windowsill, his bare chest heaved, and a pain like none he'd ever before experienced lanced through him.

He didn't know what he thought, what he believed anymore. If the doubts themselves, stirred once more to life upon Alena's arrival on Cadvallan, hadn't been enough, the bitterly angry words of Norwin and the haunted, helpless look in Twyla's eyes had. He hadn't realized until this evening in the tavern how much stock he'd placed in being able to win over his brother, in Dorian's innate humanity. But now . . . now he feared that his brother was no longer the man he'd grown up with, thought he'd known—if he'd truly *ever* known the real man his brother was.

Memories of Dorian's pettiness, of his jealousy and sullen silences whenever Galen had received praise or recognition, of his undermining ways, rushed back. Yet the traits that he'd attributed in the past to immaturity seemed, in his brother as a grown man, to have evolved into a self-centered, heartless manipulation of others. And now, Galen didn't know what to do, or how to approach a man—his brother—who had become a stranger.

He'd been a fool, imagining he could stride into his home, confront Dorian with the error of his ways, and convince him to change. Yet something in Galen refused to accept the fact that his twin was as fundamentally evil as his subjects seemed to think he was. He just *couldn't* accept that. If he did, 'twould be an all-out battle between them. Even, the Mother forbid, a battle to the death.

To kill his brother or, in not doing so, mayhap allow the woman he loved to die. 'Twas a terrible choice, a bitter choice, and Galen feared he might lose no matter which way he turned. *If* he was even capable of choosing before 'twas too late.

A chill breeze gusted in through the open window brushing his bare chest with frigid fingers of air. Abruptly jerked from his morose reverie, Galen shivered, then closed the window and stepped back. He was weary to the marrow of his bones. He couldn't think straight anymore. And naught would be served by belaboring what he couldn't change. On the morrow, he would just have to face whatever came and do the—

A firm knock sounded at the door. Galen froze, knowing, before he even heard her voice, who his nocturnal visitor was.

"Galen," Alena called softly. "Open the door."

Fleetingly, he considered pretending he was asleep, but knew she'd not long be swayed by his lack of response. Sooner or later, he'd have to talk to her and settle the one matter still between them. It might as well be now.

Striding over to the door, Galen unlocked it and pulled it open. Alena stood there, her pale hair cascading about her shoulders, her luminous eyes wide and uncertain. He stared down at her for the longest time, caught up in the sight and scent of her. A knot formed in his chest, swelling to a throbbing mass as it rose to his throat. He needed to speak, wanted to speak, but suddenly feared he couldn't.

She said the words for him. "May I please come in?"

He nodded and stepped aside. Alena walked past him and into the room, coming to a stop near the window. Galen closed and locked the door, then turned to face her.

"Well, Alena," he forced himself to ask, "is it time, then? Is this to be the final battle between us?"

"I wish no battle, Galen," she said. "The true battle is on the morrow. Tonight is better spent fortifying our powers, bolstering our defenses. The enemy is before us."

"You wish to force me to do what I do not wish. That makes you my enemy."

"I wish to *save* you, not harm you. That isn't the work of an enemy." Alena stepped closer. "I wish for you to hold me, kiss me. How can there be any danger in that?"

He put out a hand. "Nay, Alena. You know the danger as much as I if we hold each other and kiss. And I'll not be used, however pleasurably it might be, to do what I know is wrong."

She took another step closer. "And how is it wrong? You will not harm me, Galen. I know it. Did you kill Lydia the first or second time you lay with her?"

"Nay," he said thoughtfully. "But Dorian said 'twas a gradual draining of her life force that finally killed her. We hadn't coupled in days before I was to meet her in our secret hiding place, only to find her already dead."

"And you took your brother's word on it all?" Alena gave a disparaging laugh. "Mayhap 'twas all lies to begin with."

"I'm not and never have been so big a fool as to believe all that my brother said," Galen said tautly, stung by her words.

"I beg pardon if I offended you," Alena made haste to say. "I just suspect Dorian's hand in this somewhere."

"Aye, I've thought long and hard on that, as well." Galen shoved a hand raggedly through his hair. "And I mean to confront him on that and more, when I see him on the morrow."

"You may not like the answers, Galen."

He shot her an irritated glance. "Don't you think I know that?"

"What will you do if you anger him, if he turns on you?" She moved yet closer. "What if he tries to prevent me from rescuing Renard?"

"I won't let him harm you, Alena." His chin lifted and he fixed her with a resolute stare. "That hasn't changed and never will."

"Then you must mate with me again, Galen. This very night, or you won't possess the powers necessary to protect me."

She drew up before him, so close he could feel her warmth, inhale her clean, uniquely feminine fragrance. In spite of himself, Galen's heart began a heavy thudding. A frisson of excitement coursed through him. He reached out, grasped her arms, holding her from him.

"Alena," he warned huskily, "don't—"

"You *must* make a choice, Galen," she persisted, her tone urgent, yet strangely soothing and hypnotic. "Now, before there are no choices left to make. On the morrow, when you face Dorian, will be too late. I can do naught to help you then. Only tonight," she said, her hands rising to grasp his forearms and gently stroke them, "tonight in my arms, sheathed in my body, can I help you. And I *want* to, Galen. Not just so you'll best Dorian, not just to rescue Renard, not because in destroying Dorian I mayhap help to save the dragons, but because I desire you."

She inhaled an unsteady breath and forged on. "Aye, because I desire you but, even more than that, I love you."

He stared back at her in the moonlight, the blustering wind outside beating, like someone crazed, on the window, and thought he must have mistaken what she'd said. Finally, Galen forced words through his suddenly constricted throat.

"Forgive me, Alena, but what did you just say? I think I must have momentarily been dreaming."

"I said I love you, Galen. Is that such a hard thing to believe?"

"That you would love me?" He gave a shaky laugh. "Aye, as a matter of fact, 'tis. I thought you loved Renard, indeed, were lovers."

"Renard?" Alena frowned in puzzlement. "And when have I ever led you to believe Renard and I were lovers? Oh, aye, I love Renard as a friend—the very best friend I could ever hope to have—but I don't and never have loved him in . . . that way." She smiled shyly, almost girlishly. "Not the way I love you."

With a quick movement, Galen released her and took a step back. Confusion darkened his eyes. "It can't be. I'm not the man for you, Alena. You need a brave, strong warrior at your side, not some uncertain, broken-down sorcerer who barely has the courage to fight for himself, much less for you."

"Galen, Galen," Alena murmured, moving to stand close to him once more. Her hands lifted, slipped behind his neck, and she pressed her body to his. "Don't say such terrible things. You denigrate not only yourself, but me and my love for you. A warrior is but a man who faces whatever life puts in his way with courage and a good heart. And you, my love, have done that from the first moment I met you."

"Nay, Alena," he groaned. Taking her face in his hands, Galen lifted her gaze to his. "You're wrong. So very, very wrong. I've run from my problems; I've refused to face them. And, even now when I think of the morrow, I'm so very afraid, so terribly uncertain."

"And you don't think I'm uncertain, that I'm afraid?"

"You've been tested many times in battle. You may be

afraid, but you know that you'll come through when you have to. I don't know that and I fear . . ." His voice faded.

"What do you fear, Galen?" Alena demanded, clasping him fiercely about the wrists. "Put words to your fear. Only then can you begin to face it, to overcome it."

He pulled her to him, cradling her head upon his chest. "Ah, by the Holy Ones, Alena, 'tis too shameful to name it. I want your love, need it so badly, but I'm afraid you'll turn from me if you see me for the coward I truly am!"

"And what have you done to make you believe you're a coward?"

His chest heaved and, for a moment, Alena feared he wouldn't answer. Then, with a ragged breath, Galen began.

"I failed Lydia when she needed me most," he said, so softly she had to strain to hear him. "I used her selfishly and ended up killing her. Yet, even in the depths of my despair over what I did, I found I dearly desired that heady rush of power she gave me again—and was sorely tempted to seek out another woman to stoke those powers anew. That, even more than killing Lydia, is what terrified me so badly I turned from my magic."

"But the morrow is but a day to meet Dorian, to free Renard. How can that—"

"Magic is seductive," he rasped. "I was obsessed by it once before. I don't know what will happen if I battle Dorian. I've heard tales of what happens when two sorcerers turn against each other. The power that builds between them . . . 'tis a force unto its own. A force that seeks out the winner when 'tis all over."

Galen held her tightly to him. "What will become of me if I win, or of you, for that matter? What if all that power corrupts me once and for all? Mayhap that is the reason the sorcerers turned against the dragons. They let themselves be seduced, then controlled by their magic."

"And mayhap that was a choice freely made, not forced upon them against their wills." Alena leaned back and gazed up at Galen. "I cannot believe that a man of good heart and courage gives up his free will to anyone or anything. Only a craven, soulless coward would allow that to happen. Which are you, Galen?"

He stared down at her. The first embers of hope flared within him. "I won't give up willingly. That much I know."

"And will you fight with all your strength to do what is right and good?"

"You know I will."

A smile stole across her face. "Then you *are* the man for me, Galen Radbourne." She stood on tiptoe and kissed him softly on the lips. "I never thought to, or even wished to, find a man such as you, but I have. Now, I never want to let you go."

He smiled back, the look so beautiful and heartfelt that it took Alena's breath away. Then Galen wrapped his arms about her and, opening his mouth hungrily over hers, kissed Alena. They stood there for a time, savoring the sweet rapture of their love, before Galen pulled back.

"Though the fact you love me fills me with great joy," he gravely began, "it changes naught between us. I still cannot mate with you."

Alena frowned up at him. "You claim 'tis your magic that kills, Galen. But 'tis the wielder of the magic who determines if 'tis good or evil. And you aren't evil, Galen. So how can even this special kind of ability you possess be evil?"

"I don't know, Alena. All I know is Lydia is dead."

"Have you ever considered that she died some other way —mayhap a poisonous spider in the cave bit her—or that someone else arrived before you and killed her?"

"Aye," he growled, irritation once more beginning to thread his voice. "I'm not without some imagination. But when my father confirmed the same tale my brother told me of the effects of our powers . . . well, it seemed the most likely cause."

"Yet, knowing yourself not to be a cruel or evil man, you can accept that what flowed from you was bad?"

"Aye."

"But you *loved* Lydia, Galen. And you wouldn't harm someone you loved."

"Not willingly, nay, I wouldn't."

She stroked a gentle finger along his cheek. "And not unwillingly, either, my love. I know this now. 'Tisn't in your nature, *nor* in your magic."

Tears sprang to his eyes, followed by the beginnings of a reluctantly admitted acceptance. "Nay, I suppose not. I'm just so afraid to . . . to try again."

"Yet you must," she whispered. "For the morrow, for your land and people, and for yourself. 'Tis the only way to set aside, once and for all, the terrible guilt and self-loathing and be a whole man again. The kind of man I truly know you to be, the kind of man I need."

The tears welled and spilled over, trickling down Galen's cheeks. And, as the tears fell, he felt himself slowly cleansed, at long last, of all the pain and guilt. Felt whole, free once more. A fierce joy welled within him.

"Ah, sweet lady, I can never truly be worthy of you, no matter how hard I try," he rasped. "But I swear to you that I will never cease trying, if it takes to the end of my days." He lifted a trembling hand to cup the side of her face. "If only you promise to stay with me, love me."

"Aye, that I do, my love. That I do."

As if some thought had suddenly struck him, he paused

and cocked his head, a bemused look in his eyes. "Does it even matter to you *if* I love you, or want to keep you for my own?"

Alena considered that for a moment. "Nay. I won't hold you against your will, mind you," she hurried to explain when he reared back in surprised amusement, "but I won't stop loving you, either. You are a free man and free to love whomever you wish."

"How magnanimous of you." He released her and stepped back. "Then I suppose it truly matters not if I love you or not."

"*If* you love me, Galen Radbourne, aye, it certainly *does* matter." Alena took a threatening step toward him, then stopped. A look of uncertainty flared in her eyes. "Ah, curse it all. I'm no good at this! Do you love me, Galen?"

"Aye, Alena," he gravely replied. "That I do."

With a wild whoop, she flung herself into his arms. "You had me worried there for a moment," she mumbled from the comforting haven of his chest. "I'm not used to this playful side of you."

He laughed. "Well, I must admit, neither am I, but it grows on you. Especially," he added, a teasing lilt in his voice, "if it can unsettle you so easily."

Alena cocked her head back at him, her eyes narrowed. "And what's so special about unsettling me?"

"Oh, naught." Galen smiled and shrugged. "I just like knowing I have some power over you, however small it might be."

She shoved at his chest. "Think again, Radbourne. This is going to be a relationship of equals. I'll have no man dominating me."

He edged back, grinning. "Indeed? I was raised to believe the man was master and the woman obedient. Isn't that the way love's supposed to be?"

"Nay." Alena shoved harder. " 'Tisn't. And the sooner you get that through that thick skull of yours, the—"

Just then Galen, pushed to the edge of the bed, lost his balance. Grabbing for Alena, he pulled her down with him. They fell in a wild tangle of flailing arms and legs, bouncing down hard onto the plump, feather-tick mattress, before coming to rest. For a long moment Alena, lying atop his hard-muscled chest, her hair tousled and in her eyes, could do nothing more than glare down at him. Then, with an exasperated flip of her head, she flung her hair out of her face.

"If you think to win this argument by overpowering me, you're sadly mistaken. I've suffered far worse torments than the likes of you will ever be able to inflict."

"Indeed?" Galen murmured as he began to work free the first lacings of her tunic. "And why would I ever wish to harm the woman I love? Hmmm?" he asked as he placed a kiss at the hollow of her throat.

"I-I don't know," Alena stammered, unsettled first by his lips, then his tongue as it traced a sinuous trail of fire from her throat down to the flesh now exposed by the top of the open tunic. A delicious shiver rippled through her. She settled more comfortably against him. "There are many ways to control a person. The mating act is but one of them."

"Is it now?" With nimble fingers, Galen pulled loose more of her lacings. "And is that mayhap how I'll ultimately control you, sweet lady?"

He lowered his head once again and ran his tongue down to the cleft between Alena's breasts, thrusting it deep between the plump mounds of flesh. His warm breath, wafting over the damp trail he'd just blazed, sent wild jolts of pleasure shooting through her body. Instinctively, she arched her groin, pressing into his, and felt the hard, unyielding evidence of his own desire.

Her hand snaked down, grasped him, and gently squeezed. "And is this, *my lord,* how I will control you, then?"

He shot her a wry look. "Only if you control me there *very* gently and very sweetly." Galen paused, a roguish grin twisting his mouth. "We seem at an impasse here."

"You're the one who started it, *my lord.*"

Galen arched a dark brow. "Did I now? Mayhap my strategy was poorly thought out. My skills are rusty for want of adequate practice. Mayhap I need to retreat and try another—"

She silenced him with a gentle finger. "What you need, sweet sorcerer, is to love me. That's all I've ever wanted, even before that first night we laid together."

Startled, Galen captured her hand and pulled it from his lips. "Truly? You wanted me even before the spell?"

"Aye." Amusement quivered on Alena's lips. "What's so surprising about that? You're quite a handsome and *very* well-built man, you know."

"Well, I'll admit Lydia used to tell me that, but we were both young then and now, well, now I'm not so young."

"Young enough to suit me and old enough to know what you're doing," Alena said throatily, capturing both sides of Galen's face and kissing him soundly. "And I must admit to liking a smattering of maturity *and* experience in my men."

Galen laughed, then pulled her to him. His hands moved down her back, molding her tighter and tighter to the hard length of his body. His fingers entwined in her hair, capturing her head, guiding her mouth down to his. Their lips met and melded, Galen moving his mouth over hers with a savage tenderness, shaping and fitting her soft curves to his own.

He touched his tongue to her lips, impatiently coaxing them to part and, when they did, he thrust between them. She moaned deep in her throat, her own tongue eagerly meeting his in a hot, primitive dance. Galen's hands went as wild as his body, tugging at Alena's tunic, pulling it over her head, until he finally freed the soft, silky flesh he so desperately wanted to see and feel.

Her breasts, succulent mounds topped with velvety soft nipples, gleamed in the moonlit room. Tentatively at first, he stroked first one pouting tip, then the other. Alena trembled, arching back her head in pleasure.

"Ah, Galen," she groaned. "You make me so hot, so needing, so wild for you!"

"Do I, my love?" he whispered thickly. " 'Tis the same fire that burns in me." He grasped her hips and jerked them hard against his stiffened sex. "Do you feel it? Do you understand?"

"Aye." Alena's hands moved to the waistband of his breeches and began to tug it open. "Aye, I understand. And I want it as much as you."

The clasp of Galen's breeches sprang free, the cloth was spread, and, with an arch of his hips and a few more quick tugs of clothing and boots, he was naked. He smiled up at her, a wolfish lifting of firm, sensuous lips from white teeth.

"There seems yet to be a barrier between us," he said, suggestively glancing down at Alena's breeches.

"A small impediment easily remedied." She climbed off Galen to sit up and remove her boots. Then, scooting over to the side of the bed, Alena stood, undid her breeches and slipped them off her hips and down her legs. "Better?" she turned and asked with an impish grin.

"*Much* better." His gaze roved hungrily over her, drinking in the sight of her athletically feminine body. His sex swelled even higher and harder. He raised his arms to her. "Come to me, sweet lady."

She went to him as eagerly as a young girl in the throes of a first love, laughing, giggling, squirming, and kissing. And Galen, both overwhelmed and delighted by Alena's uninhibited response, clasped her to him, content, for long, rapturous moments to just hold and feel her. But the clamoring of a body yearning for a deeper and more satisfying union could not long be ignored.

He rolled Alena over onto her back and, shifting his weight atop hers, wedged his knee between her legs. She opened to him eagerly, a hot, feverish look burning in her eyes. As if to prolong and savor the sweet joining to come, Galen slid his hand upward to a firm, white breast, boldly capturing its softly enticing fullness. Once more, he lowered his head, his lips closing tightly around her nipple, drawing hard.

Alena writhed beneath him, plucking at his arms, his hips, his thighs. "Galen," she breathed, "please!"

He reared back, poised over her like some potent stallion, his organ huge and swollen. Then, with a primal groan, Galen grasped himself, slid a hand under her hips to lift her, and thrust into her sheath.

Alena arched back, so full of him she thought she'd either tear asunder or explode from the sheer ecstasy of his penetration. She writhed on the bed, her legs entwining about his trim hips, then began a frenzied pumping. Thrashing together violently in their pleasure and need, they were like two wild animals. Breaths came raggedly, bodies sheened with sweat, but Galen and Alena never slowed. Too much hovered just beyond their grasp, an exquisite pleasure, a fulfillment, an ultimate union that both desperately needed. The tempo of their straining bodies increased. Hands moved wildly, clasping at soft flesh and hardened muscles. Too much. 'Twas too much—

With a keening cry, the burgeoning tension within Alena

exploded. Tight, fierce tremors vibrated through her. She shuddered and shook in Galen's arms.

The crazed, little undulating movements of her sheath, clenching around him, at last sent Galen over the edge. He jerked back. His mouth opened in soundless ecstasy. His body shook and shuddered as intensely as Alena's.

And, in those fiercely sweet moments together, joined body and heart and soul, Galen tasted his victory—over himself and his magic. And knew, at long last, that what he was and did was good—and there was no taint of evil in him, not now or ever.

Through the mists and drizzling rain of another cloud shrouded day, the dark castle loomed out of the land, perched on a high, rocky outcropping far out in a bleak, barren moor. The sight of it filled Alena with a grim resolve—and a painful flood of memories. It seemed years ago now that she'd last sat here atop her horse, gazing down at the foreboding fortress from her vantage atop a hill. Years . . . and a lifetime of new experiences and startling revelations.

She glanced to her left. Galen sat calmly astride his gray gelding, his glance calm, at peace. An impulse to rail at him that such equanimity was dangerous so near the time of battle surged through her.

Alena firmly squelched it. Let him have his peace and serenity for as long as it lasted. Which wouldn't be much longer, she added grimly, if Dorian Radbourne acted true to form.

Behind them and a short distance away, Idara muttered angrily and Paddy forlornly shuffled about. Though she'd acquiesced to Galen's demand that the two stay behind, Alena couldn't help a small twinge of misgiving. She was virtually helpless without Paddy. 'Twould all depend on Galen.

Not that she didn't trust him implicitly. She did. But Dorian was cruel and crafty, and she wasn't at all convinced Galen fully comprehended the extent of his brother's malevolence, or how black his soul had truly become. That lingering naiveté could be the chink in his armor, and just the weakness Dorian needed to defeat him.

But, as much as she needed Galen to protect her, he needed her to keep him grounded, to assess the threats realistically and advise him as to the best strategy. Together, they would make a formidable team. They had to, or more would be lost than just their lives.

She smiled over at Galen. "Are you ready? 'Tis time we put an end to this journey—and quest."

"What?" He turned to her. "Oh, aye. I was just recalling the last time I looked upon my home. The land seems so bleak now, so dark, and empty and sad." He shook his head. "But mayhap 'tis just the miserable weather, or what the years do to one's memory. Mayhap 'twas always this way."

"And mayhap 'tis the ruler who sets the mood for the land and its people. A mood that could well change for the better after today."

Galen frowned. "I ride forth not to take Castle Radbourne from my brother, nor to cause him harm. You must know that, Alena, before we go a foot farther. 'Tisn't fair for me to step in, after all these years, and claim any right to rule."

"But you are the oldest, are you not? The rightful heir?"

"We were born the same day, one way or another. A few minutes' difference is hardly sufficient cause now to demand the lordship of Radbourne and its lands."

" 'Tis if 'twill make the right man lord."

Galen's eyes narrowed. "Will we get into another one of our arguments so close to the time of our confrontation with my brother, then? You won't convince me at any rate. Only the course of our upcoming encounter can, in the end."

"Aye, you'd think I'd have learned that by now," Alena muttered disgustedly. "But I still hope . . ."

He grinned. "You can be a bit stubborn at times, too, you know. I'd say we were evenly matched when it comes to strong wills."

"Would you now?" Her lips twitched. "Well, enough of the pleasantries. 'Tis past time we depart." She twisted in her saddle and glanced back at Paddy and Idara. "My thanks for your loyalty and devotion. May we soon join up again."

"Beware the sorcerers, child," Idara said. "Both of them."

Alena eyed her for a long moment, then turned to Paddy. "I'll be back for you. I swear it."

"I know, my lady." His lower lip wobbled. "I just wish . . ." He caught himself and reared back to his full height, thrusting out his chest. "Call if you need me. I'll hear, no matter how far away, and come."

Unaccountably moved by the young dragon's devotion, Alena couldn't, for a brief instant, find words to reply. Finally, she nodded and mumbled a curt, "My thanks," before shooting Galen a misty-eyed look. "Let's go," she said and, without awaiting his reply, urged her horse down the hill.

He caught up with her at the base of the hill but said nothing. Alena signaled her mare into a canter and Galen quickly did the same. They rode in silence across the treeless plain, the dark form of Castle Radbourne gradually growing larger and more menacing.

Even from the vantage of a league away, Alena could see the gates were closed and bolted, the parapets bristling with soldiers. Her mouth quirked. They must pose a real threat to Dorian Radbourne, for him to fortify the castle so heavily against two people. The realization heartened her. No matter what the sorcerer of Castle Radbourne said, his current actions spoke far louder than words.

A man's form, dressed in opulent, flowing robes, appeared on the parapet. Beside him stood a man more plainly dressed. Alena recognized the two as Dorian and his henchman, Jarvis. She cast Galen a quick glance. "It seems we're to have a formal welcome, before we're invited into the castle."

His mouth tightened. "Aye, so it seems. Pray, allow me to extend our greetings. It might come better from me, than you."

Alena shrugged. "Fine. I've naught to say to your brother, at any rate, save to demand Renard's release."

"I'd prefer to negotiate that issue as well."

She laughed wryly. "Don't trust my skills of diplomacy, do you?"

"Even you admit to a certain lacking in that area."

She halted her horse before the drawbridge and gestured up to where Dorian stood, hands on his hips, glaring down at them. "Have at it, then. Your moment of glory is upon you."

Galen inhaled a fortifying breath. He lifted his gaze to his brother's. "Hail, Dorian. May we have entrance to the castle?"

His mouth set in a thin line, his gaze cold and wary, Dorian leaned over the parapet wall and stared down at them. "Why, after all these years, have you now returned, Galen?" he demanded without preliminary niceties or preamble. "And are you now in league with that mercenary? She is outlaw in this land."

"Why, that arrogant—" Alena began before Galen leaned over and grabbed her hand.

"You said you'd let me handle this."

She scowled at him, then sighed. "Aye, that I did. Have at it."

Galen turned back to his brother. "Alena's my friend. I promise she'll cause no problems. But 'tis difficult to discuss matters shouting up at you like this. Can you not open the gates and welcome me in, brother-to-brother?"

Dorian gave a low laugh. "And aren't you still a sorcerer? Aren't your powers sufficient to open the gates yourself? Or have they shriveled away after all those years on Cadvallan?"

"They are adequate to most tasks," Galen called up to him. "I expected a more hospitable welcome, however. We are kin, after all, and this is my home."

"We are also sorcerers, and I recall your former dedication to the craft went far beyond filial loyalty."

"My former dedication went far beyond everything, even common sense at times." Galen shifted slightly on his horse to ease a muscle spasm in his side. He hadn't realized how tense he'd become, sitting here talking to Dorian. "But no more. The years have taught me that, if naught else. But the issue here is really trust, isn't it, Dorian? Trust that I mean you no harm. Just as I trust that your intentions are equally honorable."

"Aye, I suppose trust *is* the issue here." Dorian leaned over and said something to Jarvis. The man nodded, then stepped back from the parapet and hurried away. "Our bond, after all, does run deeper than life itself," he said, turning back to Galen. "As does your debt to me in saving your life fifteen years ago."

Slowly, Galen nodded. "Aye, that it does, and I haven't forgotten. That I swear."

Dorian smiled. With a creak of iron hinges, the huge, wooden gates swung open. "I'll hold you to that." He gestured down toward the gates. "Pray, come in, Brother dear. I find this issue does indeed bear further discussion. Come in, and let us plumb the depths of your trust and gratitude."

CHAPTER SIXTEEN

Galen arched a dark brow at Alena, his mouth twisting in a wry smile. "Do you see what diplomacy can do for you? We now have an invitation into the castle without one threat offered or sword drawn."

" 'Tis also to his advantage to have us inside. Escape will just be all that harder within well-fortified walls."

"I envision a more pleasant conclusion to our visit than a desperate attempt at escape."

"And I say you are a hopeless dreamer," Alena muttered, nudging her horse forward.

They rode over the drawbridge and the murky, foul-smelling moat, past the imposing gatehouse, and into the outer bailey. Its appearance hadn't changed much from Alena's last visit. 'Twas still ill-kempt, she thought sourly, with stinking piles of refuse stacked along the walls and horse droppings scattered liberally about. On closer inspection this time, she also noted chinks in the crumbling mortar between the stones sealing the outer wall, and the skeletal remains of some unfortunate men hanging by their hands from chains hooked high above into those same walls.

For a panic-stricken moment, Alena wondered if one of those men was Renard. She scanned the skeletons more closely. Relief swamped her. Nay, none possessed the breadth or length of bone to support a body as large and strong as her partner. There was still hope that he lived.

Dorian awaited them at the head of the broad stone steps leading to the keep. As she gazed up at the richly garbed sorcerer, the mottled gray walls behind him suddenly seemed to acquire a life of their own, alternately metamorphosing from hollow, haunted eyes to open maws mouthing soundless warnings and mournful cries. She blinked frantically, dispelling the disconcerting images. By the Holy Ones, Alena thought, were the images mayhap a warning of what was to come?

In spite of herself, her hand crept to her sword hilt. Its substantial heft felt reassuring, solid, in a reality teetering on the brink of unreality. She shot Galen a quick glance, striding there beside her, tall, and strong, and sure. Ah, how she loved and trusted him!

A fierce swell of confidence filled her anew. Together, they *would* prevail. Even against the evil, terrible tests still to come.

Dorian Radbourne, dressed in a stiff robe of amethyst-colored silk and brocade, the same milky pendant as Galen's hanging from his neck, calmly stepped forward when they reached the top of the steps. With hand outstretched, he walked up to Galen.

"Welcome, Brother," he softly said, his darkly mesmerizing eyes gleaming with a warm affection. "I beg forgiveness for my earlier inhospitality, but I had to be certain you were still the same man I sent to Cadvallan all those years past."

Galen grasped his hand. "And am I?"

Dorian smiled. "Aye, or at least in all the ways that matter. You're still a sorcerer, and you're still my brother."

They hugged then, standing for a time clasped in each others' arms. Alena watched the filial display with a growing sense of unease. If Dorian swayed Galen to his side, she was doomed. Mayhap 'twas best if she—

She cut the disquieting thought short. Nay, she'd not allow herself to doubt Galen. He was no fool. He dearly wished to win over his brother and convince him his ways were wrong, but he was no fool. He'd not long or easily be led by Dorian's insincerity or trickery.

"Come," Dorian said at last, releasing Galen and stepping back. Ever so fleetingly, his glance scanned Alena. "Bring the woman and come inside. I've given orders that a simple repast be laid for us, and I prefer the privacy of my reception chambers to a public display of affection before the commoners of the keep."

Though his words were that of a consummate host and loving brother, the sorcerer's eyes, nonetheless, betrayed his hatred for Alena. Yet beneath his thinly veiled animosity there burned a savage desire for her, too. She couldn't help a small, involuntary shudder. A man like him, feeling like he did about her, would be a viciously cruel lover. A lover who she'd not long survive.

"We'd be honored, wouldn't we, Alena?" Galen asked, turning to her.

Shaken from her unpleasant thoughts, Alena stared up at him, momentarily taken aback. "Oh, aye," she muttered. "And can we mayhap invite Renard to this little meal? 'Twould make for a most cozy foursome, wouldn't you say?"

Something dark and ugly flared in Dorian's eyes. "He lives, if that is what you're asking," he growled. "But before I release him to you, there are a few minor matters we need to discuss. Considering the circumstances, I think a few hours more or less longer in my dungeons will be permissible, don't you?"

"Nay, I don't." Alena stepped forward, her hand gripped about her sword. "I think, instead—"

"That's enough, Alena," Galen sharply cut her off. " 'Tisn't proper to insult or threaten a host within his own home. Nor," he added a bit more gently, "the proper way to accomplish what we came here to do."

Alena's lips tightened, but she restrained her harsh retort. With a curt nod, she stepped back, her hand falling from her sword.

Dorian, watching the interplay, chuckled. "I see you've had some success in taming the wench. I must admit 'tis a most pleasurable consideration—her taming, I mean."

"Alena is a reasonable woman, when treated reasonably," Galen said, riveting his attention back on his brother. "One of my hopes for this meeting is to prove that and span the chasm of misunderstanding between you two." He arched a dark brow. "Mayhap 'twould be wise, though, to have Renard fetched from his cell to attend our little gathering. As a gesture of your good intentions, shall we say?"

Dorian's teeth flashed white in a lazy smile. "Indeed? *My* good intentions, you say? And what gesture of good intent do I get from you in return?"

Galen shrugged, lifting his hands, palms open in a sign of trust. "We are here, are we not, within your castle?"

"But not exactly defenseless, either."

"Alena's sword is rather useless against your powers."

"Aye," Dorian conceded, "but your magic is yet to be tested."

"And need never be, between two brothers."

A grim smile played about Dorian's lips. " 'Tis true enough." He motioned to Jarvis who had suddenly appeared from the doorway. The man strode over, shot Galen, then Alena a glowering look, and bowed to his master.

"Aye, m'lord?"

"Bring Renard to us. We'll await him in my reception chambers."

At Dorian's words to Jarvis, who bowed once more then turned and strode away, Alena's heart leaped within her breast. With Renard beside them, the chances of making good their escape improved greatly. If Galen could just use his magic to disable Dorian . . .

She squelched that wild hope, forcing her attention back to the present. First things first. And the most vital action of all right now was to remain alert to Dorian and his next moves. He, too, might well have his own plan for them, and a particular timetable for carrying out that plan.

They followed him into the keep and its shadowed, cavernous hall, the sound of their booted feet reverberating hollowly off the walls and rafter lined ceilings. Past the blazing hearth and the coat of arms of the dying dragon, they walked. This time, however, Alena comprehended the full significance of the gruesome crest. Only through the annihilation of the dragons could the sorcerers gain the ultimate power.

Instead of entering through the doors to the right of the hearth and into Dorian's large reception hall, he led them past the hearth to a smaller door off to the side wall. A richly furnished chamber, lush with cushioned chairs, velvet curtained windows, and richly embroidered wall tapestries, welcomed them. A smaller hearth, ablaze with a crackling fire, and a long side table laden with food and drink, completed the sense of a warm, hospitable room.

"Pray, help yourself to the food," Dorian said, walking over to the side table. He picked up an etched silver ewer and began to fill four delicately fashioned, narrow-stemmed silver goblets. "Take a cup of wine, as well. After such a long journey, I'm sure you're a bit parched." He took three of the four goblets and walked back to where Galen and Alena stood.

"Here. The wine is quite safe." Dorian handed a goblet to both Galen and Alena. He lifted his own cup in a toast. "Let us drink to a successful reconciliation between us," he said, briefly meeting Galen's gaze before swinging to Alena, "and to a fresh start at a special friendship with you, fair lady."

At the hypocrisy in the sorcerer's words, anger flooded Alena. Summoning all her skills at diplomacy and subterfuge, she masked the heated emotion behind a bland smile. "Indeed? We'll have to see about that, won't we?"

Dorian lifted his cup to his lips and drank deeply. Alena's questioning gaze met Galen's. He smiled and nodded. She took a careful sip of her wine. 'Twas untainted. She took another sip. The wine was one of the finest she'd ever tasted, and she'd had her share of fine liquors as booty in her years as a mercenary soldier.

"You like it, don't you?" Dorian inquired, a tinge of amusement hovering about his words. "You're also surprised that I didn't try to drug or poison you, aren't you?"

Alena smiled thinly. "Aye, I suppose so. But then, a man of your considerable powers doesn't need to stoop to such desperate tactics, does he?"

"Nay, I don't. 'Tis wise of you to realize that. 'Twill make things go—"

A sharp knock sounded at the door. Dorian turned, a look of anticipation on his face. "Ah, that must be Jarvis with Renard." He glanced at Alena. "Will you do the honors, fair lady?"

Not bothering even to offer a reply, she turned on her heel and rapidly strode to the door, her heart pounding. What would she find on the other side? Alena wondered. Was this but a cruel trick or would Renard truly be there? And how would he look, what would be his condition, after over a month in the dungeon?

She grasped the bronze door handle and pulled the door open. There, Jarvis behind him and two guards holding him by his arms, stood Renard. His clothes were dirty and frayed a bit at the edges, his face had lost most of its tan, and he looked several pounds thinner, but he appeared reasonably healthy.

"Renard? I—" Suddenly, Alena was at a loss for words. The hopes, the fears, the frustrations swelled within her, filling her with a confusing mix of emotions. Her throat tightened. Her eyes burned with unshed tears. But her pride wouldn't let her display her true feelings before these men, her enemies.

"Let him go," she hoarsely commanded the two soldiers still holding him. "Now."

"Do as she says," Dorian softly said, coming up to stand behind her. "He is now as much a guest as my brother and this woman."

The guards released Renard, who remained standing there, unmoving, his hooded gaze wary, waiting. Alena managed a small smile of encouragement. "Come in, Renard. These halls are cold and the room is warm with a brisk fire." She took him by the hand. "Are you hungry, or would you like a cup of wine to ease your thirst?"

"Aye, some wine would be welcome," he rasped before following her. A questioning light, however, still flickered in his eyes. She gave him two quick squeezes to reassure him, the only signal she dared that he'd recognize as one of their secret signs. Recognition and relief flared, then died, but 'twas enough to tell Alena he'd caught her surreptitious gesture.

When they reached Galen, Alena drew to a halt. "Renard, this is Galen," she said by way of introduction. "Not only is he quite obviously Dorian Radbourne's twin brother, but he's a sorcerer as well. He has been away for many years and just returned with me today. Galen is my friend and came back to help me free you from your, er, unfortunate incarceration in Castle Radbourne."

"Very tactfully put, fair lady," Dorian said, walking up with a fourth goblet of wine in his hand. He offered it to Renard.

The big warrior accepted it, his eyes swinging from Dorian's to Galen's to Alena's. He didn't drink from it, though.

Alena knew his quiet acceptance of the strange turn of events was due to his uncertainty as to their plans and the strategy of the game being played out here. 'Twas also why he chose to follow temporarily where he normally liked to lead. For the time being, at least, Alena knew he'd emulate her actions and take his cues from her.

She sipped from her cup. He took a drink. She lowered her cup. So did he.

"My thanks for your willingness to so readily free Renard," Alena said, looking over at Dorian. The man watched them with dark, assessing eyes, like some predator sizing up his prey. "I think, though, 'tis past time to move onto the business at hand. Or, at least what business Galen still has with you. I've finished mine with Renard's release."

"Aye, 'tis evident there are issues we've yet to discuss." Dorian motioned to the cushioned chairs clustered before the fire. "Come, let us sit and talk."

Alena glanced at Galen, who had suddenly become uncharacteristically quiet. She found his gaze riveted on Renard, who stared back unblinkingly. They took the measure of each other, both as potential allies and, she knew with a woman's instinct, as to their place of importance in her life. The former effort, she knew, was the mark of an intelligent and cautious man.

She didn't begrudge them that, especially considering the strange and strained circumstances in which they'd first met. But she'd no time nor patience with masculine possessiveness over a female. And especially not over her. Dorian Radbourne already avidly sought chinks in their defenses. She'd not allow Galen and Renard to give him more.

Stepping over to Galen, she took his hand and tucked it in the crook of her arm, then pointedly stared back at Renard. "Aye, come, my friends. Let's finish what we came here for."

Dorian waited until they were all seated. "So, Galen. Tell me true. Why have you really come back? And how did you escape the spell over Cadvallan?"

"A spell you laid over the isle and refused ever to lift?"

His brother took a swallow of his wine, then shrugged. "Father thought 'twas best. He imagined you a broken man after . . . all that had transpired."

"Did he now?" Galen smiled but it never quite reached his eyes. "Well, 'tis a moot point now, isn't it? I am here."

"And the reason for your return?" Dorian prodded.

He must tread carefully from here on out, Galen knew. All could be won or lost on the way he worded things. And more hinged on this meeting than just Renard's freedom. Far, far more.

"When you took Renard prisoner, Alena came to Cadvallan to fetch me. She knew she couldn't hope to prevail against a sorcerer of your prowess, without another sorcerer of equal powers. I was reluctant at first to help her or leave Cadvallan, but when I heard of the problems afoot in Wyndymyll . . ."

"Aye?" Dorian leaned forward, the image of concerned attentiveness. "And what problems were they?"

"An abuse of power. Rumors of maidens being taken and never returned. And a growing vendetta against the dragons, to the point it had now become a concerted attempt at their total annihilation."

"Galen, Galen," Dorian chided. "You have long known of

the sorcerers' war with the dragons. It began well before our birth. I didn't start it; our ancestors and those of the dragons did that."

"Aye, I'll admit I accepted that explanation, too, all the years of my youth," Galen said. "But after living on Cadvallan with the dragons these past fifteen years and learning what I learned on this quest, I find the old answers not good enough anymore. We must cease this pointless, mutually fatal battle with the dragons, before 'tis too late for us all. And that, Brother, is why, in the end and above all else, I am here."

"Indeed?" A muscle flicked at the corner of Dorian's mouth. "To do what? To take Castle Radbourne from me? To cast me aside and reclaim your inheritance as the true lord and heir?"

Galen saw the rage smoldering beneath his brother's quietly taunting words. Step carefully, he reminded himself, and inhaled a steadying breath before forging on. "Nay, Dorian. I don't want to take Radbourne from you. I want only to assist you in the tasks that lie ahead. Once the land is healed and the dragons safe, I don't know what I'll do." He smiled. "Most likely go back to Cadvallan and whatever dragons choose to remain there."

"What makes you think I need your assistance?" In a swirl of shimmering robes, Dorian rose. An aura of barely contained anger encompassed him. "I certainly have never wanted it."

Galen gazed up at his brother. Curse it all, this was going to be even more difficult than he'd originally anticipated. "We are brothers. In times of need, we should stand beside each other."

"There is no need, you fool!" Dorian cried. "Don't you understand? *No one* needs you or your help anymore!"

Beside Galen, Alena's hand reflexively moved to her sword. Renard went tense, his hands fisting. Frustration flooded Galen. "Dorian, listen to me before 'tis too late. You abuse your power. Our people fear you. The land is dying before our eyes. You must stop this. You must!"

"And do you imagine our people would accept you any more readily than I—you who killed the woman he supposedly loved?" Dorian flung the question back at him. "Do you think they'd fear you any less? We are cut of the same cloth, possess the same powers that require sustenance from the life force of others."

"There are ways to overcome that," Galen muttered. "There has to be. Together, we might more quickly discover those ways. Together, we could slowly change the perception of the people. 'Tis never too late."

"Aye, *'tis* too late." Dorian strode over to the side table and shakily poured himself another goblet of wine. Then, he wheeled about. His mouth had gone white around the lips. His eyes were rimmed in red. An almost palpable fury shimmered around him like a heated mist.

Filled with a rising presentiment, Galen stood. "Why, Dorian," he quietly asked. "No matter what has sometimes passed between us, we are brothers. *Why* is it too late?"

"Because I was a nobody, a pariah, until you left for Cadvallan," his brother spat out the words. "Father never even saw me for who I truly was until you were gone. You were always the beautiful son, the talented son, the good and kind and perfect son. *And* the firstborn son."

"That wasn't my fault." A belated recognition of his brother's secret anguish all these years filled Galen. Guilt rushed in to join the bitter recognition. Had he, however unintentionally in the self-centered preoccupation of youth, contributed to Dorian's pain?

"By the Holy Ones," Galen cried, "I *never* meant to throw any of my successes up into your face. I never even sought out the praise and attention I received. I just tried to do the best I could. Should I have done less, turned everyone away, just to make you look better?"

"Aye," Dorian snarled. "A truly loving brother would've done so. But, nay, you were too greedy, too full of vainglory, too full of yourself, ever to see my need. And you thought me stupid, inferior to you, too."

"Nay, 'tisn't true." Galen walked toward him. "I always knew you were more intelligent, more talented than I. But my holding back, purposely failing at what I did, wouldn't have made you strive harder. Only *you* could've made yourself strive harder, made yourself grow into the man you were always capable of becoming. A man with far, far more talent and potential than I. But you didn't, Dorian, and, by your own choice, your own failure, made me look so much better in comparison."

"Lies!" Dorian spat, his face purpling with his rage. "Always you try to turn it back on me. Always! But it doesn't matter anymore. I am finally more powerful than you. And I intend to grow and grow and grow in my magic, until there is no one, neither sorcerer nor dragon, who can best me. And I will, Brother dear. You can be certain of that!"

Galen halted. Behind him he heard Alena and Renard rise from their chairs. A sense of urgency, of impending doom, flooded him. "Dorian, I don't care if you're more powerful than I," he began again, his voice going taut with his rising anxiety. "You can be the most powerful. You can rule Radbourne and its lands until the end of your days. I just can't let you go on this way, hurting others, destroying the dragons and the land."

His brother gave a shrill, disbelieving laugh. "*You* can't let *me,* Galen? And how, pray tell, are you going to stop me?"

"Dorian," Galen pleaded, once more moving toward him. His hands lifted, opened in supplication. "Don't push this to a fight between us. We just met again, after fifteen years apart. I know you don't trust me, but won't you give us a chance? Give us time to get to know and understand each other? What happened between us as boys doesn't have to follow us the rest of our lives. We can change the past, rebuild our relationship, and make it better than before."

"Can we?" Dorian's eyes shifted restlessly. He rubbed his arms, shuffled his feet. Then, as Alena moved to stand at Galen's side, he went still, his gaze turning black and hard. "You speak of trust, of changing the past. Well, prove to me how sincere you truly are. Prove to me with actions, not pretty words."

"How, Dorian?" Galen demanded hoarsely, a flicker of hope flaring in the depths of his rising dread and despair. "How?"

"Give me Alena," Dorian said, a savage smile twisting his lips. "Give her to me to use however I see fit for as long as I want her."

"And what of Renard?" Galen demanded softly, his tiny ember of hope dying as quickly as it had sprung to life. "What of him?"

"Kill him. Now. Show me those powers you claim to still possess."

"And if I don't, Dorian. What then?"

His brother's smile widened into a triumphant grin. "Then, Brother dear, you are doomed as surely as they." He lifted his hand and pointed it at Galen. "There are but two choices here. You will *be* the sorcerer and *act* the sorcerer, or you will die. Now, which will it be? I tire of waiting."

CHAPTER SEVENTEEN

"You know I can't do that," Galen whispered. "Ask for aught else that won't harm anyone, and I will give it. I'll do anything to prove my good intentions, Dorian, but I won't do that."

"She's only a woman," his brother growled, eyeing Alena with disdain. "A beautiful one, whom I'd wager you've bedded well to enhance your powers, but still a woman. Why not share her with me? You've shared all the other women you ever bedded."

Galen went rigid. "What do you mean?" he demanded hoarsely. "The only other woman I've bedded was Lydia."

Dorian chuckled softly. "Ah, my poor, trusting brother. Do you think Lydia slept only with you? She had a yearning for a noble husband and played us both to that end. I, however, recognized her game from the start and was more than happy to use her beautiful body for my own pleasure." A pitying smile played about his finely sculpted lips. "Didn't you?"

"You lie!" Galen hissed through clenched teeth. "Lydia loved me. She would have never—"

"Ah, but she did, I assure you," Dorian cut him off. "If the truth be known, either one of us could have been the one to kill her, or mayhap 'twas our combined powers. We will never know, will we?"

Galen blanched. "But you led me to believe 'twas my fault. You let me take the blame."

Dorian shrugged. "Someone had to accept the blame. You did it so nobly I hated to take the opportunity from you. Besides," he added, his mouth twisting cruelly, " 'twas only fair. 'Twas past time Father and the people saw you for the man you truly were."

"The man I truly was . . ." Galen laughed bitterly. "All those years wasted, and I never was the monster I imagined myself to be!"

Alena stepped forward and grasped his arm. " 'Tis past, Galen, no matter how unsettling this news may be. Dorian tells you this now to unnerve you, to divert you from the true purpose of our mission."

"And what might that be?" Dorian softly taunted. "Will the truth at long last be revealed?"

She wheeled to confront him. "You know what 'tis. You must be stopped before you wreak any more havoc, destroy anyone else! Though Galen truly meant to rebuild a relationship with you and help you change your evil ways, I never thought 'twas possible. You are evil to the marrow of your bones, Dorian Radbourne, and naught Galen ever did as a lad turned you that way. *You* chose to be the man you became. You and no one else!"

With a burst of mage fire, Dorian sent Alena spinning backward and to the floor. "Witch!" he spat. "Dragon's whore! Do you think I don't know who you truly are? Do you think I haven't watched as you journeyed here, insinuating yourself into my brother's heart and mind, until he could no longer think for himself? And do you think I don't know your game, that you intend to use him to destroy all sorcerers, and even him, in the end? But 'twon't be. I'll kill you before I let that happen!"

Once more, the red-hot mage fire shot from his hand. And, though Galen was too slow, still mired as he was in his shock, Renard wasn't. With a roar, he leaped between Alena and the blast of magic, taking the brunt of the sorcerer's vicious powers full in the chest.

Renard arched back and fell, sliding across the floor to stop at Dorian's feet. His mouth opened in soundless agony, then he went limp.

"Renard!" Alena screamed. She shoved to her knees and reached out to him. "Galen, help him!"

Her anguished cry wrenched the big sorcerer from his stupefied haze. He stepped before her. "Stop it now, Brother. Stop before 'tis too late."

An expression of utter disgust twisted Dorian's face. "Don't you see it yet, you fool? 'Tis already too late. Radbourne is mine. And I'll never, ever, share aught with you."

This time the mage fire spewed toward Galen. He grasped his pendant and cast a magical barrier. The fire struck the shimmering obstruction, halted, then dissipated. For an instant, Dorian stood there in shock. Then, with a grim smile, he tried again.

Blast after blast shot from his hand, to no avail. Try as he might, he couldn't penetrate Galen's magically constructed barricade. Leaning down, Dorian grabbed Renard by his tunic and half-pulled his unconscious form to his knees. A triumphant smile wreathed the sorcerer's face.

"Step aside, Brother dear," Dorian sneered. "Give it up now, before I kill Renard. Accede to me and, in my great mercy, I'll let both he and the woman go."

"And if I do accede," Galen demanded, doggedly maintaining the force of his magic. "What then?"

"You must give me your pendant and submit to my will. Without your pendant, I will rule you at last."

"Nay, Galen!" Using the solid strength of his body for support, Alena pulled to her feet. She clasped Galen's arms. "Don't do it. You're our only hope. We know too much about him now, of the source of his and your powers, and how to defeat him."

"Would you let Renard die then?" Galen rasped, his gaze burning, hot and haunted, clear through to her soul. He shook her hands aside. "After all you've gone through to save him?"

"We are both dead, sooner or later, if your brother lives."

"Well, what will it be, Brother dear?" Dorian prodded, his voice oily with a smug satisfaction. "Do you finally see what the choices are? You either stand with your own kind or with hers." He cocked his head, a considering light in his eyes. " 'Tis a hard choice. Are you man enough to make it?"

"Dorian, don't do this," Galen moaned. His hand clutched, knuckle-white about his pendant. "You're my brother, my flesh and blood. I love you!"

"Love? Love?" Dorian laughed disparagingly. "Then *prove* that love. Make amends for what you did to me all those years ago."

"I can't, Dorian. 'Tisn't right."

"Then the man dies and, in the bargain, you'll be forced to fight me."

Galen took a step forward, one hand outstretched. "Dorian, please, don't do—"

With a savage snarl, Dorian heaved Renard up and into Galen's arms. Mage fire shot from his hand. Galen flung Renard aside and loosed his own mage fire. The two forces met, melded for a fleeting instant, then exploded in a huge burst of flame.

Dorian was thrown backward, striking the side table. Food and plates scattered everywhere. The ewer of wine teetered, spilling its contents onto Dorian's head and robe. He scrambled to his feet, his face livid with rage.

"Die, you sad, sorry fool! But not before you know, at long last, who the best of us is!"

The chamber grew dim. The flames burning in the hearth and from the candles flickered and went out. A stench, foul and breath-grabbing, filled the room. The sound of voices, mournful and haunting, rose on the air, growing to loud shrieks and wails. An eerie, green glow emanated from Dorian.

"By the Mother, Galen!" Alena gasped. "He summons his powers from some place unholy. What can we do to best him?"

"Naught but stand and face him," he muttered beneath his breath. "I'd no idea he was so far corrupted."

Her hands moved to encircle his waist. She pressed tightly to his back. "I am here with you, my love—till death or victory is ours!"

"Then use your magic. Call upon Paddy. I don't know if we can best Dorian otherwise."

She nodded silently, then summoned all her strength to call to the young dragon. *Paddy, help us*, Alena pleaded. *If 'tis possible, lend your strength to ours, or we are surely doomed. Paddy, we need you!*

From far, far away, she heard his reply. *I come, my lady. I send what I can.*

With an unearthly howl, Dorian attacked. A huge green ball of whirling fire sprang from his fingers, barreling straight toward Galen. The big sorcerer flung up his hands, sending forth a magical shield to protect them. The mage fire struck the shield, wavered an instant, then penetrated the barrier.

With a grunt of pain, Galen staggered backward, taking the brunt of the fire's impact into his own body. Agonized shudders vibrated through him.

"Hold fast, my love," Alena whispered, fighting to keep

him upright. "Strike back with all your might."

He went rigid, inhaled a harsh breath, and grasped his pendant. The power filled him, then shot forth, spiraling straight for Dorian. With a mocking laugh, he deflected it with only the most minimal of efforts.

"Try again, Brother dear," Dorian taunted, "but know your efforts are doomed to failure. You cannot hope to best me after all these years. I will take you down, bit by agonizing bit, until you grovel before me, screaming for mercy. And then, while you watch in helpless torment, I'll take the woman before I kill her—just as I killed your beloved Lydia."

"Nay!" Galen roared. He sent forth another burst of fire. It slammed into Dorian. He staggered back a few steps before catching himself.

Surprise flickered briefly in his eyes, then Dorian laughed. "Is that the best you can do? 'Twon't be enough, I assure you. Not nearly enough."

Another green ball of mage fire exploded from Dorian's hand. Before he could summon a defense, it struck Galen full in the chest. With an anguished cry, he toppled over. Only the quickest of reflexes saved Alena as she managed to leap aside. She tripped and fell to her knees.

Immediately, Dorian turned on her. Alena plummeted to the floor, writhing and gasping for breath.

"Nay!" Galen cried, crawling to his hands and knees. "Stop it, Dorian. I beg you!"

"Beg me? Beg me?" His brother laughed derisively. "Do you know how ludicrous you look, kneeling there, crying out for mercy? I'm ashamed to call you brother!"

Galen shoved to his feet, teetering unsteadily. "And I'm ashamed to call *you* brother. We shared the same womb, nursed at the same breasts, were closer than any kin. Yet you have destroyed yourself. You are cursed, Dorian!"

"As are you, Brother dear," Dorian snarled. " 'Tis past time you lose what little is left you!"

Both of his hands lifted. From both hands flew twin balls of fire. Galen flung up his arms. The defensive attempt did little good. The fireballs enveloped him, consuming him in a flaming conflagration. He cried out, flailing and fighting against the searing agony.

Alena summoned all her powers. There was no time left to call to Paddy again. She had to act now, or Galen would die.

With a harsh exhalation, Alena released the white-hot force building within her. It shot through the air straight toward the window. There, it paused as if seeking out its recipient. Alena's heart sank. Paddy must still be too far away.

Suddenly, the magic grew strong and bright. Once more, flashing beams of light burst forth. The power flared, fed from somewhere outside the castle, growing in strength and force. Alena mentally joined with it, directing it back into the room toward Dorian.

The coruscating light struck the evil sorcerer. He leaped back, horror in his eyes. He glanced wildly around. "You," he snarled, his panicked gaze finally locking with Alena's. "You've joined with the dragon!"

"Aye. And 'twill be your destruction at long last."

Once more Alena summoned her powers, sent the light spiraling out toward the window. Once more, Paddy took it within himself, feeding and nourishing the power until it became a thing of greater strength and force than it had been before. The magic returned, filling the room. Alena took it and directed it, once again, at Dorian.

He screeched and flung up his hands, but 'twas too late. The light engulfed him. Within it he writhed and twisted and fought. "Stop it!" he begged. "Stop it!"

"S-stop, Alena," Galen croaked, levering himself up on

one elbow. "Even now, there still might be some way to save him. Please stop."

"Nay, Galen, he must die." She turned to face him, momentarily distracted. It was all the opportunity Dorian needed.

He sent forth a ball of fire. Alena staggered back with the impact, then crumpled into a heap on the floor.

"You're mistaken, witch," Dorian snarled. " 'Tis *you* who must die!"

Galen slammed into him, grappling for his pendant. Dorian tried to send forth more fire, but Galen's magic was too potent this close. There was naught left him but to fight in the way of common men.

Dorian's strength, however, after fifteen years of soft living, wasn't equal to that of a man who had lived that same length of time at hard labor. He tired, weakened, and, in that weakening, Galen's magic overcame his.

Dorian's black magic writhed and twisted, fighting its way up out of him until it finally broke free. There was nothing, though, no bit of good or shred of kindness to replace what was lost. Nothing to keep alive the being known as Dorian Radbourne.

With a shuddering sigh, his spirit disintegrated, snuffing out his life. Galen, belatedly realizing what was happening, jerked back, frantically recalling his magic. It was too late. Dorian went limp. Empty eyes stared back at him.

Above them, the black magic hovered like some evil bird of prey, silent and waiting. Anticipation filled the room. Both Alena and Galen knew what it sought—another magic user— and knew there'd be no way to halt it once it chose.

"Take me!" Galen cried, shoving to his feet. If one of them was to suffer because of Dorian's evil, it should be him. 'Twas his brother, his heritage, that had brought all this down upon them. "Take me, if you dare!"

The seething morass of evil hesitated but an instant more. Then with a sound of rushing wind, it descended on Galen. A fetid darkness encompassed him, sucking the breath from his body, smothering all thought and will and consciousness.

He reared back, his body bending like some strung bow. His eyes clenched. His hands fisted. He cried out, choking, gasping for air.

Terror shot through Alena. *Paddy,* she silently, frantically, called. *Help him. Ah, help him!*

I cannot, my lady, he replied. *'Tis a thing we dare not challenge, when two sorcerers battle. 'Tis a sorcerer's kind of magic. He must deal with it as he can.*

Deal with it as he can . . . Watching Galen struggle with the terrible consequences of his brother's magic, despair swamped Alena. Rather than risk the magic choosing her instead of him, he had taken the evil force into himself. He had sacrificed himself for her.

Galen, ah Galen, she silently cried. *Have I lost you, so soon after learning of your love? And if the evil vanquishes you, will you next turn on me?* Was this how 'twould all end, she bitterly wondered, here in this dark, dismal castle, one pitted against the other? And was there truly naught she could do to save him?

Anger filled her. She and Galen had come too far to lose it all now. With a fierce battle cry, she leaped forward, pulling him down with her to the floor. Cradling his tortured body in her arms, Alena held him tightly to her, rocking him, crooning a wordless melody, sending every bit of love and magic she could to aid him in his terrible battle.

And, bit by agonizing bit, the horror left him. Galen went slack in her arms. He lay there for a long while, gasping for breath, bathed in sweat. Then his eyes flickered open.

"A-Alena?"

She gazed down at him, searching for sign of the man he now was. His rich brown eyes were bleary but guileless. "Galen? Are you all right?"

He pushed her hands away and awkwardly sat up. "Aye, I think so." He rested his head in his hands. "What happened?"

"You . . . Dorian . . ." Alena gestured toward his brother's lifeless form. "You battled and you killed him."

His gaze lifted, swung to where Dorian lay. For a long, agonized moment, Galen stared at the man who had once been his brother. Then, with a choking sob, he crawled over, gathered Dorian into his arms, and wept.

"You can't mean that, Galen," Alena raged at him that night as they stood on the castle parapet. A stiff wind blew, whipping their woolen cloaks about them. Alena clutched the thick cloth tightly to her and tried again.

"Just because you had to kill Dorian and take on his magic is no reason to think you're now doomed to suffer his eventual fate. *Please* listen to reason!"

He never looked her way, riveting his gaze far out on the dark expanse of the night. "I *am* being reasonable, Alena. 'Tis too soon to tell what his magic will do to me. But I won't endanger you or anyone until I find out."

"And when you do find out, Galen, what then? If 'tis the evil that takes you over, what will you do? And if it doesn't, will you come for me, seek me out no matter where I am?"

"I don't know." His hands clenched the stone railing. His shoulders hunched and his head lowered. "If I see myself succumbing to the unholy power, I'll put an end to it, one way or another. But even if I find I can control and contain it, I still don't know what I'll do." He turned finally, his eyes burning pits of agony. "After what happened, what I experienced this day, I'm no longer so sure my kind can ever be trusted, or that we'll ever be strong enough to make peace with the dragons."

"Because of Dorian's evil? Galen, you beat him, beat his evil powers!"

Galen gave a derisive laugh. "Let's be honest with each other, Alena. I couldn't have vanquished him if it hadn't been for you and Paddy. Alone, I'd never have been strong enough."

She stepped forward and clasped his arm. "Galen, be that as it may, 'tis too soon to make a decision on this. You're still overwrought from Dorian's death and taking on that . . . that thing. Don't turn from me, send me away. At least not until you've had a time to think things through."

"Curse it all, Alena," he cried, wrenching free of her grasp. "I *have* thought about it. I don't say this lightly, when I tell you I fear the powers seething inside me. They are strong, seductive, and I crave—do you hear me?—crave them. Before, I had to struggle to control my attraction to my magic. Now, I also hold my brother's passion for it within me. I fear I'm not strong enough to resist it for long. Even now . . ."

Galen shook his head. "Even now, I find myself weakening. 'Tis but a matter of time . . ."

"And do you think I fought so hard to win your love, to save you in that horrid room, that I'll now so easily turn and leave you to this?" Alena stepped close. "Let me stay and fight alongside you. Together we've prevailed before. Paddy and I will—"

"Nay," Galen hoarsely cut her off. "You must get Paddy as far away from me as you can. You don't understand. I have this irrational need to"—he inhaled a shuddering breath—"to kill him, Alena."

He ran a shaky hand through his hair. "Do you realize what would happen if I lost control and turned on Paddy?

You'd be forced to protect him and one of us would die. I . . . don't want that to happen. By the Mother, I couldn't bear for that to happen!"

"And I say, let me stay and fight this with you. What kind of a woman do you think me to be, that I'd turn and run at the first sign of danger?" Lifting on tiptoe, Alena entwined her arms about his neck. "Do you think so little of my love?"

"Nay, I think you should save it for a man who's worthy of you." Grasping her wrists, Galen pulled her hands away. " 'Tis over between us, Alena. I'm a sorcerer. You're a *galiene*. You can choose to accept that destiny or not. But, in the end, you got what you came for—Renard. Let that suffice."

"Suffice?" Disbelief filled Alena. "Is that all you think is of import to me now? That I rescued Renard?"

"It doesn't matter," he muttered dispiritedly. "Too much has always lain between us. Leave me to my dark thoughts and even darker inclinations. If, somehow, someday, I manage to overcome them, mayhap I'll search you out. But you must let me do it in my own time and way. If you love me, you won't stay where you're not wanted; you'll set me free."

Stung by his words, Alena stepped back. He didn't mean what he'd just said, she struggled to convince herself. He was hurt, confused, and lashing out indiscriminately.

Indiscriminately . . . at life, at her, and at Lydia, who, in the end, had most likely betrayed him. Though Alena had tried to put aside the niggling doubts since the truth of Galen's first love's manipulations had been revealed, she found them now creeping back. Doubts, as to the depth of his love for her compared to how he'd loved Lydia. Doubts that, after what Lydia had done to him, he could ever truly and fully let himself love again.

" . . . *sometimes one's first love is the stuff of dreams,* " she remembered Galen saying that day at the beach on Cadvallan, *"dreams of such grandeur and magic that 'tis impossible for any other lover ever to hope to fulfill them."*

She wanted to ask him if they were true, wanted him to take her in his arms and soothe the painful, petty suspicions away. But she knew, even as the impulse to speak the words filled her that, at best, Lydia could only be part of Galen's quandary. The bigger part, the part that only he could overcome, was his fear of himself. Until he worked through that, it mattered not who he loved more.

"I told you before," Alena ground out the words, "that I wouldn't hold you against your will. You're a free man. But I'll tell you one thing more before I ride out. Beware that you don't revert to the same complacent ways that kept you so long on Cadvallan Isle. Beware that you aren't once more making a choice to run away from life, from our love, rather than face it and work through the problems.

"You once told me there should be more to life than mere existence. I think I was beginning to discover that, thanks to you and Paddy. But even as I open myself to that life, I see you now closing yourself off from it. Closing yourself off and choosing a living death, instead. But 'tis your choice in the end. I just wonder," she said, her voice breaking, "if what we had was truly ever what it seemed?"

With that, Alena turned on her heel and strode off toward the tower stairs leading back to the keep. Curse the man, she inwardly railed, her heart so close to breaking she marveled she could even find the strength to walk away. Ah, curse him! She'd not beg him to love her or allow her to stay. If he was once more bent on his foolish, pitiful self-exile, so be it.

She'd been daft to think 'twould ever work between them. Galen was too weak, too afraid, ever to face life as it must be faced. As she needed a man—*her* man—to face it.

Caught up in her tumultuous thoughts, Alena slammed into Renard, who'd been standing in the tower doorway. His strong hands steadied her. "What are you doing here?" she gasped, gazing up at him.

His teeth flashed white in the shadowed doorway. "What else? Keeping an eye on you. Rather careless for a soldier of your caliber, walking straight into someone without seeing them."

Alena twisted free of his grip. "Curse you, Renard! I don't need another one of your lectures right now! Just—just let me pass!"

He heard the taut emotion in her voice, saw the tears glistening in her eyes. "The sorcerer. What did he say to upset you so?"

"Naught." Fiercely, she shook her head. " 'Tis none of your concern. 'Tis between us."

"Well," he growled, glancing over her shoulder to where Galen still stood at the parapets, "mayhap 'tis time I *make* it my concern."

Alena clutched at his arm. "Nay, Renard. Let it be. Please."

Tenderly, he stroked her cheek, a smile softening the weathered planes of his face. "You're weary, lass. Go below and take your rest."

She exhaled a tremulous breath. "Renard, please."

"Have I not the right to take a breath of the fresh night air up here, or gaze out at the stars?"

"Aye," Alena gritted, knowing Renard would not be swayed once he'd set his mind to something. "Have at it, then." She released him and stepped around to head down the stairs. Men, she thought disgustedly. They were all alike. Stubborn, opinionated, and far too proud for their own good.

Renard waited until he could no longer hear Alena's footsteps on the tower stairs, then turned and headed out onto the parapet. Walking over, he came to a halt beside Galen. He stood there a long while in a companionable silence, gazing out onto the blackened night. Pennants flapped from the tower roof, lending a discordant sound to the windy night.

Finally, Galen sighed and turned to him. "You must take her from here on the morrow. If you care for her, you'll take her away before 'tis too late."

Renard cocked a brow. "Care for her? Is that what this is all about? You think she loves me and not you?"

Galen hesitated, then made a great show of finding sudden fascination with a crumbling bit of stone at the corner of the parapet. "Nay, I know Alena loves me, but it matters not. I'm not the man for her. My magic . . ." He inhaled a shuddering breath and squarely met Renard's gaze. "She'll just be better off with you."

"And I say, don't denigrate Alena's affections. She doesn't give them lightly." Renard smiled. "Besides, you don't know me. You can't be sure she'll be better off with me."

"I know she risked all to get me to help her rescue you. That says enough about the kind of man you are." Galen paused for an instant, then forged on. "Did she tell you that she was even willing to mate with me, if 'twould win my co-operation and strengthen my magic?"

A muscle ticked in Renard's jaw. "And did she? Mate with you, I mean?"

"Aye." Galen averted his eyes.

"And do you love her?"

Galen's mouth twisted. He exhaled a frustrated breath. "You won't let it be, will you?"

"Nay, I won't. I would know if you send her away because you've used her and are done with her, or because you truly love her."

"I truly and fervently love her," Galen breathed the admission on a shuddering sigh. His gaze swung to lock with Renard's. "If you believe naught else about me, Renard, believe that."

"I believe you, sorcerer, but, be that as it may," Renard grudgingly replied, "you've still hurt her deeply this night. I should pound your head for that."

Galen couldn't quite help a small smile. "And I'd deserve it." He gestured to himself. "Have at it. Mayhap 'twould make us both feel better."

"Alena's happiness is all I care about." Renard shifted uncomfortably. "I'm no good at this, but are you certain this is the right course, sending her away? She's never been one to run from a fight. She wants to stay with you."

"I know. But 'tis too dangerous for her to stay. She has a special destiny that calls her, one, I fear, that may well be on a divergent path from mine. And, until I can be certain of where my own destiny leads, 'tis better for her that we part."

"She wouldn't tell me much." Renard turned back to the darkened night. "I must trust you in this, man-to-man."

"Aye, man-to-man," Galen softly said, and joined Renard at the parapet once more.

CHAPTER EIGHTEEN

A faint haze hovered over the land, bathing the sunlit dawn in soft, muted shades of lavender, rose, and peach. The night wind subsided to a gentle breeze, bringing with it the scent of rich earth and springtide flowers. 'Twas yet another fresh, glorious morn, but a morn Alena found little pleasure in. Today, she rode out of Castle Radbourne with Renard once more at her side. But she rode out, as well, leaving Galen behind.

He had come down from the keep to bid his farewells, standing there in the morning light, the playful wind ruffling his dark, curling hair. Despite his new stature as lord of Radbourne, he wore but his simple black wool hooded robe, hanging open over a fine, dark blue linen shirt, black breeches, and boots. He looked, Alena thought with a sudden surge of bittersweet recollection, so much like he'd looked that morn on the beach when she'd first met him.

She swung up onto her mare, shoved her feet into the stirrups, and gathered up the reins. Glancing over at Renard, who was still exchanging a few words with Galen, she cleared her throat. Both men's gazes lifted to hers.

" 'Tis past time to depart," she said, looking directly at Renard. "I'm certain Lord Radbourne has more important matters to deal with than lingering here on farewells."

Renard exchanged a glance with Galen. "Aye, I suppose you're right. Give me a moment to fetch my horse and we'll be on our way." He strode across the bailey to where he'd tied his horse.

Alena made a move to urge her mount after him, when

Galen quickly stepped forward and grabbed the reins to halt her. She whipped her head around. "Aye," she growled, "what is it now? I'd thought we'd said all that needed to be said last night."

He stared up at her, a gentle yearning in his rich brown eyes. He took up her bandaged right hand. A curious warmth flowed into it, then 'twas gone.

"Please, Alena." Galen gave her hand a small squeeze. "Let us not part like this."

She glared down at him. "And how would you have us part?"

"As friends."

"Friends?" She laughed bitterly. "Friends don't give up on each other. Friends are loyal. Friends trust in each other. Does any of that sound like our friendship?"

He colored fiercely. "I do the best I can, Alena. Mayhap if I didn't care so much for you . . ." His voice faded.

She knew she shouldn't press so hard, knew 'twas over between them, but she couldn't help herself. "Mayhap what, Galen? You'd take pity on me and let me stay? Is that it?"

"Nay," he fiercely shook his head. " 'Tisn't pity. I told you—"

"Aye, I remember what you told me," she cut him off savagely. "And I don't stay where I'm not wanted! Never forget that, Galen Radbourne. Never!" With that, Alena jerked back on her horse. The mare half-reared, pulling free of Galen's hold on the reins. With a sharp nudge, Alena sent the horse racing across the inner bailey and out the gate.

Renard, having gained the back of his own mount, shot Alena a startled look, then glanced back at Galen. The big sorcerer stood there, a stricken expression on his face.

"Lovers," Renard muttered in disgust. "The Holy Ones spare me from such a fate." With that, he urged his horse after Alena.

She rode as if the devil were after her, galloping through the castle, out the main gate and over the drawbridge. Once free of the constraints of stone walls, Alena flattened low over her horse and kicked it into a dead run. Streaking across the land, she headed toward the distant hills.

With an exasperated curse, Renard whipped his horse into a run after her. In the state she was in, there was no telling how long Alena would push her mount. There was no telling, either, who she might blunder upon in her urgency to leave Galen Radbourne behind. He needed to catch up with her as soon as possible.

It took the good part of fifteen minutes to draw alongside Alena. She'd always been one of the finest horsewomen he'd ever met, curse her talented little hide. "Hold up!" he shouted. "Stop this crazy pace!"

When she seemed not to hear him, Renard leaned over from his galloping horse and grabbed hold of her mount's reins. "Curse it all, Alena!" he roared as he jerked hard on the reins. "Hold up, I say!"

The mare dug in her hooves, sliding to a stop. Alena bounced to a halt, then shot Renard a frigid glare.

He wasn't at all intimidated. "Are you daft, lass? I've never seen you act so foolhardy before. The man but sent you away for your own good. 'Tisn't as if—"

"You know naught of this!" Alena snapped. Her hair was a wild tangle about her head, her face was flushed, and her eyes unnaturally bright. "I suggest you stay out of it. I know what I'm doing."

Renard cocked his head. "Oh, and what might that be? Or have you decided I'm no longer good enough to be your partner?"

"What is that supposed to mean?" Alena looked on the verge of losing her temper.

"We talked for a long while last night—your sorcerer and I."

"He's not 'my sorcerer'!"

He shrugged. "Mayhap not, but I still learned a lot about what had transpired between you two in the past month. And, besides your erratic love relationship, it seems you've gone and bonded with some dragon, and have magical powers of your own." He paused to eye her intently, a wry quirk to one corner of his mouth. "Am I getting all this right?"

"The part about the dragon and my powers is true enough," Alena growled. "And the rest, well, 'tis past history."

"Indeed?" Renard shifted in his saddle to face her more fully. "And where do we go from here? Back to our army, fretting in their winter quarters, or elsewhere, mayhap to retrieve a certain young dragon?"

Alena was silent for a long while. Then, with a deep sigh, she turned to Renard. "I'm not certain where my destiny will finally lead me, but 'tis true enough that I've still some unfinished business with an old witch woman and my dragon. You are free to ride on back to our army, or go with me. 'Tis your choice."

"And what sort of partner would I be if I left you in your time of need?"

Surprise widened her eyes. "I never said I was in need."

"You don't have to. Partners know these kinds of things about the other."

The tension in Alena began to drain away. "Aye, I suppose you're right." She managed a wan little smile. "I also suppose I *could* use your help. I've some difficult decisions ahead."

"You risked all for me. I can do no less for you."

"My thanks. 'Tis good to know there are *some* friends I can still c-count on." Her voice wavered for an instant, before she

322

lifted her chin and forged on. "Idara and my dragon, Paddy, await us in yon forest," she said, pointing to the hills that lay a few leagues ahead. "We can journey on to the Boar's Tusk Inn then for the . . ."

Recalling what had happened there but two nights ago, Alena suddenly found she couldn't go on. Her right hand fisted, then slammed down hard on the saddle in a frustrated anguish. *Galen, ah, Galen,* she silently cried. *How can it all be over between us so quickly, so completely? How? How?*

Her nails dug deep into her bandaged palm and, suddenly, she was aware of what she was doing. Her wounded hand. By the Mother, had she broken it open again in her unthinking actions?

Alena glanced down at it. Curiously, for all the abuse she'd put it through in her departure from Castle Radbourne and just a few minutes ago, her hand appeared unharmed. She moved it gingerly. It didn't hurt; no fresh blood stained the bandages. She held her hand up, eyeing it closely.

"What's wrong, lass?" Renard asked.

"Naught," she mumbled distractedly, beginning to untie the bandages. "I sliced my palm open while on Cadvallan and it refuses to heal. Yet when I banged it hard but a moment ago . . ." As she unwrapped the last of the bandages and looked down at her hand, her voice faded. Her palm, save for a long, slender scar, was completely healed.

She stared at it for several seconds, dumbfounded. She'd just cleansed and rewrapped it this morn, and 'twas far from mended. How had it so quickly healed? Her mind raced, and one recollection rose to the forefront. Galen, taking her hand in his just before she rode out of Castle Radbourne . . . The strange warmth that had coursed through her as he held her . . .

Alena lifted her tear filled gaze to Renard. "Galen," she

whispered brokenly. "He healed my hand. 'Twas his parting gift . . ." She dragged in an unsteady breath, squared her shoulders, and once more met his glance. "Come. What is past is past. I must leave behind what I cannot have and forge onward. Just as Galen must seek out his own way, so must I."

"As must we all."

She smiled softly. The pain of losing Galen would heal much more slowly than her hand, but heal in time it would. In the meanwhile, there was a certain comfort to be found in the camaraderie of old friends. "Aye, as must we all," Alena agreed. " 'Tis good, though, to have you back again, Renard. 'Tis so very, very good."

He grinned. " 'Tis good to be free of that dungeon at last. I always knew you'd find some way to come back for me."

"Did you?"

"Aye, Alena." Renard's craggy face broke into a smile. "That I did."

Alena stood at the edge of the pond, watching how the water rippled and spread in the backwash of the rock she'd just thrown across its smooth surface. The glinting waves caught the luminous glow of the setting sun, sending shards of red and gold shimmering through the darkling waters. Overhead in the trees a nighthawk called once, twice, then in a great flapping of its long, pointed wings flew away.

She watched the brownish black mottled bird soar into the heavens, heading toward the darkening forest and the distant moor. A moor wherein lay a fortress—and a sorcerer she loved.

With a deep sigh, Alena picked up yet another rock and sent it skipping across the water. Four days had passed since she and Renard had ridden out from Castle Radbourne, four long, tension-fraught days in which she'd hoped and waited, and heard naught from Galen. She was beginning to wonder if she would ever hear from him again.

Squatting beside the pond, Alena dipped her fingers in the water. Though dusk now brushed the sky in strokes of deepening blues and purples, a bit of warmth from the sun still lingered in the gently lapping water. Summer would be here in but another month. The days would grow long and languorous and sultry. A perfect time to savor with a lover.

But, after tonight, if the ceremony of the Night of the Dark Moon went as Idara assured her 'twould, Galen might well be no more. The ceremony of the Night of the Dark Moon, ancient ritual that 'twas, would drive the evil from the land. 'Twas the last chance the *galienes* and dragons might have to weaken the magic of the sorcerers, to finally overcome and destroy them for all time.

Once the moment was passed, 'twould be gone for another year. Another year, Alena mused. Time enough for the sorcerers to rally against the last of the *galienes* and dragons. Time enough . . . and the outcome would all depend on her.

Twigs snapped underfoot. Bushes were shoved aside. A stone was loosened and set tumbling. Her hand grabbing for her sword, Alena wheeled around.

Paddy lumbered forward through the trees, his iridescent black scales glimmering in the dimming light. At sight of Alena, he threw up his head, his fangs bared in a toothy grin. His sudden lack of attention to the trail before him was his undoing. An exposed tree root caught him unawares. With a grunt of surprise, Paddy tripped and fell, somersaulting head over tail until he rolled to a stop a few feet from Alena.

At the ludicrous sight the dragon made, flat on his back, his arms flung out, his tail curled between his widespread legs, and a cloud of dust settling slowly over him, Alena couldn't quite hide her smile. She shook her head. "You really must take a bit more care in where you put those big feet of yours, you know. Before you're the death of you—and me."

With a soft grunt, Paddy rolled over and shoved to his feet. His tail flicked erratically, a sure sign, Alena now knew, of anxiety. She walked over to him and gently brushed the dust from his face.

"I-I beg pardon, my lady," he quavered, eyeing her uncertainly. "I try so hard, and I think I'm doing better, but every once in a while—"

Alena laughed and put up her hand to silence him. " 'Tis all right, Paddy. It goes along with a growing body. I had my own moments of awkwardness as I grew from a girl to a woman."

His brilliantly bejeweled eyes grew wide. "Truly, my lady? Then 'tis not so bad, my falling and tripping and striking others with my tail?"

"Well, 'tis still a bit painful at times, but not a crime, so to speak." Alena paused and glanced around her.

The light was fading. In the cooling air, a mist formed and rose from the surface of the still warm pond. Frogs, hiding in the dense foliage growing on the far bank, began their nocturnal serenade. She sighed, her thoughts turning elsewhere. " 'Tis almost time for the ceremony of the Night of the Dark Moon."

"Aye." Paddy carefully shuffled closer and cocked his head. "You seem reluctant to perform the rituals. Why is that, my lady? 'Twill save us from the evil of the sorcerers at long last."

"Or so Idara and the Dragon Father claim," she muttered grimly.

At the mention of the big dragon, who had arrived from Cadvallan Isle late yesterday, a premonitory shiver coursed through Alena. Strangely, when nearly all the other dragons on the isle had been too weak ever to venture off Cadvallan, the Dragon Father seemed to possess sudden strength, swooping down from the sky like some hawk plummeting toward its prey. It had been, to say the least, a magnificent but disconcerting sight. Yet when Alena had questioned him on his surprising show of powers, the big white dragon had been evasive and quickly changed the subject.

In the long run, she supposed, glancing back to the pond where, just then, a fish broke the surface to snap up an unsuspecting water crawler, it really didn't matter anyway. Whether the big dragon was present at the ceremony of the Night of the Dark Moon or not was hardly the problem. The real issue, the one that gnawed at Alena's heart and mind, was the long-term ramifications of the ceremony. And, though she tried to keep the consideration from her thoughts, how it might affect Galen.

"You worry about the big sorcerer, do you not, my lady?"

At Paddy's unexpected query, Alena's head jerked up. Her eyes narrowed. "Aye," she muttered irritably, miffed at being so easily read, "and what of it?"

The young dragon's mouth twitched, and his tail flicked to and fro. "You fear what may happen to him as a result of the ceremony. Driving out evil in the land could well kill most if not all of the sorcerers."

"Presuming all the sorcerers are evil."

"But Galen is not evil," Paddy persisted. "Therefore, he should be in no danger."

Alena gave a bitter laugh. "You forget that when he killed his brother, he took on his evil powers."

Paddy considered that for a long moment, his youthful brow furrowing in thought. "I forget naught, my lady. But magic doesn't make one evil. One chooses to do that. So it seems to me that magical powers can only be evil in the hands of an evil man."

"Galen wasn't so sure of that." She rose and rubbed her dirty palms on her breeches. "Well, one way or another, there's naught I can do now. He'll die if he has succumbed to Dorian's magic, and 'twill be for the best. And if he hasn't, then I pray he survives this night and goes on to find some peace and happiness."

"His only hope for that is if he comes for you, my lady," the dragon said. "As 'twill be the same for you, I fear."

Alena glanced up at him. "What do you mean?"

"You are life-mated, my lady. Just as you cannot be whole again without me at your side, you cannot be whole without your sorcerer. 'Tis now your destiny, as 'tis his."

At Paddy's words, a deep sadness and sense of despair swamped Alena. The dragon spoke true. She'd never be whole again without Galen. But she also knew that, after the way Galen had turned from her and back to his magic, mayhap never to leave it again, 'twas possible a *galiene* and sorcerer were never meant to join. Just as, she desperately feared, there was no longer any hope left that the dragons and sorcerers would ever find peace—until one or the other of them was destroyed.

By the Mother, but he'd never, even during those fifteen years on Cadvallan, felt so alone, so lost, so bewildered! For the tenth time since he'd given up on an early evening meal he'd had delivered to his bedchamber, Galen rose and restlessly paced the room. As he passed the bedchamber's only window, he glanced outside.

Through the narrow, arched opening in the thick stone walls, the sun dipped toward the distant hills. Hills, Galen thought glumly, that he'd watched Alena and Renard ride over not so very long ago. Hills that *he* yearned to ride toward even now, to find Alena, to beg her to come back to him.

'Twasn't as if life in Castle Radbourne was dull or melancholy. Though the castle residents had treated him with the greatest caution and deference since he'd assumed control on Dorian's death, even in the span of just four days they seemed to be beginning to relax and go about their business in a more cheerful and industrious fashion. Little by little, they had also begun to approach him with requests for work long overdue.

The stonemason had waylaid him just this morn about the possibility of repairing the weakest parts of the walls, and the cook had strode up at the noon meal and inquired what his favorite dishes might be. An ancient healer had sought him out, as well, begging permission to plant an herb garden in the weed infested, neglected castle garden plot.

Galen had been more than happy to grant their simple requests. 'Twas amazing to him, though, that any still cared, after the brutal treatment these many years. There did indeed begin to seem to be hope that something of value could be salvaged of Dorian's harsh rule.

But would the rebirth of the land and rebuilding of the fragile link with the people be enough to save them all? Galen wondered. There was still the ongoing enmity between the sorcerers and the dragons to be resolved, if indeed 'twas possible, and then there were the questions still remaining about his magic.

Though he'd watched and waited in the past days, the evil powers that had invaded him at Dorian's death seemed to lie dormant. Yet Galen knew they were there. He could feel the increase in his powers, powers now even far beyond the scope he'd gained when he mated with Alena. Powers surging, seething, seeking release.

He'd considered using them, if for no other reason than to

release some of the pent-up force. There were certainly plenty of opportunities in the run-down castle. Galen wondered what his brother had been about all these years, to let Radbourne decay to such a sorry state. Mayhap his magic had consumed him until he'd had little time or concern for the more common aspects of life.

With a soul-deep sigh, Galen strode back to the big oak chair pulled up before the hearth fire and flung himself in it. What his brother had or hadn't done was of little import anymore. 'Twas up to him to carve out his own niche now, to change what he felt needed changing—and hope that 'twouldn't all be in vain. If only he had Alena with him, if only he dared—

A hesitant knock sounded at the door. Galen wheeled around in his chair, gracing the offending portal with a black scowl. "Go away," he rasped. "Whatever 'tis, it can wait until the morrow."

Perhaps the unknown visitor didn't hear him or, if he did, didn't care. Once more, a knock sounded, more insistently now. With a savage curse, Galen leaped from his chair and stalked across the room. He wrenched it open and glared down at the old healer.

"Aye," he gritted, "what is it?"

The woman lurched back, her eyes wide. Summoning his rapidly waning self-control, Galen forced a taut smile. "I'm sorry if I frightened you, old one. My mood isn't the sweetest this eve, but 'tis naught that you have done." He stepped aside and motioned her in. "Pray, enter if you will."

She eyed him warily, then gave a curt nod and walked into his room. Striding across the chamber, she promptly took up the chair sitting opposite his at the hearth. Amused by her presumption, Galen followed and joined her there. For the first time, he noted the crumbling leather covered tome she held tucked beneath one arm.

"Come to read me a tale, have you?" he asked, making a weak attempt at humor.

"I've come to share more than a tale," the old woman tartly replied, "*if* ye are capable of grasping its truths. Yer brother never was, nor were many of his kind before him."

"And you think I am?"

"Mayhap. Ye killed yer evil brother and seem good-hearted enough, unlike most of yer kind. 'Tis also rumored that ye rode with a *galiene* and her dragon." She held up the ancient tome. "This book speaks to that. It says the only hope for the land is if sorcerers and dragons once more live as friends."

"Well, 'tis true I bear no animosity toward the dragons or their *galienes,* but I'm not so certain there's much hope left for any of us."

The old woman shrugged and offered Galen the book. "Be that as it may, I can do naught more with this and ye seem different than the rest. There's not much time left at any rate, if we're to save the land. Take the book. 'Tis past my time and powers to use, even if I'd the heart anymore for it. 'Tis a book of magic."

Galen cocked a dark brow. "Indeed? And what is this book of magic called?"

She made a great show of tilting it back to look at it, then brushed away the dust coating its cover with her sleeve. Her wrinkled brow furrowed in concentration. " 'Tis hard to read; the gilt lettering is all but gone. I think . . ." She paused to walk closer to the firelight. "I think it says *The Grimoire of . . . Brengwain . . . the Wise.*"

Brengwain the Wise . . . The name struck a chord in Galen. He'd heard it mentioned before, but where? Where?

The scene of a dark, dingy tavern flickered through his

mind. Aye, he thought, his excitement rising, a tavern, the Hogshead Inn, where he and Alena had first stayed after arriving from Cadvallan. She'd been speaking to an old man who had mentioned the name of a *galiene* named Brengwain the Wise. And mentioned, as well, a grimoire which held the

. . . the answers to the tragedy that twines tighter and tighter about us each day . . .

He reached for the book, containing the trembling of his hands with only the greatest of efforts. "I've heard of the book. I doubt if 'twill be much help in solving the problems between the dragons and the sorcerers, but I'll read it."

The old woman nodded. " 'Tis all I could hope for." She gestured to the door. "By your leave, my lord, I've a wish to depart."

Galen, already beginning to carefully thumb through the timeworn, brittle pages, glanced up. "What? Oh, aye, you've my leave."

"Fare you well then, my lord." She turned and began to walk away.

"Wait!" Galen closed the book and hurried over to her.

Startled, the woman halted and glanced back at him. "Aye, my lord?"

"Why now? Why tonight of all nights, did you decide to bring me this book?"

She smiled, a dark, mysterious smile that suddenly seemed to melt the years away until a beautiful, vibrant woman stood before him. Galen blinked, not quite believing what he saw. The old woman stood before him once more.

"Why, indeed?" she softly said. "Mayhap the time seemed right at last. Or mayhap 'twas because tonight is a special night, the Night of the Dark Moon, when all evil can be cast from the land, when all sorcerers lie at the mercy of any *galiene* still bonded to a dragon. What better night to share the final, most important secrets of all? What better night to put to rest, at long last, the painful price you've paid for your wondrous calling?"

With a soft laugh, the old woman turned and, opening the door, walked out, leaving Galen standing there, the book tucked under his arm, wondering who she really was. He realized now she'd never told him her name. Realized, as well, she probably never would.

Galen stood there for a time, until a flame-eaten log crashed to the hearth, sending sparks scattering. Galen jerked from his reverie. Clutching the grimoire to him, he turned and strode back to the hearth. He pulled his chair up closer to the firelight, then sat.

Ever so carefully, Galen once more opened the book and thumbed through the pages. There were the usual assortment of spells and directions for potions, incantations, and the like. But, as he read further, the instructions turned to the bonding between a *galiene* and her dragon, and the surprising admonitions on the importance of maintaining a close relationship with the sorcerers.

As Galen read, hope filled him anew. They had done it before, his kind living in peace and harmony with the dragons. Why couldn't it happen again? In the end, what was there to keep them apart, save the selfishness and cowardice and mistrust that had grown up between them all over the years? All failings of the heart, but not necessarily permanent nor immutable.

He needed Alena to help him in this. That much he knew. But could they make a stand together, join hearts and minds and bodies, and heal the extensive wounds wrought on the land and people after all these years? They were only two people, after all, and the damage had been wrought by so many for so long. It seemed an impossibility.

With a sigh, Galen began to close the grimoire when some lines of a strange poem caught his eye. Intrigued, he opened the book and read.

> *Magic hath its own language,*
> *Its own realities, its own laws,*
> *And a wide realm of possibilities*
> *For light, and darkness, and a misty "between"*
> *Spanning a netherland of uncertain choices.*

> *Yet though the choices bewilder*
> *And promise naught, be it good or bad,*
> *The wielder of magic must choose.*
> *'Tis the price of the calling,*
> *'Tis the price of a certain magic.*

> *A magic that springs from the heart,*
> *From love,*
> *Or from the depths of a soul-deep perdition.*

Galen didn't know how long he sat there, staring at the words, before he closed the book and set it aside. Choices, he thought. Every step of this quest had been fraught with difficult choices. Choices that promised naught, neither success nor happiness. But he had made them, one after another, as had Alena. Those choices, springing from the heart and the best intentions possible, had led them to this point.

He had made a choice when he'd turned from Alena, too. Made a choice for a living death, rather than one for life. A living death . . . just as Lydia had done when she'd chosen to play one brother against the other.

Galen smiled sadly. Poor, young, shallow Lydia. Though his memories of her were now vague and colored by the wild passions of his youth, he saw them at last for what they were. Memories. Fine and beautiful, but naught more than memories.

Alena, on the other hand, was alive and real and all the woman he could ever hope to need. Their love, born out of maturity and their struggles, was the true and lasting kind. If only he had the courage . . .

And now, there was one more choice to be made. One more choice, with no guarantee of success or happiness. Yet to turn from it would be to doom them all. Choices . . . uncertainty . . . doubts. For his magic, for him and Alena, and for the salvation of Wyndymyll.

But, as the grimoire had said, 'twas the price of his calling, the price of a certain magic that was uniquely his.

Galen rose and strode over to the window. Even now, the sun was setting behind the hills. High above, the moon gleamed in the rapidly darkening sky.

The Night of the Dark Moon, Galen thought, recalling the old healer's words. The night when all evil would be cast from the land, when all sorcerers would lie at the mercy of any *galiene* still bonded to a dragon.

A galiene still bonded to a dragon . . . Alena.

Filled with a terrible sense of urgency, Galen wheeled about and rushed back across the room to take up his black robe. He must hurry before his magic failed him for the night. Hurry, if he were to get to Alena in time.

Hurry, before 'twas too late for them all.

CHAPTER NINETEEN

"Come child. 'Tis time." Idara stepped up to the small wooden barrel she used as a tub and handed Alena a drying cloth. "The Dark Moon is upon us and yer purification bath is ended. Ye must be anointed now with fragrant oils and don yer robe."

As if in a daze, Alena rose, the cool, salted water sliding from her body. Incense filled the air, the aromatic scent of sandalwood and rose petals wafting over from the little brass censer on the floor. She allowed the old witch woman to rub her dry, then apply a fragrant, ritualistic oil of rose, jasmine, and sandalwood to her body. Only then did Idara lift the simple, long-sleeved white robe over Alena's head.

In a whisper of fine linen sliding over silken skin, the robe fell, covering her from neck to her toes and to the tips of her fingers. Alena looked down. Her mouth quirked. "I'm not used to a gown," she muttered, glancing up at Idara.

" 'Tis the dress of a *galiene* on the Night of the Dark Moon. 'Tis ceremonial garb. Ye must wear it, as ye must perform all the rituals, if the ceremony is to be successful." She knelt and offered Alena a pair of delicately fashioned white sandals.

Alena rolled her eyes, but obediently stepped into the shoes. Idara laced them up to and about her ankles, then tied them in place. Next, the old woman rose and walked over to a nearby table. She returned with a small, wooden box. " 'Tis a sacred pendant, this moonstone. 'Tis worn only for this ceremony and none other."

Alena frowned. "It looks exactly the same as the pendant

both Galen and Dorian wore. Why is that?"

"I don't know, child." Idara's mouth twisted in irritation. "What does it matter? The reason is long-buried and we've no time to ponder its significance now." She lifted it out of the case and offered it to Alena. "What matters is that it hasn't been worn in over a hundred years, and why."

Since the days when the galienes *decided to turn from the dragons, and their destruction began,* Alena thought. Wordlessly, she accepted it and put it on, momentarily overwhelmed with the sense of history, of heritage, of the brave aspirations and hopes that all the women who'd come before her had experienced. She wasn't worthy; she wasn't ready; and she wasn't even certain she was doing the right thing for any of them in carrying out this night's ceremony.

But then, there seemed few other choices left for her or the dragons. If the ceremony this night truly drove out the evil, what harm was there in that? Only the bad would suffer. If that included all the sorcerers, then so be it. They had reigned supreme for too long as 'twas. Their evil ways, whichever of them truly were evil, must be punished.

'Twas Galen's only hope to survive, though. He was not an evil man. Alena knew that to the depths of her being. He, at least, would live, no matter what destruction she wrought this night. She *had* to believe that, had to maintain her faith that he'd been able to overcome Dorian's heritage of malevolence and hatred. 'Twouldn't make up for losing him, but 'twas some small consolation, nonetheless.

She glanced at Idara. "I am ready."

The witch woman smiled. "Aye, child, that ye are." She handed Alena a cloak of the deepest blue. "Put it on and follow me. The gathering awaits us in the oak grove."

They left the little hut and walked out into the darkened forest, their way lit by a small lamp Idara held suspended from the end of a short stick. Paddy, who had waited patiently outside for them to depart, followed a close but prudent distance behind, his heavy footsteps a loud counterpart to the eerily quiet forest.

Alena glanced overhead. Through the trees, she could catch an occasional glance of the moon. Gradually shrinking as the world's presence passed between it and the sun, 'twouldn't be too long before naught was left of it but a faint glow around a blackened orb. 'Twas then, when the moon was the blackest, that, for the successful casting out of evil, the Ceremony of the Night of the Dark Moon must be held.

Renard was already at the sacred meeting place, having been sent there earlier by Idara. No man, she had informed Alena, could be present for the purification bathing ritual. Alena only wondered what her partner would think of her after this night. Indeed, she secretly wondered what *she* would think or how 'twould affect her, for good or bad, before the night was done.

A large bonfire gradually came into view as they traversed the huge, silent forest. Figures moved before the flickering tongues of flame, some walking, some dancing. Surprisingly, most were women. Alena turned to Idara. "These people. Did you summon them?"

"Aye. I called to all the *galienes* still alive to come out of hiding at last. Though, without their dragons they are powerless to conduct the ceremony, their presence and powers will aid ye in yer magic."

"I'm the least skilled, the most ignorant of them all," Alena murmured. "I'll feel the fool before them."

"Ye know what must be done. We've gone over the steps of the ritual many times in the past days. And, if that wasn't enough, ye have yer dragon with ye. These women know the power that bonding gives ye. They'll respect that if naught else."

"Aye, I suppose you're right. I just feel so . . ." Her voice faded as the huge form of the Dragon Father moved before the fire, momentarily blocking the light. "I don't like it that he's here. I don't trust him."

Idara shot the big dragon a quick glance. "In the end, he only wishes what we wish. He is not the enemy. Remember that."

"I confess to not being certain who is truly friend and who is foe in this," Alena admitted as they strode toward the clearing made by the ring of towering oaks. " 'Tisn't as if this is the usual kind of battle, with both sides clearly drawn."

The witch woman shrugged. "Mayhap not, but the stakes are no less dear."

As they entered the clearing, the women dancing about the fire stopped. As one, young and old alike, they silently gathered into a group around the altar set before the fire. Alena's heart began a staccato rhythm beneath her breast and, for a fleeting instant, she hesitated. Though these were the closest people she'd ever have as sisters, both in heritage and powers, they seemed strangers. Even the soldiers of her mercenary army seemed closer, more familiar.

But that didn't matter now. Time would mend that sense of disunity with the women. In the meanwhile, there were issues of greater import to deal with. Squaring her shoulders, Alena resolutely headed toward the circle.

The women parted to let her through. There on a long table covered with a white cloth sat two candles on either end, a long, black-handled knife, a silver bowl of water, a censer filled with more sandalwood incense, and a circlet of wild iris and jonquils.

Alena took up the circlet of flowers and placed it on her

head. She lit the candles and set the incense to smoking. Lifting the knife, she then touched its blade to the water in the bowl.

"I consecrate and cleanse this water that it may be fit to serve the Mother on this night of purification."

She next turned to the north and, moving several feet from the table with the knife held outward at waist level, began to walk a circle about the altar. As Idara had instructed, Alena tried to charge the area with her words and energy, visualizing the power flowing from the knife's blade.

"Here is the boundary of the Sacred Circle," she solemnly intoned. As Alena spoke, the night wind swirled down from the sky to brush her face and set her unbound hair to blowing. "Naught but love shall enter in; naught but love shall leave."

Alena walked the perimeter until she finally returned to the northernmost end of the circle. She placed the magic blade back on the altar. Next, she picked up the smoking censer and made the purification walk again. Lastly, she took up the bowl of water and, walking its boundaries once more, sprinkled water about the circle.

As she worked, a curious sensation pervaded Alena. The circle seemed to come alive, to breathe and pulsate gently about her. It seemed to glow, drawing in all the energy and power surrounding them. The latent power of a land long dormant, of lost hopes and expectations awaiting the right opportunity to spring forth strong and renewed.

The realization pervaded her, filling Alena with a burgeoning sense of oneness with all things. Though she had always been a part of the land and people, tonight she suddenly *was* the land and people. All depended on her to bring them out of this downward spiral of evil and destruction. *All . . . even those misguided amongst the sorcerers.*

The knowledge was startling, shattering the calm equanimity the ritual of the sacred circle had inspired. *Even the sorcerers?* Frantically, Alena delved deep into her memories. Had the tiny voice been but her own conscience, still struggling with the issue of Galen? Or had it come from outside her, from a higher, purer source?

"The moon, child," Idara hissed, as the Dragon Father and Paddy moved to stand behind her. *"Look to the moon."*

Alena lifted her gaze to the skies. There, straight overhead now, their world had passed fully before the moon. Only a thin, luminous glow encircling the dark orb remained. 'Twas time, Alena knew, to move to the part of the ceremony to cast out evil.

She picked up the black knife and, with both hands entwined about its hilt, raised it straight above her head. Arms all around her, invisible but strong, seemed to support her, strengthen her for the terrible ordeal to come. 'Twas just, 'twas good, what she did, Alena thought. Yet, through it all, that tiny voice still plucked at her.

Galen. What about Galen?

"Nay, Alena." As if summoned by her thoughts, Galen stepped from the trees. " 'Tisn't the way. Killing the sorcerers won't drive the evil from the land. The corruption will endure in the hearts of those who remain."

The women surrounding her gasped in horror. A soft growl rumbled in the Dragon Father's chest. Paddy, standing beside the big white dragon, shuffled restlessly and began to flick his tail. Idara, however, wasn't to be gainsaid.

"Don't listen to him, child!" she cried from her place outside the circle. " 'Tis but a final test of yer courage. Don't let his cunning ways turn ye from yer true path. Think of what really matters, the people, the land!"

"Aye." Galen halted halfway to the circle. "Think of the people, the land. Consider what they truly need—love, trust, and hearts courageous enough to choose what is best for all, rather than thinking only of their own petty desires."

"Like you, Galen?" Alena called to him. She lowered the knife. "Have you found *your* courage at last?"

" 'Twas always there, sweet lady. As were you, for me." A soft glow of love lit his rich, eloquent eyes. "I just couldn't see it for my fears and self-doubts."

"Fine words, Radbourne." The Dragon Father stepped between Galen and Alena. "But it changes naught. You're still a sorcerer, born and bred, and not to be trusted. In the end, you'll return to the evil that is so much an innate part of your kind. To protect us once and for all, you must die with the rest."

Galen stared up at the big Dragon and saw the animosity, unveiled and venomous, glittering in his bejeweled eyes. A sharp pain twisted beneath his breast.

"You still believe that of me," he rasped, "after what Alena and I have been through on this quest? If my efforts and devotion to her didn't prove my mettle, the sincerity of my intent, naught can. And your suspicions about me also confirms the truth of my rising doubts about you."

The Dragon Father smirked down at him. "Indeed? And what truth is that?"

"That you are as corrupt, as the sorcerers you claim to hate. There's no more room in your heart to forgive, to heal the wounds of the land, than there is in those of my kind. Because of that, you're as great a danger as them."

"You dare speak such words to me?" The Dragon Father rose to his full height and loomed over Galen, his great fangs bared, his claws perilously close. "You, who were little more than a broken-spirited calamity when you came to my isle? 'Twas I who took pity on you when the others wanted to finish you off. 'Twas I who allowed you to come near us, to work with our weak and sickly, when even your presence made me ill, constantly reminding me of what others of your kind had done to us."

"Aye, you may well have done those things and more," Galen fiercely countered, "but I now think they weren't done out of compassion, but out of consideration of the use I might be to you someday. And I was, wasn't I? 'Twould've been difficult if not impossible for Alena to have gotten this far without me."

His glance moved briefly to that of Idara, who had quietly come up to stand beside the Dragon Father. "You and the witch woman have been in league for a long while now, haven't you?" Galen demanded, riveting the full force of his rising anger back on the big dragon. "She well knew what she was doing in sending Alena to Cadvallan, and 'twasn't for Renard's sake. Nay, 'twas never for Renard's sake, was it?"

"Does it matter anymore who used whom?" The Dragon Father leaned back, a hard, flat look shattering his eyes. "What is done is done, and there's no turning back. And you, Radbourne, must die." He looked at Idara. "See to your woman. This man is at our mercy, fool that he is, daring to come out from the safety of his castle after dark. Without his magic he is helpless. 'Tis past time he be killed and the ceremony completed. Have her kill him now—or I will!"

Idara nodded and strode over to stand at the edge of the sacred circle opposite Alena. "Ye must do it, child. Finish the ceremony of the Night of the Dark Moon. 'Twill solve everything."

"Will it, Idara?" Alena set aside the knife and walked around the altar to face her. "Are you so certain of that?"

" 'Twill solve enough," the old woman snapped. "Would ye rather turn against yer kind for this . . . this sorcerer?" She made a disparaging motion toward Galen. " 'Tis yer only other choice."

Alena's glance lifted to meet Galen's. Something strong and good and pure arced between them. He trusted her, loved her, and had put his life in her hands daring to come here this night. She could do no less for him.

"Aye, 'tis indeed a matter of choices once more," she said, never taking her eyes from his. "And, aye, I choose Galen. But not over my kind or any other. I but choose him as well."

She motioned to the sacred circle surrounding her, a circle none had dared enter since she'd consecrated it. "Naught but love may enter in; naught but love shall emerge," she said with a soft smile, uttering the words she'd first used to consecrate the circle. Stepping to its edge, she held out her hand to Galen.

His heart swelling with love, he took her hand and walked inside. Immediately, a force engulfed him, swallowing him in a swirling, heated vortex. The breath was sucked from Galen's lungs. A gray mist dimmed his vision. Fear filled him.

The circle . . . 'twas of Alena's doing . . . a *galiene's* doing, he thought. Mayhap 'twas forbidden for a sorcerer to enter . . . Or mayhap, just mayhap 'twas always meant as the means of his death.

He fought against the rising doubts and panic that threatened to swallow him. He clasped Alena's hand tightly, willing his body to relax, his fears to subside. He trusted her. He would *not* waver in his love and confidence of her. If he did, they were all lost.

Almost the moment he made that resolve, the whirling maelstrom calmed, easing to a soft, soothing breeze. His vision cleared. He dragged in several shuddering breaths.

Alena stood before him, her hand still holding his. She smiled. " 'Twas one last test, was it not? I felt its power as strongly as you. But I wouldn't let it vanquish me. I could feel your hand through it all, and knew you were there, that you loved me. I knew it, no matter how terrifying the doubts and fears that assailed me."

"As I did, that you loved me."

A fierce growl pierced the pleasant haze of their mutual absorption. As one, they turned, and came face-to-face with the Dragon Father.

Fury blazed in his eyes. His nostrils flared red and his crest stood out in angry splendor about his head. " 'Twill do you no good, you traitor to the dragons and *galienes*," he snarled, glaring down at Alena. "Sacred circle or no, its protection will fade with the ebbing of the dark moon. Then I'll get to you. Your powerless sorcerer won't be able to protect you then."

Alena exchanged a glance with Galen. As one, they stepped from the circle's safety. The big dragon reared back in surprise.

"Consider long and hard before you strike at us," Alena said. "You imagine we threaten all you hold dear, that we'll destroy the plans you had for the both of us. But I say what Galen and I share is the only hope for the land. Here, at long last, *galiene* and sorcerer are bound again, one to the other, in trust and love. What better way to begin to heal the wounds of a ravaged land and tormented souls?"

"Fine words, but how am I to know the true intent of your hearts?" The Dragon Father eyed them suspiciously. "I risk much in trusting you. How can I be sure?"

Idara stepped forward. "Aye, how can we be certain, after all these years of pain and suffering? How? *How?*"

"Because *I* know the heart of my *galiene*," Paddy said, moving to stand beside Alena and Galen. "And none can gainsay my word on that."

The big dragon's glittering gaze swung to that of the

younger dragon's. "Have a care. You tread on dangerous ground when you threaten to go against me."

Paddy met his fierce look calmly. "Yet what choice have I? My place is with my *galiene,* as 'twould be for any of our kind. Would you have me deny my destiny, a destiny you instilled in me as strongly as you did in the others?"

"You would bind your powers to hers then? Use them against me?"

"I've no wish to harm you, Dragon Father," Paddy replied, dipping his head briefly in respect, "but I will not let you harm my lady. Especially not," he added, "when you are wrong about her and her life mate. 'Twouldn't be right or fair. You are wise with the wisdom of your many years. Don't let your hatred blind you now."

Alena watched the big dragon. He hesitated, but whether from the truth of Paddy's words or the realization that he was no match for the combined magic of a *galiene* and her bonded dragon, she couldn't tell. It mattered not, one way or another. 'Twould take time to heal the wounds of the older dragons, as well as the *galienes* and sorcerers. The door to that healing, though, had finally been opened.

" 'Tis over, Dragon Father," she offered gently. "Let it go at last. We are bound now, *galiene* and dragon and sorcerer. Give us a chance. That's all we ask."

The big dragon's head lowered until he was eye level with her. " 'Tis mayhap over for a time. Time enough to give you your opportunity to change what none of us has been able to change. But after that?" He smiled grimly. "Who knows?"

"All we ask for is a chance. 'Tis now our turn."

Galen wrapped his arm about her shoulders. "Aye, give us a chance, Dragon Father. You owe us that."

"Do I now?"

"Aye, that you do."

"And I say nay," Idara cried, shoving her way through the crowd that had encircled them. "I won't let this travesty occur!"

The big white dragon turned to her, wry amusement quirking the corner of his mouth. "And what will you do to stop them, if I cannot, woman?"

"Then ye give up? Is that it?" Idara demanded, her wizened old body quivering in rage.

" 'Tis as she said. We have no choice, at least not for a time."

As fast as it had filled her, the fight drained from the witch woman. Idara's shoulders slumped; her fisted hands fell open at her sides. "But what of the Night of the D-Dark Moon?" she quavered. "What of the ceremony to drive evil from the land?"

A murmur of agreement rose from the other women standing around them.

"The ceremony served its intended purpose," Alena said, her voice lifting, strong and clear, above the mumblings and restless movements of the crowd. "Served it, and more. In the past, the Ceremony of the Night of the Dark Moon served only to drive evil from the land for one night out of every year, only to have it build again until the next ceremony. But this time we have accomplished far more. In our dedication to begin anew, to strive to heal the terrible wounds, to trust and love and work together again, we have set upon a course to drive out evil every day of the year, not just one night. 'Tis a far more noble choice, to my way of thinking."

"And to mine," Renard said, moving to stand beside her.

She shot him a grateful, loving glance. Dear, gruff Renard, ever the loyal friend. She'd striven so hard to rescue him, now only to leave him. The realization filled her, bittersweet, yet undeniable. Her place was no longer at Renard's side, but at

Galen's. As her loyalties had changed, so had her life. Her destiny now called her elsewhere.

Heads nodded in agreement; murmurs of approval spread among the women. Freshened expectations flared in eyes long bereft of hope. Smiles glimmered on mouths long tight and joyless.

One by one—Idara with them, they began to drift away, back to their homes, until all that remained were Alena, Galen, Renard, and the two dragons. The Dragon Father fixed Paddy with a stern eye. "I've a wish to speak to you in private."

The young dragon turned to Alena. "By your leave, my lady?"

Alena smiled and nodded her head, secure in Paddy's unswerving loyalty to her no matter what the Dragon Father might say to him. "Aye, go. You've my leave."

The two dragons ambled off into the trees. She watched until they disappeared from view, then turned to Galen and Renard. The two men gazed back at her. Alena inhaled a fortifying breath. "Renard, I—"

He held up a silencing hand. "I already know, lass. We'll talk more later." With that, he turned on his heel and strode away.

Alena turned to Galen, a sheepish, uncertain little smile on her lips. "Well, we saved the land from evil. Where do we go from here?"

The night breeze gusted down once more from the heavens, sending the thin linen of Alena's robe billowing and dancing about her ankles, then up to her knees. With an exasperated motion, she grabbed at the offending cloth before it could rise any higher. "Cursed gown," she muttered. "I hate them!"

Galen laughed and gathered her struggling form into his

arms. "Then don't wear them ever again. It makes no difference to me. All I care about," he said, his voice dropping to a low, husky whisper, "is that you stay with me, sweet lady. You asked where we go from here. I know I presume much when I ask you to wed me and give up your warrior's life, but I need you, Alena. The land and people are in dire need of a little peace and happiness. Won't you stay and help me give it to them?"

She leaned back and eyed him narrowly. "And will I be expected to act the proper wife? Though I might never ride out as a mercenary again, I'd quickly chafe under the yoke of a noblewoman's duties."

"What would you like to do then?" he gravely asked.

Alena considered for a moment, then shrugged. "I want to take charge of the castle defenses and be responsible for the training of the knights and soldiers. That should keep me well occupied." She smiled broadly. "Well, at least for most of the time, at any rate."

"Indeed? And what will keep you busy the rest of the time?"

She threw her arms about his neck and gave him a quick kiss. "Why, what else? Pleasuring you in bed, of course. 'Tis the only proper wifely duty I know I can do joyfully and well."

At her words, spoken with unabashed pride, Galen threw back his head and gave a shout of laughter. Tightening his grip on her, he whirled Alena around and around until she breathlessly begged him to stop.

Once more, Galen lowered her to the ground. " 'Tis wifely enough and more, for me, my love," he said, all the love for her in his heart glowing in his eyes. "And if our people protest, they'll speak the words to your face and see which consequence they prefer—the wrath of a sorcerer, or a dragon, or a warrior queen with sword in hand. Whichever way, we're certain to prevail.

"Whichever way, 'tis a certain magic."